SF
WILSON
DOUBLE **Double Threat**

Wilson, F. Pau

DISCARDED
Huron Public Library

# DOUBLE THREAT

# ALSO BY F. PAUL WILSON

*Draculas* (with Blake Crouch,
J. A. Konrath, & Jeff Strand)
*The Proteus Cure* (with Tracy L. Carbone)
*A Necessary End* (with Sarah Pinborough)
"Fix"* (with J. A. Konrath & Ann V. Peterson)
*Three Films and a Play* (with Matthew J. Costello)

### The Nocturnia Chronicles
(with Thomas F. Monteleone)
*Definitely Not Kansas*
*Family Secrets*
*The Silent Ones*

### Short Fiction

*Soft & Others*
*The Barrens & Others*
*Aftershock & Others*
*A Little Beige Book of Nondescript Stories*
*The Christmas Thingy*
*Quick Fixes—Tales of Repairman Jack**
*Sex Slaves of the Dragon Tong*
*The Compendium of Srem**
*Ephemerata*
*Secret Stories**
*Other Sandboxes*
*The Compendium of F—50 Years of F. Paul Wilson* (Vols. 1–3)

### Editor

*Freak Show*
*Diagnosis: Terminal*
*The Hogben Chronicles* (with Pierce Watters)

### Omnibus Editions

*The Complete LaNague*
*Calling Dr. Death* (3 medical thrillers)
*Scenes from the Secret History*
, *Ephemerata*
*Three Films and a Play* (with Matthew J. Costello)

* see "The Secret History of the World" (page 367)

# DOUBLE THREAT

## F. PAUL WILSON

A TOM DOHERTY ASSOCIATES BOOK

NEW YORK

HURON PUBLIC LIBRARY
521 DAKOTA AVE S
HURON, SD 57350-2797

This is a work of fiction. All of the characters, organizations, and events portrayed in this novel are either products of the author's imagination or are used fictitiously.

DOUBLE THREAT

Copyright © 2021 by F. Paul Wilson

All rights reserved.

A Forge Book
Published by Tom Doherty Associates
120 Broadway
New York, NY 10271

www.tor-forge.com

Forge® is a registered trademark of Macmillan Publishing Group, LLC.

The Library of Congress Cataloging-in-Publication Data

Names: Wilson, F. Paul (Francis Paul), author.
Title: Double threat / F. Paul Wilson.
Description: First edition. | New York : Forge, 2021. | "A Tom Doherty Associates book."
Identifiers: LCCN 2021008837 (print) | LCCN 2021008838 (ebook) | ISBN 9781250776648 (hardcover) | ISBN 9781250776655 (ebook)
Subjects: GSAFD: Suspense fiction
Classification: LCC PS3573.I45695 D68 2021 (print) | LCC PS3573.I45695 (ebook) | DDC 813'.54—dc23
LC record available at https://lccn.loc.gov/2021008837
LC ebook record available at https://lccn.loc.gov/2021008838

Our books may be purchased in bulk for promotional, educational, or business use. Please contact your local bookseller or the Macmillan Corporate and Premium Sales Department at 1–800–221–7945, extension 5442, or by email at MacmillanSpecialMarkets@macmillan.com.

First Edition: June 2021

Printed in the United States of America

0 9 8 7 6 5 4 3 2 1

HURON PUBLIC LIBRARY
521 DAKOTA AVE S
HURON, SD 57350-2797

*For*
*Chris Morgan.*
*Thanks for the inspiration.*

## ACKNOWLEDGMENTS

Thanks to my wife, Mary; my beta reader, Kim Bryson; and the stalwarts at my publisher: Tom Doherty, Bob Gleason, Robert Davis, and my longtime copyeditor, Rebecca Maines.

# AUTHOR'S NOTE

When I was a guest at San Diego Comic-Con in 2007, Chris Morgan wandered down from LA to hang out for a while. I'd met him years earlier when he did a rewrite on the *Repairman Jack* script for Beacon (his is still the best version) and we'd stayed in touch. He was then into his long relationship with the *Fast & Furious* franchise. While we were jawing he mentioned how he loved my novel *Healer* and wanted to do a film someday. I said too much of it takes place inside Dalt's head. He said he'd make Pard visible—but only to Dalt. And I thought: *Brilliant.* The idea festered and festered until (with his blessing) I took a mulligan to reimagine and rewrite *Healer* from scratch as a contemporary novel. *Double Threat* is the result. Thus the dedication to Chris. This book never would have happened had he not dropped that simple remark.

I must also thank Chris for introducing me to Rick Loverd, program director of the National Academy of Sciences' Science & Entertainment Exchange, who put me in touch with John Vidale, Ph.D., a seismologist at USC and a member of the National Academy of Sciences. He eventually put me in contact with Egill Hauksson, Ph.D., Research Professor of Geophysics at Caltech's Seismology Lab in Pasadena. Dr. Hauksson showed me around the Southern California Earthquake Center at Caltech and gave me ideas and a ton of info on earthquakes (which have a bearing on the events in this volume and more so in its sequel). Any errors herein are mine, either out of ignorance or because I needed to stretch the truth.

# DOUBLE THREAT

# 1

The very idea of hiding in a cave gave Daley the deep creeps.

This one was shallow, basically a cleft in the rocks, maybe twenty feet deep. She'd done an inspection using the mini Maglite she always carried on her key chain and found nothing but a grayish mossy patch on the ceiling. Lichen, maybe? She'd heard the term but had no clear idea of what lichen was, except that it wasn't going to bite her. She'd been more concerned about finding some of the more disgusting things that liked to make their home in desert caves. Bats, for one. And rattlesnakes. And scorpions. Probably tarantulas too.

None of those, thank you. But just the thought of them . . .

She shuddered but stayed put. She needed this cave. At least for the moment. At least until she was sure a certain SUV full of angry Coachella hausfraus had given up on finding her. What was the saying? *Hell hath no fury like a woman scammed?* Something like that.

Miles away in the sandy valley below, the glittery blue of the stagnant and stinky Salton Sea dominated the view. Not high desert out there—low, *low* desert, with not a Joshua tree or saguaro in sight.

She studied the expanse of sand between her perch and the palm-tree farm that bordered the highway, looking for a dust cloud, the telltale sign of an approaching vehicle. But as she watched, she couldn't resist repeated glances over her shoulder. The cave was empty. She'd checked. So why this feeling she wasn't alone?

No dust cloud in sight out there yet, so Daley did another quick check of the interior with her mini Mag. But just like before: nada except for the lichen patch. A crazy idea that it had moved wormed into her head but she laughed it off and went back on watch.

Not her first time running the car-raffle game, but those pissed-off marks might make it her last if they caught up with her.

The game was simplicity itself: She rented a space where she could display the brand-new sports car—also rented but no one knew that. This time out she'd brought along a fire-red Mazda Miata. They go for less than 30K but look soooo sexy. As usual, a carefully chosen Talbot's wardrobe combined with her wide blue eyes and innocent twenty-six-year-old face made the raffle tickets sell like Girl Scout cookies outside a cannabis store.

The lure was winning off the books. If you win a car worth thirty grand, it's the same as winning an equal amount in a casino: The IRS and the governor want their cut. And you've got to cover that in cash, which, depending on your tax bracket, can add up. Daley's lure was to keep the lottery under the table, which meant winner take all. To some extent—in some folks more than others—everyone has a little larceny in their soul. Nothing like appealing to the dark side to add a little spice to the game.

Then comes the drawing. Daley had found that Wednesday tended to be a good day for this. The usual process is to take the winner to the display space and present him or her with a junker, explaining how the raffle's backer had, well, backed out, and this is the best Daley could do. When the winner squawks, Daley makes amends by refunding the price of the winner's raffle ticket plus a little extra to compensate for the inconvenience. The winner walks away disappointed but not angry—after all, they got back their investment and then some—and Daley walks away with the proceeds from all the losing tickets.

But in today's case, the winner—Amber Seabolt by name—returned with a crowd of her angry friends who *all* wanted refunds plus compensation. Well, Daley wasn't having any of that, so she'd been forced to beat a hasty retreat—in the junker Jeep, of all things. She'd raced south along the 86. Being a state highway instead of an interstate, it has stoplights here and there along the way. Her pursuers stayed close behind until she beat them through the light at the Avenue 66 intersection. While Amber and her posse waited for the cross traffic to pass, Daley increased her lead.

Somewhere south of Desert Shores she spotted a side road on the right through a palm-tree farm. Side *path* was more like it, running parallel to a drainage ditch. Once clear of the palms she shot off into the desert toward the hills, going totally off-road into the Santa Rosa Mountains. Of course, that was where the old Jeep started coughing and wheezing and losing power. She'd rented it from a garage in Indio—the cheapest thing they had—and it looked like she'd got her money's worth.

With the Jeep bucking and making death rattles, she spotted a group of major boulders and pulled in behind them before the thing died. Farther up the slope she spied this cave, its curved, oblong entrance looking like a toothless grin. The shadowed interior offered shade and a long view of the valley—early warning of trouble approaching. She'd accepted that offer.

Still no sign of pursuit. She'd lost them. Yay for me. But she'd also stuck herself in the middle of nowhere with a dead junker. She seriously doubted she could get an Uber or Lyft to drive out here and take her back to her own car in Coachella, which meant she was going to have to walk to some outpost of civilization along the shore of the Salton.

And that brought up the recurring question of whether these games were worth it. Just because she'd been raised by a grifter family, did she think she had to avoid the straight life?

Maybe. And maybe not.

Not like she hadn't tried straight jobs. Once she'd ditched high school and struck out on her own, she'd found herself honest work. But nothing she tried paid more than minimum wage, mostly because she lacked marketable skills—*legally* marketable skills. Even if they paid her more, she invariably found herself, after only a few weeks on the job, ready to jump off a building from boredom.

That was her problem. Everything bored her, including most

people. High school had bored her so deeply she couldn't even consider college.

Because nothing—absolutely *nothing* in this screwed-up world— gave her a jolt of satisfaction that came even close to walking away from a game with someone else's money in her pocket.

She supposed it was in her blood. Certainly in her upbringing.

After her father's murder, his extended family—"the Family"— insisted on raising her. They were all lower-lip-deep in grift. They believed in scamming rather than schooling. So, while her mom was out working a legit job as a grocery cashier—she wasn't part of the Family—her daughter was having her left leg tied up behind her with her foot nestled against her butt and being put out on the street with an older cousin to beg for money for this poor little amputee. When she got older, she graduated to the big sister of the amputee. She was also dragged along as a cute little prop when her uncles would go door to door finding customers for their driveway-coating scams because, really, would a con man bring his daughter along? Little Stanka—yeah, her given name—also learned to pick pockets and rifle through an unwatched handbag in a shopping cart.

No guilt. Her mother tried to instill some sense of right and wrong into her life, but the vast majority of her extended family— virtually everyone else she knew in the world—took it for granted that grift was life. And so it became second nature for little Stanka, and carried over to grown-up Stanka.

With the sun sinking behind her and shadows of the Santa Rosa peaks starting to creep across the desert before her, Daley figured she'd better get moving.

But as she rose she felt something slap against the top of her head.

She screamed—couldn't help it, screamed like a little girl and ran out of the cave frantically slapping at her head. Something flat and oblong and slightly fuzzy there. The lichen patch? Still running / dancing / hopping in a circle, she gouged at it, trying to work a finger under an edge and peel it off but it was stuck fast to her hair—*glued* to her head. She screamed again as her scalp began to burn, like something was seeping into her.

Then her vision blurred and her legs went soft. She dropped to her knees. As she swayed there, still clutching at her scalp, her vision cleared and she was no longer looking at a desert. The Salton Sea had expanded to a huge lake or small sea that ran as far north and south as she could see, and lapped at the Chocolate Mountains to the east. Something *huge* roiled the water as it glided beneath the surface.

And then everything faded to black.

# 1

Daley awoke in the dark with her face in the dirt.

Where—? What—? Why was she—?

It came back to her: racing through the desert, the cave, the thing on her scalp—

"Oh, shit!"

She rolled over and clawed at the top of her head. That thing, that lichen thing or whatever it was, was still stuck to her.

"Oh-shit-oh-shit-oh-shit-oh-*shit!*"

Wait . . . no, not so stuck. She hadn't been able to budge it before but now it felt loose, ready to fall off. She peeled it away and tossed it aside. Good rid—

No, wait. She might need it. The thing had poisoned her or drugged her—done something to knock her out cold for . . . for how long? Across the valley, the eastern sky behind the Chocolate Mountains was growing pale.

Almost dawn? Had she been out cold all night? God, she was thirsty. The time . . . Where was her phone? In her bag . . . but where was her bag? In the cave . . . but where was—?

All right, *stop.* Get a grip.

She was scattering. She needed to take a breath and get it together. Which she did.

Starlight and predawn glow revealed the black grin of the cave a dozen feet behind her. She stumbled up the slope to the mouth where she made out the lump of her shoulder bag. Stretching, she snatched it to her without going inside. A quick rummage found her keys and mini Maglite.

Okay. Now she had some control of the situation. The flashlight helped her find the thing that had attacked her, although now it didn't look like lichen or moss. An oblong shape, maybe five inches long, wider in the middle, tapering at both ends. Like a mini Nerf football someone had ironed flat and painted gray.

Though it looked dead as could be, Daley didn't want to touch it. She flashed her beam around, looking for a stick, and found instead a short length of two-by-four, nailed to a square of plywood. She flipped it over to reveal a sign with faded red letters.

### STAY OUT!
### DANGER!

"*Now* you tell me?"

But danger from *what?* What was this thing? She felt pretty good now. In fact, except for the thirst, she felt fine. But how had it knocked her out? She knew she'd have to find out.

Using the sign like a spatula, she scooped it up and picked her way down the hillside to the Jeep. She dumped the sign and the thingy in the rear, then tried to start the engine. Lots of clunky whining noises sounding like *forget-it-forget-it-forget-it* but not a hint of combustion.

She stepped out and looked around. Down in the valley she spotted the lights of Desert Shores. Two choices: Start walking now and risk breaking her ankle or worse in a rattlesnake hole, or spend a few hours in the Jeep and start hoofing it at dawn.

But off to her right . . . a light. She watched it for a moment or two but saw no movement. Stay with the Jeep or check it out? With thirst pushing her, the latter seemed like the best option at the moment, so she headed that way.

## 2

The light turned out to be a window in a tiny RV, with two solar panels on the roof and a jury-rigged canopy over the front door. Daley stopped about a dozen feet away. All quiet except for the hum of a generator. She couldn't tell the trailer's color but its metal skin had an odd, lumpy look.

Maybe this wasn't such a good idea. What kind of person lives out here in the middle of nowhere? Could be a whacked-out hermit, a burned-out hippie, or a *Breaking Bad* wannabe. Tons of unpleasant possibilities. But they had to have some water and she was so damn thirsty.

She kept her distance as she called out, "Anybody home?"

After no response, she was readying to try again when the door opened, revealing a squat, vaguely human silhouette.

"Who goes there?" said a scratchy woman's voice.

Relieved to be dealing with a female instead of a meth-head male, Daley said, "Just a thirsty gal whose car broke down."

"Really?" Her tone dripped doubt. "What sort of fool traipses around the desert at this hour?"

Good question. Since she didn't want to go into explaining the angry mob from Coachella, nor the thing that had knocked her out, a bit of fiction seemed in order. During a childhood rife with pervasive prevarications, she'd learned to salt the made-up stuff with as much truth as possible.

"I was exploring a cave back there and sort of lost track of time."

"Cave? You were in the *cave*? Didn't you see the sign?"

"You mean the one that was facedown in the dirt about twenty feet away from it? Yeah. I saw it. *After*. Why—?"

"Damn! How long were you in the cave?"

"I don't know. Hour or two, maybe."

"And nothing . . . bothered you?"

The question jolted Daley. "You know about that . . . that *thing?*"

"Why do you think I put up the sign? Did it land on you?"

Might as well let it all hang out. Maybe this woman could tell her something about whatever it was.

"Yeah. Square on my head. Knocked me out cold. What do you know abou—?"

"Get in here."

"What?"

The old lady stepped back from the door, and Daley could see she wore a frayed T-shirt under bib-front denim overalls. "Get in here right now."

Something new in her tone. Daley couldn't quite put her finger on it. Awe? Excitement?

But she hesitated. "Anybody else in there I should know about?"

"Do you see the size of this thing? In. Here. *Now*."

She had a point. The RV was really tiny. Daley stepped up and in.

Okay, *beyond* tiny: three hundred square feet tops. Hot in here, and kind of smelly—like burnt soup and BO. Lots of junk piled around, shrinking the already cramped living space. But otherwise empty. No one else here but the little lady . . .

. . . and her big revolver.

Daley froze at the sight of it, even though it drooped against her thigh and pointed at the floor.

"What are you going to do with that?" Daley said, pointing.

The woman opened a cabinet and closed the gun inside.

"Nothing now. That was just in case."

"In case what?"

"In case you were a rascal who thought I was a helpless lonely woman."

She wasn't as old as she'd sounded, but she wasn't young either. Her skin tones and nose and cheekbones identified her as a Native American, but which tribe, Daley couldn't guess. Lots of tribes in SoCal.

She lifted a pile of magazines from a chair and tossed them on the floor. "Sit and let me see your scalp."

"Can you spare some water first?"

The woman stepped to the micro-kitchenette and pulled a clear bottle of water from the tiny fridge. It tasted a little funny but Daley didn't care; she gulped it down.

"Now sit," the woman said.

Glad for a seat, Daley complied. She tapped the top of her head. "It landed right in the middle there."

The woman said, "Right where it needed to," and started to probe Daley's scalp with her fingertips.

"You know about these things then?"

"It's called an 'alaret,' and they tend to be deadly."

Daley's stomach did a flip. "It knocked me out but . . . deadly?"

"Very. In all my days keeping watch here, you are the first one I've seen survive. We have a saying about the alaret's victims: 'Of a thousand struck down, nine hundred and ninety-nine will die.'"

Daley could barely speak. "How . . . how long have I got?"

"Oh, not to worry. They kill you right away or not at all. But as I said, we have never seen anyone survive until you."

Relief flooded through her as she said, "'We'?"

"My people: the Desert Cahuilla—the Torres-Martinez tribe."

Well, now Daley knew her tribe. Not that it meant a damn thing to her.

The woman continued fiddling with Daley's scalp. "My name is Juana. And yours?"

"Daley."

Her fingers stopped. "No one names their daughter 'Daley.' Tell me the truth."

She sighed. "Stanka Daley."

"I'm sorry," Juana said.

Was she hard of hearing?

"I said—"

"Oh, I know what you said. I'm just sorry that's your name."

"Not as sorry as me. You know how long it takes in high school for 'Stanka' to become 'Stinka' or 'Skanka'?"

"I will guess two seconds."

"Try half that."

"Stanka . . . I've been around awhile and never heard that one before. Who would name their baby girl Stanka?"

"A Bulgarian father."

Juana frowned. "I know Bulgarians, but none named Stanka. And they are lighter than you."

"My mum said my father was what she called 'swarthy.'"

"And so are you, a little, but your eyes are blue."

"I wound up with my mum's Irish eyes. She told me my father insisted on naming me Stanka because it was his grandmother's name."

Daley understood reverence for a grandmother. Her father was murdered on the day of her birth and she lost her mother to cancer when she was thirteen. Her maternal grandmother took her in and gave her a warm and loving home.

"I shall call you Daley, as you said." Juana then showed her a handful of black hair. "You will find out soon enough so I might as well tell you now: It's falling out."

"That's *mine?*" Daley grabbed it. "Oh, shit. Oh, crap."

"Not to worry. Legend says it will grow back."

"What else does legend say?"

"That you will never be alone."

"'Never be . . .' What does that even *mean?*"

Juana shrugged. "Everything is open to interpretation."

"But I like being alone. I'm not exactly a people person."

Juana seemed not to have heard, or perhaps simply ignored the remark.

"Where is the alaret?"

"In the back of my car."

"I must have it."

Daley shook her head. "No way. I'm taking it to UCLA or USC or someplace where someone can tell me what it is."

"You already know what it is. I have told you."

"Yeah, well, I appreciate that and all, but I'm afraid folktales won't cut it with something that knocked me out cold and is . . ." She reached up, tugged at the point of her skull, and came away with another handful of hair. "And is making me *bald!*" Daley was aware of the woman staring at her. "What?"

"Dawn has come. I will drive you back where you can arrange to have your car towed."

Daley wasn't worried about the junker Jeep. She'd tell the Indio garage owner where he could find it.

"My real car is in Coachella."

"Then I will take you there."

What was going on here? "Why are you doing this for me?"

Juana smiled. "You survived the alaret. You are one in a thousand. It is my duty to help and guide you now."

Seriously? Was she talking about like a spirit guide or something? Daley wasn't in the market for a life coach—last thing she wanted, in fact—but a free ride was a free ride.

Then she thought about touching that dead thing.

"Before we go, do you have a bag you can spare for the alaret?"

Juana pulled one of those flimsy plastic grocery bags from a drawer in the kitchenette.

Daley had to laugh. "Where did you get *that*?"

"Like it says: Stater Brothers."

"But these things have been banned like forever."

"They don't go bad. And in case you failed to notice, I tend to save things." She picked up a set of keys from the counter. "Follow me."

Outside, the sun had yet to clear the mountains but the sky was turning a faint blue. In the light she was startled to see that the lumpiness of the trailer's skin was due to a random assortment of seashells glued to the metal, and the whole thing painted an awful light green.

She ran a hand over them. "Did you used to live at the beach?"

"Never." She sounded insulted.

"Then where—?"

Juana gestured to the desert around them. "Right here. This whole valley used to be underwater, from above Palm Springs all the way down to the Gulf of California, one big inland sea. Dig most anywhere and you'll find shells."

All very interesting, but Daley wanted to get back to her car.

"Fascinating, but can we get going?"

"Yes—going to Coachella. Did you know it was supposed to be called 'Conchilla'? *Concha* is Spanish for shell. But the original mapmaker screwed up and printed it as 'Coachella' and the name stuck."

"Well, I know you have the Salton Sea."

"A mere puddle on the fault."

"Which fault?"

"The big one—San Andreas. Runs right down the middle of the valley. Come this way."

She followed her around back to where a tarp-covered object sat between the RV and a big propane tank.

"I don't believe this," Daley said. "Is that . . . ?"

Juana pulled off the tarp to reveal an old Harley with a sidecar attached.

"Oh, you've gotta be kidding me."

Juana slapped the sidecar. "Take those cinder blocks out and get in."

Daley didn't know about this. She couldn't say Juana was too old to be driving a hog, but she was no spring chicken either.

"Are you sure?"

"This is how I get around."

"Who's the sidecar for?"

"It's handy. Used to be my dog's, but he up and died. Now I keep it hooked on for groceries and supplies and better balance." She handed Daley a banged-up helmet. "Put this on."

Daley took it but could only stand and stare as Juana jammed an ancient leather helmet onto her head and adjusted huge goggles over her eyes. She followed those with a long scarf she wrapped around and around her neck.

"Aren't you worried you're gonna choke?" Daley said.

"Better than ending up like Isadora Duncan."

"Who?"

"Never mind." She gestured to the helmet in Daley's hands. "What are you waiting for?"

# 3

Juana handled the Harley like a seasoned biker. It seemed she'd been back and forth to the cave so many times the bike knew the way on its own.

When they reached the Jeep, Daley hesitated after lifting the rear hatch. She stood there, Stater Brothers bag in hand, and stared at the alaret where it lay limp and flat and gray, just as she'd left it. She tried but couldn't bring herself to touch it.

"Juana, would . . . would you mind putting it in the bag?"

Still straddling the bike, Juana said, "It won't bite you. It's dead. Dead things don't bite."

"I know, but it's skeevy."

"What's 'skeevy'?" She raised a hand before Daley could try to explain. "Never mind. Your face says it all."

She stepped up beside Daley, grabbed the bag—none too gently—and, with a two-finger grip, placed the alaret inside— very gently, almost reverently. Then she carried it back to the Harley and placed it in one of the saddlebags.

Daley had felt slightly ridiculous riding to the Jeep in the side-car, but once they got on the 86 and started racing north, she felt like a totally retro dork, sending up thanks every minute for the helmet's dark visor.

She'd always traveled this route behind the wheel, never as a passenger, so she leaned back and took in the scenery. Almost sur-real. Mountain ranges to the east and west, their bases obscured by a ground-hugging haze in the low desert between—really low, as in below-sea-level low. Patches of virtually bare sand alternating with lush green farms with irrigators spraying, then back to track-less desert. She'd never really wondered where LA got all its palm trees, but now she knew: the desert south of Coachella sported acre after acre of palm-tree farms between stretches of bare sand.

She was even more thankful for the helmet once they reached

Coachella. She doubted any of her angry scamees would be out at this hour, but on the off chance they were, they'd never recognize her. She directed Juana to the Walmart parking lot on Avenue 48 where she'd left her Subaru Crosstrek.

As Daley extricated herself from the sidecar, Juana lifted her goggles and said, "Your life will change now."

She didn't like the sound of that.

"What do you mean?"

"I wish I knew. We've never had to deal with a survivor before."

This wasn't making a whole lotta sense. But then, the source was a native woman who lived alone in the desert.

"Well, thanks for the ride."

"I'll help in any way I can. You need only ask."

Daley couldn't see that happening, but said, "I appreciate that."

"You know where to find me."

As Juana adjusted her goggles and started rolling away, Daley remembered—

"Hey! You've still got the alaret!"

"And I'm keeping it."

"No, wait." Daley started toward her. "You can't. It's mine."

"An alaret belongs to no one!" Juana looked angry now. "They are sacred. We have a ceremony for their remains. They must not be defiled and their home must not be disturbed."

She couldn't be serious. "But I need to know—"

"You know *all* you need to know. Alarets have a purpose, a destiny, and you are now part of that destiny."

With that she twisted the throttle and roared off.

For an instant Daley considered chasing her, then rejected it. What was she going to do—run her off the road and wrestle her for the damn thing? Truth was, she was feeling pretty good right now. Except for losing her hair—no little thing, for sure—she seemed no worse for the incident. Probably better to simply let it go and let it be.

And, of course, stay out of caves in the future.

# 4

"I don't get it."

Rhys Pendry stared at the computer screen. He'd run last night's images as he did every weekday morning, but on this particular morning he'd run them three times, and each pass had yielded the typical array of interpretations from the scrolls. But each pass included an added message at the bottom:

*A PAIRING HAS OCCURRED*

He'd never seen it before. A "pairing"? What did that mean? A pairing of what?

Time to call the expert.

He grabbed the intercom handset and punched *1*—his father's office.

*"Yes, Rhys."*

"Hey, Dad. I just ran last night's scans and keep getting this weird message tagged on to the end: *'A pairing has occurred.'* You ever seen that before?"

*"New one on me. Run them again."*

"I already have—three times, in fact—and keep getting the same thing."

*"How odd. Shoot it over to me and I'll see what I can make of it."*

Rhys captured a screenshot and zapped the image to his father's desk, then followed on foot.

Rhys's father, Elis Pendry, had started the Pendry Fund in 1992, four years before Rhys was born. He limited his clientele to the four other families of the Pendry Clan. That way he could keep his investment strategy secret.

Rhys was learning that strategy. An ill-informed outsider would no doubt laugh it off as astrology and be done with it. But while technically correct, the comparison was as inept as it was inaccurate—like equating algebra with quantum physics. The levels of complexity were like night and day.

The door to his father's office stood open so Rhys breezed through. The Pendry Fund took up much of the first floor of the Lodge and the family lived on the second. Like his parents' master suite right above, his father's office offered a primo view. Set in the Sawtooth foothills, the Lodge had a commanding view of the lower Imperial Valley.

"You were right to bring this to my attention," his father said without looking up from his monitor. "Most odd."

A trim man in his midsixties, Elis Pendry wore his dark hair long and combed it straight back. He sported a few wrinkles around the dark eyes and some gray at his temples, but could easily pass for ten years younger. When he and Rhys were in the same room, no one ever had a problem pairing them as father and son.

Rhys cruised to the giant windows and gazed down at the patchwork quilt of varying shades of green that ran down the center of the valley, all the way to Baja.

Amazing how a steady supply of water could turn a desert wasteland into a breadbasket.

The desert wasn't vanquished, however. It waited patiently, bordering the farmlands and stretching to the base of the mountains, ready to reclaim its territory and reassert its dominance if the water ran out.

Directly below the Lodge sat the sleepy little desert town of Nespodee Springs. And out in the flat wasteland between the town and the farms lay acres of solar panels to the south, and a pinwheeling wind farm to the north.

"Negative results on a superficial search of the Scrolls for 'pairing,'" his father said. "I'm going to run a deep dive to see if anything pops up."

The Scrolls . . . informally known as *The Void Scrolls*, formally titled *Teachings of the Empty Places*, had been discovered by Rhys's triple great-grandfather Alwyn Pendry in a Cairo souq, and they'd changed the course of the clan's life.

Not necessarily for the good, in Rhys's opinion. The Scrolls had sparked Alwyn to form a silly cult of worship around the entities described in the tales they recounted.

Total bullshit.

On the good side they'd persuaded his double great-grandfather Osian to move the clan from Wales to Southern California's Imperial Valley.

Rhys loved the Imperial Valley. Too bad it was in California.

His father, a true believer, had digitized and indexed the Scrolls. He used the star charts within to guide decisions for the clan and, most important, its investments. Telescopic cameras on the roof of the Lodge took nightly photos of the skies which were digitized and run through the computers to be compared to the ancient charts in the Scrolls.

Rhys would have called *bullshit* again, except he couldn't argue with the results. The astronomy-based Pendry strategy had backed the fund out of tech stocks before the rupture of the dotcom bubble, retreated from the entire market before the post–9/11 crash, the 2007 recession, and the Internet-triggered crash earlier this month. They were now in the process of buying back in. As a result of all these moves, the financial status of the five families who made up the Pendry Clan could be summed up by the simple phrase *sitting pretty*.

A soft grunt from his father made him turn in time to see an odd expression cross his features.

"Something wrong, Dad? You look spooked."

"I'm not spooked. Just an odd conjunction in the heavens bringing up a suitably odd interpretation from the Scrolls."

"The 'pairing'?"

His father nodded. "According to the Scrolls, the 'pairing' refers to something called a Duad."

"What's that supposed to mean?"

"I'm going to have to do some deeper digging. It may be good news, it may be bad."

"And if it's bad?"

His father's eyes narrowed. "Then we'll deal with it—decisively."

*The man strides downtown along West 6th Street, slightly hunched against the February wind cutting across the open space of Pershing Square and swirling around the corner up ahead. He's hungry and looking forward to a burger and a brew for lunch. His view of the street ahead of him suddenly dissolves into a vision of a huge, contorted face leering horribly. For an instant he thinks he can feel the brush of its breath on his face. Then it vanishes.*

*He stops and blinks. What was that? He's never experienced anything like it before. He tentatively scrapes a foot forward to start walking again and kicks up a cloud of—*

*—dust. An arid wasteland surrounds him and the sun regards him cruelly, reddening and blistering his skin. And when he feels his blood is about to boil, the sky is suddenly darkened by the wings of a huge featherless bird that circles twice then dives in his direction at a speed that must smash them both. Closer, the cavernous beaked mouth is open and hungry. Closer, until he is—*

*—back on the street. The man leans against the comforting solidity of a nearby building. He is bathed in sweat and his respiration is ragged, gulping. Must find a doctor. He pushes away from the building and—*

*—falls into a black void. But not a peaceful blackness . . . hunger there. He falls, tumbling in eternity. A light below. As he nears, the light takes shape . . . an albino worm, blind, fanged, and miles long, awaits him with gaping jaws.*

*A scream tears from him, a scream with no sound.*

*Still he falls. But the horror has just begun. It becomes unspeakable.*

# 5

Daley drove straight from Coachella to her place in North Hollywood. She'd have liked someplace flashier than her dinky one-bedroom rental above a bookstore on Burbank Boulevard, but the price was right and it served her needs for now.

She faced one decision upon entering: shower then bed or bed then shower? A sudden crushing fatigue won and she dropped face-first onto the comforter and fell into a coma-like sleep.

And dreamed . . .

Strange, surreal images paraded through her dreamscape, fading as quickly as they appeared, making increasingly less sense until . . .

She awoke, feeling only slightly refreshed, fighting a strange, drugged feeling. A shower . . . a shower would freshen her up.

But the shower left her cursing at all the hair clumped in the drain—she was losing even more. As she dried off she checked her head in the mirror. No bald spots yet but definitely thinning in the shape of that damn slug—that *alaret*.

Daley kept her dark hair long enough to tie back but not long enough to be a pain. Usually she parted it in the middle but switched to a side part now to hide the thinning.

A comb-over, she thought. Can't believe I need a comb-over!

As she ran the comb across her head—loosening even more hair—she saw a flash of movement behind her in the mirror. Startled and maybe a little frightened, she wrapped the bath towel more tightly around her and peeked out.

The bathroom sat across a short hall from her bedroom. The wide-open living room/dining room/kitchen area lay to her right. No sign of movement out there.

The place felt empty, but still . . .

"Hello?"

No answer—no surprise—so she quick-checked the apartment door: locked. No surprise there either. Locking was automatic for her. She locked the sidewalk-level door and the door at the top of the stairs without thinking. A quick inspection of the rest of her small apartment confirmed she was alone.

But she could have sworn she'd seen someone dart past the bathroom door.

So . . . what? Stress? Or blame it on the alaret as well?

She shook it off and got dressed. She had business to take care of.

Down to the car and over to the UPS Store on Victory Boulevard where she pulled two manila envelopes—one fat, one slim—from her box there. On the way back she reacted and almost had an accident when she thought she saw someone sitting in the passenger seat. Just a flash and then gone. No one there.

What was going on?

Back in the apartment, she checked the slim envelope first. Oh, good. Her homeopathy certificate.

She'd taken an online course and easily passed. Halfway through she realized how the whole underlying theory behind homeopathy was total bullshit, but she went the distance anyway. Why not? The course was a cinch, the degree gave her credibility in the eyes of the gullible, and California allowed the practice of homeopathy without a license. Now she had to find a way to put it to work for her.

She put that aside and dumped the contents of the fat manila: Two dozen or so legal-size envelopes addressed to Burbank Drain and Pipe Cleaning, Inc., landed on the dining room table. The company had a box in the Burbank UPS Store. Jorge, the owner there, would empty the box whenever it filled, pack the contents in a manila envelope, and forward it all to Daley's other box in the North Hollywood store. He enclosed a bill for the UPS ground charge and a ten-dollar handling fee which Daley paid immediately via PayPal.

Each envelope contained a check for $64.35 made out to Burbank Drain and Pipe Cleaning, Inc.

Two years ago Daley had started sending out invoices to various companies all over greater Los Angeles billing sixty dollars—plus tax, of course—for "Monthly pipe and drain maintenance." She sent out hundreds. Most ignored her or sent queries as to the charge, which she ignored. But a percentage of the companies paid the bill. Those that did were added to her billing list, and the first of every month she sent them another invoice. And every month they paid. They'd added Burbank Drain and Pipe Cleaning, Inc., to their accounting software as a payee, and so its bills were honored, no questions asked.

Once she had all the checks tallied against her list, she walked over to the Citibank branch where she'd opened the Burbank Drain and Pipe Cleaning, Inc., account and deposited them. She never let too much accumulate in the business account; once a month she emptied it down to the minimum required amount and redeposited the excess cash into her personal account at Chase. As an emergency backup she kept a stash of hundred-dollar bills rolled up inside a fat, hollowed-out wax candle.

The key was not to get greedy. Sixty-four dollars and change . . . overworked bookkeepers in a busy, successful company tended not to look too closely at such a paltry sum. The $772 it cost the companies a year had no impact on their bottom line and went unnoticed on their spreadsheets. But the sum meant a lot to Daley. At the moment she had fifty-two companies on the string. That came to forty grand a year. She wasn't into high living, so that amount paid all her bills and allowed her to sock some away for the proverbial and inevitable rainy day.

On her way back from the bank, she realized she was famished and stopped at a local taqueria on Oxnard. As she ate her quesadilla at the window counter, she saw a woman staring her way from inside the beauty salon across the street. The reflection off the window made it difficult to make her out clearly, but damned if she didn't look like that Indian woman from the desert—Juana.

But then the woman stepped back into the shadows and disappeared.

Was Juana following her? Why would she do that? Daley shook it off. Lots of women around here looked like Juana. Don't get paranoid.

As she walked back to her apartment her phone buzzed with a text from Kenny.

Wassup?

                                        Nothing. Just hangin

Do the dew drop?

                                        Sounds good. 5?

CU there

The Dew Drop Inn sat just around the corner from her place, a neighborhood hang with an everybody-knows-your-name vibe. A favorite pastime there was poking fun at the bar's corny name but that didn't deter the locals from making it their go-to watering hole.

And Kenny . . . well, the two of them had shared a hot and heavy romance for about half a year as they'd tried to live together. She should have known they were doomed. Daley needed a certain amount of alone time on a regular basis and Kenny was clingy like a Siamese twin. She felt like she was suffocating and he felt rejected. The cohabitation experiment crashed and burned, but they learned they could still get along—just so long as they lived apart, as friends. The sex, though, had always been great so they'd remained friends with benefits.

Back home she flipped on the TV and landed on an all-news channel running an update on the latest hot news story, "the horrors." Daley clicked that off ASAP. The horrors gave her the creeps.

She checked herself in the mirror before heading out for some friendly faces. She debated wearing a baseball cap but decided her comb-over was hiding her hair loss just fine.


The Dew Drop housed the usual Thursday night crowd. Daley and Kenny leaned against the bar, catching up over wings and drinks—beer for him, a margarita for her. She liked Kenny, liked his longish surfer-blond hair, the dark brown eyes, the flashing smile.

The TV had been switched off its usual ESPN to a special news show and no one minded—except Daley. The horrors again.

HURON PUBLIC LIBRARY
521 DAKOTA AVE S
HURON, SD 57350-2797

The whole world was wondering about the spreading medical mystery—some kind of weird fit where the victim gets hit with whatever it is that hits him, screams hysterically, and then goes catatonic, completely cut off from the rest of the world. Cases were popping up all over Southern California and nowhere else. Once you went down with the horrors, you stayed down.

"Scary stuff," Kenny said, leaning close. "If they don't know what causes it, how do you avoid it?"

"Gotta be a virus, don't you think?" Daley said.

Kenny shrugged. "They say it's not contagious."

That was when Daley spotted the shirtless guy across the room.

"Did they change the rule about no shirts?" she said, staring at the guy's bare shoulders as he moved away through the crowd. No tats, which was unusual for this neighborhood.

Kenny turned to see. "Not that I know of. Where?"

She pointed with her glass. "Over there by the front window."

"Where?" he said, craning his neck. "Don't see him."

Neither did Daley. "Must've sat down. Probs a newbie. Better not let Edgar spot him."

Edgar had a big beard, was built like a grizzly, and owned the place. He barely tolerated tank tops, and shirtless was cause for ejection. No one knew what his problem was, but he had a *No Shirt, No Service* sign at the door and he meant it.

"Looked a lot like you," Daley said.

Kenny smiled. "Devilishly handsome?"

She'd always had a weak spot for guys like Kenny.

"Well, devilish anyway. But he keeps his hair longer like you used to, the way I liked better."

Kenny ran a hand through his hair. "Yeah, well, the new job and all. Gotta look professional and—"

"Hey," Daley said as she spotted Mr. No-Shirt. "There he goes again."

"Where?"

"I can't believe you don't see him." She pointed. "Right over there by Edgar."

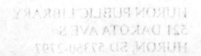

"A shirtless guy by Edgar? No way. He'd be out on his ear. I see Edgar plain as day, but as for this other guy . . ."

Daley checked Kenny to see if he was joking but he didn't seem to be. When she looked back, Mr. No-Shirt was out of sight.

Kenny grinned as he clinked his beer bottle against her margarita. "How many of these you have?"

"Not enough to start seeing things."

He leaned closer. "Enough to put you in the mood?"

"Maybe." After the last couple of days she was definitely in the mood. "You?"

"I'm always in the mood for you."

Rarely was Kenny *not* in the mood.

She drained her drink. "Let's go."

## 6

"Oh, my God." Daley rolled off Kenny and flopped onto her back, limp and sweaty. "You done good, Kenny. You done—"

She heard a strange, strangled sound and opened her eyes.

Someone was standing beside her bed. She blinked and recognized Mr. No-Shirt. But more than his shirt was missing—he was totally naked.

His mouth worked, making that strangled sound again.

She screamed.

Kenny levered up to a sitting position beside her. "Wha-wha-what? What's wrong?"

Daley was pulling the sheet over her and screaming at the naked surfer guy.

"Get out! Get outa here!"

"Get out?" Kenny said. "What'd I do?"

"Not you!" she said, pointing. *"Him!"*

"Who?"

"The guy from the Dew Drop! The one with no—" She turned to Kenny. "Is this some kinda sick joke?"

"Daley, there's nobody there!"

"Fuck you, Kenny! Fuck you and your sick friend!"

With that she grabbed her phone off the night table and threw it at the stranger—

—and watched it sail right through him.

And then he disappeared. *Pfffft!* Gone without a trace.

Daley stared at the empty space while beside her Kenny rattled on about no one there and he'd never let another guy in on them and what was she thinking? She barely heard.

He couldn't have disappeared. Not possible. Her eyes were playing tricks. Had he run out to the front room? No, he couldn't have moved that fast. She checked the floor beside her bed—nothing. The box spring was barely six inches off the rug, so he couldn't be under it.

Something way, way wrong here. Was she seeing things? *Hallucinating*—that was the word. Kenny hadn't seen Mr. No-Shirt in the bar, and the guy had been right next to Edgar who would have thrown him out on his ass . . . *if* he'd seen him. Now he was in her apartment. And she always locked both doors to her apartment—*always*.

"Kenny, check the front room."

"What?"

"Just check to see if anybody's there."

"This is nuts, Daley."

"Please."

"Okay, okay."

He hopped out of bed and padded into the front room and returned a moment later.

"Nada, babe. I checked behind the couch and the chairs, the closets. Nobody. And the door's locked."

Which meant he hadn't really been here.

"I think you're seeing things, babe."

"I think you may be right. You've gotta go, Kenny."

"What?"

"No, seriously. I'm not feeling too great. I was out in the desert overnight and I think I'm a little dehydrated."

"Out in the desert? What—?"

"I just need a little alone time."

He grabbed his jeans. "You *always* need a little alone time."

"I'm sorry. I just do. Just to rehydrate and all that."

He huffed and he puffed and stormed out. He wouldn't stay mad for long. He never did. But Daley . . . Daley was all shaky inside. What was happening to her? She'd never ever—

That strangled noise again and the naked guy flickered into view.

She yelped with surprise. He was back!

No, he wasn't. He flickered out again.

Did someone drug her margarita? Or was she going bonkers?

Wait—that alaret thing. Did it do something to her? Release some sort of toxin into her brain that was making her see things?

Whatever the cause, seeing people who weren't there was very, very wrong, and she had to do something about it. Had to get to the ER and—

No. No way she could explain this to them.

*Some weird little thing dropped on my head in a desert cave and messed up my brain.*

Right. That'll fly.

Before she started telling crazy stories to the docs she had to be able to play show-and-tell. Had to get her hands on that alaret thing and bring it in, find out what it really is. And that meant going back to the one person who seemed to know something about it.

She jumped out of bed and started to get dressed. Then stopped.

She'd never find Juana's trailer in the dark. There was dark and then there was desert dark. And Juana lived off-road.

"Shit!"

She'd have to wait till morning.

She wrapped herself in a blanket, turned on the TV, and landed on a *Storage Wars* marathon. She let it play without seeing it as she huddled on the couch. The thought of sleep was inconceivable. She was looking at an all-nighter.

Jodi Karensky . . . the name came out of the blue. Daley shivered under the blanket as she remembered . . . one of her few friends during high school. Jodi started hearing voices a couple of years after graduation, and then talking to people who weren't there. They diagnosed her with schizophrenia and eventually found a medical cocktail that controlled the symptoms. But Jodi wasn't really Jodi anymore.

Supposedly schizophrenia hit people in their twenties. Was that what this was?

No. Couldn't be. It started just hours after that cave slug had knocked her out. There had to be a connection. Had to be.

Please . . . no more noises, no more hallucinations . . . peace until I can find Juana.

# 1

The sun had cleared the Chocolate Mountains by the time Daley reached the Salton Sea.

Despite her intention to stay up all night, she'd dozed off and had strange dreams—water dreams. At some point in the past she'd heard that a water dream had meaning but she'd forgotten what it was. All bullshit anyway. She was pretty sure hers had to do with today's trip to the desert, because the desert—this very desert—had been underwater in her dream. And she'd been underwater too, but not drowning. Juana had told her how the whole Salton trough had been filled with seawater millions of years ago, so that must have stayed with her.

See? Nothing mystical or paranormal. Just lingering suggestions from the day before.

Seeing naked guys, however . . . what was *that* all about?

At least she'd made it through the night with no more appearances. The blare of a car dealer commercial on the TV had awakened her at four A.M. and she'd debated canceling the trip. She'd been symptom free, so maybe it had all been due to dehydration after all.

Then she'd heard a garbled voice say a word that sounded like *"low"* but spoken with a mouth full of popcorn. She waited, hoping she hadn't really heard it, but then it came again.

That was when she'd decided to hit the road in the dark.

Now, three hours later, she was nearing her destination in full morning light. And every twenty minutes or so she heard the voice garbling that same word.

(". . . low . . .")

There it was again.

Yeah, she needed to be back here, needed to find Juana.

She retraced her path from yesterday into the Santa Rosas. With its lower clearance, her Crosstrek wasn't as off-road-friendly as the Jeep had been, but it got the job done. She located the boulders where she'd hidden the Jeep—gone now—and pulled into the same spot.

Looking uphill she could see the mouth of the cave and couldn't suppress a little shudder. Never again.

Okay . . . she'd been a little fuzzy after she woke up, but she remembered standing here and spotting the light from Juana's trailer toward the south. A pair of binocs would have helped right now, but who had binocs? The terrain looked too rough and bouldery for her Crosstrek so, with the sun countering the chill in the morning air, she took off on foot.

After a ten-minute wander she spotted the trailer and its canopy and made her way toward it. She'd expected to have to bang on the door but Juana was already up and sitting on an aluminum folding chair outside her shell-studded home, soaking up the morning sun.

"I thought I'd have to wake you," Daley said as she neared.

Juana gave her a concerned look, then smiled. "Oh, it's you—but you look different now that you're cleaned up." The smile turned to a frown. "Don't tell me you've come for the alaret."

"It did something to me. You said you'd help me any way you could, and all I had to do was ask. Well, I'm asking."

Juana's expression softened. She pointed to a folded aluminum chair like her own, leaning against the trailer.

"Sit. Please."

Daley unfolded the chair and eased into it. "You told me my life would change. What did you mean by that?"

"Has it?"

That wasn't an answer, but . . .

"Nothing major yet, but if this keeps up, it could be huge . . . and not for the better."

"Like what?"

She saw herself in a straitjacket, but batted it away.

"I keep hearing a voice."

Juana leaned forward, intent. "What does it say?"

"Nothing. Nothing I can understand, anyway. And then last night I was seeing things . . . this naked guy."

"Naked?"

"Yeah. Looked a little like a friend of mine. That's why I need what's left of that alaret."

Juana stared at her a moment, then rose to her feet. "You want your alaret? Wait here."

She entered her trailer and emerged later with a small glass jar.

Handing it to Daley she said, "Here is what is left of your alaret."

Daley saw only gray powder inside. It looked like . . .

"Ashes? You burned it?"

"That is how we—my sisters and I—dispose of a dead alaret: the traditional way."

Daley resisted the urge to wing it at her head.

"Tradition? Your people have a tradition about these cave slugs?"

"My sisters and I do." She gestured to the trailer. "We take turns here. The sign keeps people away from the cave—"

"Not if they can't see it!"

"Perhaps it was down for a reason. Perhaps you were meant to meet an alaret."

"'Meant to'?" Daley was out of the chair. "Oh, no, lady. What's meant to happen is me going back to that cave and finding another one of those things and bringing it back to civilization where they can put it under a microscope and find out what the hell it is!"

Juana shook her head. "You will find nothing. One doesn't find an alaret—an alaret finds you. Remember: 'Of a thousand struck down, nine hundred and ninety-nine will die.'"

"How can you have any idea that's true?"

"Tradition says so. You didn't die. Perhaps you were lucky. Or perhaps you are special. Perhaps you survived because you will serve a purpose."

Daley was turning to go, but that stopped her. "What sort of purpose?"

A shrug. "Who is to say? Strange times are coming. The stars align in patterns not seen for ages. Something is brewing."

"Can you tell me anything *useful*? Anything?"

"Our tradition says the alarets came from the stars and stayed, waiting."

"Waiting for what?"

"Until one was needed."

"Needed for what?"

Another shrug. "Who is to say?"

"Damn it, lady, you're talking in circles!"

Juana looked genuinely distressed. "I didn't create these traditions. They're ancient, and they aren't handed down whole. They come in fragments. I can only know what has survived the centuries."

"And that's all you've got for me?"

Juana spread her hands. "I'm afraid so."

Shaking her head, Daley walked away. Stars aligning . . . "meant to be" . . . nothing was meant to be. Shit happened, and this time it had happened to her. And these ashes . . . what use were ashes? Who knew if they were really the alaret anyway? Could have been scooped from a campfire. She'd keep them anyway, in case of the unlikely possibility that somebody somewhere could extract something useful from them.

She called over her shoulder, "Yeah, well, thanks for all your help."

"I want to help," Juana said. "I do. I'm here to help and guide you whenever you need it."

She sounded so damn sincere.

"Right."

(". . . low . . .")

There it was again. Daley started walking faster.

Juana called after her. "Where are you going?"

"To check out that cave. If you won't help me I'll have to find someone who will—like a hospital where I can get a checkup from the neck up."

"But you're not sick. When you hear the voice, listen to it."

*Low?* She was supposed to listen to *low?*

Daley made it back to the car and stood by the rear hatch, staring up at the cave mouth. She did *not* want to go back in there.

She grabbed her flashlight and trudged up the slope. Light from the rising sun angled into the cave but she doubted it would be enough. She hesitated at the mouth, but only for a second. If she waited too long, she'd lose her nerve.

Pressing her hand over her head, she ducked inside and shone the flash beam on the ceiling: nothing but naked rock. Not a trace of lichen . . . or alaret. She leaner farther in—

("Hel . . . low . . .")

Daley yelped with surprise and jerked upright, smacking her head against the cave ceiling.

"Damn!"

("Hel-lo?")

Still garbled but definitely a word now. She stumbled back down the slope to her car.

("Hello!")

"Oh, God!"

("It's not God and I'm sorry I upset you.")

"No-no-no!"

Speaking rapidly, the voice said, ("I was trying to break my existence to you slowly. You know, let you spot me across a crowded room, then move in closer and closer, let you get used to the sight of me, then introduce myself. But I wasn't fully integrated into our nervous system so I botched it. I've spent the night working on integration. I think I've got it now.")

She reached the Subaru to find Mr. No-Shirt in the passenger seat. Calm, composed, like he was waiting for his order at a McDonald's drive-thru. Except he was fucking *naked*.

Daley was damned if she'd allow herself to scream again. But she wanted to. She didn't want to wind up like Jodi Karensky.

("You don't have schizophrenia.")

Has to be that alaret thing. It did something—

("Yes, it's 'that alaret thing' doing this.")

What was happening to her mind? Why was it playing these tricks on her?

("Nothing's wrong with your mind. You're not crazy. And I'm not a schizophrenic hallucination. I thought you'd be more comfortable conversing with a person rather than a disembodied voice in your head, so I'm creating this image in your visual cortex and translating my thoughts into a voice in your auditory cortex.")

"Please stop," she said as tears threatened. She didn't know how to deal with this. "Please go away."

And he—it—did. Simply vanished.

She needed help, big-time help, and she wasn't going to find it here in the desert. She had to get back to LA.

# 2

The apparition reappeared in the passenger seat as Daley was passing the Palm Desert wind farms. But she stayed calm. It couldn't hurt her. He—it—didn't seem the least bit self-conscious about being naked. She had to admit he had a good body, and was pretty well hung—

Wait-wait-wait! I'm thinking of him as *real*. He's not.

"You're not real," she said aloud, keeping her voice low as she made it a mantra. "You're not real, you're not real, you're—"

("Well, this image you see isn't real, but I, as an entity, am quite real.")

She remembered a poem from her childhood and began reciting it.

> *"Last night I saw upon the stair*
> *A little man who wasn't there*
> *He wasn't there again today*
> *How I wish he'd go away . . ."*

("Not going to happen, Stanka, so I'm afraid you'll have to get used to me. You've got yourself a roommate. From now on, you and I will be sharing your body.")

Daley started to reply, then cut herself off. She would not talk to a hallucination. And then she thought, why the hell not? Her brain was creating this apparition, right? So in a sense she'd be talking to herself. And she'd done that before. She'd see how far she could take this.

"In other words, I've been invaded? I'm occupied territory?"

("'Invaded' is such a loaded term, Stanka, and not quite accurate. I'm not really taking anything from you except some of your privacy, and that shouldn't really matter since the two of us will be so intimately associated.")

The fact that it was calling her Stanka was a bit concerning, since she thought of herself as Daley. Wouldn't a figment of her mind call her "Daley"? But she'd keep playing the game.

"And just what gives you the right to invade my mind—*and* my privacy?"

("Nothing gives me that right, but we have extenuating circumstances here. You see, yesterday I was a fuzzy cave slug with no intelligence to speak of—")

"For a slug you speak English pretty good."

("It's 'pretty well.' You know better.")

I'm correcting my own English?

("And besides,") it went on, ("I speak no better and no worse than you do. I derive whatever knowledge and intelligence I have from you. I know only what you know. So if you don't know something, neither do I. As an aside, although you have high intelligence, your knowledge base is quite lacking. Also, we need to work on building your vocabulary.")

"What?"

Now I'm insulting myself?

All right, maybe just stating a fact. She didn't kid herself. She'd hated school and wasn't a big reader.

("Your vocabulary is deficient in many areas, which puts limits on my ability to express myself. But to get back to your comment about 'invading,' that would be quite immoral.")

"Gotcha! You just said you were a cave slug before you invaded me. What would an ex-slug know about morality?"

("With the aid of your rational faculties I can reason now. And if I can reason, why can't I arrive at a moral code? This is your body and I am here only because of blind instinct. I have the ability to take control—not without a struggle, of course—but it would be immoral to do so. Even if I wanted to, I cannot vacate your mind and body, so we're stuck with each other, Stanka. Forever.")

Yesterday . . . in the trailer . . . hadn't Juana said Daley would never be alone again?

No freakin' way.

"I know you're not real, and we'll see how 'stuck' I am when the hospital runs some tests on me. And if you're supposed to be part of me, you know damn well it's not 'Stanka,' it's 'Daley.'"

Why not? As Uncle Seamus liked to say: In for a dime, in for a dollar. If she had to listen to this figment, it might as well get her name right.

("'Daley.'") The image made a sour face. ("I don't like it. Not feminine enough.")

"And 'Stanka' is better?"

Another face, with increased sourness. ("You do have a point. I shall call you 'Daley,' as you wish. But what shall we call me?")

"You're not going to be around long enough to need a name. Please go away. If I have to listen to you all the way back to LA, I'll run us into a bridge abutment just to get some peace and quiet."

("Oh, don't do that. If you die, I die.")

"Then go!"

("I'm gone.")

And it vanished.

At least she had *some* control over it. Or was that just another illusion?

Her phone rang. The screen read *Gram*. She picked up—always for Gram.

"Hey, Gram."

*"Hello, dearie. Just calling to see how you're doing. Haven't heard from you in a while."*

"Sorry about that. Been busy." Before Gram could ask, she added, "Car sales down in Coachella."

*"Oh. How nice."*

This old Irish lady wouldn't approve of her granddaughter involving herself in grift.

*"And would you be stopping by any time soon? Your uncle and I miss you."*

"I miss you guys too. I'll be by within the week. I guarantee it."

As soon as she straightened out her head.

*"Oh, that's wonderful. See you soon, dearie."*

"Love you, Gram."

*"Love you right back."*

Daley jumped as the apparition reappeared and said, ("I'm sensing a lot of love for this woman.")

Tons of love. She and Pa spirited her away from the Family after her mum died and gave her a loving home. So much so that she changed her last name to Gram and Pa's. Gram became the most important person in Daley's life. Still was.

"None of your business—and I thought I banished you."

("You did. I was just struck by the depth of feeling and—")

"Go! *Go!*"

("You don't have to shout.")

It vanished again.

*Depth of feeling* . . . Yeah, Gram and Pa had shown her what a normal life could be, but they hadn't been able to erase the imprint the Family had left on her brain.

And now she had something else on her brain.

But not for long.

# 3

"Well, look who's up early," Rhys said as he stepped into the din-ing room.

His mother might have been an early riser once, but for years now, with all the meds perking through her system, her morning arrival rarely coincided with the early breakfast he and Dad cus-tomarily shared. But here she was, up and about, indulging in her usual repast of coffee and vape smoke.

He pecked her on the cheek. "What's the occasion?"

"No occasion. Your father was up and down all night."

If she was annoyed, her tone didn't reflect it. The antidepres-sants had flattened her affect, flattened her tone—as flat as the desert below. They hadn't flattened her body, however. Mom had packed on the pounds in the ten years since she'd lost the baby who would have been Rhys's sister, Aerona. She blamed the antidepres-sants for the weight, and was probably right.

"Oh? Is he all right?"

"Physically, yes. He came to bed at his usual hour, but then, before I knew it, he was up and rushing downstairs for some-thing. Then he'd be back to toss and turn, then jump up and head downstairs again. This went on all night—up and down, up and down. I finally gave up altogether on the idea of sleep and got dressed."

"I wonder if . . ." Rhys stopped himself.

Mom blew a vape cloud and said, "'Wonder if' what?"

He'd started to say he wondered if Cadoc had seen him but bit it back. Doc Llewelyn had advised Rhys and his father not to mention her stillborn daughter for fear of tipping her into one of her down-ward spirals. Rhys had learned over the years never to mention her firstborn son for fear of setting off a tirade about never seeing him, never having even a simple meal with both her sons present.

He spotted Maria coming out of the kitchen with Cadoc's breakfast tray. She'd been the family cook for as long as Rhys could remember. Though gray-haired and wrinkled now, she used to be quite a beauty. He'd had a crush on her as a kid.

"Excuse me," he told his mother as he followed Maria down the hall to the rear of the living quarters.

He stood back as she stopped before Cadoc's door and slid the tray through the slot on the floor. He gave her a smile as she passed him on her way back to the kitchen.

"Just some toast and coffee for me this morning, Maria."

She nodded and continued on her way.

Rhys knocked on Cadoc's door.

"Hey, bro. Did you happen to see Dad last night?"

*"Ungh,"* from the other side. A single grunt from Cadoc meant *Yes.*

"I'm going to guess he was in and out of the library. Am I right?"

*"Ungh."*

"Was he okay?"

*"Ungh."*

"Okay, bro. Later."

You didn't say *See you later* to Cadoc because nobody saw Cadoc. Mainly because Cadoc didn't want to be seen.

So . . . Dad had been haunting the library. Rhys could think of only one reason: the mysterious "pairing" message from yesterday.

Instead of returning to the kitchen he headed downstairs to the business level. He found his haggard-looking father in the library with the translation of the Scrolls scattered before him on a desk.

"What's up, Dad?"

"Found it!" he said, slapping the papers.

Researching the printed version made no sense, not after his father had spent years digitizing the translation.

"Wouldn't it have been easier to use the computer? You've got search functions there. With the papers—"

"You'd be one hundred percent right if the Scrolls had been one hundred percent digitized. But I left out certain sections that duplicated prior information or appeared to be digressions, and heavily encrypted other sections that are too sensitive to place at risk of hacking."

"Too sensitive?" Rhys had had no idea. "How so?"

"You'll learn when you reach your thirtieth."

"That's only a year away—"

"Fourteen months, to be exact. Right now, only one living being has read those sections. When you reach thirty, that number will double. But not until then."

"But—"

"You're not ready now and you might not even be ready then, but you're my heir, after all. Leadership of the clan will fall to you. It is my duty to pass on the secret knowledge of the clan to the next generation."

. . . *secret knowledge of the clan* . . . It sounded so ominous, like it should have been accompanied by a sepulchral music cue.

"But as I was saying, I left out certain sections of the Scrolls that appeared to be digressions. And for the most part, I chose correctly. But this 'pairing' event was not on my radar."

"You found references to the Duad, then?"

"Actually Cadoc did."

"Cadoc? He helped you?" Rhys couldn't help but feel a little hurt. "I would have—"

"You were dead to the world in bed. Cadoc's a night owl. He was out and about anyway. It gave him something to do."

True. Cadoc left his room only at night after everyone else had turned in. Moved through the dark with a flashlight. He couldn't speak—his vocal cords were as disfigured as his body—but he had a sharp mind. Rhys knew that from their late-night chess games.

"But you allowed him to see the secret texts?"

"Of course not."

"He's over thirty."

"But he's not going to head the clan—that's the last job he would want. There are passages in the Scrolls he must never read. And when you take my place, you must protect him from those secrets."

"'Protect him'?"

"You'll understand once you're privy to the texts." He slapped his hand on the desk. "We keep drifting from the subject! The

Duad—Cadoc found it in the last Scroll—the *end* of the last Scroll."

"Isn't that typical? Well, don't keep me in suspense. Good news or bad?"

"Both. The Duad is bad news—it carries the threat of discord."

*The Duad of Discord*, Rhys thought. Sounds like a bad rap duet.

"What do we do about it?"

Dad shrugged. "The Scrolls give no clue as to how to identify it, so we're forced into a reactive position. Stellar conjunctions might give us a clue as to when we should act."

Try as he might—and he didn't try terribly hard—Rhys couldn't dredge up much concern.

"And the good news?"

His father's eyes lit. "The Pairing, the advent of the Duad, it's a sign that alignments are imminent for a return of the Visitors."

Rhys fought an eye roll. "Oh."

He always had to bite his tongue about this bullshit. His father was the leader of the clan and that meant he was leader of the cult that worshipped these supernatural or interdimensional or whatever beings—the Visitors. Also known as the Rymwyr, but "Visitors" was easier on the tongue. Also known as the Lords of Creation. As if. The mythology had it that they'd visited Earth millions and millions of years ago and populated various wet areas, back when the Salton Trough outside was an inland sea connected to the Pacific. But five million years ago, for some unknown reason, they packed up and left. After that the trough was blocked from the Pacific and began to dry up, evolving to its current desert state.

According to the Scrolls, when certain celestial conjunctions occurred, the Visitors could return. But to a desert? No conceivable way was the Salton Trough going to fill up with water again, so the return of the Visitors remained the ultimate long shot.

"I know you're a skeptic, Rhys, but there's so much you don't know yet."

"Then why don't you tell me."

"I believe we just had this discussion. But if it becomes clear that the Visitors' return is imminent, I may have to accelerate your education. If that becomes the case, I'll do more than tell you, I'll *show* you. Just as I've been showing you my investment secret. When I first told you about that, you were your usual skeptical self. But now?"

Rhys had to admit that the wacky idea of guiding your investments by the stars had totally put him off at first, but . . .

"Can't argue with your results, Dad."

Never hurt to give the Old Man a stroke or two, right?

"And you won't be able to argue with the revealed truths about the Visitors as the Lords of Creation once your eyes are opened."

Oh, I don't know about that, Rhys thought.

"When do you think that will be?"

"It could be soon, Rhys. Very soon. Even sooner should the Duad dare to show up in Nespodee Springs. But on to more mundane matters: Don't make any plans for Sunday. You're scheduled for the Nofio watch."

Rhys groaned. "It's been three months already?"

"Quite," he said with a slightly bitter smile. "Time accelerates as you age."

"I'm not thirty yet—as you keep reminding me."

"The Nofio is only an hour of your time."

But a *long* hour—the goddamnedest longest hour imaginable.

# 4

Daley drove straight to the ER at St. Joseph's in Burbank which, lucky for her, wasn't all that busy. She filled out the forms and then a medical assistant in scrubs with a *Sofia* name tag led her to a curtained cubicle. She did the vital signs thing and wrote down Daley's reasons for coming to the ER.

She'd just reclined on the gurney when a young Hispanic guy in a white coat, tablet in hand, and looking like he'd be more at home playing soccer for North Hollywood High than doctoring in an ER, slipped through the curtain. With Sofia standing by—probably hospital rules to have a female present—he introduced himself as Dr. Gomes.

"So, Ms. Daley, you're seeing things?"

She sat up to face him. "Not things—a guy. A blond-haired guy who isn't there."

He looked around. "Do you see him now? Is he here?"

"No."

("Yes, I am. I'm always here.")

Daley stiffened at the words.

"Something wrong?" Gomes said.

"He just spoke to me in my head."

His eyebrows rose and he scribbled on his tablet with a stylus. "So . . . auditory as well as visual. When did this start?"

"Around nine o'clock last night."

He stared at her. "Please answer me honestly, Ms. Daley: You have no medications listed. Do you take any meds or drugs, legal or otherwise, *not* listed here?"

She'd experimented with pot and speed and 'shrooms as part of her teenage rites of passage, but nothing in the past five or six years. Pot might be legal but it never did much for her, and in her line of work she had to be on top of her game at all times.

"I had two margaritas with some wings last night. Other than that, I'm clean. Any drug screen you want to do will back that up."

He nodded like a drug screen was definitely on his list. "Any headaches, blurred vision—?"

"No, but something happened yesterday that might be important. I was . . . exploring a cave in the Santa Rosas when something attached itself to the top of my head."

He looked dubious. "What sort of something?"

"I don't know. Flat and oblong, maybe five or six inches long. Ugly thing."

("I beg your pardon!")

Gomes was staring at her hair. "Where exactly did it attach to you?"

"Right here," she said, patting the top of her head . . . where she felt loose hair. She came away with a handful.

"Aw, no."

Gomes stepped closer and probed her scalp. After coming away with his own handful of hair, he made a "hmmmm" sound and starting scribbling and tapping on his tablet.

("You seem upset. It's only temporary. The hair follicles aren't dead, just shocked. Your hair will grow back, I promise.")

She found the words *It damn well better!* forming on her tongue but bit them back. If she started talking to the air she'd end up on a psych ward.

"All right," Gomes said. "I'm ordering labs and an MR to see if anything shows up. I'll be back when we have results."

He and Sofia slipped out, leaving Daley alone.

The naked surfer dude appeared again, standing at the foot of the gurney. ("They won't find anything, Daley.")

"We'll see about that." She shook her head and gazed up at the ceiling. "Listen to me—talking to someone who isn't here."

She hopped off the gurney, walked over to him—it—whatever—and waved her arm through his neck. If it had been a sword and if he were flesh and blood, he'd be headless now.

"Jesus! You're like air!"

"Excuse me," said a voice behind her. A young black woman holding a tray of needles and glass tubes had parted the curtains. "I thought I heard you talking to someone."

"I was," Daley said, waving her arm back and forth through the apparition's bare chest. "Can't you see him?"

The tech backed out slowly. "I . . . I'll be back in a minute."

Daley returned to the gurney. "But even if all this is true—and I refuse to believe it really is—how did you get into my brain—my mind?"

("I'm not exactly sure of that myself. I know the path I followed to penetrate your skull and I could describe it if you had the anatomical vocabulary, but my vocabulary is your vocabulary and yours is, not surprisingly, very limited in that area.")

"Well, here's some vocabulary for you: *Go away and leave me alone.*"

("I'm afraid I can do neither . . . Daley. But I can vanish again, if you wish.")

"I wish."

("No problem. You inhabit a most fascinating organism and I have much exploring to do before I become fully acquainted with it. So . . . so long for now. It's nice knowing you.")

Wish I could say the same, she thought. Wish I could say *Out of sight, out of mind.*

A voice in her head said, ("You can say it all you want but it won't work.")

"Shut *up!*"

"Please stay calm," Sofia said as she entered with the tech behind her. "You're scaring our phlebotomist."

"Sorry, sorry." Daley flopped back supine on the gurney and stuck out her arm. "Do your worst—I mean *best.*"

An awful thought struck her. What if these hallucinations were from a brain tumor?"

("You don't have a brain tumor. You've got me.")

Wondering which was worse, Daley bit back a scream of frustration.

## 5

"I am Doctor Holikova," said the short, middle-aged woman as she stepped through the cubicle's curtain. She had a heavy accent— Polish, maybe? "Doctor Gomes told me about you."

Daley felt her heart rate kick up. "Oh, crap. Does this mean bad news?"

They'd taken her blood, scanned her brain, then brought her back to this curtained cubicle where she'd spent an eternity imagining the worst.

Dr. Holikova looked puzzled for an instant, then smiled, showing crooked teeth. "On, no. Is no worry. All tests normal."

("Told you so,") the voice singsonged.

Daley ignored it. "You mean there's no tumor or damage or . . . anything?"

The smile held. "All perfectly normal."

"Then why . . . ?"

"Am I here? I am here *because* tests are normal. I am doing research on hallucinations and asked staff to alert me to any patient suffering from them."

"Oh, I'm suffering, all right."

Suddenly the surfer dude appeared, naked as always, standing behind the doctor with his arms and legs spread wide like that Da Vinci drawing.

("Does she mean hallucinations like this?")

Dr. Holikova was saying, "When was your most recent hallucination?"

"Right now." Daley pointed. "He's standing right behind you. Wisecracking."

To her credit, she didn't look around. "Both visual and auditory then?"

"He won't shut up."

"I find you most interesting. So many victims of hallucinations believe they are real. You know it's not."

"I just want them to stop. Can you help me? Please?"

"I will do my best. I will put you in my study. But I need further tests. Will be noninvasive and you get small payment." She handed Daley a card. "You come to my office in late afternoon and we get started. First test is EEG—recording of brain waves. Very simple. You show up, we test. You don't show up, we don't test. Is all up to you."

"Oh, I'll be there. Count on it."

With that she left Daley alone with her hallucination.

Daley checked the card: *Jana Holikova, MD*, with an office in a medical arts building on Lankershim that Daley had passed many times. An easy walk from her apartment. Definitely going to follow up on this.

("She won't find anything. I'm integrated into your nervous system.")

"Whatever," Daley muttered as she stomped out of the enclosure.

The hallucination accompanied her, saying, ("It will be good to get back home again.")

She squeezed her eyes shut to keep from screaming and collided with Juana.

"You! Are you following me?"

The older woman frowned. "Why would I be following you?"

"You said it was your duty to help and guide me. Is that why you're here? To help and guide me? Because if it is, let me just tell you I don't—"

"Maybe I should ask if you're following *me*. Because you came to *me* this morning, remember? I'll gladly help and guide you, but I'm here to see my mother."

Daley freely admitted she could use a lot of help and guidance right now, but figured it would more likely come from a specialist like Dr. Holikova than a native woman who lived alone out in the desert in a shell-studded trailer.

The hallucination leaned close to Juana. ("Look at her, Daley.")

Daley then noticed how upset the woman looked. She'd been so wrapped up in her own dilemma . . .

"Hey, you okay? Your mother . . . is she sick?"

Juana looked away and said nothing.

"Oh, hey, sorry. Is it bad?"

A shaky shrug. "No one knows. She's got the horrors."

"How awful. Is she going to be okay?"

Another shrug. "Who can say? They can't tell me what caused it; they don't know how to treat her. They've tried all sorts of meds, now they're talking electroshock. She just sits and shivers and shakes and stares at nothing. Lets out an awful scream once in a while but otherwise says nothing."

"God, that's awful. I wish I could help."

"Maybe someday you will."

("An odd thing to say.")

Daley ignored him. "Do you need anything?"

"Besides a cure? No."

"Well, then, how about me? *I* need a cure. That alaret did something to my brain. I'm seeing things more and more."

Juana stared at her. "Still the naked guy?"

Daley nodded. "And he's talking to me." She felt a sob building. "You've got to help me, Juana. It's making me crazy!"

"I don't know what to do, Daley. Truly, I don't. I don't even know if there's anything *to* do."

Great. Just great.

"Well, thanks for nothing," she said and walked off.

("Kind of harsh,") the hallucination said, keeping pace as Daley continued on her way to the exit.

Really? Correcting her manners now?

She bit back a response. New rule: She would *not* respond to her hallucination.

But yeah, she'd been harsh, and she was simply chastising herself via the hallucination for her rudeness. But damn it, she was too upset to play nice-nice with Juana.

The naked figure stayed by her side and she found it disconcerting to see people walking right through it and not noticing a thing. More proof this was all in her mind, but she couldn't help flinching at every pseudo-collision.

("As I've told you, what you see is just an image from your cortex, visible only to you,") it said, as if reading her mind. ("But if it bothers you, I'll weave around our fellow travelers.")

A considerate hallucination. Who would have thought?

As they stepped out into the midday light, she rubbed her upper arms. Despite all the global-warming talk, LA winters seemed to be getting cooler and cooler. Late February was usually warmer than this.

("You need to accept my presence, Daley. Consider your body a small business and the two of us as partners.")

"Partners!" she said, forgetting the no-response rule. "This is *my* body!"

("If it will make you happier, I'll revise my analogy: You're the founder of the company and I've just bought in. How's that sound, partner?")

"Lousy!"

It didn't seem to mind. ("As I said before, I need a name. What would you like to call me?")

"How about *'Gone'*?"

("That's hurtful, Daley.") It assumed a deep-thinking pose. ("Got it! Since we're partners, you can call me 'Pard.'")

"No way. No freakin' way!"

("*Pard* . . . I like it.")

She'd be damned if she was going to—what would you call it? Legitimize? Yeah, *legitimize* this apparition by letting it name itself. Especially not with such a totally *stupid* name.

"I am not naming you. You're not going to be around long enough to rate a name."

As she started through the parking lot she still couldn't believe it. *Pard?* From what depths had her subconscious dredged up something that would name itself "Pard"? She'd had no idea her subconscious was so totally loony . . . or so lame.

But whatever it was and whatever it wanted to call itself, it seemed she was going to be forced to look at it for a while. But that didn't have to mean watching its garbages—her Irish grandmother's name for the male accessories—swinging around all day. So she tried to imagine it fully dressed, tried to impose a T-shirt and a pair of cargo pants on it, but to no avail.

"Don't you have any clothes?"

("I don't 'have' anything, so to speak.")

"I'm trying to tell you that if I must look at you, I'd much prefer to see you clothed."

("Really? I gathered that you rather liked the male form. I tried to look like your fuck buddy, Kenny.")

"'Fuck buddy'? Where did you hear that?"

("Why, from you, of course. It's one of your designations for him.")

Well, sometimes maybe it was, but not often, and she sure as hell had never said it out loud. She preferred *friend with benefits.*

"Anyway, change. It's distracting."

Suddenly she was looking at a shapely naked blonde, D-cup for sure.

("More to your liking?")

"No! That's even worse and not what I meant."

("Well, you said 'change.'")

"I meant get dressed!"

("As you wish.") Suddenly he was back to male, wearing jeans, a plaid flannel shirt, and snakeskin cowboy boots. ("Better?")

Much. But she refused to say so.

("Or would you prefer . . . ?")

He flashed through a dozen outfits in as many seconds, from a tuxedo to tennis shorts to military fatigues and on and on.

"Stop! The first was fine."

Back in the jeans and flannel, it said, ("I can appear as either sex but I feel more comfortable as a male—'I identify as male' is, I believe, the accepted phraseology.")

God, the idea that she might be going crazy scared the hell out of her, but at least no one could say she was doing a half-assed job of it.

# 6

Daley's phone alarm woke her at 3 P.M.

She opened her eyes and rubbed her face. She'd returned home exhausted and figured a nap would be good before she headed for Dr. Holikova's. She'd been watching excerpts from *The Tonight Show* on YouTube and had dozed off during one of them. And now she awoke to find herself propped up on three pillows with her phone in her hand. She was sure she hadn't gone to sleep like this.

("Your smartphone is the most fascinating instrument,") said a voice in her head.

She sat up straight. "What? Who?"

("Just me. Remember?")

Unfortunately, she did, as it all came back. The hallucination. As she'd dozed off she'd harbored a vague hope she'd wake up cured. But here she was, barely conscious, and already the craziness was starting. Just a disembodied voice at the moment—all audio, no visual. Yet.

"Everybody has a smartphone," she grumbled. "Even homeless people."

("They've been all around you for as long as you can remember, so you're jaded. I've been sentient less than two days. This is completely new to me and totally miraculous.")

"You'll get used to it."

And then she saw all the hair on her pillow.

"Aw, no! Is it still falling out?"

("I'm assuming that's a rhetorical question,") the voice said. ("But as I told you yesterday, the follicles are still alive. The hair will grow back.")

"A lot of good that does me now!"

Dressed in panties and her Lakers T-shirt—her sleepwear—she jumped out of bed and stumbled to the bathroom for a mirror.

"Shit!"

An ugly oblong bald spot dominated the top of her head—okay, not completely bald but definitely might-as-well-be-bald, considering the scant strands that remained. She rubbed her burning eyes but the patch remained.

("Terribly sorry, but—")

"Shut up! Just shut up!"

She headed for the kitchen. Caffeine . . . she needed caffeine to wake her up and help her deal with—

She yelped in shock and did a ridiculous little dance while stretching her T down to her upper thighs—because Jimmy Fallon was sitting at the counter dressed in a voluminous terry cloth robe, sipping coffee . . .

"*What*—*?* How—?"

("Oh, sorry, Daley,") he said with his crooked smile. ("Did I startle you?")

"But—!"

Wait-wait-wait. How could Jimmy Fallon get into her apartment? And why would he want to? Yet . . . here he was.

("Oh, wow, I see that I did. My bad.")

I've gone *so* crazy . . . or . . .

"It's *you*, isn't it?"

He gave that impish, patented Jimmy Fallon grin. ("Of course it's me. Well, that is, unless you know another me.")

Daley winged a throw pillow from the couch. He didn't give the slightest flinch as it tumbled straight though him.

"It *is* you! Why would you do that?"

The hallucination reappeared as the surferish dude, still dressed in jeans and flannel. ("Well, I was sensing your attraction while you watched the replays so I thought a little visit from him might distract you from, you know, the, um, hair problem.")

"That's what you thought? You thought I'd be happy to wake up and find a stranger in my home?"

Jimmy Fallon flickered back long enough to say ("I'm not *really* a stranger!") and then it resumed the previous look.

Daley picked up her phone, activated the camera, and took a shot of him.

("What's that for?")

"I'm gonna post it on Instagram and see if anybody recognizes you."

("No, you're not.")

"Really?" She already had her Instagram account open. "Who's going to stop me?"

("It's not a matter of stopping you, it's a matter of you not being able to photograph me.")

She checked her gallery and found a photo of an empty chair in her kitchenette.

"What the—?"

Crap, he was right.

("As I told you before, I'm simply an image in your visual cortex. You're the only one who can see me. And by the way, I already am.")

"'Already am' what?"

("Used to your smartphone. What we were discussing when you woke up.")

She was developing mental vertigo from the sudden change in subject.

"I don't . . ."

("I'm telling you I'm already used to your smartphone. In fact I was doing some medical research while you were asleep.")

"How the hell did you do that?"

("Quite simple, really. While your mind was sleeping, I used your eyes and your fingers to do searches on your phone.")

She had a vague, dreamlike memory of staring at her phone's screen while her finger swiped through the pages at blinding speed.

"Do you read fast?"

A nod. ("*Really* fast. I can scan screens and store everything away for later digestion because there's an awful lot of wasted space in the human brain. You're not living up to anywhere near your potential. Neither is any other member of your species, I gather.")

As Daley rubbed her irritated eyes again, something occurred to her.

"Hey, what right have you got to pull something like that with my body?"

("*Our* body, you mean.")

Daley ignored that. "No wonder my eyes are burning. I've been reading when I could have been—*should* have been sleeping."

("Don't get excited. Your conscious mind got its time-out and

I built up our vocabulary. You're fully rested, so what's your complaint? By the way, I can now answer your question about how I entered your head. I seeped into your pores and then into your scalp capillaries, which I followed into your parietal emissary veins. These flow through the parietal foramina in your skull and empty into the superior sagittal sinus. From there it was easy to infiltrate your central nervous system.")

Daley opened her mouth to say she really didn't care, then realized she understood exactly what it was saying. She had a clear picture of the described path floating through her mind.

"How come I know what you're talking about? I seem to understand but I don't remember ever hearing those words before . . . and then again, I do."

Weird.

("Yes, it must seem rather odd. What happens is my new knowledge gets stored in your memory and is thus available to you. The result is you experience the fruits of the learning process without having gone through it. You know facts without remembering having learned them.")

"Bullshit," she said, turning on her Keurig and inserting a dark-roast pod. "I'm just dredging up things I already knew but forgot."

("What will it take to convince you? How about: I found some abnormal cells in your right ovary.")

Daley froze. Her mother had died of ovarian cancer—died horribly.

"A tumor?"

She needed to get to a doctor before it metastasized!

Somewhere within her growing panic rose the thought that a few hours ago she would have been worrying about "spread" rather than "metastasis."

("No need for concern. The cells had a long way to go, maybe twenty years before they became a threat. But I killed them off.")

"How'd you do that?"

("Cytolysis: I pumped excess sodium into their cytoplasm, causing them to absorb more and more water until they burst.")

Stunned, Daley could only stare at it.

("Do you know you inherited a mutation from your mother that leaves you prone to ovarian cancer?")

Her mother's oncologist had urged Daley to get tested for the gene but she'd been putting it off and off and off.

("No matter now. I'll keep watch for any nascent problems and nip them in the bud. Oh, and you don't have to thank me. I'm doing this for my own good as well as yours. We're partners, remember? And I don't relish the idea of walking around in a cancer-riddled body any more than you do.")

"How . . . ?"

("My consciousness extends down to the cellular level and beyond.")

"How is that possible?"

Wait . . . she was treating this figment as though it was a real thing . . . another person. It wasn't. Just the result of some screwed-up neurotransmitter ratio in her brain—too much serotonin or too little norepinephrine or—

Wait again . . . serotonin? . . . norepinephrine? How did she get to know so much about neurotransmitters? Or, for that matter, *anything* about neurotransmitters?

Then she remembered what it had said about doing research on her phone while she slept . . .

Could it be? Could she really have another mind sharing her body?

# 7

Dr. Holikova had been truthful when she said the EEG would be painless and noninvasive. What she hadn't said was that it would also be messy. Not a word about the conductive goop they used to glue the contacts to your scalp, which in Daley's case at the moment had been easy to apply to the bald patch.

She'd worn a Dodgers cap on her walk over to the office. And a Lakers warm-up because another cool day was predicted. She wasn't a sports fan, but these were cheap knockoffs that came in useful now and then.

The EEG tech had given her a strange look when she'd removed the cap, so she'd made up some semi-lame story about a toxic spill on her head. The only good part about the bare patch was how the goop cleaned up easier from there than from her hair.

The test took about forty-five minutes total, with flashing lights and the whole bit. After a fifteen-minute wait, Dr. Holikova called her into her office.

"This looks perfectly normal," she said, flipping through the seemingly endless stack of fan-folded graph paper.

("What did I tell you?")

"You're *sure* there's nothing there?"

"Quite sure. Sometimes TLE can cause hallucinations, but I see no sign of it here."

"TLE?" Somehow that sounded vaguely familiar.

The hallucination appeared wearing a white lab coat with a stethoscope looped around its neck. ("Temporal lobe epilepsy, my dear. I stored it in your memory bank.")

"Temporal lobe epilepsy," said Dr. Holikova.

He pumped a fist. ("Nailed it!")

"Would you please shut up," Daley said.

Dr. Holikova stiffened. "I beg your pardon."

"Not you. I was talking to the hallucination."

"Oh. Yes, of course." She stared at Daley a moment, then, "I most definitely want to pursue this further, with a psychiatric evaluation—"

"Now wait a min—"

"Just a formality," she said quickly. "And a PET scan to see if any areas of your brain show unusual levels of activity. All covered by the grant, at no cost to you, of course." She gestured toward the door. "My receptionist will schedule you."

("I guess that means we're dismissed,") the vision said and faded away.

Out in the waiting area, the receptionist called the psychiatrist—just down the hall—and informed Daley that the doctor didn't have an opening until next week but wanted Daley to come back tomorrow morning to take some sort of preliminary written test called the "MMPI," whatever that was.

"Really? On a Saturday?"

She nodded. "She does her testing on Saturday mornings. The imaging center is down on the first floor; they said they'll have to get back to me on the PET scan, which means I probably won't hear till Monday."

Fine with Daley. She was heading for the exit when a middle-aged woman in the waiting room began to shake uncontrollably.

"She's having another seizure!" the lady next to her cried.

The woman toppled from her seat, landing on her back, making garbled noises as she continued to thrash about. Daley dropped to her knees beside her and grabbed her wrists to keep her from hurting herself.

("Hold her!") the hallucination said.

The thrashing continued for maybe another fifteen seconds and then suddenly stopped. Slowly the woman's unfocused eyes blinked back into awareness.

("Whatever you do, don't let go!")

"But—"

("I can go in!")

"What?"

It disappeared.

"Thank God!" said her companion. "Oh, Doctor! She's just had another, even after you increased the dose."

Dr. Holikova had rushed in. She squatted opposite Daley, saying, "Can you hear me, Grace?"

Grace nodded from the floor. "I guess I had another one."

The vision reappeared. ("It will be her last.")

"How can you say that?" Daley said.

Realizing that everyone in the waiting room had heard her and

was suddenly looking at her, she released the woman's wrists and
rose.

("You don't have to talk out loud. Just direct a thought at me and
I'll catch it.")

*Like this?*

("Exactly.")

*Okay, so how can you say—?*

("I was able to go inside her!") He sounded excited. ("As you
were holding her, I sensed a passage forming. Eventually it opened
enough to allow me to make a connection and enter her. I explored
her nervous system and almost immediately saw what was going
on. I calmed the electrical storm in her brain that was causing the
seizure. I also found the source of the problem: a little scar on her
right parietal lobe.")

*But how can you say she won't have another?*

("Because I started a lytic process to dissolve the scar. It should
be complete in a few minutes. Her EEG will be normal now.")

"We'll have to further increase her dose," Dr. Holikova said.

("Tell her that won't be necessary.")

*I can't do that.*

("You must. Otherwise she'll be taking medication she no longer needs.")

*Not my problem.*

("Daaaaaleeeey. You have important information about her
medical condition. Be a good girl now and tell the doctor.")

*Damn!*

"Grace," Daley said, "you don't need a bigger dose. In fact you
don't need *any* medication."

"Don't go telling her that!" Dr. Holikova said. "That's reckless
and irresponsible!"

Grace blinked up at Daley. "How is that possible?"

"I just cured you."

("Hey! You had nothing to do with it!")

*Well, I can't very well say you* did *it.*

"That's impossible!" Dr. Holikova cried. "I can't have you filling my patients' heads with nonsense! Leave my office! Immediately!"

"Okay," Daley said. "But if you're so sure I'm wrong, maybe you should prove it. Do another EEG and I guarantee it will be normal."

She had no idea if she was right, but saw no downside for anyone.

Dr. Holikova huffed. "Nonsense!"

"What if she's right?" Grace said.

"She isn't," the doctor told her.

"I believe her," Grace said.

Dr. Holikova shook her head. "You *want* to believe her."

"What I want is another EEG. Right now."

The office door closed behind Daley then, cutting off the voices.

("This is exciting,") he said, appearing beside her. ("We've reached a milestone.")

"What? In the doctor's office?"

("No—you and I. You've accepted me as real.")

"I absolutely have not!"

"You have. You've stopped thinking of me as 'it' and started thinking of me as 'he.' That's a milestone."

As much as she wanted to deny it, she couldn't. She couldn't touch him, but he'd become real to her.

("The next step is accepting me as a partner.")

"Never. You may be real, but you're a real parasite."

("I resent that! We're partners . . . a symbiosis!")

"Parasite."

("Symbiont!")

"You hijacked my body!"

("We've been through this. So, now that I'm real to you, I say again, I want a name. I still like 'Pard.'")

She didn't want to give it a name, she wanted to give it the boot. And she'd find a way.

"What happened back there with Grace?"

("What?") he said, holding a hand to his ear. ("Is someone speaking?")

"You know damn well I am."

Still looking away, he said, ("Yes, I believe I do hear a voice, but it's not addressing me by name, so I'll simply ignore it.")

*Not addressing me by name . . .*

Did this thing really want her to call it *Pard*? She couldn't. She just . . . couldn't.

"All right, all right, damn it. But come up with another name."

("Well, the human name for me is 'alaret,' so—")

"No, I will not call you 'Al,' either."

("Well, we're back to 'Pard' then.")

"I can't. I just can't."

("Try it. It's not as if you'll be introducing me to anyone. It'll be just between the two of us.")

"Okay . . . Pard." Ugh. She still almost choked on using any name, especially this one, but . . . "As long as it's just between you and I—"

("'Me' . . . just between you and *me*.")

She repressed a scream. "Just because I accept your existence doesn't mean I accept your presence. I still want you gone."

("Understood. Not going to happen, but understood. All that aside, do you realize that I actually got into Grace's brain? When you're in physical contact with someone, I can enter and interact with them just like I can with you.")

A possibility occurred to Daley and she didn't want to seem too hopeful as she asked, *Can you transfer yourself over to them?*

("No. You'll be relieved to know that you and I are bonded and I won't be leaving you for anybody else.")

*Oh, joy.*

("I'm not sensing a burst of relief.")

*I'm hiding it.*

As they started down the stairs, Pard said, ("Isn't it wonderful? I just performed a miracle cure.")

*You only* believe *you cured her. You've no proof.*

They exited the center onto the sidewalk where the tarry stink of hot asphalt assaulted them as a crew worked at repaving this section of Lankershim. The bright sunlight cast stark shadows on the mostly nondescript buildings, reminding her of a Hopper painting.

Wait . . . Hopper? Who was Hopper? And then she knew: Edward Hopper, a painter who used bright sunlight and shadows to great effect. The chiaroscuro lighting of *House by the Railroad* and *Cape Cod Morning* flashed through her memory.

Chiaroscuro?

*Have you been reading up on art while I'm asleep?*

Pard fell into step beside her. ("As a matter of fact, yes. By the way, your laptop is much better for research than your phone. The bigger screen is excellent for art—")

Daley could barely hear him over the construction racket.

*You're wasting my sleep time looking at pictures?*

("And storing them in your memory. Your education was disturbingly deficient in so many areas, but almost nonexistent in art history—or any history at all in any measurable depth. What did they teach you in all those years?")

*I didn't go to school until I was thirteen.*

("What? No wonder I can find no early school memories. Why not?")

*It wasn't the Family way. They didn't trust schools. When my father was murdered—on the day I was born, by the way—his family wouldn't let my mother and me go. The Family insisted on raising me their way. All my cousins were illiterate. If my mother hadn't taught me reading and simple math, I'd be just like them.*

("But you have memories of high school.")

*When my mom was dying of cancer, I managed to slip away from the hospital with my gram. The Family kept trying to steal me back but she officially got sole custody—no way was the Family going to appear in court to contest it. Anyway, that stopped them from trying to get me back. They didn't want the FBI on them for kidnapping. Gram sent me to a proper public school.*

("But what did they teach you there?")

*After I got through all my remedial courses? Not much. Mostly how to get high enough scores on tests to move on to the next grade.*

("I'm amazed that you live in this culture and yet you know next to nothing about it.")

*I know what I need to know.*

("And now you know a little more. You even know what *chiaroscuro* means.")

*Well, thank you so much. I simply don't know how I lived this long without that.*

("You're welcome.")

*You do understand sarcasm, don't you?*

("I should, as it's your default mode.")

A black Stetson hat suddenly appeared on his head.

*What's with that?*

("I'm accessorizing. The hat keeps the sun out of my eyes and—")

*You don't have eyes, and this*—she touched the brim of her Dodgers cap—*keeps the sun out of* our *eyes. Lose the hat.*

The Stetson turned white as he stretched to a six-footer and became Timothy Olyphant as his character in *Justified.*

("I bet you like the hat now.")

*Oh, God, he's gorgeous, but you're not him, so quit it.*

Pard shrank to his usual self, but kept the Stetson and added a red scarf.

*Come on, lose the hat and the scarf, okay?*

("It's not a scarf, it's a *bandana.* And I think it's quite fashionable.")

She stopped and stared at him. "Are you gay?" she said aloud.

A passing woman gave her a strange look. "Did you say something?"

Daley gave an apologetic wave. "Sorry. Just thinking out loud."

*Wait a sec.*

She pulled out her phone and plugged in her earbuds.

("You're making a call? *Now?*")

"No. If I'm looking at you, I feel I should talk to you. So I'm just disguising our conversation. As long as the earbuds are in, people will think I'm on a call."

A man walking his dog passed by and didn't give her a second look.

"See?"

("Clever girl. I notice people seem to be obsessed with these phones, especially those your age. Can't get their faces out of them. And yet you . . .")

She started walking again. "My whole generation grew up with the Internet. But I'm an exception. The Family wouldn't allow us kids to have our own phones. We'd be given burners to use when we were out scamming—just to stay in touch or report trouble—but we had to turn them in when we got back home. We weren't allowed on Instagram or Snapchat or any of those because kids lose their filters online and the Family kept all their business under tight wraps. So I reached my teens knowing nothing about social media and never really got into it."

("Did you feel left out?")

"Sometimes, yeah. I wanted to join the online crowd in high school but the iPhone was only a couple years old when I moved in with Gram and she wasn't about to spring for one of those, so I wound up with a flip phone. I could text and that was about it. When I finally did get online, I had to struggle with what was all second nature to everyone else. I never caught up."

("Still, you're online.")

"Sure I am, but not as me. I'm not one for sharing personal info."

She had a bogus Facebook account under another name for when she ran a game—marks tended to get suspicious when they couldn't find someone online. But it really came down to not wanting the Family to be able to find her if they came looking. And they had an eye out for her—no doubt about that.

"But enough about me. Back to you: Are you gay?"

("You mean homosexual? I'm above all that sexuality stuff,

although I will say those orgasms you had two nights ago were quite astonishing, speaking on a purely sensory level.")

Which reminded her that she needed to make amends with Kenny for kicking him out the other night.

"So, you're *not* gay."

("I'm pure mind, Daley, with no hormones and no procreative urges, and no attraction to either sex, so I'm neither heterosexual nor homosexual.")

"Well, damn. I always wanted a gay guy as a friend."

("To give you fashion tips, I suppose.")

"Why do you say that?"

("Oh, nothing.")

"You're not getting off the hook that easy. Explain."

("Let's just say you could do with some sartorial guidance, but save that for some other time. I want to know how you can be concerned with my sexual orientation after I've just accomplished a miracle cure. Well, not *really* miraculous, but it'll *seem* that way.")

"I only have your word for this so-called cure."

("It's not 'so-called' in the least. I guarantee it.")

"Well," she said, "no point in arguing now. You've yet to prove you can cure anything. I have to go back tomorrow anyway, so I'll expose your bogus cure then."

("Quite the skeptic, aren't you.")

"When you're raised on hokum, you develop a nose for it."

## 8

The rest of the day passed in relative quiet with Pard keeping to himself. Daley wasn't sure if he was in some sort of snit or processing the results of all his speed reading last night.

Whatever.

Eventually the clock struck five: cocktail hour on Friday night. She didn't want to risk the Dew Drop with Pard—who knew what she might blurt out?—but she had vodka and she had orange juice. She made screwdrivers.

She looked up the psychiatric test the receptionist had mentioned. MMPI stood for Minnesota Multiphasic Personality Index, used by shrinks to measure a patient's level of wackiness. With all she'd been going through, Daley figured she could red-line the MMPI if she answered even half honestly.

Was she crazy? Not just quirky-crazy but deeply, off-the-rails, broken-from-reality insane? It had grown into a serious question, because Pard's current radio silence had given her time to think, and she realized she'd started accepting Pard as a separate entity—a *person*, for Christ sake. How had that happened?

Maybe because he'd been her constant companion for two days straight. Familiarity supposedly bred contempt, but it also bred . . . familiarity. People exposed to an odor or a sound long enough will stop smelling it or hearing it. Pard had totally freaked her out at first, but after two days of continuously seeing and hearing him, the strangeness of it, the *insanity* of it, had worn off. Real or not, he'd become part of *her* reality.

Acceptance of the impossible . . . two minds sharing one brain . . . whoever heard of such a thing?

Trouble was, the brain was hers.

*Hers.*

Daley didn't want to share her brain.

Maybe that was why she felt so on edge.

*. . . you will never be alone . . .*

Juana's words haunted her.

Never? Never again? This was a freaking nightmare.

I should have some say in this, shouldn't I?

The screwdrivers began to take hold. Somewhere along the way she lost track of how many she'd had, but the orange juice was gone and the vodka bottle was damn near empty.

("Please don't consume any more ethanol,") Pard said. ("I'm having trouble thinking.")

*I thought you were "pure mind."*

("I am, but the mind depends on the brain. A brain doesn't need a mind, but a mind needs a brain. And a malfunctioning or impaired brain means a malfunctioning and impaired mind. Your brain is impaired at the moment.")

Daley wasn't feeling so good herself. She wasn't a big drinker. Usually she nursed a margarita and was fine with that. Vodka definitely wasn't her drink. She kept the bottle around for the rare occasions she had visitors. But she'd felt a need for it tonight.

*I think I'm going to lie down for a while . . . just to rest my eyes . . .*

She flopped back on her bed, closed her eyes and . . .

# 1

("So . . . this is what they call a hangover.")

"You're still here?"

("I have no place else I *can* be. But about this hangover—")

"Shut. Up."

Daley didn't have much experience with hangovers because she rarely overdrank. She wasn't sure which was worse—the headache or the nausea.

No, wait. Yes, she was sure: the nausea. Definitely the nausea.

("No need to be testy with me. I'm not the one who overindulged in ethanol. For a while I'll admit the effect was rather pleasant, but then . . .")

"Aren't you feeling any of this?" she rasped. Her voice sounded like a frog's.

("No. For the time being I've blocked my awareness of the sensory input from your meninges and your upper intestine. Shall I do the same for you?")

"You can do that?"

The headache and nausea abruptly disappeared.

"Oh, my God! You're kidding me! You can cure a hangover just like that?"

("You're not 'cured' in any sense of the word. You still have a toxic level of acetaldehyde circulating through your system, and until your liver clears that, you are still officially hungover—the price one pays for intemperance.")

"It's also called drowning your sorrow."

("Is my presence so awful?")

Here we go, she thought. He's getting right down to the real nitty-gritty.

"You're not so bad in small doses, Pard. It's just that . . . it's just that I was never given a choice."

("Neither was I.")

"*You* dropped on *my* head, not the other way around, damn it!"

("And *you* entered *my* cave. My act was that of a nonsentient creature following instinct. I could have wound up sharing the brain of a coyote or a mountain lion or whatever else wanders that desert. In those cases I'd have wound up with no more awareness or intelligence than my host. But I landed on a sapient being who is very intelligent and—")

"Flattery won't work."

("I don't deal in flattery, I deal in fact. And the fact is you're an exceptionally intelligent human who was never challenged by her school and has never challenged herself and thus has no idea of her potential.")

He sounded like every teacher she'd ever had: *Stanka is not performing to her potential* . . .

She shook her head. "Won't work."

("Take it or leave it. But here's the bottom line: We are stuck with each other, Daley. We must find an accommodation that allows us to coexist with some modicum of harmony.")

Maybe the toxic level of acetaldehyde or whatever was to blame, maybe all that she'd been going through, or maybe the pervasive feeling of goddamn *helplessness* . . . Whatever the cause, she began to sob. She hated herself for it, but couldn't hold it back.

"I need alone time! I need time with just me, to be just me, with nobody watching, nobody judging. If I can't have that, I might just as well just, you know, end it all."

Pard made no reply.

"Do you hear me? I know you're listening, but do you *hear* me?"

("I do hear you, Daley. And I understand. I'm thinking . . . what if I can find a way to wall myself off from you for a set period? I won't know what you're doing and you won't know what I'm doing? Would that work?")

"Is it possible?"

("Maybe. I'll work on it.")

A ray of hope. A lifeline. Enough to pull Daley through for now.

"Okay. Maybe I can live with that. But right now I need to wash up. We've got test to take."

("'We'?")

"Well, you can stay here if you like."

("Very funny. But you've accepted me as real—we've established that. Why take a test to see if you're crazy?")

"Mostly it's an excuse to get back in that building and find out if your 'cure' from yesterday is real." She shrugged as she entered the bathroom. "And who knows? It might show I'm bipolar or some—Oh, my God!"

The mirror showed new hair, maybe an inch long, filling the former bald spot. But white—*snow white*.

("Oh, dear. I worked hard all night stimulating those hair follicles, but I didn't—")

"It's *white!* How'd it turn white?"

("So sorry. I had no idea. I was working in the dark, after all. Apparently all the melanocytes in that part of your scalp have been killed off. They make the pigment for your hair, so there's no eumelanin available to color the strands.")

She stared in horror. "I look like a freak!"

She rushed back to the bedroom and began pulling on her jeans.

("What are you doing?")

"Going out."

("Where?")

She knew of a CVS a quick walk away.

"Getting some hair dye."

("Are you sure? I think it gives you a rather interesting look.")

"Forget it, Pard. I'm not going around looking like a goddamn skunk!"

She put on the Dodgers hat, slipped into her warm-up, and dashed for the door.

## 2

The patch of white hair wanted nothing to do with the dye, shedding it like water off wax.

"I don't believe this!" Daley cried after the third failure. "Look what you've done to me!"

Pard hovered next to her, looking anxious. ("I'll work on it. I'm sure I can coax some melanocytes back into those follicles and get your hair back to normal. Just give me a little time.")

"And meanwhile?"

("As I said before, I think it's rather interesting—sort of emo, don't you think?")

"Do you hear me playing Jawbreaker?"

("I'm just saying—")

"Just say nothing for now."

Furious, Daley jammed on her Dodgers hat and stomped outside. Not only was she going crazy but she now looked like a Lily Munster wannabe. Her life was so totally out of control she wanted to scream.

When she reached Lankershim she was surprised to see the construction crew working on a Saturday. Maybe they had a deadline. They'd advanced to the front of the medical arts building and were hard at work rolling the fresh asphalt flat.

Inside, up on the second floor, the psychiatrist's medical assistant was waiting with the MMPI ready to go. To Daley's surprise, Dr. Holikova was waiting as well.

"I knew you had an appointment for testing," she said without preamble. "I need to speak to you."

"Oh?"

Daley was having trouble reading her expression, unsure whether it was guarded or hostile. She needed to feel her way here.

The doctor said, "What happened with Grace yesterday?"

Pard hovered beside the doctor. ("Oh, *yes*, I've got a good feeling about this.")

*Hush.*

"Well, it looked like she, um, had a convulsion."

"Yes, that much was obvious. It ended abruptly after you grabbed her arms. And then you told her she didn't need any more medication because you'd cured her."

Uh-oh. She'd forgotten she'd said that. Had something gone wrong? Best to play it cool.

"Yeah, well, I may have shot my mouth off a little."

("You spoke the truth!")

*Hush!*

Dr. Holikova said, "You also proclaimed that her EEG would be normal." She stepped closer and lowered her voice. "How could you know that?"

Pard did jazz hands and a little happy dance. ("Aha! Told you so!")

"So, you're saying it's now normal?"

The doctor gave a slow nod. "She's always had an abnormal focus on her right parietal lobe—a leftover from a childhood head injury. That is gone now . . . as if it had never been."

Daley could only stare back at Dr. Holikova. Pard had lived up to his boasts. He'd done it—cured Grace's epilepsy. She hadn't truly believed he'd lie, but that didn't mean he couldn't be mistaken.

He'd actually gone inside that woman and changed her.

"That's . . . that's wonderful," she finally managed to say.

"It's more than wonderful, Ms. Daley. It's unheard of. Now, I don't for a second believe that you caused that focus to vanish, and yet it is gone, just like you said it would be." She leaned even closer. "How do I reconcile those two positions, Ms. Daley? Hmmm?"

Pard suddenly became the giant floating bald green head from *The Wizard of Oz*. His voice echoed: ("Just tell her your partner, the great and powerful Pard, worked a miracle.")

*Yeah, right. A sure way to land me in the booby hatch. And go away, please?*

He vanished.

"I don't see that reconciling them is my problem, Doctor. I have no conflicts. I'm very happy with the way things turned out and I believe I'll just leave it at that. You should too."

"But I can't. You had some sort of interaction with her and now she appears to be cured."

Daley was feeling less and less comfortable with this level of scrutiny. Time to go.

"I have another appointment."

But as she was turning away, Dr. Holikova grabbed her arm.

"What is going *on*, Ms. Daley?"

Dr. Holikova's expression . . . Daley could describe it now only as *hungry*.

"Nothing's going on. Now let me go."

Her grip tightened. "Please. I need to know."

Daley pulled free and hurried down the hall. What could she say that wouldn't sound insane?

Pard reappeared as she started down the stairs.

("I gather you're skipping your MMPI?")

*I need to get away from her. I have no answers for her. But let me ask you something about this lady you supposedly cured. Can—?*

("There's no 'supposedly' about it. You heard from Doctor Holikova that Grace's EEG is normal.")

All true, but despite *wanting* to believe, Daley was having trouble making that final leap. The miracle cure was a recurring scam and her upbringing warned her against allowing herself to get sucked into it.

"Okay. You cured that lady. Can you cure others?"

("As long as there's skin-to-skin contact between you and the other, I'm in. But I need more than a simple touch. You can't just shake hands and that's it. From what I experienced with Grace, I need a few seconds of steady contact before I can assert myself.

Break that contact and I'm cut off, so total contact has to last long enough for me to do what must be done.")

"So you're saying, given enough time you can cure anything?"

("I can't cure stupid.")

Daley blinked. "Is that directed at me?"

("No, of course not. Just stating a fact. You're anything but stupid, but it would be illogical and unsubstantiated for me to say I can cure all illness. I've had experience with only one person and she had a very specific lesion. As for curing anything and everything? I doubt it. I need more study to learn disease processes.")

"You're still reading while I'm asleep?"

("I'm sure you'd be bored to tears if you were awake. But my point is: I can probably do a lot with a disease process, but not with the damage it has caused over the years. The first I can accomplish quickly, but undoing, say, all the nerve damage from multiple sclerosis or the ruined joints from rheumatoid arthritis, I don't see how that would be possible.")

As they reached the first floor, he said, ("Hey, look.")

He was pointing at an office door that read, *Dr. R. Patel—Oncology & Hematology.*

*So?*

("He treats cancer. Let's go in.")

*What for?*

("You wanted to know what I can cure, let's find out. Maybe there's someone in there I can help. Let's just take a look. Please?") He leaned close, hands folded in supplication. ("Please-please-please?")

*All right, all right.*

Daley stepped into the low-lit waiting room and saw that the receptionist's desk was empty. She took in her surroundings.

A pale young woman around Daley's age sat nearby in the front row. She had a knit cap pulled low on her head. No hair stuck out from the edges. Had it fallen out from chemo?

("There's a prospect. Go and talk to her.")

*About what?*

("About why she's here.")

*Dumb question in an oncologist's office.*

("Ask if you can read her palm—anything that involves contact.")

*I don't know . . .*

("Please-please-please?")

*Is that your new thing?*

("It will be if you don't help me out here. You wouldn't believe how long I can keep it up.")

Suppressing a growl of annoyance, Daley took the seat next to the girl. Pard seated himself on her far side.

"Hi. Can I read your palm?" She cringed at how lame it sounded. The girl leaned away. "I don't think—"

"Hey, I'm not looking for money or anything. Just to pass the time. What can it hurt?"

Still she held back. "You gonna tell me my future or something? Because maybe I don't wanna know because maybe I already have a pretty good idea."

"Don't let anybody tell you they can tell the future, because it's totally bogus."

This seemed to disarm her enough to let her stick out her hand, palm up. "Okay. Go ahead."

"What's your name?" Daley said as she took her hand.

"You tell me."

"Good for you," Daley said with a laugh. She liked her.

("Okay. Hold on to her. I need a few seconds or so to—")

Pard disappeared.

Back when Daley had turned thirteen, the Family started teaching her palmistry. They had tiny shops all over LA County, and raked in a bundle from them. Daley remembered a little of it—enough to fake it.

Pard reappeared. ("Damn, she's got leukemia. I can't do anything about that.")

*Why not?*

("Abnormal white cells throughout her bloodstream being spewed from all through her bone marrow. No way can I shut down all that.")

*But I like her. No hope?*

("She seems to be responding to her chemotherapy.")

*Well, that's something, I guess.*

("Her name's Linda, by the way.")

Daley said, "Okay, Linda—"

She snatched her hand away. "How do you know my name?"

Daley didn't miss a beat. "Just a little talent I have."

"What about my—?"

"Leukemia?" Had to be careful here. "I can't see the future, but keep up your chemo and you should be fine."

As Linda's features slackened in shock, a robust-looking man seated behind them leaned forward and thrust his hand toward Daley.

"Here. Read mine."

("An eavesdropper! Well, go ahead.")

*He doesn't look sick.*

("Maybe waiting for someone. Let me take a look.")

"Sure," Daley said and took his hand. It felt cold.

Pard waited for a few heartbeats, then faded away.

("Okay, I'm in.")

A half a minute later, he popped back into view, looking distressed.

("No use.")

*What do you mean?*

("It's his pancreas. It started there and it's spread all over—liver, lungs, everywhere. No way I can help him.")

*What do I tell him?*

("His name's Edward. He knows it's his pancreas but he doesn't know how bad yet. You should be telling him to get his affairs in order, but leave that to his doctor. Tell him something like what you told Linda.")

Feeling bad for the guy, she said, "Well, Edward, I can't see the future, but keep up with Doctor Patel and you should do fine."

"But—"

Daley jumped up and moved away before he could start quizzing her.

*This is a waste of time.*

("One more? Please-please—")

*Don't start.*

She settled near a woman who was wiping a tear from her eye.

"You seem upset. Is there anything I can do to help?"

The woman shook her head. "Not unless you can take away a spot on my lung."

"Well, I don't know—"

"I had a cough that wouldn't stop." She seemed to be talking more to herself than to Daley. "So my doctor ordered a chest X-ray and they found a spot. So they did a CAT scan and said it was c-c-cancer! Now they're sending me next door to get a PET scan to see if it's spread before they buh-biopsy it to see what kind!"

As she sobbed, Pard said, ("Take her hands and I'll check her out.")

Daley grabbed both her hands, as if trying to comfort her. "I'm sure it will be all right."

The woman tried to pull away. "You have no way of knowing that!"

("Don't let go. I'm going in.") Pard faded from sight. After a few seconds he said, ("I've found the problem—a little tumor, still localized.")

*Fixable?*

("Finally, yeah. Tell her you're going to cure her, anything to maintain contact. Just don't let go.")

*I can promise that?*

("I guarantee it.")

*All right . . .*

Daley held on tight, saying, "I *can* know it will be all right because I'm going to *make* it right."

"How can you say such a thing?"

"Because I have the healing touch."

Pard reappeared. ("Okay. Done.")

*So soon?*

("Once I got in there it was easy peasy, as the saying goes. Her name's Lynn and her malignancy is a thing of the past.")

Daley released her hands and stood. "There, Lynn. You won't need that biopsy because you're now tumor-free."

"That's impossible!"

"You'll see." Daley waggled her fingers in the air. "Magic."

"Are you one of Doctor Patel's patients?" said a strange voice.

Daley looked up to see a large woman in scrubs towering over her. The receptionist, she presumed.

"Um, no. Just entertaining the troops."

"You'll have to leave."

"Let her stay," Lynn said, looking slightly dazed.

"Sorry. Patients and family only. Leave or I'll call security."

("Better do as Nurse Ratched says. My work here is done.")

"No problem," Daley said.

At the door she took a peek out into the hallway to make sure Dr. Holikova wasn't around, then hurried outside into the bright sunlight.

("You do understand, don't you, that you were laying it on rather thick back there. I mean, magic fingers and all.")

*Let's just hope you live up to your own hype.*

Suddenly he became Justin Chambers, dressed in scrubs. ("The tumor is history.")

*Oh, we're doing* Grey's Anatomy *now?*

("Well, it's one of your favorite shows and I feel like a hero surgeon, so maybe this will help you think of me as one.")

*You cut out the tumor?*

("No, I strangled it.")

*Meaning?*

("I closed off the blood vessels that were feeding it. Without oxygen, the cancer cells died. Then I sent in an army of phages to gobble up the corpses.")

*You're pretty proud of yourself, aren't you.*

He puffed up his Justin Chambers chest. ("Hero surgeon.")

*Lose it, okay?*

Abruptly he was back to Pard.

("Anything you say, partner.")

*And we're not partners.*

## 3

("I have to say that was very tasty—messy but delicious.")

"You can taste?"

("I taste what you taste.")

Daley had brought a cheeseburger and a chocolate shake home from In-N-Out—animal style, of course—and virtually inhaled it. She hadn't realized how hungry she was. The fries never even made it home.

Pard had sat opposite her, eating his own burger—well, the image of a burger. Just so she wouldn't have to eat alone, he'd said.

Couldn't say her parasite wasn't gentlemanly.

"Sometimes I forget to eat, and then I overeat. I need to organize my life and get on a schedule."

Pard slouched back in his chair. A toothpick appeared in his hand and he started sucking on it.

Okay, not a perfect gentleman.

("I've sensed some self-assessment going on.")

She wondered how much Pard was privy to her private thoughts. She could communicate by thinking *at* him, but how about when she was mulling a problem? She could ask him, of course, but could she trust the answer? He might not want her to know he was listening in.

"Yeah, well, I'm twenty-six and I'm wondering if it might be time to set a new course for my life."

("And the destination?")

Daley leaned back, not exactly sure what to say.

("Am I sensing inner conflict?")

"I'm thinking I'd like to accomplish something in my life."

("Like?")

She shrugged. "I dunno. Anything."

("Well, you're only twenty-six. Plenty of time to—")

"Not going to accomplish much on the road I'm on, living off fake invoices and mid-level scams. But . . . whatever. It's all moot if I don't get my life back."

*Moot?* She'd never used "moot" before. Pard's vocabulary-building again.

Daley grabbed her warm-up jacket and headed for the door. "Let's go check on Lynn and see how she did with her scan."

("Wait. Aren't you going to clear the table?")

She glanced back. She'd taken out a small plate to catch the animal-style droppings and a fork to finish them off.

"Later."

("You have a dishwasher. It will take you ten seconds to put them in.")

Was he kidding?

"No one's going to steal them."

("I find this very disturbing.")

"Okay. *You* put them away."

("Not funny. Please?")

Oh, hell. He said *please*.

"Have you any idea," she said, grabbing the plate and fork, "how anal you are?"

("There's a right way and a wrong way. I prefer the right way.")

She decided not to argue. She jammed everything into the dishwasher and resumed her exit.

Back again along the same route. She'd soon be wearing a groove in the sidewalk.

("I hesitated bringing it up back at the apartment, but did you ever consider arranging all the forks and knives and spoons together in the dishwasher? It would make unloading—")

An inarticulate howl escaped her, triggering worried looks from passersby.

("What's wrong?")

*I'm seriously thinking of throwing myself in front of a bus right now.* ("Forget I said anything.")

She'd calmed down by the time she passed the repaving crew and stepped into the medical arts building.

("FYI: Her full name's Lynn Graverson but there's all sorts of laws controlling the release of medical information.")

*She said she was scheduled for the scan today and that was a couple of hours ago. We'll take a peek.*

The imaging center took up half the ground floor across the hall from the oncologist's office. Daley tried there first, telling the receptionist she was here to pick up Lynn Graverson. But Lynn had been and gone. Daley tried without success to get her phone number.

("Well, if nothing else,") Pard said as they returned to the hall, ("it's good to know they take privacy seriously.")

*But a pain in the butt for us. Let's try the oncologist.*

("You really think Nurse Ratched will be more help?")

*We'll never know if we don't try.*

Daley entered Dr. Patel's office and went straight to the receptionist window. Still about a half dozen people seated in the waiting room, but a different half dozen. She had no plan beyond winging whatever conversation ensued.

"Hi," she said. "Remember me?"

Instead of a narrowing of the eyes and a command to leave, Ratched's eyes widened.

"Doctor Patel!" she said, calling toward the rear of the office. "Doctor Patel, she's back! She's here!"

*Hmmm . . . I'm not sure I like this.*

("Perhaps the good doctor doesn't like people telling his patients they're cured—even when they are.")

A stubby, bespectacled Pakistani in a white coat emerged from the rear, moving fast, closely followed by Lynn Graverson.

He pointed to Daley, saying, "This is her?" first to Ratched, then Lynn.

When they both said "Yes," he burst into the waiting room, Lynn following.

"I must speak to you," he said.

*What's going on?*

("I'm pretty sure we're about to find out.")

"Okaaaay," Daley said slowly. "What about?"

"You told my patient you cured her tumor. 'Magic,' you said."

Not sure where this was headed, Daley said, "Oh, well, I was just—"

"But it's gone!" Lynn blurted as tears filled her eyes. "The PET scan showed no tumor, just like you said! There's nothing to biopsy, just like you said! I'm cured!"

"Now, now, Lynn," Patel said, "we can't be one hundred percent sure of—"

"Do you hear that, people?" Lynn cried out to the waiting room. "This girl cured me of lung cancer just by taking my hand!"

A half dozen people were suddenly on their feet, saying "What?" "How?"

"Do you see what you're doing?" Patel said, visibly angry now. He leaned closer. "You're giving them false hope."

"She did it for me," Lynn said to the others. "Maybe she can do it for you."

("Now she's done it.")

Daley wasn't sure what Pard meant until the other patients started clutching at her with a chorus of "Can you? Can you?"

Their desperation was so palpable, Daley instinctively backed away.

"She can!" Lynn said. "I know she can! I'm proof!"

Feeling as if her throat were closing, Daley broke free and back-pedaled toward the door. But they followed. She yanked the door open and burst into the hallway, making for the exit.

The tinted glass doors to the outside lay straight ahead. Daley pushed through and squinted in the sudden burst of sunlight. She heard a babble behind her. A quick rearward glance showed the whole group, including Lynn, charging after her, crying out to her, reaching for her.

Thoroughly frightened now, she broke into a stumbling run.

("I don't think they want to hurt you.")

*They might not want to, but who knows what'll happen once they catch up to me.*

Another glance over her shoulder showed them closer, so she picked up speed. Maybe if she crossed the street . . .

As she veered leftward her foot caught on something and she fell forward with her hands flailing before her. She tumbled off the curb just as the road roller was reversing. Her left hand went under the drum and she screamed with pain like she'd never felt in her life.

# 4

Daley lay on her back and saw a blurry guy in a blurry white coat standing next to her. She blinked to clear her vision and expected to see Pard but, no, this guy had black skin. She saw now that he wore a white lab coat over green scrubs. He stood to her right; a scrub-garbed nurse adjusted an IV on her left.

"Stanka?" the nurse said. "Stanka?"

"Call me Daley."

"Ah, you're awake," the black guy said. "That's good. I'm—"

"Where am I?"

"Saint Michael's Medical Center in Burbank."

"I had a brain scan here yesterday."

"Yes, I reviewed your records. I don't know if you remember my name—you were quite distressed and in a lot of pain when I arrived—I'm Doctor Stabler. I'm a hand surgeon. You're in the recovery room now."

"Recovery? Hand surgeon? Why—?"

And then it all came rushing back. The fall, the road roller's drum crushing her hand, the pain, the screams—hers and others—and then passing out. Coming to with the EMTs, the ambulance ride, the ER, injections that made her fuzzy, and now . . .

She tried to raise her gauze-swathed left arm but it wouldn't move. She blinked for a better look at all that gauze and padding and—

"My hand!" Her left arm was too short. "What happened to my-my-my—?"

"We couldn't save it," Dr. Stabler said.

No-no! Couldn't be! Had to be a bad dream, the worst nightmare ever!

He took her right hand in his. "My team and I tried our best but the injury was too severe. The bones were virtually pulverized, the vasculature torn, the little muscles that move your fingers were crushed and, well, partially cooked from the heat of the asphalt. We had to amputate."

"You cut off my *hand*?" She could hear her voice escalating in tone and volume.

"I'm so sorry, Stanka—Daley. We did everything we could but it was simply impossible to save it."

"But you had no right!"

The nurse said, "The possibility was explained before surgery and you signed the consent."

"I don't remember . . ."

"We had no choice, I'm afraid," Stabler said. "If we'd left it attached it would have become necrotic and infected and threatened your life by spreading infection throughout your system."

More details came back . . . She remembered falling, putting her hands out to keep from landing on her face, her left hand sinking into the fresh, hot asphalt and the roller going over it. Her scream made the operator slam the brake, but he stopped with the roller atop her hand. She was screaming *Get it off! Get it off!* when he jumped down to look, and his scream joined hers when he saw her. She'd passed out as he jumped back up to the controls.

My-hand-my-hand-my-hand-my-hand! *Gone!*

A scream rose to her lips but she bit it back. She did sob, though. Deep, wracking sobs from way, way down. She didn't want to go through life with one hand. How was she ever going to manage that?

Dr. Stabler was rambling on about the wonderful things they were doing with prosthetics these days but she barely heard him. Her mind was numb to the future . . . a maimed, one-handed future.

They injected something into her IV line and the next thing she knew she was alone in a private room. No, not alone. A familiar figure stood close by the bed.

Pard.

("I'm so sorry this happened, Daley.")

"Pard . . . you're still around."

A grim smile. ("I am with you always. But this is all my fault.")

She stared at the foreshortened end of her mummy-wrapped left arm for a long moment. "I still can't believe it happened."

("I take full responsibility.")

"I'm perfectly glad to blame you, but how do you figure that?"

("Pure hubris on my part. I healed that woman and then goaded you into bragging about it on my behalf.")

"'Bragging'?"

("Absolutely. I could have simply done my work and then just let her discover she'd been healed. But I pushed you into announcing it.")

"I sort of got into it. Remember 'magic fingers'?"

She remembered waggling her ten fingers in the air . . . and a lump formed in her throat as she realized she'd never do that again.

("Still . . . I prompted you.")

"I don't get it." She pointed to where her hand used to be. "What's all that got to do with this?"

("Don't you see? Doctor Holikova and those others associated you with the cures, and the lung-tumor lady wanted you to help all her sick friends. They never would have been chasing you if I'd just told you to keep the cures between us.")

He had a point . . . sort of.

"All right, maybe you are to blame in a roundabout way, but there's no way you could have known this would happen."

She smacked her lips. Thirsty. She pointed to the water pitcher on the nightstand.

"Pour me a glass of water, will you?"

Pard gave her a dubious look, then went to grab the pitcher. His hand passed right through it.

("Have you forgotten that I'm just an image in your brain?")

Well, damn, she had forgotten. He looked so solid. Showed how real Pard had become to her. And how useless he was. Worse than useless—she'd lost her hand because of him!

She didn't know if it was the drugs they were feeding her or what. Maybe it was just . . . everything, but suddenly she felt helpless, trapped in a life that seemed hopeless and awful. She began to sob.

"What good are you? I mean, really? You've done nothing but mess up my life. Three days ago I was happy and I was *whole*! Now look at me! *Three days!* That's all it took you to totally fuck up my life! I wish I'd never gone into that cave, or maybe I wish I'd fucking *died* in there! Anything's better than this. Why don't *you* just die and leave me in peace!"

Talking only worsened her thirst. She'd have to buzz for the nurse. But she'd close her eyes first . . . just for a few seconds . . .

As she faded away she heard Pard say, ("I'm going to make this up to you, Daley. I'll make this right, I swear . . .")

# 5

"Ungh."

Cadoc's gray, papery hand appeared and slid his queen two diagonal spaces. Then he tapped a finger once on Rhys's king, the signal for "check."

Rhys hadn't seen that coming. As he studied the board he realized he needed to pay closer attention. Forget the distractions of the day and focus on the game.

He enjoyed his regular Saturday night chess game with his older brother, although the conditions could get off-putting at

times. Cadoc insisted they play in his heavily curtained suite at
the rear of the Lodge, and that the light in the room be limited
to one small gooseneck lamp with a high-intensity bulb sharply
focused on the board. As a result the board seemed to float in
empty blackness.

Rhys went along with his brother's obsessive privacy about his
appearance. No mystery as to why the guy did not want anyone
looking at him. He'd been less guarded as a child and Rhys had
become familiar and even comfortable with Cadoc's papery gray
skin. His voice hadn't been affected yet and he spoke normally,
but as time went on, Cadoc's condition became worse, wrecking
his voice, and he grew less and less comfortable with his appearance until he adopted a lifestyle of keeping himself locked away in
the daylight hours and venturing out only after everyone else had
turned in.

Okay, it came down to more than just papery skin. Every member of the Pendry Clan—all five families—had a patch of rough
gray skin somewhere on his or her body. The Pendry Patch. Some
were large, some were small, but no one on record had the Patch to
Cadoc's extent. The poor guy looked like a cross between a paper
wasp nest and a peeling river birch.

Rhys forced his attention back to the board, littered as usual
with gray flakes of Cadoc's skin. You could always tell where Cadoc
had spent some time. Rhys spotted an easy escape from check and
took it.

Cadoc didn't hesitate. He moved his queen again and tapped
Rhys's king twice.

"Ungh."

Two taps . . . checkmate.

"Rats! You knew I'd fall for that!"

Rhys looked for a way out but found none. When Cadoc said
'mate, he meant it. He leaned back.

"Hey, sorry I didn't give you a better game, Cad," he said, rubbing his eyes. "My mind's all over the place tonight."

A sheet from Cadoc's ever-present notepad dropped onto the chessboard.

Papa?

Cadoc always referred to Dad as *Papa*.

"Yeah, well, who else? He's become obsessed with this 'pairing' message and the 'Duad' he found in the Scrolls. But will he let me have a peek at his off-limits sections? Nooooo."

The faint sounds of a pencil scribbling, then another sheet dropped on the board.

Papa is quite mad, you know

"'Mad' as in pissed off or crazy?"

Crazy

Rhys laughed. "Yeah. Crazy like a fox. Speaking of Dad, where is he?"

At regular intervals—usually before a Nofio—he'd disappear late at night. Rhys would hear him go out and come back a few hours later.

Out

"I know that. Where out?"

Desert

"What's he do there?"

His business

"You don't know?"

Cadoc tapped the *His business* note. Rhys figured if his brother knew, he wasn't going to say. He switched to another line of inquiry.

"Dad was telling me how he let you see some of the undigitized Scrolls and how you found something about this Duad thing."

"Ungh."

One grunt: a yes.

"Anything interesting? Anything I should know?"

Vague

"Yeah, that's what Dad said. That vagueness is what's driving him nuts. And he's taking me with him."

Seen all translations

"Who? You? Even the sections he's encrypted?"

<u>All</u>

"He told me he wasn't going to show you, damn it."

Doesn't know

Cadoc must have accessed them during one of his late-night rambles through the Lodge.

"Wh-what do they say? What's he keeping from me?"

Bad stuff

Crazy stuff

Awful stuff

"*What*, damn it!"

no tell

"C'mon. You can tell your best bro."

Can't tell

Trouble

"Dad will never know, so—"

It's Sat night. Should be out

with Fflur, not babysitting me

"Don't try to change the subject."

Cadoc's hand shot out and gave the last note two insistent taps. *Respond.*

Fflur . . . Flur Mostyn, the girl the clan Elders had chosen for Rhys to marry. A nice enough girl, not bad looking. Everyone said they'd make a fine couple. They were scheduled to be married when he turned thirty—everything happened after he turned thirty. But he was in no hurry for the wedding. Something was missing between him and Fflur. He wanted sparks. Was that too much to ask? Or were sparks something that happened only in books and movies?

"I'm not babysitting, Cad. I'm playing chess with my only brother. I can always go out."

I'll be out later

"Where? Up on the roof?"

Out and about

I roam

Rhys blinked. "You mean . . . out and about down in town?"
                              All over—solar & wind farms & trailers
"Oh, crap. You could be seen. I know you don't want that."
                              Very careful
"But what do you do out there in the dark?"
                              Watch & see things
                              Listen & hear things
"Like what?"
                              I know things
"C'mon, bro. Like what?"
                              Someday I tell
Was Cadoc doing a Peeping Tom thing down there in Nespodee
Springs? Getting caught would be devastating for him. They'd
treat him like a freak, make a spectacle of him, everything he
wanted to avoid.
    "I can't tell you what to do, bro, but you're courting disaster out
there."
                              I know
                              Risk = life
Jesus. Most people would say life equaled risk. Rhys sensed his
brother meant what he wrote.
    "Please be careful."
                              Only no moon or new moon
"Still . . ."
                              Thanks for game, Rhys
"You don't want a rematch?"
                              Done tonight
    "Okay, then. Might as well turn in. I've got lifeguarding the
Nofio to look forward to tomorrow."
                              Fuck the nofio
"Whoa. Where's that coming from?"
                              forget it
"No, seriously. What's the issue?
                              so much you don't know
"Enlighten me then."

> you learn soon enough

Rhys was getting really sick of hearing that. He rose and gathered up the note sheets. He wanted to keep these.

Cadoc blew his flakes off the board, then rapped on the table and held out his hand.

"I'll chuck these out for you." A lie, but . . .

Another pair of knuckle raps. *Give.*

"All right, all right."

He handed them over then headed for the door. "But remember what I said about being careful."

"Ungh."

As Rhys closed the door behind him he heard the note sheets ripping. He stood in the hall, thinking about one of Cadoc's notes: *Bad stuff / Crazy stuff / Awful stuff*

How much of that could he believe?

# 1

Daley was suddenly wide awake.

A voice was saying, ("Time to get out of here.")

She looked around. Here? Where . . . ?

Oh, yeah. The hospital room . . . because of her hand . . .

. . . *we had to amputate* . . .

Oh, God, her hand . . . her hand was gone! How could she have forgotten? Then again, they'd been pumping morphine into her all night.

Pard stood by the bed. ("Daley, get up and get dressed. We need to leave.")

Daylight seeped between the blinds. Morning already?

"Leave? What are you talking about?"

("We can't let them see your hand. They'll be serving breakfast soon and then that Doctor Stabler will be in to check on your stump.")

"Yeah, well, that's his job."

("Yes, but you no longer have a stump.")

Did he just say—?

"What?"

("I spent the night growing you a new hand.")

She levered up in bed and raised her arm. *"What?"*

("Be careful with that. The muscles are rudimentary and stretched out, and the bones are nowhere near fully calcified yet, so it'll be weak and fragile for a while.")

She stared at the end of her mummy-wrapped left forearm. Last night it had looked horrifically, sickeningly shortened . . . *abbreviated*. Now something was stretching out the gauze at the end where her hand should be . . . *used* to be . . .

. . . was again?

She wiggled her fingers and saw movement under the gauze.

Oh, God, my hand—*my hand!*

Okay, calm down.

She'd thought yesterday was a bad dream, and now today she had to be having another dream, a good dream, but an impossible dream, because, well, she knew crabs could grow a new claw and lizards could grow a new tail, but humans simply couldn't grow a new hand. They just couldn't. So this was another dream, a wish-fulfillment dream that—

("Daley, please! We've got to go. I should have thought of this last night but you were so upset and I was so anxious to make this right for you that I overlooked the fallout that would ensue if it was discovered.") Pard was moving back and forth between the bed and the closet like a dog who had to go out. ("Please move. I'd bring your clothes out to you but I can't.")

"What's the big hurry?"

("You can't let the staff see what I've done. How will you explain it?")

"Did you really do it?" Could this be true . . . she had a left hand again? She reached for the gauze. "I want to see."

("No-no-no! Leave the gauze alone. I rearranged it to hide what I did.")

"But—"

("You have the rest of the day to admire my handiwork, but if you don't leave right now, you'll regret it for the rest of your life.")

"Isn't that a bit of an overstatement?"

("You like your alone time? How much alone time do you think you'll have when you're known as the only person in human history ever to regenerate a limb?")

The truth of that struck like a blow. He was right. She had a vision of herself on the cover of the *National Enquirer*.

"Oh, shit! Shit-shit-shit!"

She threw back the sheet and began to slide off the mattress when she noticed the IV tube running into her left arm.

"What do I do about that?"

("I emptied it during the night because I needed the glucose. Pull it out.")

"Just like that?"

("It'll bleed some but that's the least of your worries right now.")

She loosened the tape and gauze pad over the insertion site and pulled out the needle. A little clear fluid dribbled from the tip, and blood leaked from the hole in her skin. She pressed the gauze over it and rushed to the closet where she found her shoes and jeans, her cap, and her somewhat ruined blouse—whoever had removed it had slit the left sleeve first.

Dressing with one hand wasn't easy but she managed. After retrieving her phone and ID folder from the nightstand, she was ready to roll.

"Now what?"

("Now we improvise. First thing we do is get the lay of the land—or, in this case, the hallway.")

Improvise . . . Daley could barely focus. She had her hand back—*her hand was back!*

She pulled the door open to check the hall—

—and found herself face-to-face with Juana.

Daley jumped back in shock but Juana seemed unfazed. "You are leaving?"

"What are you doing here?"

Juana pointed down the hall. "My mother, remember?"

"Oh, right." Awfully early but—whatever. "Okay, yes, I'm leaving. I need to get out of here without anybody seeing me."

"You have a plan?"

"I'm thinking I'll walk to the elevator like I've been here visiting someone, like you, take it down to the lobby, and stroll out the front like I haven't a care in the world."

Juana pointed to Daley's left arm. "You will have a hard time sneaking past the nursing station with all those bandages. You'll need a distraction."

"You're volunteering?"

Juana nodded. "I believe I can handle it."

Daley met the woman's dark gaze. "Why would you do that?"

"To 'help and guide you,' remember?" She looked around, then pointed to the left. "The elevator is that way. Give me half a minute."

Daley thought she should ask: "How's your mother?"

Juana shook her head. "The same. Which means not good."

As Juana moved off, Daley stepped back into the room but left the door open six inches or so.

("I think she's following you.")

*I get that feeling too. But why would she want to follow me?*

("Maybe she feels responsible.")

*No cause for that. For some strange reason I get a feeling that you and she are connected somehow.*

("That woman and I? Connected? Ridiculous. How would that be possible?")

*No idea. Just a feeling in—*

Somewhere out in the hall a woman began wailing in pain.

"I believe that's our cue."

("I'm curious as to the nature of her diversion.")

*Well, we're not risking a look. We can ask her next time we see her— which I'm betting will be soon.*

Keeping her face half-turned toward the wall, Daley quick-walked to the elevator and jabbed the DOWN button. After something like a half-century wait, the doors slid open and she slipped inside but kept her back turned. When they whispered closed with no one raising an alarm, she released a breath she hadn't known she was holding.

*Made it.*

# 2

The Nofio . . .

What a way to waste a nice Sunday afternoon, Rhys thought as he watched half a dozen fully clothed pregnant women wade around in hot spring water. Not that he would have preferred to see them in bikinis. But you'd think the Elders would allow them to wear one-piece swimsuits for the Nofio. Nope. Tights and long-sleeved T-shirts were the style du jour. The clan had strict rules on what women wore.

Osian Pendry, the patriarch who moved them from Wales to SoCal, had chosen to build his family lodge over a hot spring. Admittedly, the Pendry spring wasn't anywhere near as big or elaborate as the one the Tadhaks had claimed for their spa, but the area hosted such a network of geothermal activity, hot mineral water was never in short supply.

This spring ran in a trickle under the Lodge foundation and pooled in a depression that ran maybe twenty feet on a side, arriving from the uphill side and dribbling away downhill into an underground channel that took the waters to . . . wherever.

The Nofio was just one more clan ritual that made no sense to Rhys. Mindless tradition. Ask why they did it, the answer invariably came that they'd always done it. And so they kept on doing it: Four times a year all the pregnant women in the clan would trek to the underbelly of the Lodge and immerse themselves for an hour or so in the warm pooled spring water. After they were through, they'd dry themselves off, go back home, and no one would visit the pool until the next Nofio.

While the women were immersed, the head of the clan—these days, that meant dear old Dad—would read a passage from the Scrolls that supposedly invoked a blessing upon the unborn from the absent Visitors.

For safety's sake, a younger male member of the clan would watch over the bathers to make sure no one drowned. Typical of the clan, women weren't considered capable lifeguards. The pool water never rose past chest height, so drowning was unlikely, but Rhys couldn't argue with erring on the side of caution. He did argue with his name being in the pool of lifeguards, but didn't raise much of a fuss. With the way the rotation worked, it came down to one hour on one Sunday a year. He could donate that much to the family, right?

*Fuck the Nofio . . .*

He'd been shocked to read that from Cadoc, who rarely used profanity in his notes. Rhys had mentioned the Nofio a number of times over the years, but had never evoked that sort of response. Just last year he'd joked about adding Cadoc's name to the lifeguard rotation list, to which Cadoc had replied, *Do you want to cause a rash of miscarriages?*

Yeah, he'd had a sense of humor about it once. But now . . .

What had changed in the past year?

*You'll know soon enough* . . .

Yeah. In less than two years, when Rhys hit thirty, all secrets would be revealed. But *what* secrets? What did Cadoc already know?

*Watch & see things* . . . *Listen & hear things* . . . *I know things* . . . *someday I tell* . . .

Obviously he'd learned something that had turned him against the Nofio.

Rhys was beginning to wonder if learning the clan's secret lore should be something to look forward to, or something to dread.

### 3

Scissors ready, Daley stood over her bathroom sink.

"And now for the big unveiling. Ready?"

Pard popped into view beside her, dressed in surgical scrubs, a mask, a cap, and latex gloves.

("Ready.")

"You're kidding, right?"

("I thought it appropriate.")

"It's not."

("You're no fun.") He flashed back to flannel and jeans. ("I think I should warn you that the fingers might be a little short. After all, I was working in the dark. But short is no problem because I can always make the bones grow a little longer.")

"I've got my *hand* back, Pard. Do you think I'm going to quibble about finger length?"

Slowly, carefully, Daley began snipping away at the gauze.

("You need to go on a high-calcium, high-protein diet,") he said at a machine-gun cadence, ("because I stole calcium from your existing bones and—")

"You sound nervous."

("I suppose I am. I've never done this before. I found the gene that acts as the master control switch for EGR and turned it on, then I worked at breakneck speed. You have no idea how I taxed your system. Mistakes might have been made.")

Somehow she knew that "EGR" meant early growth response and that it controlled regeneration. The gene was normally turned off in humans.

("You should start taking calcium pills for a while so I can strengthen the bones. I also broke down some of your existing muscle into amino acids so I could build new rudimentary muscles in the fingers.")

As Daley kept snipping away—damn, she was wrapped like a mummy—she said, "You stole from other muscles? I don't feel weak anywhere."

("Mostly your glutei.")

"My butt? You stole from my *butt?*"

("Not to worry. I didn't need much and with a high-protein diet we can rebuild it in no time.")

"That's okay. My butt was too big anyway."

She stopped cutting and began unwrapping the gauze. First she saw fingers, and then a thumb and a palm. The skin was unnaturally smooth, with no wrinkling or whorls or creases by the finger joints. She flexed them, making a fist. The skin felt tight, like a too-small glove. As she straightened the fingers, she couldn't help it—she began to cry.

("What's wrong?")

"I'm so huh-huh-happy!"

("Oh. So am I . . . except with the color.")

Daley wiped her eyes. She turned the hand this way and that, then held up her right to compare them. Except for the smoothness, the fingers looked perfectly formed, same length and caliber left and right, except . . .

"It's yellow."

("I'd say it looks more gold than simply yellow.")

"You would."

("Either way, I don't know where the pigment came from. However, in my defense, I will remind you that I was working in the dark, sight unseen, as it were.")

She kept rotating her hand back and forth. She couldn't stop staring at her wonderful, wonderful new hand.

"First my hair, now my hand. What's your prob with pigment?"

("I can fix it. I'll have the skin tone matching the right hand in no time.")

"Don't you dare."

("You *want* a golden hand?")

"For a little while, yeah. Might serve as a reminder to a certain know-it-all that he makes mistakes too."

But that wasn't the only reason. A plan was taking form in the back of her mind.

("I can only assume you're referring to me. Well, let me tell you—")

"Thank you, Pard."

("For what?")

"For giving me back my hand."

("You mean *our* hand. And thanks are not in order. I had no intention of letting us spend the rest of our lives in a maimed body.")

The reality of her situation settled over her with an inescapable finality.

"We really *are* partners, aren't we."

("So, you've finally accepted that. Another milestone! All for one and one for all. For better or worse. Till death do us part . . . I'm running out of clichés.")

Daley said, "Hmmm."

("'Hmmm'? I'm not sure I like the sound of that.")

"It means I'm seeing dollar signs."

("Where?")

"In my head. My hand aside, first Grace, then Lynn . . . if we can cure them, we can cure others. There's got to be a way to monetize this."

("What? You can't be serious!")

"Why not? Doctors charge for their services. Why shouldn't I?"

("Because they're not *your* services. They're *mine*.")

"Ah, but where would you be without me? Stuck on a cave ceiling, maybe?"

("That's hurtful, Daley.")

"You said you were pure mind. How can you have feelings?"

("You denigrated my humble origins.")

Did she? She hadn't meant to. Maybe she was still angry for what had happened to her hand. As she stared at its replacement, an obvious question came to the fore.

"Where do you come from, Pard—besides a cave ceiling, that is? I mean are you a rare life-form or some sort of alien or what?"

He put on a puzzled expression. ("I honestly don't know. I've wondered that myself. I had no awareness before I began to integrate with you, so I have no way of knowing.")

Daley returned to her front room.

"Are there others like you?"

("Again . . . I don't know.")

"We should find out, don't you think?"

("Absolutely. We should start with Juana. That woman knows more than she's telling.")

"No doubt. We'll have to get on her case next time we see her. Meanwhile . . . remember I said I wanted to accomplish something? I think I'd like to be a healer."

Pard began to pace the room. ("A healer? You mean put on some sort of modern-day medicine show?")

Daley narrowed her gaze. "How do you know about medicine shows?"

("Because *you* know about them. I know whatever you know, remember?")

"Oh, right. Okay, but I'm not talking about putting on a medicine show, because that's a scam. I'm talking about doing real healing."

("No, you're talking about *me* doing real healing.")

"We're partners, remember? Your word. And you can't heal anybody without my touch. I see us on network TV in worldwide syndication."

Pard adopted a scandalized expression. ("You want to be a *televangelist?*")

"I want the money to roll in so fast we can't count it."

("Is that all you're interested in—money?")

She'd grown up poor, with Mum working crummy jobs and trying to stretch every dollar to the max. Money had been a day-and-night concern, as in *Where's the next dollar coming from?*

"Mostly I'm interested in not having to worry about money—ever again. As for televangelists, they're fakes and everybody with half a brain knows it. We'll have no religion connection, but we *will* be providing miracles. That'll be our thing: We'll be dealing with truly sick people and truly healing them!"

("Doing well while doing good, in other words.")

"Exactly! And doing *very* well. We'll have reputable doctors do before-and-after exams to verify the cures. As you said yourself, what you did *seems* like a miracle."

Pard stared at her. ("Real cures on TV. You don't see a problem there?")

What was he talking about?

"I see a lot of people who won't be sick anymore."

("You'll be an instant, international celebrity, recognized everywhere. You won't be able to show your face without—")

"I'm a homebody and I'll be able to afford all the privacy I need."

("Okay, then, here's another question: How do we stop?")

"Stop what?"

("Healing. Consider: We've shown the world that you can cure people of life-threatening or life-ruining conditions without surgery or harsh medications, simply by touching them. Now, after years of doing that, we're older and tired of it, burned out. We want to stop. How do we manage it?")

Daley shrugged. "We simply cancel the program—pack up and go home."

("Do you really think you'll be allowed to do that—deny sick people your healing power, your miracle touch?") Pard shook his head. ("You'll be considered public property—a national resource. You quit and you'll be vilified like no one else in history, you'll be hounded to the ends of the earth. You'll never know a day's peace.")

"Stop trying to harsh my mellow, Pard. 'Vilified'? You mean an army of trolls dumping on me on Twitter? I can live with that."

("No, I'm talking about riots, Daley. I'm talking about a mob breaking into your home and burning it to the ground.")

The doorbell rang. Daley stepped to the window and looked below. Dr. Holikova stood at her front door.

What on earth did she want?

The bell rang again. And again.

("I don't think she's going away.")

"Oh, hell."

Daley hurried down the stairs to her front door but didn't open it. She watched Dr. Holikova through the peephole.

"Can I help you?"

"Stanka? I check at hospital and they say you leave AMA this morning."

*AMA? American Medical Association?*

Pard appeared beside her. ("You've heard it on *Grey's Anatomy:* 'Against medical advice.'")

"You are all right?" the doc said. "I just want to see how you are after terrible accident yesterday."

Yeah, sure.

Daley held up her new hand . . . *My new hand.* How many people in all the history of humanity had been able to say that? Still hard to believe what Pard had done.

She said, "It wasn't nearly as bad as it seemed at the time. I'm okay now."

"Please let me in, Stanka, just for minute. I must speak with you. Is very important. And is not just about Grace. I hear from Doctor Patel downstairs that young woman with dark hair and Dodgers cap like yours held patient's hands and tell her she is cured of her lung cancer and . . ." Dr. Holikova seemed to struggle with her next words. "And PET scan done right after shows no cancer. So you can see is important I speak to you."

She glanced at Pard. *What do you think?*

("Bad idea. You can't let her see that hand. Not yet. Even if she thinks it was merely injured, it looks too good.")

Daley leaned her head against the door. She really and truly had lost control of her life. But then again, when had she ever had complete control?

"Just curious, Doctor Holikova—how did you find me?"

The only addresses people had were her two mail drops.

"You gave my address when you had EEG."

Oh, right. Dummy! Why had she given her apartment?

She checked the doctor again through the peephole and noticed a group of about a half dozen women crossing Burbank Boulevard and angling her way.

"You didn't happen to give it to some people from the oncologist's office, did you?"

"I would never give privileged information to anyone. But group of patients have been hanging around the building. They ask me about you, but I tell them nothing. I think they're waiting for you to reappear."

The group was closer now and Daley recognized Lynn leading the way.

"Not anymore, they aren't."

"What do you mean?"

"Those people behind you look awfully familiar."

She turned and gasped. "They must have followed me! Let me in before they get here!"

"Not a chance, Doc."

Daley hurried back up to the top of the stairs and paused on the landing, listening. She heard faint arguing below, and then the bell started ringing as fists hammered on the door. She stepped inside her apartment and locked the door.

"What do we do?"

("Unfortunately, like most buildings around here, this one has no fire escape, and that new hand of ours is in no condition for any acrobatics. So I guess we wait them out.")

The banging didn't go on for too long. Daley watched from the window as the owner of the ground-floor bookstore chased the women away with a threat to call the police.

Suddenly restless, she began wandering the room and checking the street again and again.

"I'm feeling trapped." She glanced at Pard who was sitting in the recliner with his legs crossed, looking like he hadn't a care in the world. "How can you just sit there when I'm all on edge?"

He tapped a finger against his temple. ("Pure mind, remember? I'm not really sitting and I'm not subject to mood swings.")

"I feel like I'm going to jump out of my skin."

("Why? Usually you're pretty much a homebody. Except when running one of your tawdry scams—")

"'Tawdry'? 'Tawdry'? You don't know what I do."

("I know everything you know, remember? Scams are beneath your intelligence and dignity. Just because you were raised that way doesn't mean you have to live that way. But be that as it may, when you're not sullying yourself as a grifter, you tend to be perfectly happy to stay home.")

"But then it's *my* choice. I'm not being given a choice at the moment." She checked the window again. "No sign of them for a while now. Looks like they've been chased away."

("I wouldn't suggest we go for a walk.")

"How about a drive?" She'd parked her car just around the corner. "I need to pick up some groceries anyway."

("You can have them delivered.")

"I need to get *out*, Pard."

("Very well, then. Not as if I have much say in the matter anyway.")

"Exactly."

Gathering her phone, shoulder bag, cap, and jacket, Daley hurried down the stairs to the front door. The peephole showed no
lurkers so she stepped out onto the sidewalk and quick-walked to
the end of the block. Pard glided along at her side. She rounded
the corner and—

("Uh-oh.")

Eight or nine women huddled near her car.

*Oh, shit!*

She couldn't tell if they knew the Subaru belonged to her or
had grouped there simply by convenience. She did a one-eighty
and started back, hoping to retreat around the corner before they
spotted her—

"There she is! That's her!"

No such luck. Daley broke into a run but skidded to a halt at the
sight of three more women at her front door.

One of them pointed at her. "It's you!"

Just like in Dr. Patel's office, they all converged on her at once,
tugging and pawing at her, beseeching her to help them. She fought
them off but they wouldn't give up, backing her toward the curb.
She was desperate enough to consider trying to dash across Burbank
Boulevard when she heard the roar of a poorly muffled engine.

Juana pulled to the curb on her hog.

"Let's go!" she said.

Daley didn't need any more than that.

As she hopped into the sidecar she blurted, "What about Pard?"

Juana looked around. "Who?"

"Never mind. Go!"

As Juana hit the throttle and they roared off, Daley shook her
head in chagrin. At first she'd denied Pard was real, now he was
almost too real.

("As if you could leave me behind.")

A grinning, bareheaded Pard winked from the hog's passenger seat where he'd wrapped his arms around Juana. A long scarf trailed out behind him. Daley remembered Juana's Isadora Duncan remark and suddenly realized she now knew who she was: a famous dancer whose long scarf had caught in the wheel of an open touring car back in the 1920s and broke her neck.

More of Pard's research, she supposed.

As they drove Daley pulled the helmet from the front of the sidecar; she reversed her cap and put it on over it. Juana crossed Cahuenga Boulevard and pulled to a stop.

"They're not following us," she said.

Daley lifted her visor. "But *you're* following me. Why?"

"You know why: to help and guide. And you definitely needed help just now with those ladies who think you can cure them."

Her words jolted Daley. "How do you know about that?"

"Been keeping tabs on you."

"That's kind of creepy."

"Not at all. 'To help—'"

"'—and guide.' I know, I know."

Juana pulled her goggles down and let them hang around her neck as she stared at Daley's hand. "What—?" she said in a shocked tone.

"Oh, the color? Left over from the injury that put me in the hospital."

"The injury to your hand," she said softly, then shifted her gaze to Daley's eyes. "Well . . . can you?"

"Can I what?" But Daley knew exactly what.

"Cure them?"

Daley couldn't bring herself to say *yes*.

"That remains to be seen."

("You're not being entirely honest.")

*Well, you told me you couldn't cure everything, didn't you?*

("Yes, but . . .")

*Then let me handle this.*

After a long stare, Juana said, "Where to now?"

"Well, I don't think I should go back home just yet. I need a place to crash."

"I'm staying in Sherman Oaks with family but there's no room for you there. I'd offer you my trailer but that's three hours away. Do you have any friends?"

She had Kenny, but crashing with him could get awfully complicated right now, especially after Thursday night.

"Not really."

Juana gave her a strange look—which she deserved.

("Why don't you have any friends?")

*I never learned how to make friends. I wasn't allowed to have any growing up—at least not outside the Family. All my contacts were limited to the Family until I moved in with Gram. She sent me to a real high school, but I was pretty much relegated to outsider status all the way through.*

Gram . . . a possibility. Although she'd promised a visit just last Friday, Daley didn't want to impose. The old woman didn't have a spare room but her couch was good for a bit of snooze.

"My grandmother has a place in Tarzana. Could you drop me there?"

"No problem."

She readjusted her goggles and they were on their way. Daley was glad she'd worn the warm-up—the cool air was growing even cooler.

# 4

"We made it," Daley said to no one in particular as they rolled toward the entrance to Gram's senior development.

("Just barely. You do realize we had three near-death experiences on that little twelve-mile jaunt.")

*You're telling me.*

She'd expected Juana to stick to surface roads. Instead she'd roared up onto the 101 and driven like a demon, weaving in and out of traffic, cutting off pickups and semi-trailers alike. Daley kept shouting at her to slow down, but between Juana's leather helmet and the combined roars of the traffic and the Harley's engine, any attempt at communication was futile. She did manage to call Gram at the outset and say she was coming for a visit.

They cruised past the sign at the community entrance.

### ENTRÉE

Sounded like it might be a French restaurant, but the second line burst that bubble.

#### The Finest in Adult Living

Daley directed Juana to Gram's building where she pulled up before it and killed the engine.

"I was thinking about you as I drove," she said, lowering her goggles.

("Oh, so that's her excuse. Because she obviously wasn't thinking about safety.")

Daley pulled off her helmet. "New and better ways to help and guide me?"

("When not trying to kill you?")

"As a matter of fact, yes. Exactly what I was thinking. Are you serious about this healing thing? Do you want to give it a try?"

("How odd . . . just what you and I were discussing before Doctor Holikova interrupted.")

*Really odd. What's Juana's story, I wonder?*

Daley said, "I've been thinking about it, but after that scene back at my place, I'm not so sure."

"I think the key will be to start low and slow . . . locate an out-of-the-way venue, a small town where you can find your bearings, get your footing while you work discreetly."

"Leave LA? I don't know about that."

"Too many people here," Juana said. "Too many loudmouth crazies. One misstep and you'll be branded a fake."

"Torn to pieces in the Twitterverse."

"Exactly. You want a small, quiet place where you can engage in trial and error. You may fail miserably, or you may have some success and find you don't like it, want no part of it. Or you may find it's exactly what you were meant to be. Either way you can then return to LA with your head straight and some experience behind you."

"Why do I get the feeling you already have just such a place in mind?"

Juana's smile transformed her face into a mass of wrinkles. "I have a possible locale in mind. We'll have to do a little research first. Can you find my place again?"

"Yeah, pretty sure."

"Stop by tomorrow morning and we'll do reconnaissance."

"What time?"

She pulled up her goggles. "Any time. I'll be there."

She kick-started her hog and roared off.

("She appears to be taking this 'help and guide' mission very seriously.")

*Seems more like she's edging into "nudge and manipulate" territory. What kind of "small town" is she thinking of?*

("I suppose we'll find out when—")

"There you are!" said a voice.

Gram waved from the doorway of her unit.

"Hey, Gram."

A lean, lanky woman with high color in her cheeks, Gram's hair used to be as red as those cheeks but had gone mostly gray. She was always a pretty woman, but she'd lost weight since Pa's death, leaving her cheek lines sharper and her chin more prominent. *Rawboned* might be the word for her now. But her blue eyes never lost their shine.

"What was that horrible racket?" she said.

"Just my ride."

"Well, come in, come in, or you'll be catching your death of cold."

*Death of cold?* Well, the temperature had dipped into the fifties, and that was pretty much a hard freeze as far as Gram was concerned.

Daley followed her inside.

("I'm feeling that burst of love again. No one else in your world triggers that.")

*She's the best.*

Back somewhere around the dawn of time, Gram and her brother Seamus did what most intelligent Irish folk did back in the day—got out of Ireland as soon as they were able. They came over together from the Auld Sod to spend the summer working in the Hamptons. They liked America so much they decided to stay and headed for the warmth of Southern California.

After more than fifty years here you'd think they'd have lost their accents. But no. They both sounded like they'd just stepped off the boat. Daley suspected an unspoken competition to see whose speech could remain the least Americanized.

When Pa died, Gram had found the empty house unsettling, so she and brother Seamus, a widower for almost a decade, moved in together. They'd started their lives together, so why not end that way? Besides, it was lots cheaper.

So they bought this two-bedroom, two-bath, free-standing ranch unit with stucco walls and a barrel-tile roof in a brand-new senior development. The good part about their arrangement was they provided company for each other. The bad part was they were the stubbornest pair this side of Alpha Centauri.

Daley stepped inside and was immediately reminded of the two things she would always associate with Gram: heat and smoke.

("Do they live downwind from the county incinerator?")

*You'd think so, wouldn't you.*

("I feel like we've stepped into a house-size ashtray.")

Daley worried about them, worried herself sick about losing Gram to lung cancer. But despite her entreaties, they refused to quit the ciggies. They'd say they know they're poison but they *can't* quit. Daley knew they didn't *want* to quit.

Uncle Seamus's Jack Russell terrier barked once as he charged her, then jumped against her leg, tail wagging. She patted his head.

"Hey, Brendan."

He trotted after her as she wound through the haze of the living room.

("Do they realize they have too much furniture?")

*When they moved in they each insisted on keeping their own furniture. Neither would budge. If I hadn't taken some of it for my place, this room would be impassable.*

("It looks like a used-furniture store on clearance day. On second thought, considering all the pictures and statues of saints on the walls, it looks like a combination devotional chapel/secondhand furniture store.")

Daley angled around to the front windows and opened one.

"Lookit after what you're doing now!" Gram cried. "You'll be letting in the night air!"

Daley coughed. "And letting out some smoke."

Gram had this thing about night air—somehow it was bad for you.

She rubbed her upper arms through the sleeves of her housedress. "I'm going to get a sweater before I catch pneumonia!"

That didn't seem likely since she and Seamus kept their thermostat set on *sauna*. Daley suspected they'd Krazy Glued it there.

As Gram scurried into her bedroom, Seamus, cigarette dangling from his lips, came out of his. He was built like Gram, but there the resemblance ended. Seamus sported a white chinstrap beard—stained nicotine brown around his mouth, to be sure—a shiny pate, and twinkling eyes. Give him a shillelagh, a cocked hat, and a shamrock, and you'd have a leprechaun.

She waved as she passed on her way to the kitchen at the rear.

"Hi, Unk."

He blew a kiss from the other side of an overstuffed sofa. "Coming to stay for spell?"

"Just until the wee hours."

Back with these two less than a minute and already she was adopting their lingo.

In the kitchen she opened the window over the sink and sighed as she felt fresh air begin to flow.

Gram coughed as she returned, rubbing her hands. "I was about to pour meself some nettle soup. Will you be having a bowl?"

"I'll take a rain check, Gram." Daley had never been fond of nettle soup, but then Gram put on her hurt look so Daley said, "Okay, just a taste."

"That's my dearie. It's anti-aging and you're not getting any younger, you know."

"Thanks, Gram."

Gram's belief system was what Daley had come to call voodoo Irish. Ostensibly a Catholic—she'd dragged Daley to Sunday mass during her teen years—she carried all this baggage from Ireland's pagan past. She believed in God and Jesus, and the Virgin Mary— *loved* the Virgin Mary—but also believed in leprechauns and banshees and even the Morrigan.

Plus she'd never met a patron saint she didn't like. The living room/dining room area looked like a shrine to any saint who'd ever set foot on Irish soil. She'd collected statues of about a dozen or so.

Pard said, ("Where does she find these?")

*She has a revolving charge account at the Discount House of Holy Stuff.*

("Rampant religiosity.")

*But it works for her. Let me give you an example of the voodoo. When Gram put her house on the market, the first thing she did was bury a statue of St. Joseph in the backyard to help the sale. I laughed when I heard. I mean, I know they've got a patron saint for everything, but I'd never heard of one for real estate deals. But wouldn't you know, she wound up with three potential buyers who got into a bidding war. Gram walked away with twelve thousand more than her asking price.*

("Coincidence reinforces superstition.")

*And how. That statue—all cleaned up now—occupies a place of honor on her night table.*

Uncle Seamus, on the other hand, was anticlerical to the point of atheism, but could never quite bring himself to step over that line. A skeptic who accepted Pascal's wager about believing in God: *"If you gain, you gain all; if you lose, you lose nothing. Wager, then, without hesitation, that He exists."*

The nettle soup was soon ladled and the three of them hovered around the kitchen counter to partake.

"Will you be leaving that hat on?" Gram said.

Daley didn't want to explain the white patch.

"If you don't mind. My hair is a mess."

"I don't mind. But what happened to your hand?"

The gold skin . . .

"I was working with some dye and it's very stubborn. Let's try your soup."

Daley tried but had to stop after two spoonfuls. *Blech.*

"Billy Marks has been stopping by," Gram said.

Daley felt her gorge rise. If the nettle soup hadn't been enough to put her on the edge of hurling, mention of that name just about pushed her over.

"What's he want?"

"What do you think?" Seamus said. "Looking for you."

Billy Marks was some sort of distant uncle on her father's side— her father's cousin. He was the man who murdered her father on the day she was born. Oh, he denied it up and down and no one had ever been able to prove it because of a questionable alibi, but her mother never had a doubt he'd done it.

"What's he want with me?"

"What else? To involve you in one of his scams."

She felt shaky inside. She wanted nothing to do with the Family—especially Billy Marks.

"You didn't tell him where I am, did you?"

"Never!" Seamus cried. "I've had a mind to get out me Webley and make a few holes in him!"

"Leave the Webley where it is, please."

Seamus had an old revolver—known as a Webley-Fosbery, as she recalled—he'd brought over from Ireland. He'd taken Daley to a shooting range with it now and again when she was a teen. The antique still fired and always caused a stir with multiple offers from collectors to buy it. She was pretty sure it hadn't left his bedside drawer for a long time now.

Billy would probably end up with a few holes in him someday, but please not from Seamus.

"You look peaked," Gram said. "Have you eaten dinner?"

"Had a big lunch."

("We've had nothing since your so-called breakfast of Pop-Tarts.")

Gram coughed. "Well, then I'll be fixing you something right now. The pork chops aren't even cold yet."

Daley knew Gram's pork chops: suitable for use as a roofer's hammer.

"That's okay, Gram. Not hungry."

("That name upset you,") Pard said. ("You might want to consider a little food.")

*I'm okay now. Just surprised is all. And Gram's pork chops aren't exactly food.*

No one could ruin a perfectly good piece of meat like Gram, mainly because she'd never met a piece of meat she considered overcooked. That old Irish thing again: Cook it until it has the texture of jerky, then cook it some more. Daley had once considered getting a sign for over her front door: *Abandon All Hope of Flavor Ye Who Enter Here.*

"A wee bit of stout then?" Seamus said. When Daley shook her head he held up a bottle of Jameson's. "A touch of whisky?"

*Watch his reaction when I say . . .*

"Don't you have any Bushmills?"

His eyes fairly bulged. "Oh, you cheeky thing, you! You know I'll not have Protestant whisky in this house!"

("I take it this isn't the first time you've played this scene.")

*Nor the last. But I could use a shot to settle my nerves.*

("This Billy Marks really upsets you.")

*I want to see him dead.*

"Maybe just a wee dram, Unk."

Seamus poured and Daley sipped her Jameson's while he and Gram had at their soup. As soon as they finished they immediately lit up cigarettes.

Daley coughed.

Gram offered a sour smile. "We know that's a fake cough, dearie. Why do you keep doing it?"

"It's not fake. It's the smoke."

Then the dog coughed.

"See? Even Brendan's got a cough!"

# 1

Daley found herself abruptly wide awake in the dark on one of Gram's couches.

("It's four A.M. Time to move.")

*Did you wake me up?*

("We agreed on four o'clock to return to our place unseen.")

*So now it's "our" place?*

(*"Su casa es mi casa."*)

Pain shot up Daley's spine as she sat up. *Oh, my back. I'm too young to have backaches.*

("This couch was not made for sleeping. You should have taken your uncle up on his offer.")

Seamus had wanted her to take his bed while he took the couch.

*Wouldn't think of it.*

She'd slept in her clothes so she was ready to go. She checked her phone, wondering if she could get an Uber at this hour, but no problem. One was ten minutes away.

Once back in North Hollywood she had the Uber drive around her block once but spotted no lurkers.

("It appears your fans have gone to bed.")

In her apartment she packed an overnight bag and emptied her candle safe of the fat roll of Benjamins she hid there. She figured it might be best to stay away a few days until her "fans" gave up.

She jumped in her car and headed for the desert.

# 2

"There it is," Daley said as she spotted the casino.

It sat west of the 86 with nothing but desert around it—as if plopped there by a giant hand.

("About time,") Pard said from the passenger seat where he'd spent the trip.

The sun was climbing the clear winter sky. Traffic hadn't been bad but still the trip had reached the three-hour mark. Daley had called Juana as they reached the Salton Sea and been instructed to meet her at the Red Earth Casino just south of Salton Sea Beach.

She found Juana waiting with her Harley near the entrance to the parking lot. Red Earth had its own gas station and convenience store—one-stop shopping for gamblers. She held out her hand as Daley unfolded herself from the driver seat.

"Here," the older woman said, handing her a seashell.

"For me?"

"They're everywhere." She pointed to an area of disturbed sand a few feet away. "I kicked that up while waiting for you."

"Looks like an oyster shell."

"Except it's six million years old."

"You're a morning gambler?" Daley said as she tucked the shell into her bag.

"Not any sort of gambler. I realize your Subaru has all-wheel-drive but it's built low to the ground. It would have been slow going on the path to my place, and then you'd have had to turn around and go back the same way. Better we meet here." She gestured at the casino. "My tribe owns this."

*What's her tribe?*

("It's buried in your memory—Desert Cahuilla.")

"Desert Cahuilla, right?"

She smiled. "Good memory. You drove through our reservation a few miles back."

Daley had seen the signs and remembered it as pretty desolate with no paved roads. "The government should have given you part of the San Fernando Valley instead."

She shrugged. "You know how that goes: As soon as it became worth something they'd have kicked us out. Besides, my people have always lived here. These are our tribal lands."

"Is this what you wanted me to see?"

"No. We're headed fifty miles southwest as the crow flies."

"Southwest? That's all empty desert."

"Pretty much, but not quite. Since we're not crows, we've got maybe seventy miles by road. Less than an hour and a half. You follow me."

"What is this place?"

"Small resort town with mineral waters and a spa. It's called Nespodee Springs."

"'A small resort town,' she said," Daley muttered as they drove the main drag. "I feel like I'm back in the old west riding into Tombstone. Where's Wyatt Earp?"

("You've never been to Tombstone.")

"No, but I've seen the movie."

They'd followed Juana south to somewhere between Brawley and El Centro where they came upon a big sign with a bright red arrow pointing west.

### YOU'RE ALMOST TO NESPODEE SPRINGS!

A right turn took them onto a desert road. After nine or ten miles of sand and sagebrush, the utility poles disappeared. Just . . . stopped.

("That can't be good,") Pard had said.

Daley couldn't argue. But then the white poles and spinning vanes of a wind farm appeared in the distance and she felt a little better.

"Somebody's cranking out voltage ahead."

They reached a *Welcome to Nespodee Springs* sign and the road suddenly improved. Rows of mobile homes lined both sides; farther to the north the cluster of three-bladed wind turbines they'd seen from afar pinwheeled in the breeze. To the south lay a huge, glittering solar farm, and beyond that some weird-looking tower like a giant skeletal mushroom.

Pard had ridden shotgun the entire trip. When Daley looked left, he looked left; when she looked right, he looked right.

"Why are you mimicking me?"

("It's more like synching. I can see only what you're seeing.")

"You see what I'm seeing whether you turn your make-believe head or not. It's annoying."

("Sensy-sensy.") He faded out. ("I'll simply monitor from within.")

And then they arrived at what might be called a town: two rows of one-and two-story wooden buildings flanking a strip of asphalt that ran westward up to the nearby foothills. A planked boardwalk ran along in front of the storefronts, just like in a Wild West town. A sign advised them that the Nespodee Springs Hotel and Spa lay beyond the town, farther up the slope toward a thick cluster of palm trees.

("Oh, look,") Pard said as they rolled on. ("One of the hallmarks of western civilization: a laundromat. And a no-name gas station with a car wash.")

Daley spotted the Nespodee Springs Market, Arturo's Cozy Coyote Café, a beer-wine-liquor store, a used furniture store with couches and chairs out front, and a no-name bar with a corrugated steel awning over its boardwalk. She saw a storefront with *Thomas Llewelyn, MD—General Practice* on the window, along with a couple of empty units.

Pard reappeared. ("Her advice was to start small but this is beyond small. It's minute.")

"I'd go so far as to say it's microscopic."

("Beyond that. It's subatomic.")

"It's quantum—even though I don't know what that means."

("Nobody does, but at least you admit it. The big question is: Can this tiny place support a doctor *and* a healer?")

"Maybe he's here for his health—you know, the desert air?—and has very limited hours."

("Maybe. But I sense friction ahead. Even so, I think I like this place.")

"You do?"

("I can't tell you why, but it has a homey feel.")

"It's 'homey' only if one has spent most of one's existence clinging to the roof of a cave. Oh, wait. That would be you."

("That's hurtful, Daley.")

"Deal with it."

Up ahead Juana parked nose in before a real estate storefront. Daley pulled in beside her. She checked the outside temperature on her dashboard: *70*. A good fifteen degrees warmer than LA. She wondered what the thermometer read in July.

### 3

The same notice about the "pairing" had appeared on Rhys's screen three mornings last week. They didn't run analyses of the stellar images on weekends, so now he waited to see if Monday morning was going to be the same. His father stood by his shoulder as he scrolled to the bottom of the screen. His shoulders tightened as the message appeared:

*THE DUAD APPROACHES*

Similar, but the difference was ominous.

Rhys said, "I'm guessing that means this 'pairing,' this 'Duad' is on its way here."

His father shook his head. "I can't see any other way to interpret it."

"But I'm still not clear on what 'a pairing' means. A pairing of what? Are we talking two people? A couple? What? And why is it—they—coming to a godforsaken corner of nowhere like Nespodee Springs?"

"To interfere with our destiny."

Rhys couldn't hide his annoyance and impatience. "Who is this 'our'? It doesn't include me, because I've never been briefed on this destiny."

"You will be soon enough, but right now only I and the heads of the other families are involved."

Rhys could only growl with frustration.

"Forget the investments for today," Dad said as he laid a gentle hand on Rhys's shoulder. "I'll watch the indexes while you watch the town."

"And how am I supposed to do that?"

"Reposition one of the sky scopes to focus downhill."

Oh. Of course. Simple enough. The roof scopes were all on servos that allowed them to be pointed in almost any direction; they fed their images directly to the Lodge's server and from there to any of the monitors. He got to work on it as his father walked away. In no time he found a scope that could angle toward Nespodee Springs's main thoroughfare.

He settled back for what he anticipated to be a long, boring morning. But almost immediately he spotted a motorcycle approaching. He focused on it and upped the magnification.

Only Juana. She sure as hell wasn't the pairing or Duad. That strange native lady kept popping in and out of the town. Practically a fixture around here. Back in the day her tribe called much of the valley their own, but still, what was the attraction in Nespodee Springs that kept her coming back?

She pulled into her usual spot before the real estate office. She and Jason Tadhak seemed to be tight. Hung out a lot. Rhys couldn't imagine they had anything romantic going on, so what was the attraction? Juana wasn't in the market for—

Hang on a sec. A car approaching. A Subaru Crosstrek pulling in next to Juana. He focused on the driver as she got out. Wearing a baseball cap with a short dark ponytail out the back. Her face was shaded but she looked slim and, best of all, young.

But only one of her. If she was part of the Duad, where was her other half?

And then she glanced up and her face turned Rhys's way. Add good looking to the slim and young.

Things were suddenly looking up in Nespodee Springs.

## 4

Daley joined Juana on the boardwalk before a window signed with *Tadhak Realty*.

Juana said, "I called this morning and asked if they had any commercial space available and they do."

"I'm not surprised," Daley said. "The place looks dead."

"Appearances can be deceptive," said a dark-haired, thickset man as he stepped from the real estate office. He wore a gray suit with a white shirt and no tie. He extended his hand. "Jason Tadhak."

"Daley," she said, shaking hands.

His bushy eyebrows rose. "That's all? No 'Miss' or 'Ms.' or 'Mrs.'? Just 'Daley'?"

"For now."

He stared for a few heartbeats. He was built straight up and down: broad shoulders that flowed into a thick waist that blended into wide hips.

"As you wish. Call me Jason." He turned to Juana. "Still riding that Harley, I see."

"It gets me where I want to go."

Daley said, "Obviously you two know each other."

He smiled, showing perfectly even teeth. "Everyone knows Juana. But I'm guessing you don't know much about Nespodee Springs."

"Never heard the name until a little over an hour ago. I've heard of Borrego Springs and Jacumba Springs, and Palm Springs, of course."

Jason gestured around. "My family has been here quite literally for centuries. We run the spa and hotel and we built this town. We have a natural hot spring that gushes wonderful mineral water with a steady temperature of one hundred and four degrees. Nespodee Springs was very popular throughout the twentieth century—not as popular as Borrego and Jacumba, I'll grant you, but we held our own, especially with the Hollywood crowd. Bette Davis and James Cagney were regulars here during the thirties. Even little Shirley Temple came a few times."

Daley widened her eyes and tried to look impressed. "Wow!"

*Do you have any idea who he's talking about?*

("He mentioned Hollywood, so . . . old movie stars, I guess?")

"But then, as the popularity of soaking in hot mineral springs diminished, so did our trade. And consequently, our population. We're down from our peak of fifteen hundred or so, but we're still home to five hundred souls and still experience steady tourist traffic."

*Only five hundred?*

("A micro-town.")

"A good place to get your healing feet wet," Juana said.

("More like get your toe damp.")

"I don't know . . ."

Jason pulled a set of keys from his pocket. "Let me show you what we have."

Just then a bus came downhill and rolled past, all white with no markings and heavily tinted windows. Looked weird, almost sinister.

"From the spa?" Daley said.

"No, they're workers at the wind farm."

"Yeah, but the wind farm's down there," she said, pointing in the direction the bus was headed. "Where are they coming from?"

"My family compound," Jason said. "The wind farm is a family project, so we Tadhaks work it. We've found it best to keep it all in the family."

Yeah, well, whatever.

He led them to a pair of empty storefronts side by side at the end of the building row. An unpaved driveway divided it from the laundromat in the next group. He keyed open the door to the end unit. The inside was dusty with empty shelves, display cases, and counters, but spacious.

"The previous tenant ran a gift shop here. I'd warned her she'd be competing with the spa's gift and souvenir shop but she opened it anyway. Didn't last six months. You, on the other hand . . . Juana said 'healing.' What kind of healing? Holistic? Naturopathic? Reiki?"

Daley hadn't thought this all the way through yet. Should she mention her degree in homeopathy?

Nah.

"It's . . . it's my own style. I haven't given it a name yet."

(*"Your* own style? My-my-my!")

*I'm riffing. Don't break the flow.*

"Well, let me be frank with you: A lot of our guests at the spa— I'm not going out on a limb when I say *most* of our guests at the spa—are into alternative and holistic medicine. They obviously believe in the healing powers of a natural mineral hot spring or else they wouldn't be here. But many hold New Age beliefs, like crystals and pyramid power and such. It's a big tent and if your system fits under it, you could do well here."

"But your town already has a doctor. I don't want any trouble."

Jason grinned. "Doc Llewelyn? He's a pussycat. And semi-retired. His family is part of the Pendry Clan and they keep him pretty much as busy as he wants to be."

"The Pendry Clan?"

"A cluster of Welsh families who moved here early in the last century. They own that monstrosity up there."

Daley followed his point and saw a massive two-story house jutting from the hillside. Its flat roof and horizontal planes gave it a Frank Lloyd Wright look.

Frank Lloyd Wright? Who . . . ? And then she knew. Pard again.

"'Clan'?"

"Five families. Pendry, Llewelyn, Mostyn, Baughan, and Gwynn, but you need only remember Pendry. They're the ones who run the show up there. All very insular."

"And all living in the hills," Juana said. "Won't live down here with us flatlanders. Have to be above us all."

("Do I detect a note of hostility, hmmm?")

Tadhak said, "They do come down to buy their groceries and support the town, so you'll see them around. The women are easy to recognize by their clothing. They keep to themselves, home-schooling their kids and all that. Don't expect them to consult you. They won't use anyone but Doc Llewelyn. He's one of them." He pointed to the hillside home. "The big place—they call it their 'Lodge'—is their meetinghouse and home of the current head of the clan, Elis Pendry."

"What do they do here?"

"Some have small businesses in Brawley and El Centro, a lot of them work the solar farm. Elis Pendry invests their money for them and he's very good at it, I'm told." Jason winked. "Mostly they have babies."

"What about all those solar panels I saw?"

"My family runs the wind farm to supply energy for the town—we're all electric here, by the way. The solar array is a Pendry project that's connected to one of their less conventional endeavors."

"Like?"

"Like their Tesla tower," Juana said.

"Has that got something to do with those electric cars?" Daley said.

"Not a thing." Tadhak gestured around the store. "What do you think?"

("I think he wants to move from the subject of the Pendry Clan.")

*Well, we were getting off topic.*

("Still, I get the feeling he's not too fond of the Pendrys. And Juana certainly isn't.")

"What do I think?" Daley said as she did a slow turn. "It has potential."

She was trying to sound noncommittal and didn't have to try too hard. She had her doubts about Nespodee Springs being the right place for her.

"I think you should give it a try," Juana said.

("She's right. I like this town. It agrees with me.")

*Yeah, but I'm the one who's got to pay for it.*

"Here's my situation," Daley said. "I've got another five months left on my apartment lease back in LA. No way can I commute from LA, so that means getting another place nearby. Two apartments plus the rent here means this place has to more than pay for itself—and pretty damn quick—or I'll go broke."

Jason jiggled the keys in his hand. "I think I can solve your problem." He pointed to the ceiling. "This store has a furnished apartment directly above. It's empty now. I'll let you have both for free for the remaining five months on your LA lease."

The offer stunned Daley. "Really?"

"I'll even throw in a cleanup."

She glanced at Juana who seemed unfazed. What was the connection between these two?

"Why would you do that?"

"Well, first off, I like you."

"We just met."

"Yes, but you've got an air about you that gives me confidence."

("He's sensing my presence, no doubt.")

*No doubt. What else could it be?*

("Do I sense sarcasm?")

"Secondly, I think a healer will be good for this town. And last, I don't much like the idea of the tourists heading to and from the spa seeing empty storefronts on Main Street. It makes Nespodee Springs look down on its luck. It's not. Sure, it's seen better days, but it's not dying."

("Makes sense to me.")

*You're already sold on the place, so he's just saying what you want to hear.*

Her upbringing was reminding her that if it sounds too good to be true, it most likely is.

"What if, after the five months are up, I'm losing my shirt?"

He shrugged. "Then you walk away, no strings."

"And what if, after five months, I'm doing well?"

Here she saw potential for a rip-off: If she was making a go of the healing, he could jack up his asking price for the rent. And she'd be forced to pay it, because if she didn't, she'd have to walk away from the successful reputation and traffic she'd built.

"I charge every tenant the same rate per square foot. You'd be no different."

What was she missing here? Where was the catch?

He seemed to read her mind as he smiled and said, "There's no catch, Daley. I don't need the money. I have a successful energy storage business that feeds and houses my extended family very well. This is just a sideline for me. You might say I'm emotionally invested in Nespodee Springs. My goal here is full occupancy."

("I don't see a downside, Daley.")

Neither could she. But she couldn't commit just yet. This was happening too fast. She felt like she was bring pushed into something. She couldn't escape the feeling that this meeting was a setup, engineered by Juana. But why?

("What's holding you back?")

Even Pard was pushing.

"I'll tell you what," Jason said. "I'll even throw in the utilities, including cable TV—we have our own dish—for those five months."

No question: He really, really wanted her here. Again, why? She couldn't buy into full occupancy as the whole reason. Some other agenda was in play. But what? How could she possibly be important to this town?

("Well, that ices the cake, as far as I'm concerned.")

*Not for me.*

Daley held up her hands. "This is an important decision. Can I have a little time to think about it?"

"Of course," Tadhak said. "I wouldn't want it any other way. Take all the time you want."

"I'm just going to sit in my car for a bit. Just to gather my thoughts."

"Of course."

Daley returned to the Crosstrek and rolled down the windows. She watched Juana and Jason walk back to the real estate office. Both of them cast furtive glances in her direction.

("What's wrong? Isn't this what you wanted?")

*I don't know what I wanted.*

("This seems perfect.")

*Exactly.*

("Sorry?")

*Juana is setting me up.*

("Right—setting you up in the business you wanted.")

*Do I want it? I'll be walking a tightrope. I'll have to let people know they're sick, and yet . . . if I let them know that I—we—cured them, I could wind up in the middle of scenes like the one outside my apartment.*

("The solution might be a surrogate.")

Daley's immediate thought was a surrogate mother, but then she realized it also meant someone acting in place of someone else.

*You mean give someone else credit for the cure? But that'll put them in the very position I'm trying to avoid.*

("Not some*one* else, some*thing* else.")

*Like what?*

("Let me think on it while you seal the deal with that Tadhak fellow.")

*You really think we should pull the trigger on that store?*

("I absolutely do. You're risking nothing except your time, and . . . I don't know why, but somehow this place feels like home to me.")

Shaking her head, Daley stepped out of her car and headed for

the real estate office thinking that just might be the strangest
thing Pard had ever said.

## 5

Rhys's father joined him at the monitor as he centered the image
of Juana, Tadhak, and the new girl on the screen.

"You just missed the handshake between Tadhak and the girl,"
Rhys said. "They were all in that empty store down a ways. I think
she's renting it."

"She's opening a business? What's she selling?"

Eye-roll time. "Maybe if the telescope was equipped with a
long-range mic I could tell you, but as it is—"

"Just thinking out loud, Rhys. What would the Duad want
with a store?"

"You think she's the Duad? How can she be? Takes two to
make a Duad. Where's the rest of her? It can't be Juana, can it?"

Dad shook his head. "Doubt it. Juana's too much of a fixture
around these parts. But . . . you never know."

"What's the next step?" Rhys said. "If there is one."

"Oh, there most certainly is one: a welcoming committee of
one—you."

What?

"Me? I think *you* should go, being the patriarch and all."

"No, that would attract too much attention, attach too much
importance to her presence."

He couldn't believe this. "You're kidding, right?"

"It has to be you. I can't exactly send Cadoc, now can I? Head
down there now, size her up, see what she's planning."

. . . *size her up, see what she's planning . . .*

Well, she *was* kind of cute from a distance. No harm in getting
up close and personal to check her out.

After a trip to his quarters where he ran an electric razor over
his face and splashed on a little aftershave, he headed down the
hill. He decided to walk. The breeze was pleasant and he could do

with a little exercise. Not a bad trip going to town—all downhill that way since clan rules stated everyone had to live in the hills—but it could be a real chore coming back on a hot day.

He checked in at the real estate office but Jason Tadhak wasn't there.

Tadhak was a mystery. His battery company had to have made him a millionaire a dozen times over, yet he still spent a lot of time hanging out at his family real estate office. Yeah, his ancestors had built the town and the spa and still owned all the buildings, but he had to have more profitable ways to spend his time.

Rhys moved farther along and found Tadhak in an empty store with Juana and the newcomer. The door was open, so . . .

"Anybody home?" he said, knocking on the door frame.

Juana and Tadhak registered shocked recognition—had to be the first time in a long time they'd seen him in town—while the newbie simply looked curious.

"Mind if I come in?" he said into the silence.

"Rhys, right?" Jason said, stepping forward and offering his hand. "I haven't seen you in a dog's age."

"I keep pretty busy up at the Lodge. And how are you, Juana?"

She frowned and stayed behind Tadhak. "You know me?"

He gave her his warmest smile. "Everyone knows Juana and her Harley."

She nodded stiffly. "I'm good, Mister Pendry."

"Oh, please—it's Rhys. My father is Mister Pendry." He turned to the new gal. He saw now that her cap carried the Dodgers' logo. He wasn't a big baseball fan himself, but he leaned toward the Padres. "And who might you be?"

"I might be Daley," she said, stepping forward and offering her hand.

She had a firm shake. He liked that.

"'Daley'? Is that a first name or last?"

Her blue eyes nailed him from beneath the peak of her cap. "It's an *only* name."

"Like Beyoncé? Or Adele?"

"More like Plato."

Rhys found himself taking an immediate liking to her. She had attitude. And he liked her looks. That slim, lithe body, the impish twist to her lips. She had a waiflike quality, and the face peeking out from under the cap brim reminded him of Sarah Silverman. He placed her at just a couple of years younger than he but she seemed to house an older, more experienced person.

He noticed her left hand then. What was the story with that golden color? He figured it would be rude to ask.

"I'm going to go out on a limb and assume you're renting this space?"

She nodded and appeared about to speak but Tadhak butted in before she could answer.

"Well, well, well. What brings you down to town from on high, Rhys?"

A dig—a gentle one, but still a dig. Rhys ignored it. The Pendrys immigrated to the area more than a century ago, but the Tadhaks had been here even longer. Forever, it seemed. Rhys's people had bought their land from the Tadhaks and the relationship had always been cordial, but Jason seemed to have a perpetual chip on his shoulder where the clan was concerned—not a big one, but noticeable.

"Just taking in some of the last of the winter air."

"Yes, I imagine it gets a little stuffy up there in the Lodge."

That chip again . . . but Rhys focused on Daley.

"What sort of business, if I may be so bold to ask?"

"New Agey healing stuff."

That sounded harmless enough.

"Partnering with Juana?"

The answer was important: If the two of them were linked they could be the Duad.

"No," Juana said. "Daley has her own thing."

*Her own thing* . . .

Well, damn. That was no help. But maybe Dad would finally get over his Duad obsession.

"Can I ask why here instead of, say, San Diego?"

Juana answered for her. "I suggested Nespodee Springs as a place to start."

Rhys fought a dubious frown. Start what? *New-Agey healing stuff?* That seemed a stretch. Why was this gal really here?

Daley said, "And Mister Tadhak here made me an offer I couldn't refuse."

Interesting . . .

Rhys gestured around at the empty shelves and counters. "Looks like you'll be needing some stock."

Daley raised her eyebrows. "Ya think? I'm going to check into that tomorrow."

He'd learned what he'd needed to know, but felt an inclination—no, a desire—to hang around.

"Well, if you need any help setting up, just call up to the Lodge and I'll come down and pitch in."

Rhys bit back a laugh as he saw Jason Tadhak's jaw literally drop open.

"Thanks," Daley said. "I probably won't need to take you up on that, but I appreciate the offer."

Taking that as his cue to exit, Rhys made the appropriate nice-meeting-you and good-seeing-you noises and left.

As he headed back uphill toward the Lodge, Daley's image stayed with him and he felt a strange lightness of spirit. He figured in the coming week he just might show up at Daley's shop and help her set up, whether she asked him or not.

Just to continue his investigation, of course. Nothing more than that.

# 6

Daley wondered at Jason Tadhak's slack expression as he stared at the empty doorway and said, "That was . . . surreal."

"I gather he's not the sociable type," Daley said.

"Not Rhys in particular, but the Pendrys as a breed are totally self-absorbed. For one of them to offer to 'pitch in' and help a newcomer set up . . ." He shook his head. "And Rhys, of all people. He's the heir apparent to the head honcho."

"You must have made an impression on him," Juana said.

Daley shrugged. She wasn't looking for a relationship. Kenny, however, would be four hours away. Maybe . . .

She shook it off. She had to focus on getting this place up and running and start honing her healing chops.

("Admit it: You found him attractive.")

*He's good looking, sure.*

("And charming.")

*If you say so.*

"If he's such a recluse," Daley said, "why was he here?"

"To check you out," Tadhak said. "Don't ask me why, but it seemed pretty obvious he wanted to know who you were and why you came to town."

"Well," Juana said, "my work here is done. I'm heading home. What's your plan?"

Daley shrugged. "Find a place to sleep, I guess."

"I'd offer you a room at the spa's hotel," Tadhak said, "but we're full up. The power's off here but I'll have it turned on tomorrow. El Centro's the best place for a motel."

"Then that's where I'll head."

He shook her hand and walked out. Juana followed.

Pard popped into visibility. ("Do you get the feeling those two are in cahoots?")

*Cahoots? Did you really just say cahoots?*

("Well, we are out in the desert. And it's in your vocabulary.")

*Never! You lie!*

("I never lie. But back to Juana—I'm wondering if she's getting a finder's fee for you.")

*Well, if she is, good for her. And good for me since I wound up with five rent-free months here.*

("Yes, there's that.") He gestured to the shelves and counters. ("What do you want to stock this place with?")

*The usual New Age junk—healing crystals, Reiki stones, scented candles, aromatherapy oils, and on and on. Just got to find a place that sells it wholesale. I'm hoping for San Diego since it's a lot closer than LA.*

("Road trip tomorrow?")

*Unavoidable, I'm afraid. But let's check out this El Centro place. If they've got motels they've gotta have fast food joints and I'm starving.*

("You think they'll have an In-N-Out Burger?")

*Good bet. They're pretty much everywhere.*

("And you'll order animal style again, right?")

*Is there any other way?*

Pard rubbed his nonexistent hands together. ("Oh, goody!")

# 7

"I'm telling you, Dad," Rhys said, "she's not the Duad."

They were watching on the telescope feed as Daley got into her SUV and drove off.

"It has to be her. Who else can it be?"

"You should be asking *how* it can be her. She's one person."

"The stellar configurations are yielding a consistent message from the Scrolls."

Rhys wanted to scream *Forget the damn Scrolls!* He was sick of hearing about the Scrolls. He bit his tongue.

"Not only is she just one person, she's got only one name."

*"Daley."* His father snorted derisively. "You mean she *uses* only one name. She's got a legal name. You need to find out who she is. Check out Facebook, Twitter, Instagram, and Snapchat and the rest of that nonsense. She's there, I guarantee it. She's twenty-something. She's your generation and none of you can stay away from those places."

"Hard to get very far with just 'Daley' to work with."

"We have her license plate number. The sheriff owes me a few favors. I'll have him run it for me. We'll get her full legal name and then we'll track her down and learn all about her."

"She's still only one person, Dad."

Dad's face reddened. "Stop saying that! You sound like a broken record. She's the Duad. I know it! I feel it in my gut! And tomorrow's configurations will prove me out."

Rhys idly wondered what a broken record sounded like. He'd never owned any vinyl.

# 1

### THE DUAD IS HERE

"Didn't I tell you?" his father said. "Didn't I tell you?"

Rhys hid his dismay. He'd been hoping analysis of the stellar images would yield that same "*The Duad approaches*" message as yesterday, but no such luck.

"I still don't see how one person can be considered a 'pairing' or a 'Duad.'"

"Only one person is new to town—the mystery girl. The sheriff got back to me on her plates and the car is registered to a Stanka Daley from North Hollywood whose age is in line with this girl."

Rhys couldn't help making a face. "Stanka? Really." What an ugly name for such a pretty girl. "No wonder she goes by her last name."

"The sheriff ran a check on her and she's got no record of any sort."

"There. You see? So what's the worry?"

Dad pointed to the screen. "'*The Duad is here.*' *That's* the worry."

"But that's just it: She's *not* here. She drove out of town last night and hasn't come back yet."

"Stop splitting hairs and check out the social media. Get me some history on her."

When his father was gone, Rhys accessed his own Facebook account and started a search. The results shocked him.

With well over two billion people registered on Facebook worldwide, he found not one Stanka Daley. A couple of search hits came close with spellings that were only slightly off, but the associated photos didn't match the girl he'd met yesterday. Twitter, with only—only!—a billion point three registered, came up empty as well. Same with Instagram and Snapchat.

He buzzed his father.

"Are you sure you got the name right?"

*"Of course. Why?"*

"Because there's no Stanka Daley on social media."

A long pause and then, *"All right, now it's my turn to ask: Are you sure?"*

"Absolutely. I didn't believe it either, but a number of repeat searches yielded the same results."

*"The only reason I can think of that someone her age isn't on social media is she's got something to hide."*

"Well, she could be using a phony name. But believe it or not, there are people with nothing to hide who can't be bothered."

His father said, *"Maybe the thing she's hiding is herself."*

That gave Rhys a moment's pause. "You mean like the witness protection program, something like that?"

*"She could be a fugitive."*

"Do fugitives open stores?"

*"I'm telling you right now, Rhys, that young woman is either hiding something or hiding from something. I'm assigning you to find out what."*

## 2

"Girl, that's gotta be the most fucked-up patch of hair I have ever seen."

Daley had driven to El Centro last night where only rare buildings rose to a second story. She'd located the anticipated In-N-Out Burger. After inhaling dinner there she noticed it shared a parking lot with a reasonably priced Comfort Inn—a veritable skyscraper at three stories—where she'd spent a fitful night on a not so reasonable mattress.

With morning, the first order of business was to find a solution to her patch of white hair. After grabbing a roll and a coffee from the motel's complimentary breakfast, she asked the receptionist for the name of a good beauty salon.

So here she was in Sandra's Hair & Nail Palace on South Fourth Street to see what a professional could do for her. The owner herself had taken up the challenge but to no avail. The hair rejected any and all pigment.

Daley stared at her Lily Munster image in the mirror. Sandra, a hefty Hispanic woman with small hips, a large bust, and cotton-candy pink hair done in a bob, had tried two different dyes but they wouldn't take. She'd suggested simply coating the hair with black pigment but that would mean applying the pigment every morning because it would wash out in the shower.

Pard appeared. In place of his usual sandy hair he sported a black mane with a white patch on top. He did his jazz-hands thing.

("What do you think?")

*Are you making fun of me?*

("Not at all. This is a gesture of solidarity. Since I'm responsible, I think it only fair that I share your predicament.")

*Well, undo it. Looking at you like that only reminds me of my own Munsterness.*

His hair abruptly switched back to the usual.

("I still think it's a good look for you.")

*That's because you aren't human.*

"Well, thanks for trying," Daley said to Sandra. "I guess I'm doomed to wearing hats all the time or looking like a skunk."

"Not necessarily," Sandra said. "I have one more option."

"I'm listening."

"We can bleach the rest of your hair to a matching white and make you a platinum blonde."

"With my skin tone?"

"You've got some pigment but not a lot. Except for that hand of yours. What's up with that, if I may ask?"

Daley waved her golden left hand and recited what she'd settled on for her standard answer: "Got dipped in some dye that won't come off."

"Girl, you got all sorts of color issues, don't you?"

"I suppose."

"Well, anyway, you ever seen Etta James, that gal who sang 'At Last'? She went platinum with lots darker skin than you. I'll be glad to make you platinum but, you know what? Looking at you now, I don't think this is a bad look for you."

Pard pumped a fist. ("Aha! Vindication and validation from one of your fellow humans—and a coiffeur professional to boot.")

*One with pink hair!*

"I don't know . . ."

"What do you do for a living, honey?"

*How to put this . . . ?*

"I'm opening a shop in Nespodee Springs for—"

"Nespodee Springs? What can you sell in a crazy-ass place like that in the middle of nowhere?"

"Healing things, like crystals and—"

"You mean like paranormal, New Age stuff? I *love* that kinda shit. You should open up right here in El Centro. I'd be in there every day. So, you gonna put out healing vibes and all that?"

*Healing vibes . . .* One way to put it.

"I hope to."

"Well, then, you want to stay just the way you are and keep on looking just like you do. Black hair that's got a white spot in the middle, and a golden hand—that's your healing hand, honey. Take it from one who knows: Make that your healing hand. People gonna look at you and say. 'Oh, yeah, that bitch can do it, that bitch can heal.' And that's what you want. One look at you and they're already half sold. I can hear 'em right now, saying, 'Take my money! Take my money!'"

("Listen to this woman, Daley. She's a natural, and she's right. From what I've been reading, a key ingredient in successful therapy— *any* kind of therapy—is *believing* it will work. If they believe they're going to get better, they're already on their way to a cure.")

*I don't know . . .*

("Listen to me: The type of people who will seek you out will not be looking for a typical professional in a white lab coat with a stethoscope around the neck. They can find that anywhere. You'll be offering something different.")

Daley was beginning to think that Pard—and Sandra—might be on to something.

## 3

Next stop was the Sign Factory to order a banner to hang inside the store's front window. Four feet wide and one foot high looked about right.

She bought some linens at Bed Bath & Beyond, then they headed for the New Age supplier Pard had looked up in San Diego.

Interstate 8—also called the Kumeyaay Highway—cut right through El Centro, so they hopped on that and rode it west past another wind farm—smaller than the one in Palm Desert but larger than Nespodee Springs'—and into the Laguna Mountains where some of the upgrades were so steep she wondered if her Subaru would make it. Then, after a peak altitude of four thousand feet, a wild ride down to sea level in San Diego.

Pard rode shotgun the whole way and a couple of times Daley had to stop herself from telling him to fasten his seat belt. They traveled mostly in silence as they gloried in the scenery. Daley had lived her whole life in California but predominantly in and around LA with an occasional trip to San Francisco. Spend too much time in LA and your unconscious begins to assume the world is paved. This wild, unpopulated side of California was new to her. So much unsettled land, so much green on the western slopes.

The Rare Earth Center for the New Age occupied a two-story brick building with a giant blue eye in a golden pyramid painted on its side.

She eased from the car and stretched—a too-soft mattress and a long ride had stiffened her back.

Pard said, ("You forgot your cap.")

"I'm going to go *au naturel* and see how these folks react."

Inside she found a cornucopia of New Age paraphernalia: quartz crystals in varying shapes and colors, rune stones, chakra healing crystals, Reiki stones, tell stones, palm stones, and on and on. She picked random aromatherapy vials. The geodes and candles would look good in the front window. She stocked in all of them, but took special care with the various colors and shapes of the large palm stones. These might come in handy. She threw a beaded curtain into her cart as well.

"I really dig your hair," said the ponytailed guy working the cash register. "Striking. Who does it for you? My girlfriend—"

"Nobody does anything to it," Daley said. "This is the way it grows. The result of a terrible accident."

("What?")

"Oh, I'm sorry."

"Not as sorry as I."

("Oh, thanks, Daley. Nothing like a stab in the back. I thought we were friends.")

*Oh, lighten up. Just having some fun.*

("At my expense!")

*That's what makes it fun. Ready to head back?*

("Not until you've had a fashion makeover.")

*I don't need—*

("Look at you: worn jeans and an embroidered peasant blouse. Nobody's going to believe that someone dressed like that wields any sort of healing power. We passed a vintage clothing shop a few blocks back. Let's check it out and find you something with a little more style, something that goes with your hair.")

## 4

*I look like a Goth chick.*

As soon as they'd stepped into the clothing shop, Pard morphed into Tim Gunn in a gray business suit. He picked out a long-sleeved scoop-neck top and a black tube miniskirt over black tights.

("First off,") he said, smoothing his suddenly gray and receding hair, ("black is mysterious. Second, you've got great legs so you should show them off. Third, the long black sleeve draws attention to the gold of your left hand. And finally, all that black pops your patch of white hair.")

In all the scams she'd worked, the aim of her clothing had been to look anything but mysterious, to project a look that inspired trust.

("This completes the picture, and it inspires a different sort of trust—trust that you have some mystical power. All that's left is to do something about those eyes. You know, get all Cleopatra with the eye shadow and eyeliner.")

*Nope-nope-nope-nope. That's where I draw the line.*

("Trust me on this. I—")

"No!" she said aloud.

A number of women nearby turned and gave her wondering looks.

*Let's get out of here.*

# 5

Hands on hips, Daley looked around her shop. True to his word, Jason Tadhak had had the place cleaned up before Daley arrived.

She'd driven from San Diego to El Centro where she picked up her banner at the Sign Factory. From there straight to Nespodee Springs. She'd stocked her shelves with the various New Age knick-knacks and hung the beaded curtain over the alcove at the rear of the space where she'd do her "consultations."

("Despite all our purchases,") Pard said, ("the place looks kind of bare. No, wait—let me rephrase that to something more euphemistic: The shop emits a 'minimalist vibe.'")

"It does look sparse, doesn't it. Maybe I should put off the grand opening for a while."

("Getting cold feet?")

"I wouldn't call it that, exactly. It's just that . . ."

She had to admit she still wasn't entirely comfortable with the situation, couldn't escape the feeling that she'd been maneuvered in some way. But by whom? She knew Tadhak had wanted to fill one of his vacancies, and he'd succeeded there.

But Tadhak hadn't lured her out here. Juana had. Ever since the incident in the cave, Juana had been popping into Daley's life. Really, was her mother truly in the hospital with the horrors when Daley had been there? Was her mother even alive? Yeah, Juana was the most likely suspect as the manipulator. But if so, what was she getting out of it?

A roar outside as Juana pulled up on her Harley.

"Well, speak of the devil."

("You think she's evil?")

"Not at all. But I think she's got an agenda with me, and damned if I know what it could be."

("Maybe she truly wants to 'help and guide' you.")

"But guide me toward what? Will it be a place I want to go?" She watched as Juana pulled shopping bags from her sidecar. "Why don't you disappear now."

("What? But—")

"When I can see you I tend to talk to you and that causes confusion and maybe raises a few questions about my mental status."

("I have a few questions myself. But I create this image only for your convenience, you know.")

"I appreciate that, but sometimes it's *in*convenient. Like now. So go on—evaporate."

Pard complied, but with deliberate slowness.

Toting a shopping bag in each hand and dressed in her uniform of faded T-shirt and bib-front denims, Juana pushed through the door and stopped dead. She dropped the bags and stared.

"Your hair . . ."

Daley touched the top of her head. "You've seen that."

Juana shook her head. "No . . . not till today. You always wear that Dodgers hat."

"Yeah, well, I wear it so people won't give me that look you're giving me right now."

"Sorry." Juana shook herself. "It took me by surprise, but I guess it shouldn't have."

Daley frowned. "What do you mean by—?"

"Nothing. Just talking." She picked up the bags and looked around. "Despite the *CLOSED* sign on the door it appears you're ready to go."

"Just about."

She upended one of the shopping bags and emptied it onto the counter in front of Daley. Circular and semicircular shapes with strings and feathers and beads . . .

"Those look like—"

"Dream catchers," Juana said. "They're not part of any Desert Cahuilla traditions—they started in northern tribes—but some of the ladies on the reservation make them for gift shops and paranormal shops and such. Would you display them? They'll go halfsies on the price. They're raising money for my mother."

"Well, hell, they can have all of it then."

"Thank you. My mother could use it. But are you sure?"

"It's for a good cause. And since I have no overhead to speak of for the moment, why not?" She gestured around at the array of crystals and geodes and candles and posters she'd stocked in. "I'll be selling this junk but really they're just props to add some New Age ambiance—you know, help reel in the kind of—" she caught herself before she said *mark*—"client I'm looking for."

Juana reached into her second bag and brought out a flattened, softball-size rock with a spiral design, then another with humanish figures, and others until they totaled six.

"Cahuilla rock art," she said. "These are definitely part of our own culture, but they're not antiquities. They're all new, done by the same ladies who do the dream catchers. And for the same cause."

"Fine. You set the prices and display them where you want. Just make it clear they're not museum pieces."

"We can add some handwoven baskets too."

"Bring 'em on."

Daley had no problem with helping raise money for Juana's mother, or helping the local natives make a few bucks for themselves, but she didn't want to get busted for bogus antiquities. That would cast doubt on her main line of business, and people needed full faith and belief where healing was concerned.

"Ready to hang out your shingle?" Juana said, setting her bags on the floor. One landed with a soft *thunk*. Another art stone?

"Just about," Daley said. "I had a window banner made in El Centro."

"Let me guess." She waved an arm toward the window. *"DALEY: HEALER."*

"That occurred to me but it seemed kind of in your face. And frankly, it promised too much. So I came up with this."

She pulled the banner off a shelf and unrolled it atop the dream catchers and stones.

## HEALERINA

Pard reappeared and said, ("I repeat: dumb name.") He'd complained about the name when she'd ordered the banner and apparently hadn't changed his mind. ("Too much like *Healerama,* which sounds like a used shaman dealership.")

*Used shamans?*

("We can do better, Daley.")

*It'll grow on you.*

("So will a fungus.")

Juana cocked her head as she studied it. "Healerina . . . I like the way it rolls off the tongue . . . like 'ballerina.' What does it mean?"

"Aha. Just the question I want people to ask when they see it. 'My-my. Look at that . . . *Healerina* . . . whatever does that mean? Let's go in and see.'"

Juana nodded slowly as a smile played about lips. "You're a clever girl. I think all this is going to play out just fine."

*See? Juana gets it.*

But Daley wasn't sure if "all this" referred to the shop or something else entirely.

"Help me hang it?"

"I'd be honored."

Together they managed to center the banner on the front window and tack it to the top of the frame. They stepped outside to see how it looked.

Juana was nodding. "Easily visible from the street. I've got a good feeling about this."

("So do I,") Pard said.

Daley held back as Juana returned to the store. She wasn't so sure. She saw pitfalls ahead. She was going to have to walk a tightrope to avoid them.

("Why so worried?")

*We have to cure people to make this work—I mean, you've got to beat whatever's ailing them—but we can't let people think I cured them.*

("Really? Then why are we doing this?")

*They have to associate me with the healing but not directly credit me.*

("Tall order—*very* tall order. How are you going to make that happen?")

*I'm working on it.*

As she stepped back into the store she saw Juana staring at one of the smaller rock art stones. She shoved it back in the bag as Daley entered.

"What's that?"

Juana smiled. "Nothing."

"Let me see what's on the stone. Don't you want me to sell it?"

"Oh, no. This is one of the ancient stones. Not for sale. Never for sale."

Why was she so evasive?

"Can I see it?"

"No, really, it's . . ."

Daley thrust out her hand. "Juana . . . give."

The older woman hesitated, then with a resigned look, pulled a silver-dollar-size stone from the bag and handed it to Daley—

—who gasped when she saw the drawing: a head with a crude, featureless face, long black braids, and a white patch in the hair at the top of its head.

"You put me on a stone?" Daley said. "But I thought you hadn't seen my hair before today."

Juana, usually the picture of unearthly calm, looked upset. "I hadn't. That stone is hundreds of years old . . . maybe older."

Daley stared at her and knew she wasn't putting her on. Her gut tightened into a knot. "But that's not . . . not possible."

"So you would think."

"Is that why you were so shocked when you first saw my hair?"

"Yes. I realized I'd seen you before . . . on this stone."

"It's got a hole drilled through it."

"It was meant to be worn around the neck. I give it to you to wear."

Daley shook her head. "Oh, no. I couldn't."

"But you must. It was meant for you. Long ago someone in my tribe saw you coming."

## 6

Juana had roared off, leaving behind nothing but questions.

("I'm at a total loss to explain that,") Pard said as Daley locked up.

"There's a logical explanation. Gotta be."

("Well, when you come up with one, let me know.")

Daley was relieved to see that Tadhak's cleaning team had hit the upstairs apartment as well. To call it sparsely furnished was being generous. She would have to make a trip back to her apartment. She didn't relish the seven-hour round trip but figured she could pack the Crosstrek with enough stuff to make this place feel like home.

Though spotless, the bathroom had ancient fixtures, especially the tub: solid steel with an enamel lining on four ornate legs.

"This is the kind of bathtub they have in old cowboy movies."

("I don't think the building's been here that long. At least it's clean and got running water. You don't have anyone who can bring you buckets of hot water.")

Her phone said seven o'clock by the time she'd put sheets on the bed and hung towels in the bathroom. Her stomach grumbled.

"I'm hungry. Let's try out Arturo's Cozy Coyote Café."

("Your Pepto-Bismol is back in North Hollywood.")

"Hey, how bad can it be?"

("Looks like we're going to find out.")

She went to the window. Night fell quickly in the desert. The street was already dark.

"It's right across the street and we should support our fellow businesses, so—"

("It looks closed.")

Pard was right. No lights on in the café.

"I'll bet it's just a breakfast and lunch place—no dinner. Well, damn. I'm hungry."

("El Centro's In-N-Out is only thirty miles away.")

"Again?"

("You love their cheeseburgers. Admit it.")

"Not as much as you. All right, let's go."

As Daley headed out of town she was struck by how *dark* it had grown. She'd never driven in the desert at night.

("Pull off the road,") Pard said from the passenger seat.

"What? Why?"

("Just trust me for a couple of minutes.")

So she pulled off to the side and stopped.

("Now turn off the lights and get out and look up.")

"Are you sure?"

("You'll thank me.")

Despite her reservations, Daley stepped out of the car and looked up.

"Oh. My. God!"

The moonless sky was ablaze with stars. She immediately spotted the pale haze of the Milky Way, smeared across the sky. And the seven sister stars of the Pleiades were sharp and clear and—

Wait. How did she know this?

"Pard, have you been studying astronomy?"

He suddenly changed into a black man with a mustache and a bright smile.

("I wouldn't say 'studying,' but I have been browsing.")

"So now you're that guy from *Nova*?"

He rose into the air. "See this line of three stars?" He touched each one as he spoke in Neil deGrasse Tyson's voice. "That's the Belt of Orion."

"You can fly now?"

("And this oblong glow, dangling below the belt like a penis, that's the Orion Nebula complex.")

Daley laughed. "'Like a *penis*'? I don't think that's how he'd describe it."

She climbed onto the hood and reclined with her back against the windshield. Starshine from the moonless sky painted the flat, featureless desert a drab gray.

Just like the landscape of my life, she thought.

("Is that what you really think? How you really see your life?")

"What other way is there? I look back and I don't see anything worthwhile. Fatherless from the get-go, then motherless. Scamming for change, picking pockets. 'Tawdry'—your word—scams as an adult."

("Are you proud of those scams?")

"I'm not ashamed of them. Not much different than scams like Powerball or Megamillions."

("It's not a scam if there's a real chance of winning—")

"How do you call one in three hundred million a 'real chance'?"

("Because someone *does* eventually win.")

"But millions and millions of people *lose*, just like my losers lost the car."

("*No one* was ever going to see the new car you showed them.")

"Doesn't matter. I chose the winner fair and square, so no matter what the prize turned out to be, the losers are still losers. Maybe the car they lost wasn't the one they bet on, but they were destined to wind up with zero either way. And if all goes according to plan, they never know that. The last game was ruined by someone catching on."

("How can you say 'ruined' when you walked away with a hefty cash payout?")

"Money is only part of it. The real high is walking away with the cash and leaving the marks thinking everything was on the up-and-up, with no clue they've been scammed. Nobody is mad or unhappy. And the reason for that is because they bought one hundred percent into the illusion I was selling."

("And that's important?")

"Crucial. I wasn't out to make people unhappy, I just wanted them to give me their money."

("I note the past tense.")

"Not sure I want to go on like I've been. Like I said, I'm not ashamed of what I see when I look back. I'm not about to shout it from the rooftops, but no regrets. But without it, what have I got? I don't see anything ahead."

("There's this new venture, opening tomorrow.")

"And it's going to give new meaning to my life, right?"

("Well . . .")

"I'm not holding my breath. Because really, what's the point? What's the point of anything?"

("That's the kind of thinking that leads people to jump off bridges.")

She laughed. "No worry. I'm not suicidal. But you know, if a big extinction asteroid were to clobber Earth tonight, I'd be okay with that."

("Well, aren't you Little Miss Sunshine tonight.")

"It's the truth."

("I'd be anything but okay with that. There's too much to learn.")

"Like what?"

("Like *everything*. Perhaps it's because I've been sentient only two weeks, but I don't see how you can dismiss this wonderful planet you live on, or the mind-boggling universe around it.")

"Newbiespeak. You'll get over it." She waved a hand at the stars.

"You call it 'mind-boggling' but that doesn't keep it from being meaningless."

("You sound like Camus.")

"Who's Kamu?" The name rang a bell but she didn't track it. "Sounds like a new killer whale at Sea World."

("C-a-m-u-s. A French writer who thought that death makes life absurd.")

"Well, he was half right. Even if we were immortal, life would still be absurd. I mean, why am I here?"

("That question implies that you think someone put you here.")

"Well, it wasn't my idea."

("You're here because you're here. And the universe out there doesn't care one way or the other. If you want meaning in your life, you're going to have to make your life meaningful.")

"Wait—let me write that down."

("Have you ever considered the possibility that your sarcasm might be a defense mechanism?")

She knew she was acting like a bratty adolescent, but bad enough she had a second consciousness in her head, she had one that felt obliged to come up with inspirational aphorisms.

"Seriously? 'If you want meaning in your life, you're going to have to make your life meaningful.' I'm thinking I should paint that on the ceiling over my bed so that when I wake up in the morning I—"

Something moved in the sand off to her right.

*Did you see that?* She didn't want to use her voice.

Pard disappeared and spoke in her head. ("Of course I did. If you saw it, so did I. But what was it?")

*I was hoping you'd know.*

("I haven't a clue.")

Faintly lit by starlight, the flat, sandy expanse was broken by clumps of scrub brush and—

*There it is again. No, it's another. And there's another!*

("Daley, they're *big*.")

They looked like cacti—head-size barrel cacti popping out of the desert floor. At least half a dozen now, with more appearing. As the number reached a dozen, Daley squinted in the starlight and could swear she saw the glint of eyes, as if they had faces. That was enough.

She ripped open her door, jumped inside, hit the ignition, and turned on the headlights. Yes, faces—not human, but *faces*, all looking at her. She peeled into a sharp U-turn back to town. In-N-Out could wait.

"Ohmygod! What were those things?"

("Lizards? Giant lizards? *You've* never heard of such a thing. *I've* never heard of such a thing . . .")

"*Maybe* lizards . . . but not like any lizards I've ever seen. I mean, who's ever seen lizards that big? Can I say, What the fuck, Pard? Can I just say, What the *fuck*?"

("You may. Say it for me as well.")

Daley screamed at her windshield: *"WHAT THE FUCK?"*

# 7

Cadoc heard her voice as soon as he entered the empty apartment.

He'd been out on one of his nocturnal creeps when he saw her speed around the back of her shop, leap out of her car, and race up the stairs to the door of her apartment.

He'd been curious about the mystery woman—everyone was curious about Daley and her Healerina shop—and now was as good a time as any to ferret out some answers.

He'd eased up the stairs to the empty apartment next to hers. Robberies were unheard of in Nespodee Springs and so security tended to be lax. A thin strip of plastic was all one needed to get past a locked door.

Cadoc followed the sound of her voice to the kitchen. Not only were the walls thin, but the previous tenant here had stolen some fixtures when he left, a couple of the kitchen cabinets among them, leaving a gap in the wallboard.

Cadoc stepped up to the opening and listened.

"We did see what we saw, right?" she was saying. "I mean we can't blame it on a trick of the light, because those stars were pretty damn bright out there." A pause, then: "No, it was *not* an optical illusion."

She sounded like she was on the phone. Cadoc wondered who was on the other—

"Don't give me that, Pard," she blurted. "You see what I see and I saw heads sticking out of the sand and staring at me."

*What?* Heads sticking out of the sand?

Cadoc noticed a sliver of light where the wallboard on Daley's side had separated from the stud. He put his eye to it and saw her alone in her kitchen holding a soft drink in one hand and gesturing to the empty air with the other. She wore no earbuds or AirPods.

"How do *I* know what they were attached to? But they had to be attached to bodies! I mean they can't be just heads. They didn't roll up like tumbleweeds. *They popped out of the sand!*"

Could she mean . . . had she seen the porthors? No . . . not possible.

But who was she talking to? She wasn't thinking out loud, she was looking and gesturing as if someone else were there. But unless her companion was invisible, she was alone.

"No, I *shouldn't* have gone into the bar. I've never been in there and I don't know what it's like, and I'm not about to start asking the local boozers about giant lizards." After a pause: "Oh, fine for you. I'm the only one who can see you, but *everyone* can see me. Just my luck some drunk would take a shine to me and follow me back here. No, thanks."

She opened the refrigerator door, then closed it.

"It can wait. First thing tomorrow—yeah, I know it's opening day, but first thing we do is start asking around. We can't be the first to have seen them." . . . "Good idea. I'll start at the café. Maybe I should go up the hill and ask that Pendry guy." Her tone turned sour. "No, it's not because I think he's 'cute.' His family's

been here forever, supposedly." . . . "You want a logical explanation? Okay, here's one for you: *giant lizards!*"

With that she stormed out of her kitchen.

Cadoc leaned against the common wall and tried to make sense
of all this. Papa had become obsessed with the Duad coming here
to interfere with the clan's plans. He'd been sure it was the new
arrival, but Daley had remained alone, confounding him.

But *was* she alone?

*I'm the only one who can see you . . .*

Was she some sort of dual personality? Although that indicated
mental instability, it might qualify her as a pseudoDuad. Or was
she the genuine article: two people in one body? Her conversation
just now might indicate it.

*I'm the only one who can see you . . .*

What did that mean? An imaginary friend, or someone who
was truly invisible?

Cadoc couldn't go with an invisible man. Well, not yet, at least.

But overshadowing all that was her claim that she'd seen giant
lizards popping their heads out of the desert and staring at her.
If they hadn't been the hallucination of a schizophrenic mind,
then they could only be the porthors. But porthors hide from
everyone . . . show themselves only when called.

Why would they reveal themselves to her?

# 8

Daley felt an urge to scream.

This wasn't her. She usually handled stress pretty well—thrived
on it, in fact. Tomorrow was opening day and tonight she'd either
seen giant lizards popping their heads out of the ground or she'd
hallucinated them.

Either way . . . not good.

And then there was Pard. That guy standing over there was
definitely a hallucination, but one deliberately created by the being

in her head. The problem was he was *always there*. Even when she couldn't see him, he was *there*—seeing what she saw, hearing what she heard. And commenting . . . always commenting. He had opinions on everything, but could he keep them to himself? Noooooo!

"I need some alone time, Pard. I need a hot soak and no one else in my head. Can you take a nap or something for a while?"

("I believe that can be arranged.")

"Really? How?"

("I've figured how to give myself a time-out from your consciousness by blocking all your inputs. A virtual, windowless, soundproof room. It's good for you because it will allow you the alone time you say you need.")

Daley was so relieved to hear this, even though she'd been too busy of late—until tonight—to feel the need for solitude.

("And it's good for me as well,") Pard continued, ("because it removes distractions and allows me to concentrate on the data I've stored away but not fully digested. Will two hours do?")

"Very nicely, thank you."

("Any time. What are you planning to do?")

"Gonna take a long hot soak in that ancient tub and let the only voice in my head be my own."

("I understand.")

"But will you be gone? Really gone?"

("No, I can't go. We're locked in to each other.")

"What I mean is you won't be just hanging back and keeping quiet?"

("Believe it or not, I have lots to keep me busy. I'll be 'gone' in the sense that we'll be cut off from each other. Even if you want to ask me something, I won't hear you. You'll have to wait until the two hours are up. That's what you want, isn't it?")

"Most definitely."

("Then I'll see you soon.")

Silence.

Was he gone? Really gone? She didn't feel any different. How would she know for sure?

"Pard? Pard, are you there?"

Silence.

No reason for Pard to lie about this. He wasn't the lying type. If he couldn't do it, he'd simply say so. She had to trust him on this.

Okay, he was gone. Now what?

After locking the doors, she got the water running in the tub. She'd learned the water came from the local spring. It had a vague sulfurous odor but nothing she couldn't handle. She didn't have any bath salts or suds, but she had a bar of soap and she had two hours.

She needed this.

She checked the temp as the tub filled, then pulled off her clothes and slipped into the water. The old-fashioned tub was angled away at the end opposite the faucets, perfect for leaning back and reclining, and she did just that.

A loud sigh escaped on its own. She'd never been a bath person. Soaking in water that contained whatever you were washing off was not her idea of getting clean, but oh-dear-god it felt so good to sink up to her chin in hot water and close her eyes and just be *alone*.

*You will never be alone* . . . Juana's words. Did she know about Pard?

"Hey, Pard?"

Oh, right. She couldn't ask him what he thought because he couldn't hear her. You get so used to someone being around all the time, you take their availability for granted.

She'd ask him later. Right now . . . she put tonight's lizards and tomorrow's grand opening aside and luxuriated in the sensuous feel of the hot water against her skin. She closed her eyes.

So good.

After a few moments she slipped her hand between her thighs . . .

# 1

("Rise and shine.")

Pard was back. She'd gone to bed after her bath and he must have ended his time-out after she dozed off.

"It's too early."

("You scheduled our grand opening for ten A.M., which leaves us time to ask around about whatever we saw in the desert last night.")

"All right, all right."

She wanted a few answers herself. She pulled on some clothes and headed across the street to Arturo's Cozy Coyote Café for coffee and info. Along the way she paused to allow the Tadhak white bus to roll past. She couldn't see anyone on the other side of the dark glass but could feel them staring at her.

*Is that creepy or is that creepy?*

("Well, it seems unusual, that's for sure.")

She introduced herself to Arturo as the owner of the new shop, and during the welcomes and good-lucks and explaining her name and getting a free cup of coffee, she noticed how he kept staring at her head. Then she remembered she'd forgotten to wear her cap.

She pointed to her hair. "Yeah, my hair just up and turned white there one day. Can't do much about it."

"Oh, hey, I didn't mean to stare." He was a big man wearing a backward Padres cap and a grease-stained apron. At the moment he was both waiter and short-order cook, but had only two other customers in the place, both seated at the counter. "It's just I never seen nothing like that before. And I'm not saying it looks bad or anything. I kinda like it."

"Well, like it or not, I'm stuck with it." She hit the subject she came for. "Listen, Arturo, I was out in the desert last night, looking at the stars and—"

"They're amazing out here, ain't they?" he said with a grin. "But it's even better up by Borrego Springs—that's an official Dark Sky Community. No light pollution up there."

"I'll have to check it out," she said, pushing to get back on topic, "but I've got to ask you: What have you got living out there in the sand?"

"Pardon me?"

"The stars were great but when I looked down I saw these giant lizard heads popping out of the ground."

His grinned broadened. "What were you smoking?"

"What?"

"Lots of folks toke up when they watch the stars."

"I'm not a pothead, Arturo."

"No worry. It's been legal for years—Proposition Sixty-four, remember? I voted for it myself."

"I don't own a single joint. It's not my thing. I—"

"Peyote, then? Those cactus buttons can show you some strange sights."

"Arturo, I was as straight as I've ever been and I saw these big lizards popping their heads out of the sand."

Arturo turned to the two breakfast eaters farther down the counter. "Anybody hear tell of any giant lizards out in the desert?"

Both shook their heads.

Arturo winked at her. "Guess you're the first, Daley. But I'll keep my ears open and let you know if I hear anything."

"Thanks for the coffee."

("And for nothing else,") Pard said.

*We didn't imagine those things, did we?*

("I don't imagine things. We saw them. They were real.")

*Then why aren't there local legends about them? Why don't we see signs for nighttime tours to "See the Giant Gila Monsters!" or whatever they were?*

("I guess that's always an option if the shop fails.")

*Very funny.*

As she stepped outside she spotted Jason Tadhak unlocking the door to the real estate office up the street.

*There's someone who'll know.*

("He did say his family's been here for centuries.")

But after working through the hair stare and explaining the white patch, she found Tadhak as much help as Arturo.

"Giant lizards?" he said, casually leaning back in his swivel chair. "You saw giant *lizards?*"

"People-size lizard heads," Daley said. "Smallish people, but still people-size."

"You sure you weren't . . . ?"

"Chemically enhanced? Very sure. Why is that the first thing everyone asks?"

"Because in all the time my family's been here we've never heard anyone talk about seeing giant lizards."

*Why us?*

("Indeed.")

"You've got pictures?" he said.

"Pictures?"

"Yes. Photos, movies—with your phone. Everyone records everything these days."

"I never even thought of it. I was too shocked and scared."

"Well, if it happens again, you—"

"Aren't you concerned? Or curious? Even a little?"

"If there are more sightings, of course. But it might have been just a trick of the light out there."

Daley started to protest but Pard said, ("He's blowing you off, Daley. And who can blame him? We have no evidence to back us up, so let's drop it.")

*Damn, why didn't I think of my phone?*

("Maybe because you were raised without one? Anyway: next time.")

*I don't want a next time!*

"Hey, this is your big day, right?" Tadhak said. "What time do you officially open?"

"As soon as I get back there and change and turn the *CLOSED* sign around."

"Well then, I'll have to stop by and buy something." He rose and reached across his desk. "Good luck to you, Daley. And I mean that—in every sense."

("'In every sense' . . .") Pard said as they left the office. ("He put such emphasis on that.")

*Obviously it's in his interest that I make a go of the shop.*

("Of course. But it seemed more than that.")

*Nobody believes us that giant lizards are crawling around at night out there and you're worried about how our landlord is emphasizing words. I think you need a little perspective, Pard.*

("I have plenty. And I have a sense that they're *both* important.")

# 2

She changed into the black outfit Pard had picked out for her. To complete her look, she strung Juana's flat little Cahuilla art stone with a strip of rawhide and tied it around her neck. She opened Healerina at ten sharp. Pard, reduced to six inches tall, appeared on her shoulder.

"What—you're Jiminy Cricket now?"

("I don't want to get in the way.")

*That's going to be too distracting. Sit on the front window shelf. No one's going to go over there.*

Only a few people wandered in and out during the first couple of hours, and no one bought a thing.

At one point Daley spotted a pair of Pendry girls, maybe ten or twelve years old, lurking on the threshold. Each wore a long-sleeved dress that covered her from neck to knees over tights. A Mennonite look. She wondered what that felt like in the blazing desert heat of summer. The dresses were uniform in style, but at least they varied in material. The redhead wore a light blue print and the brunette a red paisley pattern.

"Come on in, girls," she called.

They jumped as if startled and ran away.

Shy things.

A little after noon, a frail, pale-looking woman stopped inside the front door, looked her up and down, and said, "You're quite the package, aren't you."

"Sorry?"

"I mean you all in black, the hair too, except for that patch. Quite striking. Should I assume you're Healerina?"

Daley waved around at the shop. "The whole place is Healerina. I'm Daley. Welcome."

"I'm Estelle." Her gaze roamed the shop. "Quite the place you've got here."

Daley gave her a smile. "Just getting started. How can I help you?"

"Well . . . I'm not sure."

So pale . . . her skin seemed almost translucent. But well dressed, hair nicely done, and that wasn't costume jewelry on her fingers and around her neck.

"Well, take a look around and—"

"When I saw 'Healerina' I thought you might be, you know, a healer."

*Okay, Pard, I think we may have our first healee.*

("'Healee'?") he said from his window seat.

*Figure it out. Be ready.*

("Aye, sir.")

"What I do is facilitate the body's own healing powers."

Her face fell. "Oh."

"Hang on now. Hidden deep within every human body are amazing recuperative powers. They should be circulating freely but modern civilization has suppressed them. I, however, have learned the secret of setting them free so they can do what they were always meant to do: heal."

("You're really slinging it.")

*Tell them what they want to hear. That's the key. I'm wrapping your abilities in a self-empowerment fantasy. Who doesn't want that?*

("But it comes down to you telling her that you're not doing the healing, her own body is.")

*You got it.*

"So you're saying that you won't be healing me, I'll be healing myself?"

("Didn't I just say that?")

"Exactly."

Pard said, ("I'm not sure I'm following you.")

*I took your suggestion from the other day: I'm creating a surrogate.* Daley picked up a red quartz palm stone. *This.*

"Okay, Estelle. Come back to my little imprinting room here and—"

"'Imprinting'?"

("'Imprinting'?")

She answered both at once: "Yes, imprinting. You'll see."

Daley led her through the beaded curtain to the table and two chairs set up in the intimate space.

"I was driving by on my way to the spa when I saw your sign," she said as she sat down. "That word, 'Healerina,' it just stayed in my brain and I had to come see."

*Did you catch that, Pard?*

("Okay. Score one for you.")

"Glad to hear it, Estelle. Where are you from, by the way?"

"Pomona."

"Nice. Okay . . ." She pressed the blood quartz palm stone into Estelle's hand. "Now, what I want you to do is take this bloodstone and hold—"

"But don't you want me to tell you what's wrong first?"

"Let's see if I can discover that on my own."

She closed Estelle's hand around the palm stone, then clasped both her own hands around hers.

"Your hand . . ." Estelle said, noticing the color for the first time.

"Yes . . . golden skin. I'm going to give the stone time to become familiar with you—what I call 'imprinting.'"

("Shocking how the New Age hokum flows so effortlessly from you.")

*I was born for this.*

Daley closed her eyes for dramatic effect. "So let's sit here like this and let it happen."

This would give Pard the time he needed to establish contact with Estelle's body. He disappeared from the window, and then, after a short wait . . .

("Okay, I'm in.")

*What's going on?*

("She's pretty healthy except for this bleeding ulcer. It's making her anemic.")

*Can you fix it?*

("It's been there a long time but I'm pretty sure I can stimulate some new lining to fill it in.")

*Go for it.*

After another wait . . . he reappeared.

("Okay. Done. The gastric membrane cells lining the margin of the ulcer were unresponsive at first. I had to boot them into action. They're multiplying now and should fill the ulcer crater in a day or so.")

*Excellent!*

She released Estelle's hands and leaned back. After a dramatic pause she said, "You're anemic from a bleeding ulcer."

Estelle stared and almost dropped the stone. "How can you know that?"

She had the woman's confidence now. The next step was to build on that.

Daley shrugged. "It's what I do. What I don't understand is why it hasn't been diagnosed before this."

"Oh, but it has!" The words came in a rush. "I can't tell you how many times I've been endoscoped and biopsied and cauterized. They've tried everything but it just won't heal. I'm so tired all the time. I keep getting transfusions and I feel better for a while but it keeps bleeding and then I'm anemic again. I'm so sick of this. They say the only way to cure it is to cut away the part of my stomach with the ulcer, and I don't want that. Can you help? Please say yes."

"As I said before, I can't heal you, but I can help your body heal itself."

This was a point Daley wanted to drive home. She had no license to practice medicine, so she wanted to avoid setting herself up for that charge. By offering no cure and simply facilitating a self-cure, she could skirt the law and avoid the wrath of the medical community.

"I'll do whatever you want."

"Okay, the first thing to do is keep that stone with you at all times. Hold it when you can, and when you can't, keep it in a pocket. I even want you to sleep with it."

Estelle gave a tremulous smile. "That seems easy enough."

"The second thing to do is contact your specialists as soon as you get back home and say you want another endoscope."

Here was another safety buffer: refuse to get between the healee and her regular physicians. This way no one could say Daley interfered with accepted standards of care.

"Again?"

"You'll want to prove to them that the ulcer is healed and you don't need the surgery."

Estelle blinked. "You're . . . you're pretty confident, aren't you."

"I'm confident in your body's ability to heal itself."

"I . . . I don't know," she said, staring at the stone as she turned it over in her hands. "My husband's always accusing me of being gullible."

Daley shrugged again. "Everything else has failed. What have you got to lose?"

"Well, for starters, whatever you're going to charge me for this stone and the 'imprinting.'"

And now for the clincher . . .

"Oh, I'm not charging you anything."

Estelle's jaw dropped. "Nothing?"

"You walk out of here with the stone free and clear."

("Color me shocked, Daley. For someone who loves money so . . .")

"But . . . but that makes no sense," Estelle said. "How do you make a living?"

("Yes, please, I want to hear this too.")

"I'm counting on you to show your appreciation once your specialists tell you the ulcer is healed."

"Appreciation?"

"Yes. Make a donation to the shop in the amount you think this encounter was worth to you. I leave the amount totally up to you."

"I've never heard of such a thing."

Daley rose and held the beaded curtain aside. "There's a first time for everything. Remember: Contact your specialists right away."

Clutching her stone, Estelle wandered through the main area of the shop in a daze, but she did buy a dream catcher and one of the Cahuilla art stones before she left.

("Guilt purchases. And that money goes to Juana's people. At this rate, Daley, you'll be out of business in record time.")

*We'll see.*

# 3

The day had started off weird. Rhys had transmitted the analysis of the celestial configurations to his father who called a few minutes later.

*"You're sure these are correct?"*

Rhys knew he'd done everything according to protocol. "Absolutely. Why?"

*"It's giving me a clear message to sell. Which means we'll have to start divesting."*

"But we're just getting back in after that Internet mess."

*"That's all changed. The message is very clear: Divest."*

"Okay. Techs? Large caps? What?"

*"According to this, everything."*

"Everything? You're sure?"

*"Yes. The Scrolls gave me similar warnings just before all the other sell-offs. I listened then and I'm listening now."*

"You're expecting a meltdown?"

*"It looks that way. We'll proceed at a measured pace. Don't want to attract attention. But I want us divested and completely in cash by mid-March."*

"Then what?"

*"I don't know yet. Depends on subsequent analyses."*

And then he hung up.

Well, his father would do the actual selling. Rhys would be saddled with the paperwork. This could be kind of exciting, actually . . . watching the market sink from the safety of a mound of cash.

And then, less than half an hour later, his father came storming into Rhys's office and slammed the door.

Oh, shit. Had he made a mistake with the analysis?

"Have you heard what she's up to?" Dad said.

"Who?" But Rhys had a pretty good idea. He hid his relief that this wasn't about him.

"That—that girl you assured me is no problem."

"Daley? With the New Age shop?"

Rhys couldn't imagine what she'd done to rile him like this.

"Don't you listen to what's going on in town?"

"Not particularly."

In truth, not at all. But where was this going?

"She's asking around about giant lizards she saw out in the desert last night."

Rhys laughed. "She probably saw an iguana!"

"Let's hope that's what people think she saw. As for me, I've heard her description and I've no doubt she saw porthors."

That killed Rhys's laughter. "Porthors? They're a myth—bogeymen from the Scrolls."

Dad was shaking his head. "There's so much you've yet to learn. The porthors are real. I've seen them many, many times."

He was talking crazy now.

"Dad . . . ?"

"There's an excellent reason you think they're myths. First off, the clan Elders want it that way. And second, because the porthors never show themselves unless summoned. I'm quite sure this young woman did not summon them, because if she had, she wouldn't be asking everyone she meets what she saw. That leaves us with the very unsettling possibility that they revealed themselves to her *without* being summoned."

"So?"

He slammed a fist on Rhys's desk. "They *never* reveal themselves to *anyone* without being summoned. What is it about this girl that would cause them to do that?"

Rhys was at a loss for words. Dad was asking him to accept the existence of these make-believe creatures, and then explain their behavior.

His father leaned into his face. "Find out, Rhys. Get to know her, befriend her, become her lover if that's what it takes. I don't care how, just find out who she really is and why she's *really* here."

"Sure, Dad," he said as his father turned away. "Just as soon as you apologize."

His father froze, then did a slow turn.

"Apologize for what?"

Rhys rose and faced him. "For talking to me like that. I'm not your errand boy, I'm not your gofer or your troubleshooter or your fixer or your private eye. I'm an analyst and I—"

"Okay, okay," his father said, hands up, palms out. "I get it. That was harsh of me, and I apologize. But this is a stressful time, so many things coming to a head. I need your help. We need to step out of our comfort zones and think outside the box."

Rhys wanted to tell him to put a lid on the jargon, but that might sidetrack the apology.

"So I'm asking you," he continued. *"Asking* you, Rhys, to put on your game face and zero in on this girl. Learn all about her—for my sake, for your own sake, for the sake of the clan. Can you do that? *Will* you do that?"

"Well, she's not my type," Rhys said, "but if you put it that way, sure. All you had to do was ask."

"Then we're on the same wavelength?"

"Locked in."

Is he losing it? Rhys wondered as his father walked out.

Didn't hurt to let Dad think he was reluctant to pursue Daley when Rhys was anything but. She intrigued him. He'd never met anyone quite like her. Investigating her was going to be fun—for both of them, he hoped.

He knew the outcome already: Daley was different from the usual Nespodee Springs resident, and different from the tourists who came through to visit the spa, but in the end she'd turn out to be a normal human being, not a pairing, not a Duad.

Nothing special, nothing different, nothing to make her a threat to whatever Dad was seeing in the stars.

# 4

The rest of the day at Healerina progressed slowly, with desultory traffic, mostly people from the spa wandering through town and stopping in. A few bought some New Age knickknacks, but most just browsed. An occasional local dropped in, mostly out of curiosity.

Daley wandered the shop ceaselessly, like a cruising great white.

("Your boredom is tangible.")

*I shouldn't be bored? I feel like a bloody shopkeeper.*

("Well, this is a shop and you are its keeper. What do you expect?")

*I'm supposed to be a* healer.

("And that's exactly what we did with Estelle. Be patient. You can't advertise so you're going to have to depend on word of mouth. It will be slow going at first.")

Near closing time, Jason Tadhak stopped by as promised and bought a clear palm stone.

"This'll make a nice paperweight," he said, then smiled. "Can I expect anything else from it?"

"Like for instance . . . ?"

"Will it heal me?"

Oh, no. Was he sick? Daley sort of liked him. After all, he'd been very generous to her.

"Depends on what's wrong."

"Well, nothing, I hope. I'm in good health as far as I know."

"We could retire to the imprinting room and I could bond you with the stone and—"

He backed up a quick step. "No-no-no. That's okay."

"It's free for my landlord."

"Thanks but not necessary."

He slapped a ten-dollar bill down on the counter and hurried out.

*What just happened?*

("No idea, but that offer definitely scared him off.")

*What's he afraid of?*

("Some folks figure what they don't know can't hurt them.")

*He's too smart for that. Doesn't he seem a little sad to you?*

("Yes. Definitely.")

*I wonder what he's got to be sad about.*

("Maybe the same thing that's making him so angry.")

*Angry? I didn't get that.*

("I can see the rage boiling off him.")

*But—*

Rhys Pendry sauntered in. He wore a lightweight burgundy sweater with his hands thrust into the pockets of his gray slacks. He looked like he was just killing time.

"Happy opening day," he said with a grin.

Daley returned the smile. "Welcome."

His grin turned to a frown when her hair registered.

She shrugged. "Yeah, I know. It insists on being white there. I have nothing to do with it."

"Was I staring? I didn't—"

"It's okay. Everybody stares at first."

"Can you blame them? I mean, it's kind of cool. And I repeat: Happy opening day."

("Good recovery.")

"Another five minutes and you would have missed it."

"Closing?"

She gestured to the empty shop. "As soon as I usher out this crowd of customers."

"Well, why don't you do that and I'll treat you to an opening-day libation at our swanky local watering hole."

"Deal."

("You like him, don't you.")

*He's kinda cute.*

("This is his second trip to town 'from on high,' as Mister Tadhak put it, and both times to see you. I'm thinking the feeling is mutual.")

Daley liked that idea. But to avoid attracting extra attention, she donned her Dodgers cap, then flipped the *OPEN* sign to *CLOSED*, and locked the door.

*How about another of those time-outs?*

("Are you saying three's a crowd?")

*Exactly what I'm saying.*

("Fine with me. I've got things to do. See you later.")

Good. She'd find it easier to relax and be natural—and to spin a tale, if need be—without Pard hanging around and commenting on everything.

"Have you tried the Thirsty Cactus yet?" Rhys said as they strolled the hundred or so feet along the boards to the cantina.

"Is that its name? I've never seen a sign."

"Used to be one hanging from the awning, but it fell off and the owner never rehung it. It's the watering hole for the locals. Those who don't have jobs in Brawley and El Centro work the solar array, and a lot of them like to stop by for a cold one after work."

"They're in from the wind farm too, I imagine."

He shook his head. "That's Jason Tadhak's baby—totally family run. And the Tadhaks . . . well, people think the Pendrys are dour, but at least we know how to have a good time when we get together. But the Tadhaks live behind a wall and have got to be the most non-fun people on earth."

This town keeps getting stranger and stranger, she thought.

The shade under the corrugated steel awning carried a chill. Inside, the walls were of the same rough wood planking as the floor and studded with license plates. The old *Thirsty Cactus Cantina* sign from out front hung over the bar where two pairs of workmen stood at opposite ends. In a corner a Hispanic couple hovered by the jukebox as it played a song in Spanish. They all gave Daley and Rhys the once-over as they entered, then went back to whatever they'd been doing. Except for one. A bearded guy in his forties with overdeveloped muscles, loads of tats, and a cutaway denim jacket fixed his gaze on Daley and followed her as she and Rhys found a table away from the jukebox. The phrase "undressing her with his eyes" took on a whole new level of meaning.

"I hear this place can get pretty raucous on occasion," Rhys said. "A couple of guys get overserved and start throwing punches, but nothing serious enough to call the sheriff."

Daley didn't remember seeing any evidence of law enforcement about.

"This place has a sheriff?"

Rhys laughed. "No, the *county* has a sheriff. We're too small for our own police department so the sheriff's office sends someone out if there's trouble, which there almost never is."

"Hey, folks," the bartender called from behind the bar. "Just an FYI: We don't got table service."

Rhys smiled. "Can you tell I'm not a regular?" He rose and

gestured toward the bar. "Come along. You might as well meet a fellow businessman."

At the bar he introduced Daley as the proprietor of the new shop up the street and the bartender introduced himself as Jake Wasserman—owner, bartender, glass washer. Daley ordered a Coors Light and declined a glass.

"Arrogant Bastard," Rhys said.

"Pardon me?" Daley huffed in her most offended tone.

Rhys laughed. "Nothing personal. It's a local ale, brewed just over the mountains in Escondido."

Daley knew that. They stocked it at the Dew Drop, though she didn't much care for it.

When they were served, Rhys held up his bottle. "To the success of Healerina."

"I'll drink to that."

"Hear, hear," Jake said as he leaned over the bar and joined in by clinking his glass of club soda to their bottles.

"Speaking of hearing," Jake added after they'd all taken a swig, "I hear you was asking Arturo about some kind of giant lizards you saw out in the desert last night."

"My, my," she said, looking from Rhys to Jake. "Word gets around fast."

Rhys gave her a curious look. "Giant lizards? How giant are we talking about?"

Daley heard the biker guy mutter to his buddy, "Yo, Benny, I gotta giant lizard for her," which got a laugh from Benny.

Rhys had obviously heard it too because he started to turn. Daley reached out to stop him—she'd heard way worse walking past a construction site—but he was too quick.

"Is that any way to welcome a newcomer to our town, Mister Kendrick?"

The biker looked surprised to hear his name. Close up now he seemed to have a slight native cast to his features. "Do I know you?"

"You know my father."

A blank look while this penetrated, then a frown. "You're Mister Pendry's kid?"

"I am."

He gave a twisted half-smile. "Yeah, well, sometimes my mouth don't check with my brain before sayin' stuff. No hard feelings, okay?"

"None taken," Daley said with a quick wave.

In truth, the remark hadn't bothered her. Almost funny in a way.

Rhys motioned her back to the table. When they were seated again he said in a low voice, "That's Jeff 'Karma' Kendrick, ex-biker and foreman at the solar array as well as all-around utility player for my father."

"'Karma'?"

"I think he was some sort of enforcer for the Gargoyles. When someone who crossed the gang wound up hurt, they'd simply say, 'It was Karma.'"

She guessed the Gargoyles were some sort of biker gang. She glanced up and found Karma's eyes locked on her. Very uncomfortable.

"But tell me about these lizards," Rhys said.

Damn the lizards. She'd met this guy only two days ago. She didn't want to scare him off.

"Okay, first off—before you ask—I don't do drugs. And second, I'm beginning to think it was a trick of the starlight."

"So how big were they?"

"Can we talk about something else?"

"Of course. But I can't help being curious. What did they look like? Did they have tails?"

"Just some sort of optical illusion. Why the third degree?"

That came out a little harsher than she'd intended, but she didn't want to be branded the town crank.

He leaned back and raised his hands, palms out. "Sorry, sorry. It's just that you're new and have no idea how dull it is around here. I mean *nothing* happens. So anything, even an optical illusion, is a big deal."

"You must do *something*," she said, desperate to switch the topic off her. "How do you spend your day?"

He went on about helping run the Pendry Fund and managing the payroll and insurance and benefits for the solar workers, and so on. Never failed: Get a man talking about himself and the conversation never flagged.

She liked Rhys. He displayed an odd mix of self-confidence and vulnerability she found appealing. Along the way he mentioned a degree in economics and she could see him trying for a sophisticated air, but sensed that deep down he was something of a rube.

When he turned the conversation to her past, she told the truth about being an orphan but said nothing about her questionably legal activities, opting instead for a tale of years of study with various naturopathic and holistic and homeopathic healers.

She was so glad Pard was on time-out. If he were present he'd be distracting her with a barrage of corrections and comments.

Rhys said, "I've got to say, this seems an awfully out-of-the-way location for a shop like yours."

"But that's what I want. Isn't the desert where all the ancient prophets went to find clarity? I'm looking for a way to synthesize everything I've learned into something new and unique and wonderful. In a city I'd be distracted by the noise and the crowds. Out here I can think . . . and dream."

Oh, she was rolling now. Being raised in a family that treated the truth like Play-Doh, shaping it any way they wished, offered certain advantages. Her kin lied at every turn—not out of necessity but simply on whim, simply because they *could*. And this tale . . . she'd have to remember this one: a thing of beauty, a work of art.

Pard would be yammering on and on about the truth if he were here.

Rhys raised his beer—they were on their second now. "To clarity."

"Clarity." She quaffed the end of her Coors and slammed the bottle down. "That's it for me. Time to go home."

"What are you doing for dinner?"

Yeah, he was interested. And so was Daley. But she sensed downshifting to a lower gear might be best for now.

"I'm fasting tonight," she said. "And meditating. But I'll take a rain check if that's all right?"

*Fasting and meditating* . . . She wanted to laugh out loud. Where did she come up with this stuff? Good thing Pard hadn't heard; he'd never let her forget it.

"A rain check—you've got it." He leaned forward on his elbows. "But tell me: What time do you open tomorrow?"

"Ten A.M. Why?"

"Just wondering if you'd like a tour of the solar array. Morning's the best time because it can get hot out there, even in winter. After that, I can give you a tour of our Tesla tower."

Tesla . . . She realized with a start that somehow she knew a lot about Nikola Tesla. Pard again, she guessed. She sure as hell hadn't read anything about him herself. At least not while awake.

"Is that the contraption I've seen from the road?"

It stood off to the south, backed up against the foothills, the thing that reminded her of a giant skeletal mushroom.

"That's it."

"What's—?"

"I'll explain it all tomorrow. Date?"

She didn't want to put him off a second time, and besides, she was interested in that tower.

They arranged to meet outside Healerina at eight. He escorted her back to the shop where she left him to go "meditate."

# 5

"What's up, bro?" Rhys said as he closed Cadoc's door behind him and dropped into a chair.

A note had appeared under his bedroom door just as he'd been about to turn in. *Talk in my room.* Cadoc rarely sought him out between their chess games, so maybe this was important.

A note dropped on the table before him:

You like her?

That could only mean Daley.

"You're referring to the town's newest shopkeeper? Yes. Quite a bit. She's an interesting girl."

I like her too

Oh?

"And what would you know about her?"

I listen

Rhys's gut tightened. "You mean when you're creeping around town? You're not doing a Peeping Tom thing on her, are you?"

No eyes

Ears only

"Well, good, because peeping is big trouble." Although Rhys had to admit he wouldn't mind seeing Daley in an au naturel state.

She talks to herself

That took him aback for a moment; then he realized—

"You probably just heard her on the phone."

No phone

She's alone

Speaks to empty room

Rhys felt a sudden chill. He couldn't say why. He didn't find it spooky or anything, just . . .

"You're not getting into Dad's Duad fantasy, are you?"

Maybe

"Don't do this to me, Cad. There's got to be another explanation."

Crazy?

"Well, she's into all that New Age crap. Maybe she's talking to her spirit guide or something."

Talked about you last night

"She did?" Okay, this was interesting. "What she say?"

She thinks you're <u>cute</u>

A warm little glow replaced the chill from before.

"No kidding?"

So maybe she <u>IS</u> crazy

Or bad eyes

He laughed. "Thanks a lot!" A thought struck. "Hey, listen. Don't mention her talking thing to Dad. This Duad idea really has him going. I'm trying to get him back on the rails. If you say something . . . I mean, who knows, right?"

Lips sealed

Doesn't consult me

"I'm seeing her tomorrow, giving her a tour of the solar farm and the tower."

Not tower

Papa won't like

"He won't know. And he's got nothing to worry about. Daley is just what she says she is. A little flaky, maybe—but good flaky. She means no one any harm."

Cadoc gathered up his notes, which was his signal that Rhys should think about leaving. He turned at the door.

"Thanks for telling me all this, Cad. I appreciate it. I really do."

"Ungh."

Rhys closed the door and started down the hall.

*She thinks you're cute . . .*

Well, how about that?

# 1

Since she didn't know when she'd next get a chance to eat, Daley ordered eggs and sausage and toast at Arturo's. She'd worn her cap to avoid any discussion of her hair, but had to put up with his ribbing about whether she'd seen any more giant lizards.

*Am I ever going to live this down?*

("We saw what we saw, Daley.")

*Yeah, but did we see what we think we saw?*

She took an extra coffee for the road and was standing in front of her shop when Rhys showed up in a Highlander.

He started to get out but she opened the passenger door and called out, "I got it."

She appreciated a guy holding a door for her, but waiting for someone to run around the front of a car to open a door she could easily handle herself—awkward. Worse than awkward: total bullshit.

They made small talk along the way with Rhys asking some rather pointed questions as to whether she had a partner in the shop.

Finally she said, "Look, I'm probably going to go broke running the place by myself. A partner would only mean I'd go broke sooner. You should understand that, Mister Degree-in-Economics."

"Only if it's a given that you're going to go broke. I don't accept that premise."

"Well, my predecessor didn't last."

"Yeah, but she was competing with the spa's gift shop. You're offering something completely different. Apples and oranges."

"You have more faith than I do."

He winked at her. "I have faith in *you*."

("Oh, he likes you,") Pard said from the back seat. ("He *really* likes you.")

*Time for another time-out?*

("Absolutely not. I want to see his Tesla tower.")

Rhys turned south and drove them along a chain-link fence that rimmed the solar array. It ran about ten feet high and was festooned with *NO TRESPASSING* signs.

"If you look uphill to your right," he said, "you can't miss the Tadhak compound."

Daley saw a high, long beige wall that looked like poured adobe. All angles and sharp edges had been smoothed over, like ice cream left out of the freezer too long. She could see nothing of whatever lay beyond it.

"Actually I could miss it. Really blends into the scenery."

("Could have been designed by Gaudí,") Pard said and somehow Daley knew exactly what he meant. Would she ever get used to this?

"People think we Pendrys keep to ourselves, but the Tadhaks take insular to a whole other level. Nobody outside their family has ever seen behind those walls."

They continued on about a mile south of town to a gate in the fence. The fellow in the guardhouse waved them through. The south-tilted panels of the array lay straight ahead. The car was approaching from the east, so they were lined up edge on. And looming above and behind them all: the Tesla tower.

"The solar panels take up about four acres of the six we have fenced off. The lack of clouds out here in the desert makes our array super-efficient, exceeding a one-megawatt capacity."

Daley shook her head. "Is that a lot? I have no idea what that means."

"It would allow us to supply more than a thousand homes on a steady basis year after year."

Shocked, she said, "A *thousand*? Your clan owns a thousand homes? Where are they all?"

He laughed. "No, not even close. We plan to use the excess for the tower. If you want to get out and walk around, we can, but otherwise I'll just drive you around the perimeter."

"Seen one solar panel, seen them all, I guess."

"You've got that right. Of course I could take you inside one of the buildings and show you the inverters."

"Sounds exciting."

("Sarcasm, Daley.")

*What's sarcasm?*

("Try to sound interested.")

*Gotcha.*

"What do they invert?"

"The PV cells produce DC power. We have to convert it to AC to make it usable."

"You really know how to show a girl a good time."

("Daley!")

But Rhys laughed. "Let's get you down to the tower. It's a helluva lot more interesting." He glanced at the dashboard clock. "And we should get moving. The engineers are up at the Lodge for a briefing before they do the final wiring for the test run tonight."

"Testing for what?"

"To see if we can send power through the air."

("Never happen.")

"Is that possible?"

He shrugged. "Tesla thought so. The Pendry Elders are true believers in Tesla's theories about wireless broadcast energy."

("I'm afraid I can't count myself among them.")

*Hush.*

"How's that going to work?"

"Good question. They've invested a small fortune in the tower, so let's hope Tesla was right."

"And you're testing it today?"

"Tonight. And you're invited."

"I don't know . . . sounds dangerous."

"You'll be safe. Interested?"

("Say yes! Yes-yes-yes! I want to see this in action.")

*Sounds boring.*

("Please do this for me.")

"Okay," she said. "Sure."

("Thank you.")

*You owe me.*

As they passed the inverter building—is that what they called it?—she spotted Karma Kendrick having a smoke outside. He spotted her as well and treated her again to his strip-stare.

But then the road curved around and suddenly the tower lay dead ahead, claiming her full attention.

"God, it's massive. You don't sense its size from the road."

"We've built it exactly to the dimensions of Tesla's original Wardenclyffe tower, which means it's one hundred and eighty-seven feet high."

("Very impressive. And you don't have to ask about Wardenclyffe because, thanks to me, somewhere in your memory bank is the datum that it's a now-defunct town far out on the north shore of Long Island.")

*You're so wonderful.*

("More sarcasm?")

Rhys pulled to a stop outside another ten-foot chain-link fence festooned with *No Trespassing* signs. Concertina wire coiled along the top all the way around.

"Wow," Daley said. "You *really* don't want company in there."

"A lot of copper up in the cupola, and copper's valuable."

Scattered among the *No Trespassing* signs were warnings about dangerous high-voltage electric currents.

"Is it safe?"

"Yeah. Everything's insulated and re-insulated."

She pointed to the padlocked gate. "How do we get in?"

"Easy when you've got a key."

Karma came striding up as they got out of the car.

"You can't go in there."

"It's okay, Kendrick," Rhys said. "My father is—"

"I know exactly who your father is and he's the one who told me to keep everyone away from the tower except the engineers and the Elders. So I can't let you in."

Rhys jangled a key ring. "It's all right. I've got keys and I'll take full responsibility."

Karma said nothing but he didn't look happy.

Rhys unlocked the gate and they stepped inside. Daley stopped and gazed up at the maze of crisscrossing struts and trusses tapering up to a circular platform that supported the gleaming, copper-studded, mushroom-cap cupola.

A heavy steel pipe ran through the center from the top into an opening in the base. The tower had eight sides and so did the concrete pad that supported it.

"Looks like you're almost finished."

"Pretty much." He patted a sheet metal enclosure on one of the supports. All eight supports boasted the same. "Just finished installing the base isolators."

"Base—?"

"A kind of shock absorbers to make the tower earthquake resistant. Like I said, the clan has a *lot* of money sunk into this."

"You're not going to enclose it?"

"Nah. The inside would cook in the summer. Cooler to leave it open. Tesla never enclosed his tower."

Daley waved a hand in the air. "It this really going to work?"

"We hope to find out tonight. We may learn there's still a lot of kinks to work out."

Daley noticed a ladder leading up to the cupola.

"What's the view like from up there? Can we go up?"

Rhys hesitated. "People go up, but . . ."

"But what?"

"It's there for workers, not sightseeing. I'd never forgive myself if you fell."

Daley decided then and there she was going up, and started walking around the base.

"Don't worry about me." She pointed to a thick insulated cable running up the inside of one of the supports. "Is it electrified?"

"The dome? It's not live. Still some wiring to finish. It'll be done by tonight for the trial run."

"Good."

When she reached the ladder she started climbing.

"Daley," he said from behind and below, "I wish you wouldn't."

Pard floated beside her. ("And here's where I *do* agree with him: This ladder is just a bunch of open rungs without a safety cage. It's much too risky.")

*I'll be fine.*

("Please . . . if you get killed, I die too.")

*Nobody's going to die.*

As she continued her ascent, she glanced down and began to wish for a safety cage around the ladder. Because, damn, the ground looked awfully far away. She noticed Rhys climbing below her.

Good for him.

She was winded by the time she reached the opening in the platform and climbed through, and was still chasing her breath when Rhys arrived.

"You're crazy," he said, panting as well. "You know that, don't you?"

("Again I find myself in agreement with this man.")

"Could be. What I do know is I seem to be out of shape. And I also know the view from up here is spectacular."

She stood and saw the whole lower Imperial Valley spread out before her. A sliver of the Salton Sea gleamed silver to the north while the whole area south of it showed a patchwork of startling green.

"The miracle of irrigation," he said, following her gaze. He stood by the central steel pipe. "All those veggies . . . with two crop cycles instead of one, this part of the desert has become known as America's Salad Bowl."

She ran a hand over the copper fittings of the dome. "And this is going to send electrical power through the air?"

"That's the hope." He pointed toward Brawley and El Centro

and the more populated areas of the valley. "If it works, and if you've got the right kind of antenna and transformer, you should be able to run your household appliances with electricity from the air."

"No offense, but it sounds kind of dangerous."

"Yeah, it does. I guess we'll find out when we start testing it. We're in *terra incognita* here. Nobody's ever succeeded at this."

"And your people think they'll be the first."

He shrugged and smiled. "Someone's gotta be first."

("I beg to disagree. *No one* is going to be first if it's impossible.")

Her attention was drawn to the donut-shaped coil encircling the steel pipe.

"What's that?"

"A type of resonant transformer known as a Tesla coil. Don't ask me to explain any more than that. We have electrical engineers in the clan who understand it, but electricity remains a mystery to me." He smiled uncertainly. "Can we go back down now?"

He was trying to hide it but he looked unsettled.

"Tell me: Are you afraid of heights?"

"I wouldn't say 'afraid.' Let's just say that standing in the open almost twenty stories up doesn't top the list of my favorite things."

"You could've stayed on the ground."

"I was afraid you'd fall. I wanted to stay behind you so I could catch you if you slipped."

*Well, well, well . . . my hero.*

("Still more sarcasm?")

*Not at all. I'm touched.*

("Sometimes it's hard to tell with you.")

*Yeah, well, that's not a new problem.*

She smiled. "That was sweet of you. Okay, then, let's get back to earth."

"I'll go first."

"To catch me if I fall?"

"Well, yeah," he said in a *Duh!* tone.

*You know, I could get used to this guy.*

("I hope you do. He has a core of decency I find very attractive.")

*I thought you said you weren't gay.*

("I'm not. I'm simply free from hormonal taint, which allows me to appreciate people for what they are regardless of gender.")

She followed Rhys to the ladder. The descent was a lot hairier and seemed a lot longer than going up, but they made it to solid ground without mishap.

"Well now," he said, brushing off his hands, "you may think you've seen the tower, but you've seen only the part that goes up. The rest of it goes down."

"Down?"

"More than a hundred feet down. Come on. I'll show you."

Daley followed as he ducked under the trusses onto the tower's base and led her to a low wall bordering a large, squarish opening in the concrete, maybe a dozen feet on a side. The steel pipe running through the center of the tower vanished into its shadowy depths. The walls of the shaft appeared lined with steel, supporting an elevator that was little more than a platform running on two vertical tracks. Rhys lifted the cover of a junction box to reveal a toggle switch. He flipped it and a vertical row of bulbs began to glow down the length of the shaft.

"Want to take a look?" he said

"Why not?"

They stepped onto the elevator platform and Rhys closed the waist-high gate. The air grew cooler as they descended. Daley noticed another thick insulated cable running down along a seam between two of the wall sections.

"Did you hit water on the way down?" she said.

"The Livermore Lab did a groundwater survey back in 2008 that showed you have to go pretty deep in this area of the valley— like almost a thousand feet—before you hit water.

The shaft ended at a rocky floor where another Tesla coil was attached to the steel pipe. The pipe continued into the earth.

"We stopped here because this is the depth where Tesla stopped. This, however"—he tapped the pipe—"keeps on going down."

"How far?"

"Another three hundred feet."

"What? We're already a hundred feet down—"

"A hundred and twenty, to be exact."

"Okay, fine. What's the point of another three hundred?"

"Tesla had this idea of anchoring the tower deep into the earth so he could 'make the planet quiver with energy'—his words—and turn the earth itself into a giant conductor."

Daley shook her head. Rhys might as well have been talking Hindi for all she understood.

"Don't take this wrong, but that sounds crazy. What's it even mean?"

"Well, we've known for well over a hundred years that electric currents run through the upper layers of Earth's crust. They're called telluric currents. Tesla wanted to create standing waves in the planet's crust as a means of transmitting power."

"Oh, well, that clears up everything."

He laughed. "I don't pretend to understand it either."

She leaned closer to the coil. "Do you hear a hum?"

He cocked his head, then nodded. "Yeah. I guess they've already completed the wiring down here."

"So it's running?"

"Not at all. I've seen films of these coils. They shoot sparks and arcs in all directions. Very impressive."

She spotted four smaller galvanized metal passages—pipes really, but wide enough to crawl through—heading off into the ground in different directions.

"Where do those go?"

"Ventilating shafts running up to the surface to keep a little air circulating down here. They can also be used to help in an extraction in case of a cave-in."

"Cave-in? You've got steel walls here."

"Yeah, but the valley's a hotbed of seismic activity. The San Andreas runs partway down, and we're practically on top of the Cerro Prieto and Superstition Hill Faults here. And the Laguna Salada Fault runs nearby too."

Daley suddenly felt hemmed in.

"You know how you didn't like being on top of the tower? Well, I'm starting to feel the same down here at the bottom of this shaft."

Rhys smiled. "Well then, let's get back topside."

("A little claustrophobic, are we?") Pard said, hovering beside the platform as she stepped back on the elevator.

*I never thought so. I still don't think so. I just think I can find better places to spend my time than a hundred and twenty feet underground in an area that's "a hotbed of seismic activity."*

("Can't argue with you there.")

When they returned to the top of the shaft they found a half dozen serious looking men waiting.

"Rhys," said the oldest, "you're not supposed to be here."

Rhys looked miffed. "I don't see why not."

"I'm afraid you'll have to leave."

"Really?" Rhys said. "What's up?"

"We're waiting for your father and the other Elders. They have a meeting scheduled here."

"I hadn't heard."

"Just the Elders and us."

"We were just leaving."

Once they were back in the Highlander, Daley said, "Who are they?"

"The clan's engineering crew." He nodded toward a couple of big SUVs pulling up. "There's my father and the other Elders. Let's go."

*Does he not want his father to see me?*

("I have a feeling he doesn't want his father to see *him*.")

# 2

As he stepped from the car, Elis Pendry spotted a familiar-looking SUV driving away. Karma Kendrick was standing nearby so he motioned him over.

Despite—or maybe because of—Kendrick's felonious past with a biker gang, Elis had given him a job. He had certain security concerns, especially about the tower, that he wanted covered and Kendrick's reputation as a ruthless enforcer had been a plus. To his credit, he'd proved himself a hard worker who could keep a crew in line. A task-focused personality.

But he appeared to have fallen down on this task.

"Wasn't that my son?"

"Yeah, boss."

"He looked like he was coming from the tower."

"Yeah, he and his girlfriend were all over it."

"Girlfriend?"

"Yeah, the one who opened that weird store."

The Duad . . . well, he'd told Rhys to get to know her and learn all about her. But he'd never intended for him to show her around the tower, of all places.

"One of your jobs here, Kendrick, is to keep everyone except Elders and the engineers away from the tower."

"I do that."

"Well, tell me, then, into which category does my son fall? Elder or engineer?"

"Hey, he's your kid and he's got a set of keys and he tells me he'll take full responsibility. What am I supposed to do—rough him up and kick his ass outa here?"

Elis didn't like his tone but had to admit that Rhys had put Kendrick in a bad spot.

"Okay, I see your predicament. If it happens again, just say you have to check with me before you let him in." He glanced over and saw the other four Elders waiting for him. "That's all for now. We have a meeting here so you can return to whatever it is you do around the array."

Kendrick nodded and stalked off while Elis joined the Elders and the three clan engineers.

"Well," he said, "are we ready for tonight?"

Rolf Gwynn, the chief engineer, nodded. "All the wiring is complete. We tested the cupola yesterday at low voltage and all the connections worked."

Elis was more interested in the subsurface setup right now, but didn't want to let on, so he followed up on the tower's dome.

"Will the circuitry up top be able to handle the full voltage?"

Gwynn shrugged. "We think so, but only a full test will answer that."

"And what about below?"

"We haven't tested the circuits yet—that's why we're here this morning."

Gwynn stepped to a post near the shaft where two junction boxes were attached—the one for the tower situated above the box for the subterranean section. He unlocked the lower box and swung the door open to reveal a rheostat to control the voltage being fed down the shaft.

They all crowded up to the waist-high barrier around the edge and peered below.

"Will we be truly be able to open a passage?" Elder Mostyn said.

Elis gave him a sage nod. "The celestial configurations will align with the solstice. A path through the void will be possible if the tower works the way it should."

"The solstice . . . less than four months away."

Actually, the alignments would occur at the coming equinox, mere weeks away. Elis was keeping his fellow Elders in the dark as to the date. He'd let them know at the last minute. Two of the four he could trust with anything, but two ran their mouths and it wouldn't be long before the whole clan knew. Certain clan members were too emotional, too mercurial to be trusted with the truth. They would know when it was a fait accompli.

"Yes. That's why we need to start testing. If we miss the solstice window, I don't know when we'll have another."

"But if we open it, will they come?"

"The Visitors will have to decide if they like what they see. If not, all our efforts will be for naught."

Elder Baughan leaned closer. "You know the Scrolls better than anyone, Elis. What is your gut feeling?"

"I don't trust my gut. But I do trust the stars. I've let them guide our investments and they've yet to fail me. Right now the stars are telling me to divest and I've started the process. Something's coming with a negative effect on investments. The return of the Visitors will gut the markets. I've started to sell."

"Then let's make this work," Gwynn said, stepping to the power control. "This will be at ten percent power."

Leaning over the fence, Elis saw only a black pit with a large pipe running down its center. He hadn't turned on the lights because the Tesla coil—if properly wired and connected—would provide plenty of illumination, even at low power.

A hum echoed up the shaft and then sparks started to arc from the coil where it encircled the shaft one hundred and twenty feet below. Elis and the other Elders burst into cheers and applause.

It worked! The stage was set to change the world.

## 3

Rhys dropped Daley back in town in time to open Healerina at ten sharp. She'd enjoyed her time with him this morning and sensed he felt the same. They'd exchanged cell numbers before parting so he could arrange to pick her up for the test tonight. This might lead somewhere. But even if it didn't, at least she'd made a friend in town.

Shortly after she'd opened her door, an older, gray-haired gent strolled in. He wore twill pants and a plaid dress shirt with a string tie. He paused to examine the homeopathic certificate she'd hung on the wall, then approached her straight off with an extended hand.

"Welcome to town," he said. "I'm Tom Llewelyn. Nice to meet you."

Llewelyn . . . Llewelyn . . .

("That's the name on the doctor's office across the street,") Pard said from his window seat.

"Oh, Doctor Llewelyn. Nice to meet you."

She introduced herself and ran through the obligatory just-call-me-Daley rap.

*Why is he here?*

("Can't say. Looks friendly enough, though.")

"So," she said in her best, most sunshiny voice, "what can I do for you on this beautiful morning?"

He shrugged. "Nothing much. Just wanted to say hello and wish you luck."

Whoa.

"Okay, can I be blunt and say that's not the reception I expected from the town doctor."

He smiled. "Why not?

"Well . . ." Wasn't it obvious?

"We're not in competition," he said. "I'm part of the Pendry Clan and they use me exclusively. I couldn't lose them as patients even if I tried, although a few I could do without." He shook his head. "Some of them really set my teeth on edge. But I live up there on the hill with them. They're in my face all the time."

"Oh, right, somewhere I heard you folks had a rule that you all had to live up there. That true?"

"Yes, in a way. The idea is to set down your roots above sea level."

"Sea level? Why?"

"For when the ocean comes back. This whole valley used to be underwater, part of the Pacific."

"I know, but—"

"The ocean *will* be back. The ocean always gets its way. So that's why we live on the hill."

What did she say to *that*?

But he wasn't looking for a reply, apparently, because he hit her with, "So what alternative school or theory do you follow? I noticed a homeopathic certificate on the wall but you don't seem to stock any homeopathic products."

"That's because they're total bullshit."

He stared at her for a few heartbeats, then burst out laughing.

"I can't believe you just said that! I agree one hundred percent, but I didn't expect to hear it from you."

She waved at the certificate. "That's there because I needed something to hang on the wall. But basically I do my own thing."

"Which is . . . ?"

"I don't have a name for it yet."

"Does it work?"

"Too early to tell, but I hope so. I'm pretty sure I won't be making people worse."

He nodded. *"Primum non nocere."*

"Sorry?"

"The beginning of the Hippocratic Oath: 'First do no harm.'"

"Well, I'm certainly not looking to do harm."

He didn't respond and she noticed a tragic expression and a thousand-mile stare. Finally he shook it off and offered his hand again.

"Good to hear." He winked. "And when you come up with a name for what you do, let me know."

When he was gone, she muttered, "Well, that was different."

("Seems like a nice old gent.")

"Those are the ones you have to look out for."

A strange, vague tingling began to run up and down her arms.

*Do you feel that?*

("Of course I do.")

*What is it?*

("Your tactile nerve endings are picking up something.")

*So it's not coming from you or me?*

("No . . . from outside. I—")

And then the floor began to vibrate, the quartz stones began to rattle in their trays, and dream catchers tumbled from their wall shelf.

"What the hell?" Daley cried and grabbed the edge of a counter.

She'd experienced earthquakes before—no one growing up in California was a stranger to them—but she doubted she'd ever get used to them.

The tremblor was over almost as soon as it had begun.

Pard said, ("Well, that was exciting. My first earthquake.")

She couldn't help remembering what Rhys had said about the area being "a hotbed of seismic activity."

*Let's just be glad it didn't happen when we were way down in the base of that tower.*

("At least it wasn't the Big One.")

After every little one, people always talked about the Big One. She guessed Pard was no exception.

*Hey, wait. What do you know about the Big One?*

("I read, remember?")

*You really think there'll be a Big One?*

("No doubt. The only questions are when and just *how* big.")

## 4

After closing up for the day, Daley changed out of her Healerina duds and into something more comfortable—and warmer since she'd learned the hard way how cool the desert could get after sundown. She chose a quilted down vest over a sweater and jeans.

("I'd hardly call that a seductive ensemble.")

"I'm not out to seduce, I'm out to stay warm."

("But he likes you and you like him.")

"That seems to be the case, and if so, my 'ensemble,' as you call it, shouldn't affect that."

("I can give you larger breasts if you want.")

"You mean, like, implants?"

("Not at all. Breasts are largely fat. All I have to do is increase the adipose content. You're a thirty-four B now. I can make you a C. It will take a week or so but—")

"You can do that?"

("If I can rebuild your hand . . . what do you think?")

Did she want bigger boobs? They'd be real, not fake, all hers . . .

"Nah. I'm good. B-cup is fine. FYI, my priority isn't a relationship right now."

("Then why go at all?")

"Because I want to see if this Tesla thing works. I mean, broadcast power? That's such a game changer."

("*If* it works, which it won't.")

"And you call me Little Miss Sunshine. What if it does? Don't you want to be present at the moment the world changed?"

("Am I detecting a hint of enthusiasm here? Has young Mister Pendry managed to lighten your crushing ennui?")

"At least it's not the same-old same-old."

She was standing out front when Rhys arrived at 7 P.M. sharp.

"Any damage from the quake?" he said as she belted herself in.

"A few things rattled off the shelf but that's it." The aftershocks had been negligible. "You?"

"About the same. No structural damage. We were worried more about the tower but it can handle a three-point-six just fine."

"Is that what it was? I hadn't heard."

"That's what they said on the news: three-point-six Richter with an epicenter not too many miles away along the Cerro Prieto Fault, somewhere in the neighborhood of the prison."

"What prison? We have a prison?"

"Centinela State Prison, right here in the Imperial Valley. No damage there, either, by the way."

"You realize, don't you, that the quake hit just an hour or two after you warned me about all the seismic activity down here."

He smiled. "I forgot to tell you I'm psychic."

Daley had expected him to drive through the solar array as he had this morning but instead he flashed past the entrance.

"We're not going to the tower?" she said.

"*To* the tower? No. We're going to set up about a mile away."

"Set up what?"

"I've been assigned to aid in the test run and I thought you might like to be part of it."

"Depends on what I have to do."

"Basically it comes down to seeing if we can get a couple of lightbulbs to glow—even a little bit. We have people setting up a hundred feet from the tower, a hundred yards, a quarter mile, half a mile, and one mile—me. Or, rather, us."

Daley's participation came down to holding a flashlight as Rhys set up two odd pieces of equipment. The first was a small bulb in a socket attached to two wires. He inserted the metallic prongs at the ends of those wires into the desert sand by the Highlander's front bumper.

"You think current might come through the ground?" she said, feeling an urge to get back in the car. "Isn't that dangerous?"

"Tesla is reported to have been able to light bulbs through ground conduction miles from his Colorado Springs lab back in 1901 and no one got hurt. And, according to Pendry family tradition, supposedly all the way from Long Island to Wales."

The other piece was a box about the size of a cigarette carton with an antenna and a bulb jutting from the top. This he placed on the Highlander's hood.

"This one's to test air transmission."

("Interesting contraptions,") Pard said, leaning on the fender. ("But an exercise in futility.")

*Debbie Downer!*

("I prefer Ralph Realist.")

"Now we wait," he said.

"For what?"

"For the tower to start transmitting."

She could make out the tower due to the lights around its base. Still an imposing structure even at this distance.

"How will you know? They're gonna call you?"

He smiled. "Oh, don't worry. If what I've been told is true, we'll know when she's powered up."

They leaned against the grille of the Highlander and faced west toward the mountains. In the distance, faint light from a quarter moon lined the tower's copper cupola.

"Orion is up there somewhere" she said, remembering Tuesday night as she searched the sky. "Look for three stars in a—"

A flash in the darkness ahead cut her off.

"Here we go," Rhys said.

Another flash followed by yet another. They looked like bolts of lightning arcing through the air, except they weren't coming from the sky; instead they radiated from the dome atop the tower. Soon they flashed in such rapid succession and in so many directions she lost count.

"It's beautiful and awesome," she murmured. "And kind of scary."

"I'm told the arcs are relatively harmless—don't ask me to explain why they don't fry you like a lightning bolt, because I don't understand electricity."

("I can explain . . .")

*That's okay. I don't plan on getting anywhere near something like that anyway.*

"My father put out a press release and gave the sheriff and the various police departments a heads-up so they'd all be prepared if worried calls started coming in."

"You mean *when* they start coming in. Those sparks must be visible for miles."

# 5

Elis ignored the dramatic electric arcs shooting high into the night sky and concentrated on lower levels, just above the horizon. If it appeared, that was where he would find it. He and the four other Elders had spaced themselves around the valley, with Kyle Mostyn afloat on the Salton Sea.

Everyone not an Elder had been locked out of the tower enclosure tonight. This included the engineers. Just as they'd been locked out and sent away this afternoon. After they'd gone, Elis had unlocked the control box for the subterranean section and ratcheted the rheostat up to maximum output. Then he and the Elders had stepped back and waited.

This resounding success of this afternoon's test had left them giddy—a 3.6 quake!

But that had been the subterranean component. Simple waiting would not cut it where the tower was concerned—and only the tower was powered up tonight. No, gauging the tower's success would require careful observation. If they didn't pay close attention, they might miss it.

Elis pivoted his head back and forth like a radar dish, keeping a grip on the binoculars suspended from his neck. They weren't to be used for scanning because they narrowed the field of vision. Only when he spotted something would he then focus in on it with the binocs.

He'd told everyone to use their peripheral vision where the human eye sees mostly black and white. They were looking for black.

So far, nothing. Then . . .

*"I see something!"* Kyle Mostyn cried in Elis's headphones.

Mostyn . . . out on the water.

"What . . . what do you see? Describe it!"

*"An area of the sky maybe twenty degrees above the horizon to the north of me just turned black."*

Elis couldn't help thinking, Well it *is* night . . .

"Elaborate 'black.'"

*"Black-black. No stars. They disappeared for a short while. Like a hole in the star field . . . like a billion stars faded out and then turned back on."*

Elis pumped a fist. That was what they'd been hoping for. And it made perfect sense that it would manifest over the Salton Sea.

# 6

Rhys said, "How're we doing with your bulb?"

Daley checked out the one sitting on the hood—"her" bulb. Dark. She bent closer, trying to detect the faintest glow, but it remained dark.

"Not looking too good here, Rhys," she said.

*Dead as Kelsey's nuts, as Uncle Seamus would say—as long as Gram was out of earshot.*

("Who's Kelsey?") Pard said from the far side of the hood.

*No idea.*

("And why were his—? Never mind.")

Rhys was bent over the in-ground setup. "Same here. Damn. I'll call it in."

He turned away as he jabbed at his phone but she could still hear him.

"No action out here at one mile . . . No, not even a glimmer . . . How about closer in? . . . Shit . . . Yeah, well . . . What, tonight? . . . Now? . . . Can't it wait? Okay, okay, I'll be there . . . Might be a little late, though."

"No luck anywhere?" she said as he ended the call.

He looked disappointed as he shook his head. "Not a glimmer. And to make matters worse, the Elders' Circle has called a meeting for all involved to review the test."

"That means you, I take it?"

"Unfortunately, yes. I'll have to drop you back at your place, then go to the meeting. I was hoping we could grab some dinner but this could drag on."

"Dinner?"

He smiled. "Or are you fasting and meditating again?"

("That smile says he might be on to you.")

*Not a chance.*

She put on her duh-everybody-knows tone: "No one fasts on a Thursday."

"Really?"

"It's simply not done."

"News to me, but . . . another rain check then?"

"Sure. I'll file it with the last one."

*Just as well.*

("Don't tell me you're looking forward to another frozen dinner tonight.")

*I'm kinda tired. And we've got sriracha chicken and rice—yum!*

("Yuck.")

# 7

Rhys hid a yawn.

Was this meeting never going to end? Really, how much was there to talk about? The transmission failed, so back to the drawing board, right?

But no. They'd all gathered in the Lodge's main meeting room, and everybody—except the grunts like Rhys who'd helped with the testing—seemed to have something to say. The whole Circle of Elders was in attendance—Dad plus the heads of the other four families—and they all had to have *their* say. Then the clan's engineers were called on to explain why they thought the test flopped. They got all sorts of defensive and said they were following Tesla's circuit diagrams to the letter—checked and double-checked—but explained how they might well have been drawn by an assistant, because Tesla developed his diagrams in his head without writing them down.

All fine and good, and maybe even true, but something was off. It all had a rehearsed feel . . . some sort of dog-and-pony show. The Elders, including Rhys's father, sat in a pack and seemed oddly jubilant—hardly consistent with a failed test run. Why such a happy, almost celebratory mood?

Rhys kept looking around, trying to spot Cadoc lurking in the shadows, but saw no trace of him. He had no doubt his brother was somewhere within earshot. He wouldn't miss this for anything.

Finally his father rose and addressed the crowd. His cheerful demeanor with the other Elders had turned somber now.

"It appears we still have work to do to achieve our dream. As we've heard from our engineers, success depends on two requirements: The tower must be able to broadcast power, and the transformers must be able to receive it. If one end of that equation is faulty, the process fails. The crucial question is: Where does the fault lie? Transmission? Reception? Or both?"

"What's the next step, then?" someone said.

Dad didn't hesitate. "More power."

"But our home lights dimmed during the test as it is," someone else said. "How much more do we need?"

Rhys hadn't heard that and it surprised him. The solar array produced far more power than the Pendry homes needed. To use all the excess and then some indicated an impressive drain.

An engineer said, "The array is producing all it can under present conditions, but it's not yet spring. Maybe in summer?"

"For a number of reasons, we can't wait that long for testing." Dad pointed to Rhys. "My son and I will talk to Jason Tadhak tomorrow to see if he can augment our power supply."

We will? Rhys thought.

# 1

The police showed up at Healerina on Friday morning.

Juana, dressed as usual in her bib-front denims, had stopped by with a clutch of dream catchers. They were proving a popular item and she'd brought some new ones to replenish the stock.

("One could wish she'd try a different ensemble,") Pard said. He'd taken up his usual position by the window and Juana was hanging over him, looking out.

*Why? It's her signature look.*

("Well, then, one can at least hope she owns more than one pair.")

"A sheriff's car just pulled up," Juana said.

Daley joined her. Sure enough, a white patrol car emblazoned with *Imperial County Sheriff* in bright green letters had nosed into the curb in front of the shop. A buff-looking, dark-haired guy in a dark green uniform unfolded himself from the unit and stepped toward the door.

"This looks like official business," Daley said, feeling a touch of the jitters.

Had the folks she'd scammed in Coachella tracked her to Nespodee Springs? One of them might have spotted her on their way to or from the spa.

"That's Sam Alvarez," Juana said.

"You know him? How?"

"Over the years I've gotten to know most of the department."

("From which side of the bars, I wonder.")

"Officially he's a sheriff's lieutenant but we call him 'deputy,'" Juana added. "Don't worry. He's good people."

"He may be, but I'm pretty sure he's not here to buy a dream catcher."

He stepped inside and looked around. "Looks like you made it through the earthquake okay."

"Good morning, Deputy Alvarez," Juana said.

He looked surprised as he smiled. "Juana. I didn't expect to find you here."

"I'm everywhere," she said. "You should know that by now."

"I'm here to see the owner." He looked at Daley. "Would that be you?"

"That would be me. Is something wrong?"

"Depends."

("Uh-oh.")

"On what?"

"On whether you're practicing medicine without a license."

*So soon? I knew this would happen, but this is only our third day open.*

("Has to be Doc Llewelyn. He stops by yesterday and the storm troopers stop by today. My statement contains a logical fallacy, by the way.")

*A what?*

("Well, you see—")

*Later.*

Struggling to keep the disappointment from her expression—she'd liked Doc Llewelyn—Daley said, "Wherever did you get that idea?"

"Well, the name of your business does have the word 'healer' in it, and the sheriff heard from the State Department of Consumer Affairs that they received a complaint about how you might be practicing without a license."

"'Might be'?"

"Well, the caller said he wasn't sure what you were doing, but he suspected a problem."

"And just who was this caller?"

"A doctor in Pomona."

("Then it's not Llewelyn after all. Estelle said she was from Pomona.")

*I'm guessing she went back to her GI guy and told him I cured her.*

("You never said that.")

*But that doesn't mean Estelle didn't. Wishful thinking, you know. And her specialist wouldn't have scoped her again already—it hasn't been two days yet.*

Though hardly welcome, this was kind of a relief. She'd known all along that, given enough time and opportunity, she'd raise the ire of the medical community. She'd rather deal with this than a swindling charge.

"I see," Daley said, gathering her thoughts. She gestured around the shop. "Well, as you can see, I have no meds for sale—of any kind. I'm just a guide, deputy. I don't prescribe, I simply help people heal themselves."

Deputy Alvarez pulled out a small spiral notepad and flipped a few pages.

"Here we go: According to the complaint, you told this doctor's patient that she didn't need surgery anymore."

("That is *not* what you said.")

*Tell me about it.*

Daley shook her head. "I most certainly did not. I don't know if the woman said it wrong or her doctor heard it wrong, but what I told her was to return to her specialist so he could check her over and see if he thought she *still needed* surgery. I never *ever* get between a patient and her licensed professional."

("Did you just say 'licensed professional'?")

*I did. Sounds official, doesn't it?*

("An excellent command of Officialese.")

Alvarez started scribbling in his notebook. "DCA checked for a website and said you don't have one."

Daley realized she'd never thought of starting a Healerina website. But now that the deputy had mentioned it, she figured the shop was still way too nascent to invest in one.

*Nascent?* Where'd that come from? Pard again.

"What do they care about a website?" she said.

"That's where quacks"—his hand snapped up—"not that I'm saying you're a quack, it's just that the website is where quacks make their most outrageous claims. That's where they hang themselves."

"Maybe it's a good thing I don't have one."

He smiled. "What would it say if you did?"

Daley had a feeling the question was more important than he was making it seem.

"I'd probably put: 'Helping Californians heal themselves since last Wednesday.'"

He gave a polite laugh, then said, "Is that what you do? Help people heal themselves?"

Had to be careful here . . .

"Yes, but only while keeping up with their regular doctors. I like to think of myself as a sort of self-health counselor."

("Did you just make that up?")

*On the spot.*

("That's pretty good. I like it.")

*So glad you approve.*

("Was that sarcasm?")

As Alvarez transcribed her response, Daley said, "Why didn't the Consumer Affairs people come themselves? Why a guy with, you know, a gun? Did they want me arrested?"

A smile. "They have their own Division of Investigation but the complaint had no specifics, just a suspicion. If you had a website with claims that stepped over the line, they'd be here. But since you have no website at all, and don't advertise, they have only hearsay to go on. And, since they're headquartered up in Sacramento, and you're way down here, they asked us to look into it."

"And what do you plan to report?"

He looked around. "That I didn't find any basis for the complaint.

You're not offering treatment and not, as you say, getting between patients and their licensed professionals. But it's not my decision. DCA will have the final word. Right now I think they'll let it go but keep their antenna up. If more complaints come in, you'll be hearing from them directly."

*Well, isn't that just ducky.*

("Inevitable, I'm afraid. If we have any success—and I guarantee we will—people will talk about you and you can't control what they say to others, no matter how careful you are about what you say to them.")

"Any suggestions?" she said. "On how to stay off their radar, I mean?"

"Keep it low-key like you have it. If you advertise, don't make promises you can't keep, or offer cures for things like cancer and AIDS. That's a big red flag. I've seen DCA come down hard on some naturopaths and chiropractors in the county who start promising results that their licenses don't qualify them for. You're not licensed for anything, so you've got to be extra careful."

"Thanks for that."

"No problem." He folded up his notebook. "Mind if I look around?"

"Not a bit."

Daley watched him wander over to Juana and exchange a few pleasantries, then browse the displays. He spent extra time examining the quartz palm stones.

*Seems like a decent guy. Good-looking too.*

("If you say so.")

Finally he headed for the door. "Have a good day, ladies."

Daley joined Juana at the front window.

"Well, well, well," Juana said. "Seems you've hit the radar of both the county sheriff's department and the state consumer affairs folks. Congratulations."

"Lucky me," Daley said as she watched Deputy Alvarez drive away. "How come I don't feel like celebrating?"

# 2

"Now that's interesting," Dad said as Rhys parked the Land Rover in front of Tadhak Realty, right next to Jason's old Mercedes. "A sheriff's car leaving the Duad's shop."

Rhys watched the white-and-green unit pull away. He wondered . . .

"Your doing?"

"What do you mean?"

"Getting her in trouble, making life miserable for her, chasing her out of town. You know, that sort of stuff."

His father smiled. "I don't need the sheriff. When I want her gone, she'll go, and I won't need to get a third party involved."

Rhys forced a laugh. "You're kidding, right?"

"Not even close."

Rhys found his deadpan expression disturbing. He had to be kidding.

His father added, "I assume you've learned nothing about the Duad."

"She has a name, Dad—Daley."

"Actually, it's Stanka."

"Yeah. Stanka Daley, but she goes by 'Daley.'"

"She saw the porthors, Rhys. Or rather they showed themselves to her."

"Well, that's more than they've done with me."

*Porthors* . . . How could he believe in that junk? But then Daley had seen *something*—she'd been asking all over town about it. What?

"All in good time, Rhys. But something is going on here and I want to know what it is. Where nearing a crucial juncture and I don't want her interfering."

"I can't see how she can be a threat to anything, but I might have found out something more about her over dinner last night if I hadn't been stuck in that useless meeting."

"Not useless at all. I sold the Circle on the need for more power."

"'Sold' them?"

"The Elders took a vote after the rest of you left and we agreed to have the Pendry Fund underwrite whatever the Tadhaks charge us."

"But why go to the expense, and what's the rush? In three months or so we'll hit the solstice and the array's output will peak."

He leaned toward Rhys. "The solstice will be . . ." He hesitated, then said, "I want to be prepared. The heavens are aligning. We must be ready."

"Ready for what?"

"The Return is imminent."

Rhys suppressed a groan. The Return of the Visitors . . . His father was such a brainy guy. Rhys couldn't believe how thoroughly he'd bought into all that garbage in the Scrolls.

"And your girlfriend is a threat to that," he added.

"She's not my girlfriend, although . . ."

"Although what?"

He wouldn't mind a girlfriend. Not one bit. But . . .

"Nothing."

"You have a fiancée. Remember Fflur?"

"Of course I remember her. A nice person, but hardly a fiancée. It's not as if we've had a relationship and I proposed. You and the Elders figured we'd go well together and made a match."

"Arranged marriages work. Take your mother and me. We've had a solid marriage for three decades. Sometimes you have to put the stability and integrity of the clan ahead of your own personal desires."

"Take one for the team, in other words?"

"You make it sound like getting shot!"

"Well, spending my life married to someone chosen by a bunch of old men sounds pretty much just like getting shot."

"Just don't get sweet on the Duad. I've a feeling she won't be around too much longer."

That sent a little jolt of alarm through him. "Oh? You know something I don't?"

"Just a feeling. That's all, just a feeling. Let's go in."

Jason Tadhak was waiting for them—Dad had called him earlier and arranged for a meeting. After greetings and pleasantries, and Jason commenting how he hadn't seen Rhys in years and now twice in a week, they sat and got down to business.

Dad said, "Well, Jason, the future of this whole conversation depends on two questions, and the second is contingent on your response to the first."

Dad was a compulsive prefacer. Rhys wanted to nudge him and tell him to get to the point.

"The first is whether or not your wind farm produces more power than you need to supply the town."

Jason smiled. "*Tons* more."

"That's what I like to hear! Okay, now the second: Would you be interested in selling your extra wattage?"

Jason leaned back and steepled his fingers. "This has to do with your Tesla tower, I assume?"

"Yes. We need stronger current."

"That was quite a display last night. Very impressive. And you need *more* wattage?"

"Yes, we do."

"I think I can speak for my family—in fact, I know I can—and say that our answer is yes. We will supply whatever you need up to the point where it impacts the town."

His father looked stunned and didn't reply for a moment. Then, "You're serious?"

"Absolutely. But it won't come free, of course. My family will require compensation."

"That goes without saying—as long as it's within reason. How much per kilowatt?"

"We have plenty of cash in the family coffers. We're looking toward the future. If your project is successful, it will change the world. And the people who control that technology will have unimaginable wealth and influence. We can remake the world into a paradise. We want a piece of the action instead."

Dad frowned. "Meaning?"

"We will give you all the wattage you want or need—up to the limitation I mentioned—in exchange for part ownership of the project. No cash, just partnership points."

Did I somehow wind up on *Shark Tank*? Rhys wondered.

A knock on the door interrupted. A young woman poked her head in. She wore an Indiana Jones hat and a safari jacket embroidered with *SCEC*.

"Sorry to interrupt. I'm Doctor Heuser with the Southern California Earthquake Center. Just doing a damage survey on yesterday's tremblor. How'd we do here?"

Tadhak said, "No broken windows, just things falling off shelves. The only breakage was in the grocery store with glass bottles hitting the floor. I manage all these properties, so if something more serious had occurred, I'd know about it."

She nodded. "Pretty typical for a three-point-six. Thanks. You've saved me some time. Another question: Did any of you notice anything strange before the shaking began?"

His father frowned. "Explain 'strange.'"

"We've had numerous reports of a vague tingling of the skin prior to the shakes."

Rhys hadn't felt a thing. The three men looked at one another and shrugged, then denied any sensation.

She made a note, saying, "Okay, that fits. The mentions came more from down in the valley, less from the higher elevations."

As she started to close the door, his father said, "Excuse me, but we get a lot of quakes here."

"We know. You have faults all over the place."

"But this is the first time someone from the Earthquake Center has come calling."

"This quake was a multi-fault rupture."

"'Multi-fault,'" Dad said. "I've heard of those."

Dr. Heuser said, "It's when a rupture in one fault propagates over to another nearby fault. Unfortunately they're becoming more common. And that's bad because when multiple faults are involved, you multiply the intensity and the result can be a very damaging quake."

"Wasn't the 1812 San Jacinto earthquake multi-fault?" Dad said.

She smiled. "You know your seismologic history. Yes, and very destructive. We didn't have any instruments to measure severity back then, but we guesstimate it at M-seven-point five. Another reason I'm out here is because our seismic sensor network picked up an odd signal in this area before the quake and we're trying to track down the source."

"Odd how?" Tadhak said.

She shrugged. "Odd in that we've never seen it before and can't identify it."

Dad said, "Fascinating. Can I contact you sometime if I have questions?"

She stepped inside, saying, "Well, we're pretty busy right now, but when things calm down, sure. I'm with the seismology group up at Caltech."

She handed a card to each of them, then waved and left.

Rhys examined his card. *Rebecca Z. Heuser, Ph.D.* It carried the same SCEC logo with an *NSF + USGS Center* below it.

He looked up. "'NSF'?"

"National Science Foundation and United States Geological Survey," Dad said.

"I had no idea you were so into earthquakes, Dad."

"I have no choice *but* to be interested. We're due for a big one around here and knowledge is power." He tucked the card away as he turned back to Tadhak. "And speaking of power, where were we?"

"We were discussing how many points I get in your project in return for letting you tap into my wind farm voltage."

"Ah, yes. How many do you think it's worth?"

He didn't hesitate. "Twenty-five."

Dad gave a soft laugh. "I'd never be able to sell that to the Elders. But I can give you ten."

"Make it fifteen. I can't go any lower."

His father nodded. "I can get them to agree to fifteen."

Jason Tadhak rose and stuck out his hand. "Then we have a deal? Fifteen percent ownership in whatever technology arises from this?"

Rhys was shocked when his father shook Tadhak's hand and said, "Deal."

He knew it wasn't his place but he felt he had to say something. "Shouldn't we think this over?"

His father shrugged. "What's to think over? We need the voltage, Jason's willing to part with some of his without the clan putting up cash. Enough said."

"This will be easy to arrange," Tadhak said. "The town's main transformer is oversized and just happens to be on the south side, with a straight shot to the tower."

"When can we get started?" Dad said.

Tadhak shrugged. "Start trenching today if you want. The land between the tower and the transformer is already yours, so no problem there. I'll even throw in some extra heavy-duty cable we've had left over from powering up the town. As soon as the deal memo is signed and you lay a cable, we can hook you up to our transformer. After that, the ball, so to speak, will be in your court."

Rhys couldn't believe how accommodating Tadhak was being. He seemed to want to get the project up and running as much as Dad. Rhys couldn't help phasing out as they discussed details of the deal, about having the Tadhak lawyers talk to the Pendry lawyers, blah-blah-blah.

He jumped as he felt a hand on his shoulder.

"Earth to Rhys," Dad said. "Time to go."

He shot from the seat. "Sorry. My mind drifted."

He shook hands with Jason and followed his father out to the Land Rover.

"I was afraid you were going to nod off in there," Dad said.

Rhys let his annoyance show. "Well, why not? I had nothing better to do. No part in the conversation or the negotiations. Why was I even there?"

"To see how things get done, to see how to handle a negotiation, that's why."

He turned to his father. "Seriously, Dad? You call that a nego-tiation? He asked for twenty-five freakin' percent! And you gave him fifteen!"

"What would you have done?"

"I would have paid for the wattage and kept one hundred per-cent of the technology."

"That's because you don't know how much we've poured into that tower. It's been hellishly expensive. I'm talking millions. I walked in there ready to pay too, but I intended to bargain like hell for a low price. But when he asked for a percentage, I almost fell off the chair."

"He seems to want in very, very badly."

"That he does. I probably could have got him down to five."

"Why didn't you?"

"Because I wanted to seal the deal."

"But fifteen percent?"

"I would have given him fifty."

*"What?"*

"What's fifty percent of nothing?"

Rhys stared at his father. "What does that even mean?"

Dad waved him off. "Forget I said it."

"Oh, no. Dad, you can't leave me hanging like that. 'What's fifty percent of nothing?' You need to explain that."

"Nothing to explain. Just running my mouth. Take us home."

Rhys could see he wasn't going to get anything more out of his father. Grinding his teeth in frustration, he drove them back up the hill to the Lodge.

# 3

What the fuck?

Karma couldn't believe it: Some guy had got inside the tower fence. Not only that, he was just stepping off the elevator. He'd been down the shaft!

Shit-shit-shit! Pendry would have his ass. He'd been pissed

enough that his own son had got into the tower. Now a stranger? And the very next day? Goodbye, job, hello, unemployment line.

He raced over and yanked on the gate but found it locked. How the fuck had he got in?

The guy spotted him and ducked around to the far side of the tower. Karma opened the padlock and ran after him. He found him halfway up the fence, climbing toward the jacket he'd draped over the concertina wire.

Okay, the *how* question was answered, now to get to the *why* and *what* he'd done down in the shaft.

He ran up, grabbed the back of the guy's belt, and yanked him off the fence. As he landed on his back he held up his hands and started yelling.

"Okay! Okay! I'm busted! I give up!"

He had curly sandy hair and a scraggly beard. Karma kicked him in the side.

"Damn right, you're busted, fucker! What? I didn't put up enough no-trespassing signs up for ya?"

The guy reached into his breast pocket and pulled out an ID folder. "I'm a reporter, checking on the earthquake and the light show around here yesterday."

Karma grabbed it and checked. Yeah, it had his photo. Allen J. Puckett, reporter for . . .

"*The Light*? You work for the fucking *Light*?" He pointed toward the tower. "You think you're gonna find a flying saucer or something down below?"

"Hey, the paper's not like it used to be. We do legit news now."

Bullshit. Karma saw issues when he waited in checkout lines in Brawley and El Centro. Martian babies and secret messages from inside the earth and shit like that.

Puckett added, "I came looking to see if there might be a connection between the earthquake and the light show last night."

"Well, you didn't find none, so you can haul your nosy ass—"

"*Au contraire*," he said with a grin. "I found *something*. Not sure what it is but there's definitely something going on down at the bottom of that shaft."

Oh, shit. This kept getting worse and worse. Pendry'd throw a shit fit if he found a fucking reporter had gotten *near* his precious tower, but then if that reporter started writing crazy stories about it . . .

This guy was bad news . . . made Karma's beard itch.

"Like what?" he said.

"You're going to tell me you don't know?"

"I'm just a guard dog. Supposed to keep mutts like you out."

"You've never been down there?"

"Why would I wanna go down there?"

"Hey, can I get up and show you?"

"Yeah, sure," Karma said, playing along. "Why not?"

Puckett got to his feet and led the way to the tower where they ducked through the struts and crossbeams to the low wall around the shaft.

"There's a big pipe going into the ground down there and all sorts of weird electronic equipment at the bottom." He pulled out his phone and held it up. "I got pictures and everything, but I need a human angle. You've got to know *something* about this thing. Fill me in and I'll put you in my write-up. You'll be famous. The ladies will be all over you."

Yeah, he thought, they're all crazy about out-of-work guys.

"Weird shit down there, you say?"

"The weirdest."

"Maybe you better take another look," Karma said and gave him a hard shove.

Puckett screamed and his arms and legs were going every which way as he disappeared into the darkness. He screamed all the way down. And then all noise stopped.

Okay, reporter problem solved, replaced by a dead-body problem. But Karma had lots of desert available to him out there.

He went and got his pickup and backed it up to the tower fence gate. Then he turned on the shaft lights and took the elevator down to the bottom where he found Puckett looking very broken and very dead. The guy hadn't been kidding about all the weird electronic shit down here. Karma had never seen anything like it.

He accompanied the body back up to the surface where he struggled it onto his shoulder and hauled it to his pickup.

As he tossed it onto the cargo bed, he heard a voice say, "Well, well, what have we here?"

Karma's heart damn near stopped when he looked around and saw Elis Pendry watching him.

"Mister Pendry," he said. "We got a dead trespasser."

Pendry didn't look shocked, just troubled.

"How did this come to be, Kendrick?"

"He climbed over the fence and I chased him and he fell down the shaft. He was talking about the sparks from the tower causing the earthquake."

Pendry said, "You do realize, don't you, that the tower put on its show well *after* the earthquake."

"Right, so it couldn't've caused the quake."

"Exactly. And what are your plans for the deceased?"

"Well, we can call the cops, if you want."

"This is something I most definitely do *not* want. I cannot have the constabulary crawling all over my tower and attracting the press who will inevitably concoct wild and irresponsible theories about it."

"Okay, then, just between you and me, I know place out in the desert near—"

Pendry's hand shot up. "I think you'll agree it's better for both of us if I don't know the particulars."

"Yeah, I guess so. Let's just say I can bury him where no one will ever find him."

"Well, Kendrick, by doing so you will go a long way toward redeeming yourself for letting him get over the fence in the first place."

Well, at least it sounded like he still had a job.

"I'll get right on it."

"He must have a car somewhere that will need disposal, as well as a phone."

"Leave it all to me."

Pendry smiled. "That's what I like to hear, Kendrick. Make it happen."

Karma slammed the tailgate closed. Wouldn't be the first time he'd buried someone in the desert.

# 4

A knocking noise . . .

She'd just been dozing off—Friday night in Nespodee Springs was *so* exciting.

But really, who knew that doing next to nothing for ten hours in a virtually empty shop could be so exhausting? She'd tuned in the late news on a local station. Besides the latest updates on the continuing spread of the horrors throughout Southern California, the big story in this corner of the county was still last night's flashes from the tower. Someone driving along a county road near Ocotillo had recorded a video on her phone and sent it in. Daley's eyelids had started to droop as the newswoman droned through a press release from the Pendrys explaining the Tesla tower and how the display was harmless.

More knocks.

She straightened from the sofa and looked around, trying to locate the sound.

("'Some late visitor entreating entrance at my chamber door,'") said Pard from where he sat in the easy chair.

The shop below had front and back doors, but the apartment had only one—through the kitchen from the outside stairs.

She checked her phone. "Almost midnight."

The eat-in kitchen—would you believe a linoleum floor?—took up the rear of the apartment with the door to the right and a window over the sink. She leaned over the sink to see who was out there. Faint moonlight lit a long flight of stairs running up to a small landing outside the rear door. She squinted but could make out only a dark shape.

She called out, "Who is it?"

No reply. Her gut twisted. He must have heard her. This wasn't good.

She flipped on the light over the landing but nothing happened. Not good at all.

Then she noticed a slip of paper slide under the door. It read:

                    You don't know me

*He's slipping me notes?*

("Well, he's honest, at least.")

Totally weird.

"If I don't know you," she said, "I'm not going to let you in."

Another note slipped through.

                    Don't want to come in

"Then why are you here?"

                    Just want to say hello

She found that somehow touching, but remained on high alert.

"Why not just tell me your name?"

                    Can't speak

"You're mute?"

                    Yes. And very ugly

Another note quickly followed.

                    So please don't open the door

She had no intention of opening the door, so if he was trying to disarm her, he was succeeding.

("This is very puzzling.")

*Tell me about it. What's he up to?*

("Well, the door's locked, so you're safe. You can tell him to go away or play this out.")

*As if this town isn't weird enough already. All right, I'm going to play it out. I mean, why not? And how ugly can he be?*

And besides, she was bored.

She knelt next to the door and said, "You know . . . what's ugly to some people isn't ugly to others."

Despite my ugliness I am vain

Please respect that

God, this was weird.

"Okay. The door stays closed."

She looked up to find a T-shirted Jason Statham standing by the door with a grim expression and his trademark stubble.

*What are you doing?*

("Just want you to feel safe while you're interacting with this nut job,") he said in a decent imitation of Statham's Brit accent, which Daley loved.

*He might be a nut job, but I don't think he's dangerous. I appreciate the thought, but you can return to your generic self.*

("I kind of like this look.")

*Suit yourself.*

She turned to the door: "Why are you here?"

To get acquainted

"Through a door? With notes?"

I have no choice

"Oh, right. I'm sorry about that."

Did you enjoy the show last night?

"You mean the tower?" Of course he meant the tower. "Very impressive to watch. Too bad it didn't work. Loved the sparks, though."

It's all a show

Like fireworks on the 4th

"Were you there?"

where I could see the show

yet not be seen

"You keep calling it a 'show.' Is there a reason for that?"

I tell the truth

it's a distraction

"Distraction from what?"

I hear you talking at night

The abrupt change in subject was jarring, but the words themselves gave her a definite chill.

"You've been eavesdropping on me?"

> I listen to the town
> I know its heartbeat
> You are part of its heartbeat

"That's kind of creepy. In fact it's a *lot* creepy."

> So I've been told
> Who do you talk to?

"All right, you're making me uncomfortable now."

("Want me to get rid of this tosser?") said Pard-Statham.

*What does that even mean?*

("No idea, but tough Brits say it in films. Should I jolly well give
him the old heave-ho?")

*Stop it . . . please.*

> Sorry
> I'm harmless
> just lonely
> Won't listen anymore
> I'll go now

Now she felt bad for him.

Wait. Why was she assuming *him?* Why not *her?*

"Are you male or female?"

> male

Thought so.

"Where will you go?"

> Home

"Where's that?"

> Can't tell
> can I come back sometime?

Her instincts shouted *NO WAY!* But she sensed something
sweet about him.

"This is very strange but . . . yeah, I guess so."

> Thank you!
> I won't abuse it

An odd thought occurred to her.

"You didn't happen to be out in the desert Tuesday night, were you?"

You did not see me there

Still Statham, Pard said, ("Dig it: He's not saying he *wasn't* there.")

*Dig it?*

("You don't think Jason Statham would say that?")

*Maybe . . . if this was 1955.*

Back to the door: "Well, then, what did—?" She broke off.

*I almost said "we!"*

("Careful!")

She cleared her throat. "What did I see?"

The moon was new

Hard to see anything

"You keep track of the phases of the moon?"

moonrise/moonset important

if not to be seen

"But what did *I* see?"

I cannot say

"Does that mean you don't know or won't tell me?"

I cannot say

I can tell you other things

I know secrets

"Like what?"

Another time

Tell no one about me

"Why not?"

Just don't

Can I have my notes back?

"Yeah. I guess. Sure."

Daley gathered them up and slipped them back under the door. She heard footsteps on the outside stairs, and then all was silent.

"What just happened?" she said as she rose to her feet. "And I don't need a bodyguard anymore."

Jason Statham vanished as Pard reverted to his usual look.

("I'm not sure. This town becomes stranger by the day.")

"Well, you're the one who insisted on settling here."

("I do not argue the point. Yet despite the escalating strangeness, I still feel very comfortable in Nespodee Springs.")

"Well, that makes one of us." An odd mix of feelings coursed through her. Unsettling to have a stranger hovering at her door, yet never once had she felt threatened. "Do you think that was someone we know?"

("Who? Rhys Pendry? Jason Tadhak? No need for them to play games to 'get acquainted' with you.")

"Creepy Karma Kendrick?"

("I sensed a gentleness in our mystery man . . . and a palpable loneliness. That hardly fits with the tactless lout with all the tattoos.")

Daley couldn't argue. Ah, well . . .

"I wonder if he'll be back."

("I think we can count on that.")

Oddly enough, Daley found herself looking forward to another encounter.

One note had said, *I know secrets . . .*

I'll bet you do.

She had a feeling this town was rife with secrets. If she was going to stay here, she wanted in on them.

# 1

Early on Saturday she checked the light over the back door to see what bulb she'd need to replace it and discovered it worked fine once properly tightened in its socket. Her mysterious visitor must have loosened it. She noticed odd gray flakes, delicate and papery, littering the landing.

"Do you think these are from Note Man?"

("I can't think of anyone else it could be,") Pard said. ("Is that what you're calling him? Works for me.")

During the morning Healerina saw a fair number of weekend tourists who were spending a couple of days at the spa, but none of them was looking for healing.

Noon brought Karma Kendrick, beard, tats, cut-off jean vest, the works.

*Oh, joy, I have a feeling this isn't going to go well.*

Pard spoke from his window perch. ("He doesn't appear to be in need of healing. Well, spiritual healing, maybe.")

Daley watched him wander among the display cases, finger the feathers on a couple of dream catchers, then amble over to where she was standing.

"Remember me?" he said.

"I do."

He was staring at her white patch, which she figured was a couple of feet above where he usually stared at a woman.

"What the hell happened to your hair?"

("His middle name should be 'Tact' instead of Karma.")

"It just grows that way."

"I don't remember—"

"I was wearing a cap the last two times you saw me."

"Oh, yeah. So you do remember me."

"I even remember your name: Karma."

He grinned through his shaggy beard. "Do you, now? I guess I must've made a big impression on you."

("The last thing you want to do, Daley, is encourage this guy—not even a little.")

"Well, your name did. Never met anyone named Karma before."

("Oh, well, that should chase him right off.")

"Girlie," he said, stroking his beard, "you've never met anyone *ay-tall* like me before."

"That's probably true."

*Girlie? Really?*

("I assume this passes for charm in his world. And don't forget, he's at least fifteen years your senior.")

He said, "And tell you what: I don't think I ever met anybody like *you* before. I mean with that gold hand and that white patch of hair. You're really somethin' else, y'know that?"

What did she say to that?

"That's probably true too."

He flexed his huge biceps. "See those guns? No steroids, just hard work. And hard as rock. Check 'em out."

*Touch him? Is he kidding?*

"I'll stick with 'seeing is believing.'"

He hesitated, then lowered his arms and made a show of looking around. "So what is this place? You, like, heal people?"

("Careful . . .")

"I sell stuff. Want to buy something?"

A wider grin. "I gotta feeling what I'm looking for ain't for sale."

*Puh-leese!*

She refused to respond to that.

"Say," he said, "what time you get off?"

"Why do you ask?"

*As if I didn't know.*

"Well, I was thinking you and me could go down to the Cactus and have a beer or two."

"I don't know . . ."

"After that we can wander over to my place. It's the double-wide right next to the big dish."

Time to shut this down.

"Thanks, but I don't think that will work."

The grin vanished. "Why not? You got something better to do?"

"Nothing personal."

He started nodding. "Oh, you got something going with that Pendry kid."

("It would never occur to him that it might have something to do with him, now, would it?")

"That's unlikely, since I've known him less than a week."

"So what is it then?"

Had to be careful here . . .

"I just don't think we're a good match."

"Yeah? How do you know if you ain't tried it?"

"Some things a girl just knows."

His expression darkened as he leaned in close. "Listen—"

"Well, if it isn't Karma in the flesh," said a man close behind Kendrick.

Daley hadn't noticed him come in, and neither, apparently, had Kendrick, who stiffened at the words.

He looked familiar . . .

"Oh," Kendrick said. "Alvarez. What're you doing here?"

Deputy Alvarez . . . of course. He looked so different in civilian clothes.

Alvarez indicated the little girl whose hand he held. "Brought my daughter to do a little shopping. You behaving yourself?"

"Course I am. Just like always."

"Glad to hear it."

Alvarez stared hard until Kendrick shrugged and moved away.

Kendrick pointed a finger at Daley and said, "To be continued," as he strolled out the door.

Alvarez watched him go, then turned to Daley. "He bothering you?"

"Just asking me out. Not happy that I wasn't interested." She didn't want to say how glad she was that the deputy had chosen that moment to stop by, so she quipped, "Don't tell me you've had another complaint already."

He smiled. "No, just looking for a little doodad for Araceli here."

"Araceli," Daley said to the dark-haired, dark-eyed little girl in a pink dress. "What a beautiful name."

"It means 'Altar of the Sky,'" her father said.

"How old are you, Araceli?"

The girl didn't answer, just leaned hard against her father's leg and whimpered as she rubbed the right side of her head.

"She's four," he said, "and she's not feeling too great today."

"Oh?"

"Headache. Her pediatrician says she's got childhood migraines. Her mother gets them and they're known to run in families, so . . ." He shrugged. "I thought one of your pink stones would cheer her up."

"They won't help her migraine, I'm afraid."

Daley wanted to be sure to get that out in the open to this cop.

He laughed. "Oh, I didn't expect that. It's just that I saw them here yesterday and she loves pink. I mean *loves* it."

Daley waved a hand at Araceli's pink dress, pink hair bow, and pink sneakers. "I never would have guessed." To the child she said, "Want me to show you the stones? I have different sizes."

She shook her head and clung closer to her dad.

"She's not herself when one hits. I'll take her."

He lifted her and carried her over to the display. Some of the palm stones were pink quartz and Daley wondered . . .

*Think I should offer him one on the house?*

("That's iffy. I say not. He might think you're trying to influence his report to Consumer Affairs.")

*But it's a good report—he said so himself—and it's probably already in.*

("Then he might think you're rewarding him.")

*So either way my motives come off as questionable.*

("That's how I see it. On the other hand—")

Araceli made a retching noise as a cascade of vomit erupted from her mouth. She began to wail as it soaked the front of her dress.

Daley grabbed the roll of paper towels she'd been using to clean the front window and rushed over. Alvarez still had her in his arms. Daley tore off a couple of sheets and, gripping the child's upper arm, began to wipe at the dress.

"That's okay, honey," she said. "I'm going to get this mess off your pretty dress."

"Hey, I'm so sorry," Alvarez said. "They told us to expect this with a migraine but this is the first time it's happened."

"No biggie," she said as she wiped away what looked like curdled milk and half-digested Cheerios. "Poor kid."

("Keep hold of her,") Pard said. ("I'm going to take a look inside.")

Araceli began to struggle against Daley's grip. She wanted her daddy and only her daddy. But Daley held on and kept wiping.

*Hurry it.*

"Just give me a second here, honey," Daley cooed, "and we'll get most of this off."

Araceli screamed then and her father pulled her away, breaking contact.

"I'd better get her back to the car," he said as he carried her toward the door. "Sorry for the mess."

"What mess? It's all on her."

Pard appeared beside her. ("She's got a brain tumor, Daley.")

"What?" she said aloud through her shock.

Alvarez gave her a questioning look as he went out the door.

*You're sure?*

("Of course I'm sure.")

*Well, did you fix it?*

("I didn't have time. I was just assessing the situation when she broke contact.")

*We've got to tell him. They think it's migraines.*

("You can't come flat out and say she'd got a tumor. There's no way you can know that. Well, there's me, of course, but—")

*I've got to tell him something!*

She hurried out to the street where Alvarez had just finished strapping the child into her car seat in the rear section of his double-cab pickup.

"She needs a brain scan," she blurted.

He slipped behind the wheel and rolled down the driver window. A half smile. "Are you practicing medicine now?"

"I'm telling you she's got to have a brain scan ASAP."

He stared at her. "Her doctor wanted one but her mother's had migraines since she was a kid and she said no."

Daley had to get through to him.

"Deputy Alvarez, listen to me, please. I have . . . an instinct for these things. Something serious is going on with Araceli, much more serious than migraines. Please-please-*please*, have her scanned. I'm begging you."

He started the truck. "I appreciate your concern, I really do, but—"

"Do it!" she said, slamming her hand on the driver door as the truck eased back. "Do it or you'll never forgive yourself!"

He looked startled and braked for an instant, then kept rolling. He gave her a half-hearted wave, then roared off.

*Did I get through?*

("I couldn't tell. But I suspect your Parthian shot will eat at him all the way home, wherever that may be.")

*You mean about not forgiving himself? Well, he won't. I can tell he loves that little girl.*

("Well, it's out of our hands now.")

But not out of Daley's mind.

# 1

Happy Day of Rest, Rhys thought as he watched the sweaty workers lay the cable.

Really, was Dad crazy? What was the big hurry?

The first thing Dad had done after returning from Tadhak's office on Friday was arrange the rental and delivery of two ditch witches—basically giant chain saws on wheels designed for cutting through dirt instead of wood. Yesterday Rhys had been assigned to await their arrival and position one digger at the transformer and the other at the tower. The delivery had been delayed, so while he was waiting he'd wound up with the added task of trolling the trailer park to lure solar array workers with double-time wages to give up a day off to feed Dad's OCD.

Saturday had been pretty well shot by the time he'd finished.

Today they'd started at daybreak, with one ditch witch trenching from the tower toward the transformer, and the other working out from the transformer. As promised, Jason had delivered two reels of his surplus heavy-duty electrical cable. One reel rolled along after each ditch witch, unspooling into the fresh ditch, while a couple of men with shovels followed to fill in the trench by hand.

The good news was that Tadhak's main transformer was located on the south side of town. Had it been on the north side, laying the cable would have been far more complicated and taken days longer.

How convenient to have it here in direct line to the tower. The mystery to Rhys was why it had been placed here on the opposite side from the wind farm in the first place. Almost as if Tadhak had anticipated this. But of course that couldn't be. The transformer had been here well before the tower.

Which dragged his thoughts back to yesterday's surreal "negotiation." He'd always heard that a good negotiation ended in a compromise, which meant each party walked away with something less than everything they were looking for. Yesterday, from all appearances, both his father and Jason Tadhak had walked away delighted with the outcome.

*What's wrong with this picture?*

And Dad's parting remark still bothered him.

*What's fifty percent of nothing?*

What the hell was he saying? Was he going to cheat the Tadhaks? His father could be ruthless—extremely—but he valued his reputation. So what did he mean by *fifty percent of nothing?*

Something very not right there.

Karma sauntered up. He was experienced with foreman duties at the array so he'd been running the show here today.

He pulled a hand towel from his back pocket and wiped his face as he said, "That's extra-heavy-duty cable, a lot bigger than what we need, and tough to work with. I never thought we could do it, but it looks we're gonna have it all buried before we lose light."

Sundown was officially somewhere around five-thirty, but out here, close to the mountains, it disappeared earlier as it sank behind the peaks looming to the west.

"Good job."

"Your father promised me a bonus if we got it done today."

"Well, you earned it, Kendrick. Just submit a list of names and the hours they worked, and you'll all receive an extra check this week."

He nodded and stared south toward the tower. "This is all for that thing? What's up?"

"What do you mean?"

"I mean that was one helluva light show the other night. Now you're pumping *more* juice into it?"

"It's complicated."

"I'll bet. Just like that chick you've been hanging out with."

Rhys tensed. "What about her?"

"Well, I was talking to her yesterday in that weird store she's got. Not exactly the friendly sort."

Rhys had to smile. He had that right.

"No, she doesn't give away much about herself. Which reminds me—I've got an errand to run. Release the men when they're done and my father will settle up in the next couple of days."

He hurried to his car and drove to Healerina but saw the *CLOSED* sign on the door as he pulled up. Daley had closed up shop already. He got out for a closer look and saw a *Closed Monday* note on the glass.

He went around back where she parked her car but it was gone.

Damn. He'd wanted to take her out for dinner but had been so busy all day it slipped his mind. Where had she gone?

## 1

"Oh, crap," Rhys muttered when he saw the display.

### THE DUAD MUST GO

The divestment process had been proceeding in a slow, steady, orderly fashion. The Pendry Fund would easily meet Dad's mid-March deadline to be out of the equity market. But now this.

Good thing his father wasn't around. He'd gone out first thing this morning to harass Jason Tadhak into hooking the new cable to the transformer. Even Rhys knew the procedure was a lot more complicated than making a few connections. Not only was the deal memo not ready, but they needed to build a mini substation to handle the switching and regulate the voltage.

But what did this mean here? *Go?* Did that mean leave town? Or something a lot more sinister?

He was tempted to run last night's scans again, but he'd already been treated to a number of these cryptic messages in the past few weeks, and repeat runs had never made a difference.

Okay. He'd fix this—only a temporary fix, he knew, but it would buy some time. He took screen shots that cut off the message and forwarded them to his father's computer.

Then he jumped in his car and drove down to Healerina. The trip proved a replay of yesterday: the door locked, the *Closed Monday* sign still in the window, and no car around back.

Where the hell was she?

# 2

Daley slept in.

She hadn't realized how much she missed her old bed until she'd collapsed into it last night. And somehow hugging the pillow until late on a Monday morning seemed the height of decadence.

With no return visit from Karma, Sunday had proved blessedly uneventful. So Daley closed the shop a little early to accommodate the long drive back to LA. She'd brought along an audiobook—a mystery thriller to help pass the time—but couldn't concentrate on it. All she could think of was that poor little girl and the thing growing in her brain.

She made it to North Hollywood and crashed, grateful for the oblivion of sleep.

One of the reasons for the trip had been to move some of her stuff south and make her Nespodee Springs place feel more like hers. The other had been her monthly billing chore. Yesterday had been the first of the month, and that meant bogus invoice time.

("Do you really want to continue this?") Pard said as her label printer began spitting out address stickers.

"I don't see I have a choice. Healerina isn't exactly a cash cow, and I've still got rent and taxes to pay."

"I know, but it's just . . . beneath you."

Funny how she never used to see it that way, and now . . .

"I hope to phase it out."

"Before you get caught and arrested for fraud. And even if you do phase it out, these kind of things don't go away entirely. They're always out there, waiting to come back and haunt you."

She sighed. "Yeah, there's always that."

She'd insulated herself to some extent. The bank had her address and that of Burbank Drain and Pipe Cleaning listed as the Burbank UPS Store. The Burbank UPS Store listed her at the North Hollywood store and vice versa. Round and round and round she goes . . .

But she wasn't kidding herself: A determined investigator could unravel it all fairly quickly.

She printed out the invoices, folded them into envelopes, and attached the address stickers. Ready to go.

Keeping a constant watch for her fan club from the Medical Arts building, she spent the early afternoon packing her Crosstrek with smaller pieces of furniture and various odds and ends, including her candle safe. Fortunately nobody showed and she was able to get the job done with time to spare.

"I've got an itch to see Gram again," she said.

Dressed in shorts and a Hawaiian shirt, Pard looked up from where he lounged on the couch, a position he'd held all day. A couple of times she'd almost yelled at him to get off his ass and help her load the car but bit it back when she realized he couldn't lift a toothpick.

("Well, scratch it, then.")

So she called.

"Hey, it's me," she said when Gram picked up. "Got any plans for dinner?"

*"The usual. Will you be coming over?"*

"Love to. But—"

*"I'll put on another pork chop then."*

"No-no. What say I bring over dinner for you and Seamus tonight?"

*"Oh, you don't have to be doing that. You're too busy as it is."*

"I'll pick up a steak and some sides, you just save your appetites."

*"You won't be trying any of that nuveen cuisine on us, will you?"*

Nuveen cuisine . . . Daley had first heard the expression as a teen and had to look it up: Gram's term for *nouvelle cuisine,* which meant any dish that came with a sauce or "took on airs." Any time Daley had tried to introduce a different kind of food to the table, it had been dismissed as "nuveen cuisine."

"No nouvelle cuisine, I promise."

*"Well . . . all right, if you really want to . . . but at least let me do the afters."*

"Deal. I'll be over around five-thirty."

Pard said, ("How does someone who lives on frozen dinners plan to cook this?")

"Oh, I'm not cooking anything . . ."

She stopped at the post office to mail her invoices, then headed out to a butcher shop in Burbank that sold precooked steaks—just heat and eat. She picked out a marinated London broil and mixed-green salad. On impulse she added a pound of broiled asparagus that looked delicious.

When she arrived at five-thirty sharp, Brendan gave her a welcoming bark; Seamus took the food and found his way through the smog to the kitchen where he set it on the counter. Dressed for dinner now in khakis and a button-down shirt, Pard sat on the kitchen table.

Daley said, "How'd you fare in the earthquake, Unk?"

"Barely felt it up here. A vibration was all. Can I be opening you a stout, dearie?"

She'd never been a stout fan—even the name was unappealing—but that didn't mean she couldn't have a little fun.

*Watch this . . .*

"Got a Guinness, Unk?"

She didn't want a Guinness any more than she wanted a mint julep, but she always liked the reaction.

Seamus glowered at her. "You know damn well I'll not be serving that swill in me house."

("Ah! Similar to his 'Protestant whiskey' reaction.")

"And I'll not be having you say 'damn' in *my* house," Gram said, charging in from her bedroom.

Seamus pointed at Daley. "She asked for a Guinness!"

Gram turned to her. "Dearie, why would you be tormenting the man?"

("I was about to ask the same question. Let me hit the memory banks. Oh, yes, I see . . .")

The two of them came from County Cork where the Murphy's brewery sits right on the edge of Cork city. Seamus's father had worked there all his life and Seamus put in a short spell among the vats himself before coming to America. Murphy's biggest rival was the eight-hundred-pound gorilla of stout, Guinness, which was brewed in Dublin. As a matter of Cork pride, they drank only Murphy's.

"Come on, Unk," Daley said, not ready to give it up just yet, "have you even *tried* Guinness?"

He turned up his nose. "Never!"

She loosed a dramatic sigh. "Well, then, if you haven't got Guinness, I suppose I'll just have to make do with the wine I brought."

She'd picked up an oversized bottle of Argentinean merlot on the way. Red and on sale—what more did she need to know?

"Great heavens!" Gram said, eyes wide as she stared at her hair. "What in the name of the saints have you done to your hair?"

Daley gave an elaborate shrug. "It just turned white there. And I can't change it."

"Well, no one on my side of the family's ever had hair like that." She eyed the rest of her. "And will you be looking at yourself, all dressed in black. You look like a widow. You need some color, you do."

She'd worn her Healerina garb because time would be tight getting down to the desert tomorrow morning in time to open the shop.

"Black is a color."

"Well, you'll never be attracting a man if you're goin' about looking newly widowed."

*No comment.*

The steak came in its own aluminum pan which Daley put in the oven along with the asparagus.

"Aren't you going to boil them?" Gram said.

"No, they're *broiled.*"

"I've never heard of such a thing. This is nuveen cuisine, isn't it?"

"No, not even close. You'll love it. Trust me." She had to get her to stop hovering. "How about you dish out the salad while I get the wine out of my car?"

"Of course, dearie," she said as she took a sip of her whisky. Gram preferred her Jameson neat, poured a little bit at a time into a juice glass. She called them "shorts."

With a cigarette dangling from her lips, she began forking the salad onto plates.

("This feast isn't getting off to a great start.")

*It'll turn out fine. I'm sure of it.*

She hadn't enough arms to carry in the wine along with the food, so she'd left the bottle behind. As she retrieved it from the front seat she almost dropped it at the sound of a man saying her name.

"Stanka, Stanka, my, how you've grown."

She whirled to find a smiling, neatly dressed man standing by the rear bumper. Though the sun was down, she still had plenty of light. He appeared to be in his fifties and looked vaguely familiar.

"I'm sorry . . . do I know you?"

"You mean you don't recognize your Uncle Billy?"

She almost dropped the bottle again. Billy Marks had put on weight and gone a little gray since she'd last seen him—when she thought she'd seen the last of him.

And yet, here he was . . . the last person she wanted to see.

"You're not my uncle."

"I'm your father's cousin. That makes me an uncle of sorts—a distant uncle."

"*Very* distant. What do you want?"

"That's not a very friendly greeting."

"How do you expect me to greet the man who murdered my father?"

His smile vanished. "That's a lie your mother spread and you know it. The Family council completely exonerated me. I wasn't even in the same town when it happened."

His alibi had been his brother, and Daley would never buy that.

She began walking toward Gram's door. "I have nothing to say to you."

"But I've got matters with you. I heard how you messed up your game in Coachella."

She kept walking . . .

"You shouldn't be running games without giving the Family its cut."

. . . and walking . . .

He added, "And I know Consumer Affairs has an eye on you."

That made her stop and turn. "How do you know what Consumer Affairs does?"

The smile returned. "I've got a source keeps an ear out for anything involving the Family—just so we get a heads-up on any trouble coming our way. I don't know what you're running down there in the desert, but you better give the Family a slice."

"I left the Family behind at thirteen. I'm so far gone you're not even in the rearview."

"You're never out of the Family, Stanka. Besides, we can help you, make sure you don't screw up this new thing like you did Coachella."

"It's not a 'thing,' and I want nothing to do with you or the Family—especially you."

"Consumer Affairs lists you as 'Healerina.' It better not have anything to do with the horrors, because I'm developing a game on the horrors and I don't need no interference."

She resumed walking away. "Rest easy, Billy," she said over her shoulder. "I'm not interested in the horrors."

"Keep it that way, or there'll be trouble."

A burst of rage wheeled her around and drove her toward him. What she felt must have shown in her face because he raised his hands and took a step back.

"Whoa! Whoa!"

"That wouldn't be a threat against Gram, would it?" she said through clenched teeth as she got in his face. "*Would* it?"

"No, of course not. I don't stoop to messin' with no old woman. *You're* the one who should watch out."

"Well, that's fine. But if you ever lay so much as a finger on Gram, I'll have your eyes. Got that? Your *eyes*! And then I'll stick a knife in your heart like you did my dad."

She turned and stomped back inside where she closed the door behind her and leaned against it, shaking.

("Your heart is pounding.")

*I thought I was through with him and the Family.*

("Did he really kill your father?")

*They had a blood feud. He told my father he'd get even on the happiest day of his life. The day I was born he was found dead, stabbed in the heart.*

("I'm so sorry. We've never discussed this.")

*What's to discuss? My dad was never part of my life—obviously. Just a name and a picture my mother carried. But still, he was my dad . . . and Billy Marks killed him.*

("And that burst of protective instinct . . . it caught me off guard. You don't have that for anyone else in the world.")

*I thought he threatened Gram.*

("But you . . . you said you'd have his eyes. You meant that metaphorically, right? You didn't mean literally gouging—")

*If he hurt Gram? Of course I would. I don't think I could stop myself.*

("Well, now . . . that's scary.")

*Nobody hurts my Gram—nobody.*

"Are you all right, dearie?" Gram called.

"On my way."

*Help me put on my game face for the old folks.*

("Okay . . . I'm blocking some of that adrenaline to slow your heart and unjangle your nerves. There. Feeling better?")

*As a matter of fact . . . yeah.*

And she did. She suddenly felt calmer, less shaky.

*All right . . . showtime.*

Well, it could have been worse.

Daley poured everyone some wine. And soon a second for her. It further relaxed her and brought back her appetite.

She served the salad, then the asparagus, and placed the platter of sliced steak in the center of the table.

Seamus started off by poking at his salad. "And what would this be?"

"Salad, Unk. Try it."

"Salad's got lettuce." Poke-poke-poke. "Where's the lettuce?"

"Those are called tricolor greens. There are other kinds of lettuce than your usual iceberg."

Gram, ever helpful, said, "It's that nuveen cuisine."

Poke-poke. "Looks like stuff I'll be pulling out of the garden." Poke-poke. "You wouldn't be feeding us weeds now, would you, dear?" He caught himself and smiled at her. "If you brought it, I'm sure it'll be delicious."

He took a leaf and gingerly pushed it into his mouth, chewed, swallowed. His smile definitely looked forced this time.

"Different. Good, yes, it's good. But different."

"It's nuveen cuisine, I tell you."

Gram used the meat fork to examine the steak slices.

"It's not cooked," she said.

It came out medium-well. Daley liked her steak rare to medium rare but hadn't dared leave anything redder than a faint pink. God forbid. A steak caught in the Hiroshima blast might pass muster as adequately cooked.

"Of course it's cooked. If you want overdone pieces, take from the ends."

Gram speared herself a blackened tip, cut it in half, and tasted it.

"Quite good, dearie. Lovely flavor from that marinade. I'm just wishing it was cooked a little more."

Daley shrugged it off. She knew Gram and Seamus had grown up eating bully beef. She noticed Seamus half out of his seat, looking back toward the kitchen.

"You forgot to put out the poppies."

"No potatoes tonight, Unk."

He looked at her as if she'd called him a name. "No potatoes? Not even crisps?"

"Try the asparagus instead. It's different and delicious."

He made a face. "Asparagus makes me pee stink."

"Mine too," Gram said. She was holding up one of the broiled stalks and examining it. "Dearie, I'm afraid these are overcooked."

Daley never would have guessed that word existed in her vocabulary.

"They're supposed to be a little crisp, Gram. They can't help being a bit crisp after broiling."

She got a pained expression. "Crisp asparagus? That's nuveen cuisine if I ever heard of it."

Daley could feel her patience slipping away. "Just. Try. One."

Gram took a hesitant bite, chewed, and then her face lit.

"Why . . . why, it's delicious." She dug into her serving. "You must be trying these, Seamus."

Seamus sighed. "All right, but I'm going to pay for it. Don't even like to be in the same bathroom with meself when me pee starts to stink."

Not knowing whether to laugh or scream, Daley bowed her head and started on her salad.

("What are those dark flecks adhering to the greens? Pepper?")

She looked closer and recognized them.

("Oh, my. Cigarette ash.")

She closed her eyes and ate.


After dinner Daley was banished to the living room while Gram and Seamus cleared the dishes—since she'd done the cooking, they insisted on clearing. So she sat on an overstuffed couch with an overstuffed stomach and groaned.

*I ate too much.*

Pard slouched across from her, his belly distended to an absurd degree. ("Me too. If you're stuffed, I'm stuffed.")

*Well, I don't look like that.*

("Maybe not, but this is what it feels like. You really went to town on the meat, and finished the salad too.")

*Well, no one else was too interested in it.*

"I hope you left room for afters," Gram called from the kitchen.

("Dessert . . . ?")

"I don't think I can eat another bite," Daley called back.

"I made burnt orrrrranges." She said it in a singsong tone because she knew Daley loved burnt oranges.

("Burnt oranges?")

*A Gram special. It's 327 percent sugar. Maybe more. Besides the sugar there's butter and baked oranges in a combination of orange juice and sweet white wine boiled down to a syrup. And of course, a little Irish whisky.*

("All their desserts, it seems, contain a little Irish whisky.")

*Pretty much.*

"Okay" Daley called. "Just a taste."

("I abdicate all responsibility here.")

Back at the table, Daley was very proud she limited herself to one serving. And only one cup of coffee.

("She's pouring whisky into it!")

*Of course. You can't get coffee in Gram's without a little Jameson or Baileys along for the ride.*

("Good thing you had no plans to drive tonight. If you were stopped for a bad taillight or something, it might be hard to explain why the inside of your car smelled like a distillery.")

She pushed the coffee aside, untouched.

*I want you to run a diagnostic on Gram.*

("Ooh, is that a good idea? You may not like what I find.")

*But you may find something you can fix.*

("And I may find something I can't. I have my limits, you know.")

She knew but . . .

*I have to know.*

("Okay. Find a way to make contact.")

*I'll try the palm reading approach again. Worked in that doctor's office.*

Gram was seated across the small kitchen table, reaching for her cigarette pack. Daley grabbed her hand.

"How about I read your palm?"

"No! That's witchcraft! It's a sin!"

Gram tried to pull away but Daley held on.

"Not if you don't believe in it, and I don't. It's just a parlor game. Let me have a look."

Gram relaxed and opened her palm. "Okay. But quick now."

"Let's see," she said as she cradled Gram's hand in her own and tried to remember what she'd been force-fed at thirteen. She touched the eminence at the base of the thumb. "This is the Mount of Venus . . ."

("Okay, she's open. I'm going in.") Pard faded out.

She moved her finger across the palm. "And this is the Mount of the Moon."

"There's a life line, isn't there?" Gram said. "Where would you be finding that?"

Daley knew it ran along the inside of the Mount of Venus but she needed to drag this out.

"Let's see if I remember. Somewhere along here, I think."

"Is it long?"

"Well, I threw you a party for your seventieth birthday last year, so, yeah, it's long. Probably be longer if you didn't smoke."

Gram started to drag her hand away. "Is that what this is about? An excuse to tell me to quit smoking?"

Daley held fast. "Have I ever needed an excuse to tell you to quit?"

"Well, no."

"I do it every time I see you." She pulled hand closer. "There's a heart line here somewhere . . ."

*How we doing, Pard?*

("Almost finished.")

*Finished? Finished with what?*

("Gimme a sec . . . there. Okay. Done.")

*What did you do?*

("She has a lung tumor—bigger than Lynn's—but I choked it off. Strangled it. It's dead. I couldn't find any spread but we should recheck her in a month just to be sure. That's the good news.")

*Lung cancer is the* good *news? What's the bad?*

("Heart disease. Her coronary arteries are caked with plaque. She's a heart attack waiting to happen.")

*Well, fix it.*

("Sorry. Nothing I can do to remove plaque.")

"Crap," she said aloud before she could catch herself.

"What?" Gram said. "What's wrong?"

*Damn, what do I tell her?*

("Tell her the truth. She needs to know.")

Yeah, she did.

Daley cleared her throat and said, "Trouble with your heart line."

Gram snatched her hand away and pressed it against her chest. "Me heart? What are you finding wrong with me heart?"

"The arteries are clogged. Do you get chest pains?"

"No. I get out of breath easy but I'm not as young as I used to be."

Daley leaned forward and fixed her with the most intense stare she could muster. "You *must* see a cardiologist—a heart doctor."

"Oh, I don't know about that."

"Please? If not for yourself, for me?"

"Well . . ."

"Promise me you'll call a heart doctor tomorrow and make an appointment. Promise?"

"Oh, all right. Seamus sees one."

"Seamus sees what?" Seamus said as he wandered back in from wherever he'd wandered off to.

"You see a heart doctor?" Daley said. "Will you call and make an appointment for Gram?"

He frowned and stared at his sister. "You're having chest pains?"

Gram rose and headed for her room, waving her hands in the air. "I'll not be feeling anything but worried right now. Make the appointment and I'll go. I don't want to be hearing any more of this. I'm going to bed."

Daley pointed a finger at Seamus. "Make sure she goes. I'm counting on you, Unk."

"Oh, don't you be worrying, dearie. I'll get her there."

"And while you're at it, she needs to quit smoking. Now. And she can't quit while you're puffing away in front of her. I know you love her, so you know what you've got to do."

He sighed, then nodded. "The heart doctor has been after me forever about that. I guess we're both overdue."

He left Daley alone in the kitchen. Well, not alone. Alone was a thing of the past.

*Thanks for handling the tumor.*

("She means a lot to you, and you mean a lot to me.")

*Aw, I didn't know you cared.*

("Why are you so uncomfortable with gestures of affection, or someone simply saying something nice to you?")

Daley's throat tightened at the thought of Gram dropping dead from a heart attack.

*Because nothing lasts. Not even Gram, apparently.*

("I'm the exception. I'm forever.")

Daley grabbed her cooling coffee and gulped, very glad for the stiff shot of Jameson in it.

# 1

"We discussed bringing in a mobile substation," Dad was saying as he paced Rhys's office, "but Tadhak says the capacity won't be enough. So we're bringing in a high-capacity model to Tadhak's specs that will—" He stopped and pointed to Rhys's computer. "What are you waiting for? Shouldn't you be running last night's scans?"

"Sorry. Just listening."

"Well, can't you listen while the computer's crunching the numbers?"

"Of course."

Rhys had the scans all loaded and ready for analysis, but he'd been waiting for his father to leave. Dad, however, seemed to think Rhys needed a rundown—the second, counting dinnertime last night—of how he'd spent yesterday. He held his breath as he pressed ENTER and waited.

The solid state drive didn't whir as it ran the numbers, so the only sound was Dad's voice. But that stopped with a gasp when *THE DUAD MUST GO* popped onto the bottom of the report.

Shit.

"Are you seeing what I'm seeing?" he said in a hushed tone.

"It's kind of hard to miss."

His father stared at the screen in silence for a seemingly interminable moment, then straightened.

"In a way, this makes perfect sense."

"How so?"

"We're approaching a critical juncture in the history of the clan and this woman, this Duad, is ready to threaten everything. And so she must go."

"What are you talking about when you say 'go'?"

"I mean out of town, gone. What did you think I meant? She's trouble and she needs to be sent packing."

"I think you're operating on some shaky assumptions there, Dad. First off, you don't know if she's really this mysterious Duad. And second—"

"The real problem, Rhys, is that you've let the clan down. You were supposed to find out about her, but what have you learned? Nothing. You took her to the test Thursday night and what did you learn? Nothing."

"I told you, I had to attend—"

"And what have you learned since then?"

"I've learned that she's out of town."

That seemed to give him pause. "Where is she?"

"I've been looking for her but can't find her. Maybe she skipped. Who knows? Maybe that message should read, *'The Duad has up and gone.'*"

"Only one way to be sure. Drive me down there."

He didn't mean in a while, he meant *now*. So a few minutes later they were both in the Land Rover.

"This will save me a lot of trouble if she really is gone," his father said as Rhys coasted them down the hill.

"What sort of trouble?"

His father stared straight ahead. "Let's leave that on a need-to-know basis."

Rhys knew his father wouldn't elaborate so he didn't bother asking. What a drama queen.

He slowed as they passed Healerina. The *CLOSED* sign was still up

"Well, that's a good sign," Dad said.

"It's still a bit early. Let's check for her car. She parks around back."

"Well, at least you've learned *something* about her."

Rhys bit his tongue and steered around to the rear. And still no car.

"Not here," Rhys said, and turned back to the street. "The mystery is: Where did she go and why?"

"I don't care, as long as she's gone."

Just as he reached the street, Daley's Subaru, stuffed with furniture and personal belongings, turned in. She gave a quick wave as she passed and kept going.

"Mystery solved," his father said. "Time for the old man to take over, I guess."

"What's that supposed to mean?"

He paused, chewing his inner cheek. Finally he seemed to reach a decision.

"You rolled your eyes the other day when I mentioned the porthors."

Of course he did. They were the equivalent of green men from Mars.

"Well, my boy, tonight you're going to see them. I don't think your introduction to the inner secrets can wait till you're thirty. With things coming to a head as they are, I see no choice but to start your education a little early."

## 2

Estelle returned to Healerina around midday on Tuesday.

Daley had conked out early at Gram's last night. The wine and the booze-infused dessert and coffee had played a big part in that, but it turned out to be a good thing because she had to be up and out extra early to make that endless trek through the desert to Nespodee Springs in time to open the shop at ten.

"It worked!" Estelle cried as she ran into the shop, arms open wide.

An instant later Daley found herself wrapped in those arms as Estelle began sobbing on her shoulder.

"Wh-what worked, Estelle?"

("I think you have a pretty good idea.")

*Of course I do, but gotta play it cool.*

Estelle backed off to arm's length and wiped her eyes with the back of her hand.

"The ulcer . . . it's healed!"

*Yes!*

Daley noticed how a pair of local women who'd wandered in were staring with wondering looks. They'd heard. Not necessarily a bad thing.

"Are you sure? How do you know?"

"I went to my gastro and told him all about you and how you were helping to heal my ulcer so I wouldn't need surgery."

("Yikes. No wonder he called Consumer Affairs.")

"That's not quite—"

She waved Daley off. "Or I said something like that. Anyway, the thing is, I demanded that he scope me again to see what the ulcer looked like. He was against it as a waste of time but I can be very persistent where my health is concerned. Well, he didn't have an opening until yesterday so he finally agreed to fit me in."

"And?"

"Just wait now. I had my healing stone and I kept it with me day and night over the weekend. And when he finished the endoscope he said the ulcer was healed!" She squealed. "He couldn't find a trace of it! Isn't that wonderful?"

"It's fabulous."

"No, wait—I should say *you're* wonderful!"

("Actually, *I'm* wonderful.")

"I can't say—"

"You *healed* me!"

"No-no. *I* didn't do it—*you* did it. You healed yourself. Never forget that. I simply put you and your stone together to focus *your own* healing powers on the ulcer."

"Well, whatever. The upshot is the ulcer's gone and I don't need to lose part of my stomach. And to show my appreciation . . ." She reached into her shoulder bag.

("Let's hope she's *very* appreciative.")

She handed Daley a check, saying, "This is for you."

Daley gave it a quick glance and tried to appear nonchalant.

*Two thousand . . . that'll help.*

"Very generous of you, Estelle," Daley said, immediately folding it and stuffing it in her pocket. Who knew? The woman might change her mind. "I'm just glad I could help."

"I'm hoping you can help my sister as well. Her back pain makes her life miserable. I brought her along . . ."

## 3

Daley stood at the window and watched Estelle and her older sister Sharon drive away in Estelle's big Lexus SUV.

("We won't be getting any glowing reviews from Sharon, I'm afraid,") Pard said from the window. ("Osteoarthritis is mostly wear and tear. I can't turn back time.")

*Estelle will make up for her sister.*

Daley had made sure to make a point of that to the sisters, but had "imprinted" a stone on Sharon anyway. If they all were lucky, she might benefit from some placebo effect.

Estelle, on the other hand, said she'd already been on Facebook raving about Healerina. Who knew where that would lead?

*Maybe there's a future in this after all.*

("I'm sure there is.")

*I'm going to have to open a bank account in El Centro and deposit this check.*

("Wow. We're putting down roots. I might go so far as to say— oh, dear.")

A Ford F-150 double-cab was nosing into the curb outside.

Daley's chest constricted. "That looks like . . ."

("It is: Deputy Alvarez.")

"Do you think she had the scan?"

She watched Alvarez lift his daughter out of the rear compartment and carry her toward the shop.

("Look at him. Can there be any question?")

He looked terrible. His clothes were wrinkled, his eyes baggy, and he needed a shave.

Yeah . . . she'd had the scan.

Unlike her father, Araceli looked fine.

Alvarez stopped just inside the doorway and stared at her.

"How did you know?" he said. "How could you possibly have known?"

"Like I said—it's an instinct."

*That is what I told him, right?*

("Right.")

"Whatever it is, I just want to say . . ." His voice choked off.

"Here . . ." She pulled a chair over to the table where the quartz stones were displayed. "Araceli, why don't you stand on this chair and look through the pretty stones and find one you like."

"Okay!" she said.

Alvarez set his daughter on the chair and immediately she began sifting through the stones. Daley drew him aside. She noticed his eyes were red.

"Tell me about it."

He took a deep breath. "Well, after we left here Saturday, her headache got worse. What you said about getting a scan kept going through my head, so I took her to the emergency room at the medical center. They know me there so they listened when I demanded they scan her head. The CT showed a growth in her brain. That's what they called it—a 'growth.'"

"I'm so sorry."

"But you knew . . . you *knew*. Anyway, they needed an MRI to get a better look and couldn't schedule that till yesterday. And it showed . . ." He choked back a sob. "They're pretty sure it's something called a malignant glioblastoma."

*Can you do something, Pard?*

("It's still small so, yes, I'm pretty sure. But I've got to get in first.")

*I'll find a way.*

("You sound pretty sure.")

*Like the song goes, I was raised on robbery.*

She cocked her head toward Araceli who was humming softly as she played with the stones.

"She looks pretty good right now. Much better than on Saturday."

"They've got her on prednisone. It's made a world of difference in her symptoms but it's only temporary. We have an appointment at Children's Hospital up in LA tomorrow." Another deep breath. "I took the week off. They say they're going to want to arrange a biopsy of the tumor because they need to know exactly what they're treating."

"Does she know about it?"

"All we've told her so far is that we're getting her help for her headaches. I don't think she'd understand brain tumor. I mean, she could grasp something bad growing inside her head, I guess, but we don't want to go there. At least not yet."

"What's the outlook?"

He pressed his mouth into the crook of his arm as a sob broke free. A tear ran down his cheek. He quickly wiped it away and glanced at his daughter to check if she'd seen. But Araceli was engrossed in the stones.

"Less than a year."

"Oh, God."

Daley's heart went out to this poor guy. Probably a real hard case with the bad guys but his daughter's illness had reduced him to a blubbering wreck.

*We* must *do something!*

("Absolutely. Get me in there.")

"Wait here," she told the deputy.

Keeping it as casual as she could, Daley ambled over to where Araceli played with the stones.

"Find one you like?"

She smiled at Daley—a totally different child than the one who'd been here Saturday—and held up a pink palm stone.

"This one."

"Pink? You like pink?"

Vigorous nodding.

"Well, good. Do you want to know a trick to make this stone special? Make it yours and nobody else's?"

More nodding.

"Okay, here's what you do. Hold the stone with this hand on the bottom and this hand on top." She arranged Araceli's hands above and below the stone. "Now you have to press real hard on it."

She sensed Alvarez slipping up behind her to watch.

"Here," she said. "Let me help you." With that she pressed her hands over Araceli's and held them there. "Now, we'll just stay like this for a minute. And you know what? I'm going to ask your daddy to time it." She glanced at him. "Would you mind?"

He lifted his wrist and checked his watch. "Not a bit."

"Old-school timepiece there," she said.

"You wouldn't believe how often during a workday I have to note the time."

Back to Araceli: "And after a minute this pretty pink stone will be yours and no one else's."

The child grinned, definitely into the idea.

*She's all yours, partner.*

("Going in . . .") He disappeared.

They held their positions and waited. Araceli became restless, squirmy.

Daley said, "A minute can seem like a long time when you're standing like this, but it'll be over soon."

"Halfway there," her father said. "Thirty seconds to go." Shortly thereafter he began counting down from ten. ". . . nine . . . eight . . ."

("Okay,") Pard said, reappearing. ("Done.")

*For a while I was afraid we'd run out of time.*

("Nasty little growth. *Very* aggressive.")

*All good?*

("Yes. I cut off its blood supply, like I did with Lynn's lung tumor.")

*Thank you. I wanted this one.*

("My, my, I guess you do have a heart.")

*You had doubts?*

("Well, where a dollar is concerned, you can be, shall we say, all business.")

*We'll discuss this later.*

As the countdown ended, she released Araceli's hands.

"There! Now the stone is yours forever."

She grinned. "Yay!"

"How much do I owe you?" Alvarez said, reaching for his wallet.

"No-no-no. It's on me."

He shook his head. "Being with the sheriff's department, and with that complaint against you, I can't accept anything."

"It's not for you. It's for her. I insist."

"And I insist on paying. How much."

She could see this going on and on, so . . .

"Okay. A dollar."

"No, seriously."

"They're on special today." She accepted a dollar bill from him. "Okay, deputy, we're even."

"It's Sam, and I doubt we'll ever be even. If you hadn't beat me over the head about getting her scanned, I still . . . I never . . ." He shook his head and swallowed, looked like he was going to puddle up again. "Thank you . . . hey, I don't know your first name. I remember seeing it on the papers from Consumer Affairs, but I'm blanking."

She ran through her I-go-by-my-last-name routine.

"Okay, Daley. Thank you for the stone and thank you for your intuition."

She found she couldn't let him leave thinking his daughter had a death sentence. She had to offer at least a smidgen of hope.

She put an arm around Araceli. "She's going to be all right."

("Careful . . . careful . . .")

He shook his head. "I wish I—"

"Trust me."

"Your intuition again?"

"Yep. This little girl is going to bust the statistics. You heard it here."

("That's enough, Daley.")

*Gotcha.*

Sam pointed toward the ceiling. "Your lips to God's ear." He lifted his daughter off the chair. "Come here, *mijita*. Time to go home."

Daley followed them to the door, then watched them drive off.

*I think we done good, partner.*

("We did.")

*I'm feeling better about this.*

("Healerina?")

*Yeah . . . in fact, I'm feeling kinda good.*

("You mean the sun has risen and brought the dark, featureless plain of your meaningless life into full bloom?")

*Let's not get carried away here. I haven't become Forrest Gump. I'm still me.*

But . . . good to feel good about something. She could get used to this.

The downside—could she ever get away from dwelling on the downside?—was the enormous responsibility.

*Are we up to this, Pard?*

("I hope so. We'd better be.")

*Seriously, how do we know if we're going about this the right way?*

("We *don't* know. That's the problem. We're treading new ground here. It's not like we can Google it to find out how so-and-so handled it. Nobody's been here before. We're on our own, Daley. That's why we have to be careful what we say.")

*You're going to tell me I've got a big mouth, right?*

("Eventually we're going to attract a lot of attention. That's inevitable. But I think we should try to delay that as long as possible. We have to explore our limits, first. I can't cure everything. I have to learn what I can and cannot do, what works and what doesn't.")

*You think I said too much to Sam?*

("If you didn't, you came damn close. When he learns up at Children's Hospital that the tumor is gone, he's going to remember the woman who told him his daughter was going to be all right—'bust the statistics' was the grammatically dubious quote, I believe.")

*And what's so bad about that? Besides, I think he's kind of hot.*

("He's married.")

*Maybe not. He never once said "my wife"—always "her mother."*

("I would call that flimsy evidence or, more appropriately, wishful thinking.")

*We'll see, we'll see.*

# 1

The plan was to meet in the Lodge's main meeting room at midnight and head out together from there. Rhys arrived at two minutes after.

"You're late," his father said.

"Hardly."

He'd told Rhys to dress for the desert and he'd done the same: windbreaker, jeans, and boots.

"My car or yours?" Rhys said.

"Mine. It's got some items we'll need. But first we leave our phones."

"Really? Why?"

"You'll understand when we get down to business." He pulled his from a pocket and placed it on a table. "There's mine. Now yours."

Reluctantly, Rhys laid his next to his father's.

"Next stop," Dad said, "the Nofio pool."

Odd . . .

"What for?"

He held up a plastic half-liter water bottle. "We'll need a sample."

And so it begins, he thought as he followed his father into the cave below: nonsense compounding nonsense. He'd come expecting weirdness, but this was starting off in a direction he hadn't anticipated.

When they reached the steaming pool, his father handed him the bottle and said, "If you'd be so kind?"

"What?"

"Fill it."

So Rhys filled it with the hot mineral water. From there to the Land Rover and down the hill. His father sat in the passenger seat holding the water bottle and a paintbrush.

"I can't tell you how bizarre this all is," Rhys said.

"Oh, we're just beginning, Rhys. Just beginning. 'There are more things between Heaven and Earth than dreamt of in your philosophy, Horatio.'"

"You're quoting Shakespeare now?"

"You don't like Shakespeare? How about the carnival barker: 'You ain't seen nothin' yet!'"

"That's anything but comforting."

"Hush, now," his father said as they entered the town. "Ease up before her shop and stop. Stay in the car while I tend to business."

. . . *Tend to business* . . . What was going on here?

Rhys had barely pulled to a stop in front of Healerina before his father was out the door and stepping up to the front window. Rhys watched him pour the spring water over the brush bristles and then start painting some sort of design on the big pane. He couldn't make out the design itself because the water didn't show up against the glass, but it seemed to involve a circle and a number of squiggly lines through it and around it. That done, he sprinkled some water on the door frame before rushing back to the car.

"Go!" he whispered as he jumped into his seat.

But he didn't close the passenger door. Instead he held it open a few inches until they were well away from the shop, then he slammed it.

"Tell me this will all make sense eventually."

"I guarantee it."

"What did you draw on her window?"

"A symbol from the Scrolls."

Rhys felt a twinge of alarm. "This is taking on a Passover vibe."

His father looked at him. "What would you know about Passover? I've never allowed a Bible in the house."

Right. No contamination by false religions.

"It's always mentioned on the news when the season comes. And I took a comparative religions course in college. Splashing that water on the lintel . . ." He bit back a hysterical laugh. "Are you expecting the Angel of Death?"

"It marks the place for the porthors."

The porthors again . . .

"Marks how?"

"For a visit."

"Why so coy, Dad? What are they going to do?"

"Mess up the place. A little wanton destruction."

"A 'little'?"

"Enough to make her consider another venue."

Shit.

"I'm not sure I like this, Dad. In fact, I'm *sure* I don't like this."

"No worry. They won't harm her. Just the things in her shop."

"'They' . . . meaning the porthors?"

"Exactly."

Okay. Daley was in no real danger because the porthors weren't real. But Dad believed they were. And that meant . . .

"You really want to do that to a harmless, defenseless woman—a *young* woman? What if she were your daughter? What if Aerona had survived? Would you want her treated that way?"

"She's not my daughter. And my daughter would never pose a threat. And don't forget: The porthors appeared to her. They never allow themselves to be seen, but they revealed themselves to her. That means she's *involved*. No matter what her age, Rhys, this woman is a threat. And she might only appear young. Who knows how old she really is, or where she came from? If you turn your back on a threat, you invite it to bite you in the ass."

No reasoning with this man.

Rhys hesitated. No, he had to say this.

"Dad, you're not going to like hearing this, but I think you need help—I mean, like, counseling, medication."

He nodded. "I know."

"You *know*? They why don't—?"

"No, I mean I know you think that, but it's not true. And I'm about to prove it. Find a spot out here where you can go off road to the right."

I can't believe I'm playing along with this.

But he didn't see how he had much choice.

"Anywhere?"

"Anywhere."

By now they'd left the pavement, passed the trailer parks and the *Welcome to Nespodee Springs* sign. The desert stretched away to either side. Rhys slowed, left the road, and headed south. The going became bumpier, but not by much.

After about two miles, his father said, "This looks like as good a spot as any. Stop here and turn out the lights."

Rhys did as he was told. Handing off the water bottle, his father got out and opened the rear hatch.

"Come on, Rhys. Time to make a believer out of you."

Biting his tongue—which he seemed to be doing an awful lot lately—Rhys walked around to the rear of the Rover and watched his father unwrap a strange oblong object from a blanket.

"What's that?"

"It has a difficult-to-pronounce name that wouldn't mean anything to you, so let's just call it a 'horn.'"

A horn, he thought. *Just when I thought the weirdness had maxed out.*

"Where'd it come from?"

"It's been in the family for generations."

"How come I've—?"

"Enough questions, Rhys. It's time for a demonstration. Follow me."

So he followed his father. All around them starlight and moonlight etched the desert and the sparse, low-lying clumps of sage in sharp relief. His father stopped a couple of dozen paces away from the car, placed one end of the horn against his lips and blew.

At least Rhys thought he blew. His cheeks puffed out and he seemed to be putting some effort into it, but Rhys heard no sound beyond the breath rushing through the instrument. Certainly nothing even remotely musical.

His father took a deep breath and blew again. And then again.

Okay, this had gone far enough.

"Dad . . ."

Movement to his right caught his eye. Seemingly from nowhere, a roundish object had appeared on the ground. And then another—this time he saw it pop out of the sand. And another and another until the ground before them was studded with head-like objects.

What the—? This was just what Daley had described. It hadn't been her imagination or a trick of the light.

And then hands and arms appeared as between twenty and thirty humanoid creatures began pulling themselves out of the sand. Reflexively, Rhys backed away.

"Dad, what . . . what . . . ?"

"No worry. They won't harm us."

Eventually the creatures stood before them. They looked like naked early humans, shorter and slighter than Rhys and his dad. As they began milling around, moonlight glinted from their eyes but Rhys could make out no genitalia.

His father gestured back and forth with his free hand. "Rhys, the porthors . . . porthors, my son Rhys."

Making introductions . . . so fucking surreal . . .

"They're real? Really real?"

"Of course. You shouldn't doubt me, Rhys. Never doubt your father."

"But where did they come from?"

"You just saw for yourself: the desert."

"You mean they hibernate there until you blow that horn or whatever it is?"

"They seem to move around under the surface."

"How is that possible?"

His father shrugged. "I have no idea. Does it matter? They come when I call."

"What *are* they, Dad? And don't tell me 'porthors.' What the fuck are the porthors?"

"You know the legends from the Scrolls."

Yeah, he did: The Visitors created them to tend to them while they were here, and left them behind when they departed. Rhys had dismissed it all as primitive bullshit, but here he was in the middle of a moonlit desert, staring at a couple dozen very real and very solid examples of that primitive bullshit.

"My guess?" Dad added. "They modified some early hominids into these things."

"But that . . . that would make them millions of years old."

"Exactly."

"But that can't . . ."

"Right," his father said in a snarky tone. "Tell me that can't be. They don't breed—at least not as far as I can tell—so we have to assume these are the same creatures the Visitors left behind."

*The Visitors* . . . Holy hell, if the porthors were real, then chances were good the Visitors were too.

"It's all true? What the Scrolls say . . . it's all *true*?"

"I'm sure there's a certain amount of confabulation involved. Stories are told and repeated and repeated and what finally gets written down is far from what started, but in the case of the *Void Scrolls*, not too terribly far, as you can see before you." He raised the horn to his lips. "Time to set the wheels in motion."

He blew again. The same note? A different one? Rhys couldn't tell. Whatever it was, the porthors stopped moving and simply stood there, as if waiting.

His father held out his hand and said, "Open the bottle."

After removing the top, Rhys handed him the bottle, whereupon he began to swing it back and forth, spraying its contents into the air like a priest anointing his flock with holy water. He tossed the bottle back to Rhys and then blew another imperceptible note on his horn.

Suddenly the creatures—the porthors—began moving, first in

a shuffle, then in a trot, all in the same direction . . . all toward town.

Toward Healerina.

"Call them back, Dad."

"Now why would I do that?"

"I don't want this, not any part of it. It's wrong, it's crazy wrong. *Please*, call them back."

He slapped Rhys on the back. "It'll be over in an hour. Less, I'm sure. Get in the car. I'll drive."

Just as well. Rhys didn't feel like driving. He didn't feel like getting in the car either, but he felt like being left miles out in this haunted desert even less.

His father drove them back toward the road in silence, but when they reached it, he turned east instead of toward town.

"Where are we going?"

"El Centro. I need some gas and the local station's closed."

"No-no-no! We've got to go back!"

"To do what? Warn the Duad?"

"No, I—fuck it, yes!"

"Damnit, Rhys! Where are your loyalties?"

"It's not a matter of loyalty, it's about warning an innocent girl that trouble is coming."

"*She's* the trouble!"

"She's got no clue, Dad. You haven't spoken to her. She's got her own thing and it's got nothing to do with us."

"Really? Well, if that's so, then she's being used. Naïve or not, she's *involved*. Remember: The porthors revealed themselves to her. Have they ever revealed themselves to you?"

Rhys saw no point in responding when his father knew damn well the answer was no.

"Have they ever revealed themselves to anyone you know? No, of course not, or you would have heard about it. I can tell you they've never appeared to me unless I blew that horn. So why did they pop out of the sand and show themselves to her? Because they recognize something in her. And so do the celestial readings. She's a threat and needs to go. It's too late to head back, but even if it weren't, you wouldn't change anything, only complicate matters."

"Goddamn it!" Rhys reached for his phone but realized it wasn't there. "Is this why we left our phones behind?"

"I know you, Rhys," his father said, glancing at him as he drove. "I know you better than you know yourself."

Rhys considered jumping his father and wresting control of the car away from him. But that was foolhardy and dangerous and, as the man said, wouldn't change anything. He pounded the dashboard a half dozen times in frustration, then sat back and fumed.

## 2

The knocking woke her.

She'd fallen asleep in front of the TV. This was getting to be a habit. She struggled off the couch and stumbled into the kitchen.

"Who is—?" Then she saw the *Hello* note lying just inside the door.

("Looks like your friend is back.")

*Note Man, yeah. Are you going to become Jason again?*

("On a first-name basis now, are we?")

*Well, he's really hot.*

("If you say so. Whatever, I don't see the need.")

Daley spoke to the door. "Oh, it's you again."

A new note.

Am here I too late?

What time was it?

A glance at the microwave showed *12:47.*

"Not at all. I was watching television."

("Sort of. More like reading.")

She just now noticed the phone in her hand. Pard had been studying again.

"What's up?"

There is talk in town
"Oh? About what?"
You
Healerina is healing?
("Already?")
"Now where did you hear that?"
I listen
Her neck tightened.
"Have you been listening to me?"
Promised I wouldn't
Keep promises
That was a relief.
"What have you heard?"
An ulcer?
*Now how . . . ?*
("I recall seeing a couple of locals in the shop earlier when Estelle started gushing about you healing her.")
Daley vaguely remembered the women. Estelle had commanded most of her attention at that moment. Apparently not Pard's.
Well?
You're not sure?
*What do I say?*
("He might come on like a confidant, but don't tell him anything you wouldn't tell the Department of Consumer Affairs.")
"I'd like to heal, but mostly I'm helping people heal themselves."
How does one heal oneself?
("I sense this might be getting personal.")
"It's complicated. The first step is believing you can do it."
Like placebo?
"Oh, I hope it's more than that."
("It is. Much more—*moi*.")
*Hush.*
Seriously
Can you heal?

("Careful . . .")

"I don't make promises."

                    Can ugly be healed?

("Knew it!")

"Ugly is in the mind. They say beauty is only skin deep."

                    But ugly is to the bone

"Sometimes pretty people are ugly to the bone."

                        My skin is ugly

                        Can you heal it?

("Watch it . . . watch it!")

*I feel sorry for him.*

His loneliness, his need for companionship penetrated the door and enveloped her.

*What do you think?*

("Matters what's wrong with him.")

"Like I said, no promises."

                        Would you try?

"Of course. When?"

                                Someday

                                Maybe

"Why hesitate?"

                        You would see me

"But—"

Daley jumped at a horrendous crash of breaking glass from somewhere below.

("That sounded like the shop window!")

"I'm gonna—"

She was rising to her feet when Note Man knocked urgently from the other side and shoved a new note through.

                                STAY!

Quickly followed by another.

                        Stay where you are!

"I've gotta go see!"

                            NO-NO-NO!

                        Stay safe where you are!

"Safe?"

Danger!

More loud thumps and crashes followed.

"You know who it is? Is it Karma?"

The biker hadn't looked too happy when she turned him down.

No

worse

"Then who?" She opened her phone. "I'm calling the police."

Don't

won't get here in time

Another note.

You will be safe

if you stay here

*What do we do?*

("We do what the man says. He obviously knows more than we do.")

# 3

Good thing Dad was driving because Rhys was in no shape to get behind the wheel.

He couldn't remember the last time he got drunk. College, maybe? Not that he was sloppy now or anything, but all the tequila he'd slugged down had caught up to him.

After filling the Land Rover's tank, Dad had suggested they find a place where they could have "a late-night snack." More like early-morning snack, but whatever. Anything to put off returning to Nespodee Springs and seeing what the porthors had done to poor Daley's shop.

What was Dad trying to do—establish an alibi? They'd be on camera at the gas station and be remembered by the restaurant.

It being a Tuesday night—or rather, Wednesday morning—El Centro was closed up pretty tight, but they managed to find a Mexican bar-restaurant still open. The kitchen was closed but they had some guacamole available and threw together a plate of cheese nachos. While Dad ate, Rhys drank—margaritas at first, then he discarded all pretense and did shots of 1800 Silver.

He was drinking to blot out concern for Daley, but also to cushion tonight's revelation that the porthors were real, and all that entailed. His father put up with it until Rhys ordered shots for the house—which had dwindled to a half dozen Mexicans by then—at which time he was informed they were heading home.

On the ride back he was kind of hoping he'd pass out and wake up in the morning. But the trip wasn't long enough, especially with Dad driving like a maniac, like someone who couldn't wait to see what had gone down in town while he was away.

They passed the *Welcome to Nespodee Springs* sign, and as they hit the pavement, Rhys braced himself for the sight of the port-hors' handiwork. The Thirsty Cactus slipped past, and then the car slowed and he saw the smashed front window and the broken furniture and display cases and shelving tossed out on the board-walk. He expected his father to keep rolling but instead he jerked to a stop.

"What?" Dad cried. "*What?*"

Rhys was about to ask what his problem was when he saw the sign in the window of the shop next door to the destroyed place: *Healerina.*

It took a while for the reality to penetrate his tequila-fogged brain, but when it did, he started to laugh. He couldn't help it: He roared.

"Stop that!" his father shouted. "Damn you, it's not funny!"

"Yes, it is!" Rhys managed as he toned his laughter down to an insane-sounding giggle. "They hit the wrong store! Now *that's* funny!"

The tires chirped as his father hit the gas and the Rover leaped forward.

"How is this *possible*?" Dad said, fuming. "I painted the symbol on the right window. You saw me, didn't you?"

Rhys had controlled himself by now, though he still had to fight back giggles.

"Yep. Right under the *Healerina* sign. Saw it with my own two eyes."

"Then how could they have ignored the symbol and attacked the store next door? It makes no sense."

"No sense at all. Unless . . ."

"Unless what?"

"Unless you got your symbols mixed up and painted the wrong one on her window. I mean, you know, maybe you mistook the symbol that says 'Trash this store' for one that says, 'Ignore this place and trash the one next door.'"

He barely got the words out before dissolving into more laughter.

"This is serious," Dad said. "Something has gone terribly wrong here and you're acting like an idiot!"

Rhys reined in his laughter. "That's because I feel like an idiot for getting involved in this nasty scheme."

Dad didn't seem to hear. "This woman becomes more and more of a concern. First the porthors reveal themselves to her, then they spare her abode when they were supposed to attack it. What is it with this woman? What connection does she have to them?"

Despite his blood alcohol level, Rhys sensed something awry in his father's assessment. True, the porthors had ignored the symbol and spared Healerina, but what had made them trash the empty shop next door? Ignoring Healerina was one thing, but attacking the place next door was something else entirely. No reason for them to go there.

Unless . . .

"The only explanation I can come up with . . ."

He shut his mouth before he could say what was on his mind.

*I'm drunk. Gotta shut the hell up.*

"Well," his father said. "I'm waiting. And it better not be more idiocy."

"It's gone," Rhys said. "Straight out of my head."

"Drowned in the lake of tequila polluting your bloodstream, no doubt."

"No doubt."

Rhys was pretty sure he knew what had happened, but he couldn't tell Dad.

# 4

Rhys knocked softly on Cadoc's door.

His brother's scribbled words from last week had come back to him in the car while pondering the mystery of Healerina and the porthors.

*I roam . . . watch & see things . . . listen & hear things . . . I know things . . .*

But even more telling had been his comment when Rhys had admitted that he liked Daley.

*I like her too.*

So now he stood—maybe swayed was more like it—outside his brother's door and knocked again.

"Hey, bro. It's me. I know you're awake. Open the door. Got a question."

*"Ungh-ungh,"* from the other side. *No.*

"C'mon, bro. I don't want to shout it."

The door opened a crack with only darkness visible beyond. Cadoc's peeling-bark hand appeared with a note.

Drinking?

"A little. Listen . . ." He lowered his voice to a whisper. "I'm asking for a friend: Is it beyond the realm of possibility that someone might have rinsed off a symbol drawn in Nofio water on the front of a certain shop in town and then redrawn that symbol on the window next door?"

"Ungh-ungh."

A firm *no . . .*

Disappointment flooded Rhys. He'd been so sure . . .

Wait . . . slowly his impaired synapses concluded that a "no" meant *not* beyond the realm of possibility.

*Yes!* Knew it!

Rhys felt a burst of warmth for his brother. He had an urge to push the door open and hug him, but that wasn't gonna happen.

"I love you, man."

A note.

> But will you love me
>
> tomorrow?

Wasn't that a song?

"You mean, when I'm sober? Definitely. I tend to love everybody when I'm drunk, but you I'll love forever. Just don't expect me to tell you again."

> That's a relief

Rhys laughed and handed back the notes. "G'night, bro."

"Ungh."

The door shut and Rhys stumbled away, thinking, I've got the greatest goddamn brother on the whole fucking planet.

# 5

Daley didn't sleep well during the night, but she'd made a point of not going downstairs until daylight. And so she was shocked to find Healerina untouched when she stepped into the shop through the back door.

Pard, dressed in his signature boots, jeans, and plaid shirt—green and white today—was leading the way. He turned and gave her a baffled look.

("All that noise . . . I could have sworn . . .")

"Are we crazy? First, seeing those lizards. Now we're hearing things?"

Through the front window she spotted Jason Tadhak standing out on the boardwalk, hands on hips as he shook his head and stared at something. Stepping outside she immediately knew what had captured his attention.

"Oh, my God!" escaped her when she saw the shattered glass and broken shelving.

He whirled toward her. "Do you know anything about this?"

She fumbled for a story. "I . . . I woke up at, like, one A.M. or so and heard some strange thumping noises, but I never dreamed . . ."

All true, kind of. She certainly wasn't going to mention Note Man—for both their sakes.

"Who would do something like this?" he said. "I mean, what's the point? The unit was empty. If they wanted to get their jollies destroying things, why didn't they—?" He gave Daley an embarrassed look. "Sorry. I wasn't wishing it on you, just wondering."

"I'm right there with you," Daley said. "I'm glad they left my place alone, but I'm wondering *why*."

Just then a sheriff's unit rolled up and pulled into the curb.

"I put in a call as soon as I saw it," Jason said.

Daley didn't recognize the deputy who stepped out and approached. She wished it were Sam Alvarez but today was Araceli's appointment at Children's Hospital. Daley was dying to know how that would go.

Jason hurried over to speak to the deputy, then led him back to the shop and inside. Daley spotted Jake standing outside his café, staring across the street at the wreckage. She started in his direction.

*I don't know what happened here, but I'm gonna leave the detecting to the sheriff's department and have some breakfast. Sound good?*

("Perfect.")

## 6

Daley put in a call to Gram and learned that she had an appointment with Seamus's cardiologist next week. Daley would have preferred sooner but as a new patient, that was the earliest available. Well, at least she was going. Gram also informed her that she'd thrown out her cigarettes.

Yay!

Rhys Pendry showed up shortly after and didn't look so hot—bloodshot eyes and a pained expression, but also a strange, haunted look.

"You all right?" Daley asked.

"I was seriously overserved in El Centro last night. But I saw the damage next door on my way back into town this morning. What on earth happened?"

"Nobody seems to know."

"You didn't hear anything?"

Daley had given a statement to the deputy, carefully elaborating on the vague story she'd given Jason Tadhak. She repeated it for Rhys.

"You didn't look out the window?"

("He seems awfully interested,") Pard said from his window perch.

*Well, you heard that deputy: This simply doesn't happen in Nespodee Springs.*

"I didn't see anything," she said. True, but only because she'd been cautioned to stay right where she was.

Rhys looked oddly relieved. "Like I said, I saw the destruction— my father was driving us home—but by then the damage had been done."

She gave him a crooked smile. "How often do you go out drinking with your dad?"

He laughed, then winced and put a hand to his head. "That hurt. But the answer is never. Just sort of happened. You know how it is."

No, she didn't know. She'd never had a chance to meet her father, let alone have a drink with him.

"He had one beer," Rhys went on, "and I . . . well, I decided to have the tequilas he would have had, had he been drinking. And when can I take you out to dinner?"

Daley blinked. "Wow. I think I just got whiplash."

He smiled. "Just trying to slip it in there before you realized where I was going."

"Are we talking a liquid dinner or will solid food be involved?"

"Definitely solid food, and drinks too, of course, although I'd like to make it tomorrow night, if that's okay. I need a day of abstinence before I face another adult beverage."

*What do you think, partner?*

("This is totally up to you. I already told you—atop the tower, if you remember—that I like him.")

"Okay. Tomorrow night it is. When and where?"

("Not the Thirsty Cactus, I hope.")

"Not a lot to choose from in the valley, but I know a couple of nice places in El Centro."

"Sounds good."

("Do I see a time-out in my near future?")

*You do indeed.*

Rhys grinned. "Great. Why don't we—?"

"Is the Healerina here?" said a well-dressed woman from the doorway.

"That's you," Rhys said. "I'll leave you to your customers. We can iron out the details tomorrow."

He gave her elbow a gentle squeeze, then made his way out.

"The whole shop is Healerina," Daley said to the newcomer. "How can I help you?"

She marched up to Daley and held out her hand. "I'm Joyce Plummer and I need healing."

Fiftyish and all business, she wore a fashionable blue suit and the large pearls in her necklace looked real. Her dark hair was cut in a longish bob, and she had a firm handshake.

"Healed of what, may I ask?"

"That's what I want you to find out. I feel awful. Something's wrong, I just know it. I want you to work a spell on me or whatever it is you do, and make it go away."

Had to watch it here.

"Where did you get the idea I cast spells?"

Her hands fluttered. "Oh, some woman in my bridge club knows someone who came to you and was cured of something or other after you sold her a magic stone."

*Wow, it's like a giant game of telephone out there.*

("Soon they'll have you levitating.")

"Okay, let's get something straight: I don't cast spells and I have no magic stones to sell."

She look stricken. "You sold them all?"

"No!" That came out a little harsher than she'd intended. "There's no such thing as a magic stone. Good word of mouth is nice, but not if it's off base and sets up unrealistic expectations. Can you tell me where in particular you—?"

"Does it matter? Does it really matter? All that matters is whether you can help me or not." She pulled a tissue from a pocket and dabbed at her eyes. Her voice threatened to break as she said, "I'm desperate!"

"Have you seen a doctor?"

A derisive snort. "Are you kidding? I've seen a slew of them. They're all quacks and incompetents. But I've heard marvelous things about you."

*What do you think?*

("I'm not sure. I don't particularly care for her attitude. And 'I feel awful' doesn't give us a lot to go on.")

*Do we have to like them to help them?*

("No, of course not. It's just . . .")

*What?*

("I don't know. Just a feeling.")

*Well, put your feelings on hold and let's see what's going on here.*

Daley gave her another once-over. She looked like understated money.

"Let me take you to our imprinting room," Daley said.

"Imprinting?"

"It's where you get acquainted with your palm stone."

"Palm—?"

"Just follow my lead. It's easier to just go with the flow and let all this happen."

"But aren't you going to heal me?"

"Just go with the flow here, Joyce. I make no promises."

Daley picked out a quartz palm stone on the way to the rear

alcove, and seated Joyce at the little table. She placed the stone between Joyce's palms, then enclosed her hands in her own. Pard appeared behind her.

"Now what?" Joyce said.

"Be patient. The stone is imprinting on you."

"What does—?"

"Hush."

*Ready?*

("Almost.")

*Can you fix her personality while you're in there?*

("I wish. Okay, going in.") He vanished.

Daley and Joyce held their position. Joyce seemed fine with it at first, but after thirty seconds or so, she became restive.

"How long—?"

"Hush. Give it time."

As with Araceli, thirty seconds didn't sound long but it could *seem* long. Time ticked on and still no word from Pard. He'd never taken this long before, but then, they didn't have a big log of encounters like this to compare.

He popped into view behind her. ("All right. I'm out.")

*Finally. What did you find?*

("Nothing. At least nothing of any consequence. She's got a few gallstones and some mild emphysema—I'm guessing she was a smoker in the past—but otherwise she's in pretty good shape.")

*Then what's her problem? Psychological? She depressed?*

("Maybe.")

*You didn't check on that?*

("I can't read her thoughts, and I can't get into her psyche with such a small window. It took me almost two days to fully integrate with your nervous system. However . . .")

*What?*

("Her adrenals are a little overactive, as if she's anxious.")

*About what?*

("I can't tell.")

*So what do I tell her?*

("Tell her to see a shrink. I can't help her.")

Daley released Joyce's hands and leaned back.

"Done."

"And?"

"I'm afraid I can't help you, Joyce."

She looked horror-struck. "You mean I'm too sick? Am I terminal?"

"No, I mean you're too healthy."

"But I feel terrible!"

"I'm sorry about that."

Joyce reached out and gripped Daley's hands, squeezing them. "But I was looking forward to a close doctor-patient relationship with you."

("Wait-wait-wait! Where'd that come from?")

*No idea.*

("It's a total non sequitur, and very leading.")

*What do you mean?*

("I smell entrapment. I bet she's wearing a wire.")

A flare of angry heat flushed through Daley.

*What? The bitch! I'm gonna call her out!*

("No. Play it cool and clueless. But be careful.")

Careful? She'd taken in this woman on good faith, only to learn . . .

Daley took a deep breath to cool herself, then smiled.

*I know just what to say.*

"That's nice, Joyce, and I'm flattered, but you do realize, don't you, that I'm not a doctor, so we can't have any sort of doctor-patient relationship."

"Then why am I here?"

("Why indeed?")

"I'm afraid that's a question only you can answer."

"What should I do then?"

After an appropriately dramatic pause, Daley said, "You're not going to like to hear it, but I think you should see a psychiatrist or some sort of therapist."

Now an offended expression. "I'm not *crazy!*"

Daley shrugged. "Well, you said none of your doctors could find anything wrong. I don't think what's bothering you is physical, so that leaves . . ."

She jumped from her seat and shouted, "Fine! Just fine! What a waste of time this was!" She stormed out without another word.

*I feel like applauding.*

("I know. Great performance. But if my suspicions are correct, it's better not to let her know you're on to her.")

*Consumer Affairs, you think?*

("Who else would care? But she's going to have to give you a good report: You didn't charge her or offer treatment for a nonexistent illness.")

*Consumer Affairs again . . . I'm wondering who instigated this. I've got a bad feeling . . .*

("You're thinking your uncle Billy—")

*He's not my uncle.*

("Well, he's—")

*NOT my uncle!*

("Got it. You think he's behind this?")

*Possibly. He said he had a source in Consumer Affairs. I could see him putting a bug in someone's ear there. He told me he's working up some scam to run on the people with the horrors, so maybe he thinks Healerina might be a competitor.*

("As if those poor people don't already have enough troubles. But the victims are catatonic most of the time. And when they're not, they're screaming.")

*He won't go after them directly. He's probably looking for a way to fleece their families.*

("How?")

*You must have heard the conspiracy theories by now.*

("Sure. So many. But how does he cash in on a conspiracy theory?")

*Well, the most popular seems to be that the horrors are the result of a government experiment gone wrong, followed by the inevitable cover-up. So if I was running a scam, I'd whip up some concoction that was stolen from the government—the CDC, maybe—a cure that they're keeping under wraps and saving for White House and Pentagon bigwigs. But lucky me, through some complicated connections, I've managed to secure a small supply. I've got more than I need, so I can sell you some for your loved one. Just a little, because there's not a lot available, and when it runs out, that's it, baby. My source dried up and nobody outside the CDC knows how to make it. So once it's gone, it's gone.*

She waited for Pard's comments but he was silent.

*Well?*

("You just made that up? On the spot?")

*Well, yeah. I know it's got lots of rough edges but—*

("You're telling me that you haven't already been thinking about this for a while?")

*Not until we started talking about Billy Marks.*

("You simply pulled this out of the air as you went along?")

*Like I said, it's not perfect.*

("That's scary, Daley. Really, really scary. I mean, if you came up with that on the fly, what could you come up with if you took time to do some deep thinking on it?")

Yeah. She had to admit it *was* kind of scary. But this was the sort of thing she'd been exposed to, day in and day out, during her first thirteen years. She'd listen fascinated as the Family's grownups worked out their schemes. It became a mind-set: How do we cash in on this? The COVID-19 pandemic had arrived after she'd left them, but she had no doubt they'd tried to find a way to profit from it.

*One thing I learned listening to my dad's people is that scams work best when you make the mark a sort of coconspirator. You know: What we're doing is illegal, and we'll both go to jail if we're caught, so if you keep this on the down low, everything will work out.*

("So if the marks catch on, they'll hesitate to blow the whistle.")

*And by the time they do, we're in the wind.*

("Fascinating. Morally bankrupt, but fascinating just the same. Are you tempted at all?")

*Tempted how?*

("To try that scam?")

*Not a bit. Some places I just won't go. I've always limited my marks
to the class of folks who won't miss what they lose.*

Too bad she couldn't say the same about Billy Marks.

# 1

"I'm still baffled," Dad said.

Rhys sat in his father's office and watched him pace. The re-appearance of *The Duad Must Go* in the morning's analysis just moments ago had only exacerbated his already agitated state.

"I just don't understand what went wrong with the porthors," he added.

Rhys could help him out there—the answer was quite simple, really—but never in a million years would he betray Cadoc's trust. Not that Cadoc had admitted in so many words that he'd washed off his father's markings and transferred them to the shop next door, he'd simply denied that such a thing was beyond the realm of possibility.

"It's a mystery," Rhys said, "one we may never solve."

His father stopped his pacing and gave him a look. "You don't sound terribly concerned."

"I'm still trying to wrap my mind around the fact that porthors exist at all. Wondering about why they deviated from your instructions will have to wait."

No lie. The implications of their existence had worsened yesterday's hangover and haunted his dreams last night.

"Well, I suppose I can understand that."

"I don't supposed you can ask the porthors."

Dad shook his head. "No, they're barely sentient." He stepped to the window and stared south—toward the tower. "We installed that high-capacity substation and it goes online from the Tadhak trans-former today. The tower's already wired in."

"I guess that means another light show soon."

"Not for a while. We need some adjustments. And I want to find out more about this girl first." He jabbed a finger toward the town below. "She knows something."

"I wouldn't count on it. When I visited her yesterday, she seemed as baffled and as unsettled as everyone else in town."

"Putting on an act, I'm sure. She knows. Mark my words, that girl *knows*."

"Dad . . ."

"Listen to me, Rhys. The porthors appeared to her and then spared her shop. She knows something and tonight you're going to find out what. Where are you taking her?"

"El Toro."

"Good place. But before you do, bring her up here."

Where the hell had that come from?

"You're kidding, right? It's a little soon to meet my parents, don't you think?"

"No, just me. Make up something—say I'm concerned about what happened next to her shop. Say whatever's necessary, but get her up here. I want to meet this girl face-to-face."

"Not to get too PC or anything, Dad, but she's twenty-six and running her own business; you might want to get used to referring to her as a 'woman.'"

"When you're my age, any twenty-six-year-old is a kid. But point taken. I'll remember that when she arrives. And then I want to look into her eyes and see what's going on there."

They're very nice eyes, Rhys thought. A lovely shade of blue.

But he doubted his father would be interested so he didn't bother mentioning it.

# 2

Healerina was empty when Sam Alvarez walked in shortly after three. Daley noted the full uniform—Stetson, sunglasses, the works.

"Deputy!" she said. "I was hoping you'd stop by. How it'd go yesterday?"

"How did you know?" he said.

"Know what?"

He burst into tears.

"Oh, no!"

*It must be bad.*

Over by the window, Pard wore an alarmed expression. ("How can that be?")

The deputy was waving a hand at her as he pulled off his shades and wiped his eyes with his sleeve.

"I'm so sorry," Daley said.

*Shit-shit-shit!*

She eased toward him. She wasn't very good at comforting people, but she'd give it a try.

("There must be some mistake.")

"No-no! It's good news. The tumor's gone. No trace of it." Another sob escaped. "I'm sorry. I've been doing that since yesterday."

("Yes! We did it!")

"That's fantastic!" Daley cried as she felt her own eyes puddling up.

"But how did you know?" he said.

"I didn't. Just a feeling."

"More than that. You stood right there and said 'She's going to be all right.' I remember those exact words because you sounded so sure and it was just what I needed to hear at the time."

"I wanted it to be true as much as you, but I didn't *know.*"

He was nodding. "Yeah, you did. Somehow you did. You said, 'This little girl is going to bust the statistics' and you told me to remember that I 'heard it here.' It's all imprinted on my brain."

"Just being a cheerleader."

("Change the subject.")

*Already heading there.*

"So, what did the doctors say?"

"They said it's gone. The tumor was definitely there on the first MRI, but no trace of it on the repeat. And her headaches are gone . . . gone like they never were."

"I'm so glad. How did they explain it? A misread? An artifact?"

*How do I know that term?*

("You're welcome.")

"That's what they thought at first but they have views from all angles and it's always there on the first scan and never there on the second. A death sentence on Monday, a reprieve on Wednesday. They couldn't explain it. None of the doctors would say 'miracle' but a number of the nurses did." He fixed her with his gaze. "But it wasn't a miracle, was it."

("Uh-oh.")

"What do you mean?"

"It was you. You healed her."

She had to puncture this balloon immediately.

"Wait-wait-wait. You know that's not possible."

"It isn't?" He gestured around. "The place is called 'Healerina,' right? You did that thing with the stone—which she absolutely loves, by the way. Treats it like a pet. But you held her hands around that stone and then you told me she'd be fine. And now she is."

"If it's gone it's because she cured herself."

He was shaking his head now. "You knew she had a tumor so you practically shamed me into getting her head scanned. And you were right. Then you did your magic with that stone and made it go away. So from now on, whenever I run into someone with an incurable illness, I'm sending them to you."

("Stop him! He mustn't do that!")

"Oh, no, Sam. I'm begging you, please. Don't do that. It'll only raise false hopes and crushing disappointment when I can't deliver. And then there'll be anger and a whole lot of trouble for me. I'm just a cheerleader, really. A facilitator. If you want to help me, just let me go on the way I've been going, and doing what I've been doing."

He stared at her a long moment.

"Is that really what you want?"

"Absolutely."

"Okay. Then that's way it'll be. But know this: You have a friend for life." He pulled a card from his breast pocket. "Here's my card. I've written my personal number on the back. Anytime you need help with anything—*anything*—you call that number and I'll come running."

("I'm suddenly hearing a Carole King song.")

*Hush.*

"Thank you," Daley said.

"Now, I know it's unprofessional, but this is personal." He spread his arms. "Can we hug?"

"Of course."

He wrapped her in his arms and squeezed. It lasted a long time, until she said, "I can't breathe."

He backed off immediately. "Sorry."

He adjusted his Stetson, replaced the sunglasses, and started for the door.

"Just remember," he said. "Any time, for anything."

"Got it."

("Catastrophe averted,") Pard said as Sam exited. ("I warned you that your super-confidence might backfire on us, and it almost did.")

*Is this an "I told you so?"*

("As a matter of fact, yes.")

*Point taken, lesson learned.* She did a happy dance down the aisle. *But isn't it GREAT????*

("It is. It absolutely is.")

# 3

Daley closed up an hour early at four to give herself extra time to shower and dress. Araceli's cure had put her in an exuberant mood so she blasted Katy Perry—a favorite from her high school days—as she dried her hair and slipped on a navy-blue shift she'd brought back from LA. So she was ready and waiting when Rhys came a-knocking at six. They'd agreed via texts that he'd come to her back door.

"You look great!" he said when she opened the door.

When was the last time she'd heard a compliment? Not that she craved them, but still . . . nice to hear one that sounded sincere.

"You clean up pretty good yourself," she said. It seemed like the thing to say, even though he always looked scrubbed and neat.

He'd gone super-prep tonight, with a sports jacket over an Izod and Dockers. Not the usual taste of guys she tended to go out with, but it worked for him.

He led her down the back steps to his Highlander where he opened the passenger door for her.

"Wow. You're making me feel like such a lady."

"Well, that's what you are. At least from all appearances."

As he slipped behind the wheel he said, "I've got a favor to ask."

"Shoot."

"Would you mind coming up to the Lodge for a moment before we head out?"

"Isn't that where you live?"

"Correct."

"It's a little early to be meeting your parents, don't you think?"

He laughed. "Exactly what *I* said! But it's just my father—his idea. He asked me to stop by with you so he could say hello to the new entrepreneur in town."

"'Entrepreneur' . . . I never saw myself as that."

"Well, starting your own business is as entrepreneurial as can be, so that makes you . . ."

He gave her an anticipatory look, so she finished for him.

". . . an entrepreneur. It sounds so capitalist. Not that there's anything wrong with that, but it always conjures up visions of paunchy guys in suits."

"And you're anything but that." He raised his eyebrows. "Well? Do you mind?"

"Not a bit." She made a queenly wave. "To the Lodge, Jeeves."

"Yes, Miss Daisy."

They both laughed as the car started rolling, Rhys because he seemed to like his own joke, Daley to hide the twinge of anxiety at meeting the leader of the Pendry Clan. She was having trouble buying that it was merely to say hello to the new entrepreneur in town. But what other reason could it be?

As they passed Healerina, she saw the blue tarp Jason Tadhak had tacked over the broken front window next door. He'd told her a glazier was on his way tomorrow with a replacement.

When they arrived, the Lodge surprised her with its size. She'd glimpsed it from downhill in the town, but up close it *loomed*.

"Built in 1925 by my multi-great-grandfather Osian Pendry."

"Did Frank Lloyd Wright have anything to do with it?"

("Frank Lloyd Wright? Really?")

*Well, I might as well sound knowledgeable when I can.*

("You do sound like you know what you're talking about.")

*In a way I do—thanks to you. And aren't you supposed to be timed out?*

("You never gave me the word.")

*Consider it given—now.*

("Can it wait just a bit? I want to see this Lodge and meet the boss.")

*Okay, but as soon as we're back in the car, you go bye-bye.*

("Deal.")

Rhys was saying, "The designer was obviously influenced by him, but no. The place did fine until the 1940 earthquake that damaged a lot of the valley. Griffwydd Pendry rebuilt it to better earthquake standards and we've upgraded a couple of times since then, so it's pretty solid now."

"Osian . . . Griffwydd . . . are weird names a tradition in your family?"

He shrugged. "We're Welsh. We've got a thing for the letter Y. It can be a pain. Do you have any idea how many people see my name and pronounce it 'Rice'? Even in college?"

"I've never seen it spelled."

Pard chimed in with ("R-H-Y-S.")

Rhys had spelled his name and was saying how he would tell people it rhymed with Reese's Pieces. Then he was leading her inside.

"Someday I'll give you a tour, but right now I want to take you to my father's office, put the meet and greet behind us, and get on our way to the restaurant. I hope you like steak."

"Love me a good sirloin."

"Great."

He led her up a few steps to the first floor, and then down a long hallway.

"My family occupies the second floor," he said. "The first floor is devoted to the clan's business."

"You have a business?"

"Making money for the five families. My father's very good at it. That's how we can afford to build things like our Tesla tower."

Finally they reached a wide open room with a huge partner's desk and filing cabinets and multiple computer monitors. Panoramic windows overlooked the valley. Not as impressive as the view from the tower, but not without its own "wow" factor. A trim, distinguished looking man with long dark hair—gray at the temples and combed straight back—had his back to her as he poured from a decanter.

"Dad?" Rhys said. "I'd like you to meet—"

He turned toward her with a smile but that vanished into a drop-jawed, wide-eyed look of shock as the decanter slipped from his fingers and hit the carpet.

Luckily it didn't break and both Rhys and his father dropped to pick it up before too much spilled. The older man reached it first and rose with it in his hand.

"So sorry about that," he said, his smile back but looking forced.

Now that she had a chance, Daley saw a striking father-son resemblance.

"What happened?" Rhys said.

"Just clumsiness on my part." He was staring at her white patch as he extended his free hand. "Ms. Daley, so good to meet you."

She shook it. "Mister Pendry." She didn't bother getting into the "just Daley" bit.

"I was so shocked to hear about the damage to the unit next door to you the other night. Things like that simply don't happen here in our little town. I told Rhys that I wanted to meet you and tell you that if there's any way, any way at all my family can be of service, you have only to say the word."

"That's very kind of you, sir. But my shop was untouched."

"Yes, so I heard." His gaze became penetrating, almost as if he were trying to see into her brain. "Do you have any clue as to what the motive might have been? I mean, an empty storefront vandalized . . . it makes no sense."

"I agree," she said. "No sense at all."

("He's a strange one. What's his game, I wonder?")

*No idea, but he's def creepy.*

("Maybe he's just intense.")

*Yeah . . . intensely creepy. Did you see his expression when he saw me?*

("How could I miss it? Almost like he'd seen a ghost.")

"I don't mean to be rude," the father said, "and please understand I mean no offense, but your hair. . . . Is that a new fashion or has it always . . . ?"

"You mean the white patch?" Daley forced a little laugh. "That just happened for no known reason."

"When, may I ask?"

"Oh, let's see. Two weeks ago, I'd say. Almost to the day."

He kept staring. "Almost to the day . . ."

Stiff small talk followed along with some stroking about how brave she was to start a business all on her own out here in the desert. He seemed awfully interested in whether or not she had a silent partner.

After her third denial she gave Rhys a penetrating look of her own.

He cleared his throat and said, "Well, as pleasant as this is, Dad, we should get moving. I don't know about Daley, but I'm starving."

And that did the trick. After goodbyes and a quick handshake, they were on their way back to the Highlander.

"Sorry about that," Rhys said as he held the door for her.

("He should be. After the seen-a-ghost look, that was like an interrogation.")

*Not so bad.*

"No problem," she said. "But he seemed awfully interested in whether or not I had a business partner. What's up with that?"

Rhys looked away as he started the car. "He's a bit of a chauvinist. Maybe he thinks a woman can't do it on her own. Anyway. You've met the head of the Pendry Clan and your life is complete." He gave her a smile. "Now let's go get some steaks."

("I don't know if I'm buying all of this.")

*Well, you'll have plenty of quiet time to ponder it during your time-out. Buh-bye.*

("Right. See you when?")

*Give it till midnight.*

("Got it. Over and out.")

### 4

Mouth dry, Elis watched Rhys drive away with the Duad.

No doubt now. All gone, vanished.

He rushed to his computer and opened the password-protected encrypted files where he had been reading about the Duad.

Rhys had never mentioned her hair and every time Elis had seen her through the telescope she'd been wearing a cap. If he'd been prepared he could have controlled his reaction, but her appearance had taken him completely by surprise.

He found the scan he sought and stared in wonder at the ancient etching of a human figure—androgynous with no hint of its gender. In fact no distinguishing features at all except the white patch centered in the dark of its hair.

Nothing in the Scroll had indicated that this was the Duad—random-seeming illustrations, some crude, some highly detailed, were salted throughout the text. He hadn't associated this one with the Duad, but now there could be no doubt.

No doubt left as to what must be done with her.

The only question remaining was how to do it.

# 5

Turned out Thursday night was country-western night at El Toro, with a live band playing at just the right volume to make conversation difficult but not impossible.

"Sorry about this," Rhys said. "I didn't know. If you want we can find another place."

"No, I'm good. I heard a lot of country music growing up."

Gram was a bluegrass fan. Said it reminded her of the music back in the Auld Sod.

She felt like celebrating but didn't want to run up the bill with champagne, so she drank prosecco. The waiter couldn't take his eyes off her white patch as he took their orders. The house specialty was steak and Daley ordered a sirloin strip. She couldn't remember when she'd had one better—medium rare, exactly as she'd ordered, perfectly caramelized on both sides and seasoned to perfection. She didn't know how she knew about caramelizing— she knew how to microwave and little else—but figured Pard was somehow at the root of this arcane knowledge.

*Arcane?*

Rhys finished his rib eye ahead of her and sipped his margarita while watching her consume her last bites.

He half-shouted, "Nothing better than dining with a person who enjoys her food."

She put down her knife and fork and leaned back, waiting for Pard to crack wise about her frozen dinners. But it never came because he hadn't heard. She'd forgotten about his time-out.

She pointed at her empty plate. "Now *that* is what I call a good steak."

When the current song ended—something about a honky-tonk bar and a whisky bottle and a broken heart—the band announced they were taking a little break.

"About time," Rhys muttered. "Now we can talk without shouting."

But that was not to be. A woman with Dolly Parton blond hair, a sparkly blouse, tight jeans, and cowboy boots grabbed the mike and said it was line dance time.

Rhys groaned.

"We're gonna start off with 'Achy Breaky Heart,'" she announced. "Yeah, I know it's an oldie, but everyone knows that dance and it'll get y'all movin'."

"Not everyone," Daley said.

She'd never line danced in her life.

As if she'd been listening in, the blonde said, "And those poor souls out there that ain't learned it yet, y'all gather over here to my left and I'll show you the steps."

Rhys leaned across the table. "I think that's our cue to leave."

She didn't know where the urge came from, but she slapped the table and said, "No. That's our cue to learn to line dance."

His expression turned horrified. "No-no-no! I can't dance. I'm terrible!"

She rose, grabbed his hand, and tugged him toward the dance floor.

"And you think I can?" She loved music but dancing had never come naturally to her. She could get by in a crowd, but could never let go like other people. "This is all new to me too. We can be terrible together."

The opening notes of "Achy Breaky Heart" filled the room.

"You'll regret this," he said as she hauled him toward the group of line dance newbies. "You have no idea how bad I am."

Turned out he wasn't exaggerating. He proved to be a truly awful dancer—absolutely no sense of rhythm. She remembered Elaine's dancing on *Seinfeld*. Elaine was better.

But Daley had to give him credit for hanging in there with her—and for his good humor about it all. They wound up learning next to nothing about line dancing, but had a ton of laughs. She couldn't remember the last time she'd laughed this much.

The band had drifted back as the line dancing wound down. As soon as the last record ended, they broke into a slow tune about—of all things—whisky and a broken heart.

Rhys held out his arms. "Okay, Daley, this I can handle."

She hesitated a second, waiting for the comment by Pard that never came, then stepped into his arms. What the hell.

He held her right hand up, ballroom style, and shuffled her around—again with no sense of rhythm. He didn't hold her too tight, didn't press her boobs against him. A perfect gentleman.

Daley decided she liked Rhys Pendry. Liked him a lot.

The frantic up-tempo of the next song—"East Bound and Down," one of Gram's faves—sent Rhys scurrying for their table.

"I've never understood dancing," he said.

"No appeal?"

He shook his head. "Not a bit."

"You mean to tell me you've never heard a song with a groove that makes you want to move your feet, shake your body?"

"Of course I have. And if I could move my feet and shake my body in a way that didn't make me look like a complete spaz, I might have a different opinion. But as it is, I don't understand why people do it."

"It's a way of connecting," Daley said.

He looked at her. "And did we connect?"

She paused, then, "Yeah, I think we did."

"Great. Then maybe dancing isn't so bad. What do you want for dessert?"

# 6

Rhys probably could have driven back to Nespodee Springs just fine. El Centro's Thursday night traffic was light and, outside the city limits, the desert roads were virtually deserted. Even though they'd hung out at the El Toro bar after finishing dinner, he seemed pretty well coordinated and his blood alcohol level was probably within legal limits. But he'd had two for her one at the bar and didn't need a lot of convincing to let her take the wheel. Another point for him.

Once back in town, she pulled around to the rear of Healerina and stopped the car by the stairway.

"Want to come up?" she said.

"Sure. I think I can handle a nightcap."

"I don't have any tequila, only vodka."

"I've got tequila up at the Lodge."

"No, my place or no place, that way you have to do the walk of shame."

She waited the few heartbeats it took for that to sink in.

He cocked his head. "Wait . . . are you saying . . . ?"

"I'll understand if you're not in the mood."

"Not in the mood? Are you kidding me? You have no idea how much I'm in the mood."

She jumped out of the car and headed for the stairs.

"Race you!"

## 7

Elis clustered under the tower with the four other Elders. The headlights from his Land Rover, parked beyond the gate, provided the only illumination. He had the lower junction box open and was adjusting the rheostat.

The substation had gone online, giving the tower access to the extra voltage from the Tadhaks' wind farm. All he had to do now was to throw the switch to send the current to the Tesla coil below.

"I'm choosing a fifty-percent setting," he said.

"How do we know that isn't too much?" said Baughan, a shadowed figure among shadowed figures.

"We don't. We're in uncharted waters here."

"But what if it's too strong? We don't want to be premature. We'll ruin everything."

He had a point—a better one than he knew. The big day was

the twentieth—the equinox. He was keeping that from Rhys as well, letting his son think they had more time. Rhys was getting too close to the Duad and . . . well, who knew what he might let slip, or what she might make him do? Better to let them think the solstice was the target instead of the equinox . . . which came exactly two weeks from tomorrow.

"Should I dial it back to twenty-five? I'm open to consensus here."

After much muttering and murmuring, Baughan said, "Leave it at fifty and pray it's not too much."

"Done," Elis said, and threw the switch.

One hundred and twenty feet below, the Tesla coil started to spark, its flashes filling the shaft.

# 8

"Doctor Heuser! Something's happening here!"

Becky Heuser had just turned off the light in her second-floor office in Caltech's South Mudd Building when Mark Hendry stuck his head out of a doorway down the hall and shouted.

"Can you be a little more specific?" she called back. She was tired and wanted to get some much-needed sack time.

"The sensors down in the desert are picking up some weird signal."

Her lethargy vanished as she rushed down the hall and followed the grad student into the data analysis center. It measured not much more than an extra-large dorm room, the walls lined with computer stations. Large black letters high on the longest wall informed you—on the outside chance you didn't know—that this was part of the Southern California Seismic Network. Below them hung two giant monitors. The one on the left displayed seismic maps of Southern California, the western US, and the world. The right screen showed multiple feeds—up to twenty at a time—from seismic sensors scattered around the southern end of the state. A neurologist had once said it reminded him of an EEG—a brain-wave tracing. Usually the feeds showed a steady, staticky pattern, but now some were tracing a strange sine wave configuration.

"How long has that been going on?" Becky said.

She and Hendry were the only members of the seismology lab still in the building.

"Just started. Have you ever seen anything like it?"

Becky nodded. "Exactly a week ago. Just before the February twenty-six quake."

"You think we've got another coming?"

"I don't know. Our sample size is one. How do you make predictions from that?"

"Do we send out an alert?"

Damn. Her gut wanted to, but she couldn't. The ShakeAlert Early Warning System had been set up to give people a heads-up that their world was about to start shaking. Lots of folks had downloaded the MyShake app so the alert came straight to their phones. It allowed a variable number of seconds—depending on how far you were from the epicenter—to get under a table or inside a door frame, or out of the building altogether.

But ShakeAlert was dependent on the fast-moving P-waves that precede the much more damaging S-waves. Sending out an alert without seeing P-waves could be the equivalent of crying wolf. If ShakeAlert was to be effective, people had to trust it.

"We have to wait," she said, hoping she wouldn't regret it. "Watch those sensors for a P-wave. The instant one appears, we'll send an alert."

He stared at her. "You sound like you expect one."

Becky kept her eyes fixed on the screen. "I do."

# 9

It was over soon, but not too soon. Rhys's enthusiastic foreplay saw to that.

"Nice," Daley said, pulling the sheet up over her as they lay side by side on the bed.

"Super nice."

"I came twice. That makes it double nice."

"You win then. Only once for me, but it was a doozy. I swear the lights dimmed."

"I thought they did too."

"Well, I guess I'm better than I thought." Rhys rolled onto his side and kissed her cheek. "I tell you, I did not expect to end up here."

"Not on a first date, right? You could say I'm easy."

"No, I wouldn't say that, and don't you say it."

"Well, with the right guy I am. After dinner tonight, I knew we'd eventually end up here, if not next week, then the week after."

"How do you know there would have been a next week or a week after?"

"Because you're crazy about me."

He laughed. "Is it that obvious?"

"Yeah. Pretty much. So I figured I could play games and put you off, or we could get down and get to it."

"When did you decide?"

"When I saw what a terrible dancer you are but you kept trying."

"That sold you?"

"Yeah, sorta. You hated it. You could have sat down and left me out there on my own. I mean, nobody has a partner in line dancing anyway. But you hung in there with me. You were already on my good side, but that was the clincher."

"That's all it took?"

"It's the little things. Guys don't realize that."

He slid his arm across her and hugged her closer. "I could get so used to this."

"Don't," she said.

"What, hug you?"

"No, get too used to this."

She sensed his body stiffen. "Why not?"

"Nothing lasts."

"Some things do."

"Okay, let me revise that: Nothing *good* lasts."

"I didn't realize you were such a pessimist."

"Realist."

"What's real is I like you, Daley. Really, really like you. Like you said: crazy about you."

She wouldn't say she was crazy about him. Not yet, anyway. She definitely liked him, but he wasn't going to get all clingy, was he?

"I like you too."

There. She said it.

"I've never met anyone like you."

"You must be very sheltered."

He laughed and sat up. "Oh, I definitely am. My family . . . the clan . . . they make up most of my social contacts, and we Pendrys make Mormons look wild and crazy."

Light filtered in from the front room and she noticed a discolored area of skin behind his right shoulder. She'd felt it when she'd had her arms around him . . . rough.

"Do you mind me asking? What's that on your shoulder?"

"Hmmm? Oh, that's what we call 'the Pendry Patch.' Everyone in the clan has one."

"Really? Everyone?"

"Yep. Different sizes, different places, but as they say, 'You're not a Pendry if you don't have the Patch.'"

Daley suddenly felt a strange tingling sensation. Some tingling could be pleasant, like the anticipation of sex, but this was nothing like that. This came with an edginess that made her uncomfortable.

She slid out of bed and found her panties.

"What's wrong?" Rhys said as she began slipping back into them. "Is it the Patch?"

"No-no. Not that at all. I don't know what it is, but I've got this strange feeling, inside and out. You don't feel weird at all?"

"I feel great. I'd feel even better if you were back in here beside me."

She didn't bother with her bra, just grabbed one of the XXXL T-shirts she slept in and slipped it over her head.

She didn't know what to say to him. Was this some sort of anxiety attack? She'd felt something like this last week before the quake. Maybe getting next to Rhys and letting him hold her was what she needed. But as she stepped toward the bed, the room jolted with a loud *boom!*

Her first thought was a *bomb*, or a truck crashing into the building, but then the floor started shaking. No, not just the floor, the room—the whole building.

"Quake!" she cried. "Another quake!"

Rhys was out of bed, pulling on his Dockers. He grabbed his shirt, then grabbed her hand and started pulling her toward the door.

"We've got to get out of here! The whole place could come down!"

He had that right. The floor was shaking as a deep basso rumble vibrated through the beams and the studs and the wall and floor planking, much worse than last week.

He pushed her ahead of him. "Go! I'm right behind you!"

She yanked open the back door and pelted down the steps in her bare feet, then ran to where she'd parked his car and put it between her and the building. Rhys joined her.

"Made it!" he said, pulling on his shirt. "Safe!"

Yeah, they were. No trees, no other buildings close enough to endanger them by collapsing.

"Unless a fault opens up directly beneath us," she said.

He laughed. "Always looking on the bright side, aren't you?"

"That's me. And don't think I don't appreciate how you made sure I got out the door first."

He shrugged. "My 'toxic masculinity.'"

Damn, she liked this guy. Had to watch that. Nothing lasts.

The ground was still shaking, rolling like ocean swells. In fact she had to lean on the car to keep from swaying back and forth.

"When's it gonna stop?" she said.

"This is a bad one."

("What is going on? Another quake? I can't leave you alone even for a few hours, can I?")

*Oh, you're back.*

("Well, it's midnight.")

*I missed you terribly.*

("Sarcasm noted. Judging from your dishabille and young Pendry's presence, I'm assuming you found a way to alleviate the despondency you suffered due to my absence.")

*Not easy, but I managed. You didn't feel the quake?*

("I cut off all sensory inputs, remember. I gather I missed out on some rather pleasurable input pre-quake?")

*Very, but really not your business. Extend your time-out, please.*

("Really? I hate to miss the quake.")

*I'm sure there'll be plenty of aftershocks.*

("Very well. See you in an hour.")

Finally it stopped rolling and they leaned back against the SUV.

"Big one," Rhys said. "And close. Too bad it didn't come a few minutes earlier so I could have claimed I made the earth move for you."

Daley threw her head back and laughed. Damn, she liked him.

# 1

("That quake really made a mess,") Pard said as he wandered ahead of her through the jumbled shop, hands on hips, surveying the damage.

Shelves had shaken off the walls, a display case had tipped over, but worst of all, the front window had shattered, littering both the inside floor and the boardwalk with sharp shards of glass. The aftershocks hadn't helped.

("I'm sorry I missed it.")

"Remember that strange tingling I had before the quake last week?"

("*Exactly* one week ago.")

"That's right. Last Thursday. This isn't going to be a weekly thing, is it?"

("Let's hope not. But I sense you're going to tell me you had the same feeling before this one?")

"The same tingling, only much worse."

("And this quake was worse. There's a correlation there, but that doesn't necessarily mean a cause-effect relationship.")

"Bigger tingle, bigger quake. I'm surprised the whole building didn't come down."

("This place has been here a long time. Probably seen a load of quakes.")

It looked like whoever had vandalized the empty store next door had come back to do the same to Daley's shop. She'd found a broom in a closet upstairs but . . .

"I don't know where to begin."

Movement at the window—or rather, the open space where the

window had been—caught her eye. Someone in bib-front denim overalls stood there.

"Juana!"

"I thought I heard you talking to someone," she said, peering around inside.

"To myself."

"Figured you'd need help."

Daley wanted to hug her. "Absolutely, but how's your place?"

"Thought it was going to tip over, but it survived upright."

"Great. But I've got only one broom."

"That's all right. I brought my own. Let me unstrap them from the hog."

("Did you see the relieved expression on her face? She was worried about you.")

*At least somebody is.*

("What about Lover Boy?")

*Up at the Lodge, working with his daddy, I suppose.*

After hanging out by the car and weathering a few aftershocks as midnight passed, Rhys had resettled her in her apartment before heading home.

("I thought you liked him.")

*I do, but he's under daddy's thumb, I'm afraid.*

("Well, his 'daddy' is one focused and forceful individual. And we, my dear, are in his crosshairs.")

Daley didn't like the sound of that.

*What do you mean?*

("Those pointed questions, verging on a third-degree interrogation, about whether or not you had a silent partner in this place.")

*He couldn't possibly know . . . could he?*

("I don't see how, but didn't our mysterious visitor say, 'I hear you talking at night'? Could he be in contact with the Pendrys? Even spying for them?")

*Could be, but not likely. I mean, if that's true, why tell us he listens? And it ignores the basic question of why anyone would care. Either I've got a partner or I don't, but what difference does it make? Why would it matter?*

("Beats me. But the fact is you *do* have a silent partner—me.")

Juana reappeared then with a push broom and a dustbin. Pard disappeared and the two of them got down to business.

# 2

Rhys found himself whistling as he walked from his bedroom to the dining room and cut it off. Wouldn't do to appear too content, now, would it? After all, he'd been out on a serious mission for the clan last night.

Yeah, last night.

Was the air a little fresher, the sky a little brighter? Probably not, but it sure seemed that way.

"I'm not surprised you're late," his father said as he arrived at the breakfast table. "You were out till well past midnight. With that earthquake and all, I was worried till I got your text."

Rhys pictured him waiting up, watching by the window.

"Well, Dad, one must always be ready to make sacrifices for the clan, right? A little less sleep is a small price to pay where the clan is concerned."

If last night was a sacrifice, he'd volunteer for similar duty every time. He still couldn't believe they'd ended up in bed. Daley was more casual about sex than any of the Pendry women—more casual than Rhys, to tell the truth—but she did seem genuinely attracted to him. And Rhys . . . well, he hadn't stopped thinking about her.

But since he couldn't let on about that, he added, "We got caught out in the quake." He knocked on the dining room wall. "The Lodge seems to have come through fine."

"With all we've spent on making it earthquake proof, it damn well better." He started buttering a piece of toast. "Did you learn anything?"

"We spent hours together, Dad, and frankly, I don't think there's anything *to* learn."

"Is that so?"

"I can't see that she's hiding anything. In fact, I don't think she has a deceptive bone in her body."

"The stars say otherwise."

Here we go . . .

"You met her. What was your impression?"

Dad chewed his toast and seemed to be considering his reply. Rhys knew he'd made an instant assessment last night.

Finally he swallowed and said, "She strikes me as something of a gamine."

"Okay, you've got me there. 'Gamine'?"

"A streetwise girl—or 'woman,' if you insist."

*Streetwise* . . . yeah, he could buy that. Daley had definitely seen a lot more in her life than Rhys. Pretty shrewd assessment on his father's part.

"Well, she's certainly no Pollyanna."

Unless, of course, Pollyanna had been very enthusiastic in bed.

"You wouldn't be falling for her, would you?"

"Falling? Not a chance."

*Falling,* as in the process of? Nope. That's over and done. I've totally *fallen.*

"Don't lose all judgment just because the Duad takes you to her bed."

Rhys had been reaching for the French press. His hand froze in midair.

"*What?*"

"I believe I spoke clearly."

"Why would you say that?"

Rhys poured coffee to hide his shock.

"I think it's a pretty fair assumption, considering how the two of you were observed in a partially undressed state behind her shop during the quake."

A protest leaped to his lips, but he realized the futility of denying it.

"I don't believe this! You were *spying* on us?"

"Don't be silly. I don't need spies to know what's going on in town. 'The night has a thousand eyes,' as the saying goes. People saw you two. And when they see something like that, they talk about it. And when they talk about a Pendry, it gets back to me."

Well, Rhys hadn't seen anyone about. But then, with Daley dressed only in panties and an oversize T, he'd had eyes only for her.

His father added, "You have a fiancée, you know."

"As you keep reminding while sending me out in pursuit of Daley."

"Rhys—"

"We've had this discussion too many times, Dad. I've got work to do."

Taking his cup along with the French press, he headed for his office.

## 3

Jason Tadhak looked harried and hassled when he showed up shortly after what would have been opening time.

"It's weird," he said, shaking his head. "All the windows on this side of the street are smashed, but just across the street, only cracked. Not that it matters as far as repairs go: They've all got to be replaced."

"I'm so sorry," Daley said, especially since she was here rent-free.

He gave her a strained smile. "That's why we have insurance."

"It seemed a lot stronger than the last," Juana said.

"Definitely a higher Richter. The last was three-point-six. The news says this was a five-point-five. Calexico and Mexicali were hardest hit. Still not as bad as the El Centro quake back in 1940. That was six-point-nine and damn near wrecked the town. You should have seen what a mess that was."

Daley laughed and he gave her a questioning look.

"Oh, not that it's funny, just that you sound like you were there."

"What?" Now he looked flustered. "Oh, no. I wasn't even born then. My father told me all about it. He took pictures. It caused a thirty-five-mile surface rupture, fifteen feet across in places."

"Now *that's* scary," Daley said.

"Damn right. Imagine having that open up under your house. I hear this new one opened up a twenty-mile crack that crosses the border, up to ten feet wide."

"That's two in a week," Juana said, "and the second stronger than the first. I hope this isn't building toward something."

"Don't we all." To Daley: "I'll send a fellow around with some blue tarp to cover the window space."

Daley had been thinking about that. "That'll make the place look closed. The town doesn't seem very buggy . . ."

"Hardly any," Juana said. "The lizards eat most of them."

Jason grinned. "The little lizards do. I don't know what the giant lizards eat."

Daley rubbed the corner of an eye with her middle finger, and he laughed.

"You can't leave the shop wide open." He backed toward the door. "Well, got to check on the rest of the tenants."

"How's Arturo, by the way?" Juana said.

"Just getting up and running when I looked in."

He waved and was on his way.

Daley looked at Juana. "I'm heading to Arturo's. You up for some coffee? My treat."

She smiled. "Well, in that case, get me a large, two sugars, lots of cream."

"You got it."

As she crossed the street, Daley noticed a lot of pedestrians about—people from the spa, no doubt, and Pendry clanners she recognized by the women's Mennonite-style dress.

("Out to survey the damage, no doubt,") Pard said.

*Some people love destruction.*

("Disaster porn.")

*At least we haven't heard of any deaths in town.*

A mild aftershock rolled down the street, triggering a surprised "Eeek!" or two and nervous laughter.

Arturo's front window was only cracked—a big crack but at least it was holding together—just like Jason had said. Inside she was hailed by all the breakfast regulars—after all, she'd become one. She didn't know why, but she took inordinate pleasure in the friendly greetings. It felt good to be known, but even better to be accepted so quickly as part of the town. She'd never dreamed it would happen, but Nespodee Springs was becoming *her* town.

While waiting for the two coffees to go, she heard a high-pitched scream from out on the street. She stepped out to see a teenage clan girl, mid-teens by the look of her, lying on the boardwalk one door down, clutching her chest. Another girl crouched beside her, screaming.

"Wynny can't breathe! Somebody help her!"

Daley ran up and dropped to her knees on the other side.

"What happened?"

"I don't know!" the other girl wailed. "She just dropped!"

Wynny was cloud white, writhing, pressing a hand against her right ribs. Daley grabbed her free hand at the wrist to make skin contact.

*Pard, can you check her out?*

("Do my best.")

Daley leaned over the girl. "Wynny, is it? Wynny, what's wrong?"

"Hurts," she said through a gasping breath. "Can't breathe!"

"Don't touch her!" cried her friend. "Get your hands off her now!"

Her vehemence shocked Daley. "What's your problem, kid?"

She screamed, *"Don't you touch her!"*

Arturo pounded up behind Daley. "Shut up, you little shit! She's only trying to help. Get Doc Llewelyn. Go on, goddamn it! Git!"

She glared at Daley and Arturo, then ran off.

"Damn weird-ass clanners," Arturo muttered. "Can't stand them."

("Going in.")

Wynny sobbed. "Hurts when I breathe . . ."

"Try to breathe slower," Daley told her. "Slow breaths . . . slowwww . . ."

She did manage to slow her breathing but Daley could tell by her expression she was still in pain.

What was taking Pard so long?

("Okay, I did what I could.")

*At last. What's up?*

("She has a pulmonary embolism.")

*Which is?*

("A clot in the lung—her right lung in this case. Came from her left leg. She's got phlebitis there.")

*Can you help her?*

("I activated a load of plasmin to start dissolving the clot, but it's a slow process. She should notice a little improvement soon.")

Doc Llewelyn, string tie and all, hurried up. "Where's it hurt, Wynny?"

She showed him.

"Pulmonary embolism?" Daley said, looking up at him with a questioning expression. She didn't want to seem too sure.

His gaze stayed fixed on the girl. "One of your legs been sore and swollen lately?"

She pointed to her left calf.

Llewelyn nodded and said, "Yep. PE. I'll get my car."

*What happened to examining the patient—you know, listening to her chest and all that?*

("I'm sure he's seen a few in his day.")

"Shouldn't we call an ambulance?" Daley said.

"By the time they get here, I'll already have her in the ER."

Wynny sobbed. "I don't wanna go!"

"I can't take care of this here, child."

He hurried off and returned a couple of minutes later behind the wheel of a big black Tahoe.

"I feel better," she said as Arturo and Daley helped stretch her out on the backseat. She took a deep breath. "See?"

("Plasmin effect kicking in.")

*Yay you.*

The doc shook his head. "You might throw another clot any minute. I'll phone your folks on the way."

After Daley snapped a seat belt around her waist, Llewelyn roared off in a cloud of dust. She watched for a moment, then turned to the other girl, who glared then spun on her heel and stomped off.

She hadn't expected profuse thanks, but maybe a bit of gratitude for trying to help.

*Did I forget my deodorant this morning?*

("Something else going on. She was half hysterical that you touched her friend.")

Daley remembered the local kids fleeing from the shop door whenever she said hello.

*I think you're right, but I've no clue as to why.*

"Come on," Arturo said, moving away toward the café. "I'll finish making your coffees."

# 4

Rhys stopped in shortly after the drama on the street. He looked good in khakis and a light-blue button-down dress shirt with the sleeves rolled up to his elbows.

"Wow," he said, looking around. "I had no idea."

"Well, we were out back."

"Got an extra broom? I'll give you a hand."

"You can have mine," Juana said. "I've got to get over to the reservation."

Daley thanked her for coming by and soon she was roaring away on her Harley.

As Rhys started sweeping, he said, "I can't stop thinking about last night."

"It was nice, wasn't it?"

And it was, but there had to be something else they could talk about.

"It was extraordinary. I would have brought you flowers but, as I'm sure you've realized by now, Nespodee Springs doesn't have a florist."

She put on a disappointed expression. "Well, Brawley does. What's the matter with Brawley? I mean, if you really cared . . ."

He looked stricken. "I do, I really—oh, wait."

Unable to hold it back, she started to laugh.

He joined her. "You rat! You had me going there."

"You should have seen your face."

"My mind was racing, thinking if I push it I can be in Brawley in twenty minutes, find a florist, maybe buy some chocolates too, and be back within the hour."

"Sorry. Couldn't resist."

He stepped closer. "You owe me a hug for that."

She opened her arms. "I probably do. But only a quick one. I'm not into PDAs." As they embraced, she said, "Poor boy, you're going to have to get used to me."

("He's not the only one.")

*Hush.*

("Is this where you drag him upstairs to bed?")

*Too much work to do down here.*

"I'd *love* to get used to you," Rhys said. "*Very* used to you."

"Okay." She broke the clinch. "That's a good hug."

He backed up a step but kept his hands on her upper arms, saying, "This isn't going to discourage you, is it?"

"What—a hug?"

"No, the wreckage. I mean, you're not going to get disgusted and close the place and pack it in, are you?"

"No way. You don't get rid of me that easy."

("Easily")

*Grrrrr!*

("Sorry.")

An odd look she couldn't decipher flitted across his face and was gone.

"The last thing I want is to get rid of you. I want you around a long time."

"Well, then, let's get sweeping."

Between the two of them they filled a garbage can with shards of glass and got Healerina—the interior as well as the boardwalk outside—cleaned up and into fairly presentable shape. That done, they had burgers at Arturo's which Daley paid for over Rhys's protests. After that, he had to get back to the Lodge.

## 5

Doc Llewelyn stopped by in the afternoon.

"That was a pretty good snap diagnosis on Wynny."

("Thank him for me.")

"Thank you."

"You had any medical training besides an online degree in homeopathy?"

Ad lib time: "No, but my mother had an embolism once."

"She okay?"

"Died of cancer."

He nodded. "Clotting can get screwed up in cancer."

"Oh, no. You don't think Wynny—"

"No-no. The clan women are prone to them. Probably the inbreeding. But she's going to be fine. Her parents are there and she's going to stay the night while she's started on anticoagulants." He turned to go. "Just wanted to let you know."

"Thanks. I appreciate that. Can I ask you a question?"

"Depends on the subject. Shoot."

"When I took hold of Wynny's wrist, her friend—"

"Catrin."

"Okay, Catrin. She got all upset, practically hysterical, screaming 'Don't touch her!' What's up with that?"

He looked embarrassed. After a brief hesitation he said, "The
clan children have been told to stay away from you. Don't buy from
you, don't even talk to you."

"Oh."

("I can feel your hurt.")

*I'm not hurt. I don't get hurt. It's just that . . . well, I feel like I have
a disease or something.*

She said, "Is it because of all the New Age stuff here?"

He shrugged. "I couldn't say, but that's the most likely reason."

"Don't you know?"

"The clan Elders have access to esoteric knowledge that guides
their opinions. Shortly after you arrived they put out the word that
you were to be avoided by the children. They don't explain their
decisions, just hand them down."

"I met Elis Pendry last night. Isn't he . . . ?"

A nod. "The head Elder. You can bet he's behind it."

"He didn't seem hostile."

("Well, he wasn't exactly warm and fuzzy.")

"I'm sure it's not personal. The clan has its own unique religion
and it's not the least bit New Agey. We're very self-contained up
there in the hills and they don't want the kids exposed to outside
influences."

*I've been called a lot of things but never "an outside influence."*

("Maybe you should scrap "Healerina" and rename the shop
"Outside Influence."")

*Maybe I will.*

"Can you tell me about this religion?"

He shook his head. "Nope. We keep that to ourselves too. Good
day to you."

*I bet Rhys will tell me.*

("I think he'll tell you *anything*.")

# 6

Rhys had texted that he'd be tied up with clan business until late, but he wanted to get together with her tomorrow. She wasn't happy, though, with the way he'd closed the text:

> Just a heads up. Its out that
> we were together last night
> and I mean =together=. After the
> quake we were seen outside
> together in the not-so-
> put-together. If you know what
> Im saying.

Well, damn. She'd wanted to ask him face-to-face about his father's problem with her.

Some other time. Tonight would be a TV night with Pard. She wasn't feeling very sociable anyway.

After a microwaved dinner—a spicy chicken and black bean bowl—she settled on the couch and caught up on the news. Nothing good going on out there, especially the word that the horrors was a spreading Southern California epidemic and nobody had a clue yet how to treat it.

Putting that comforting news on hold, she entered her Netflix ID and password and started searching the films. Pard popped into view, seated in the easy chair.

("Not a rom-com, I hope.")

"What's wrong with that?"

("You have to be one of the least romantic women in the world. Why do you like romantic comedies?")

"They always costar a good-looking guy."

("Well, if that's your major criterion, let's find something with a handsome male lead for you and a little *oomph* for me.")

"'Oomph'?"

("Something beyond boy meets girl, boy loses girl, boy gets girl back. May I suggest *A Knight's Tale*?")

"That sounds familiar."

("You've seen it. Stars Heath Ledger.")

Now she remembered.

"He was gorgeous."

("He still is—in the film, that is.")

He suddenly morphed into a chubby guy in a wrinkled corduroy jacket.

"Who's that supposed to be?"

("A deceased film critic named Roger Ebert.") His voice changed as he raised his thumb in the air. ("I give *A Knight's Tale* a thumbs-up and three out of four stars!")

"You had me at Heath Ledger." She grabbed the remote. "Let me see if I can find it."

A knock on the back door aborted her Netflix search before it started.

"Really?" she said, rising, annoyed at the interruption. "Really?"

("That knock sounds familiar,") Pard said as she headed through the kitchen.

*You think it might be—?*

Then she saw the slip of paper under the door.

*Note Man is back!*

("Knew it!")

*Let's see what he wants.*

She dropped to a cross-legged position by the door and picked up the note.

                    Care to chat?

"Sure. What's up?"

                    You came through
                    The quake okay?

"Me, okay. Healerina not so well."

                    meet Elis Pendry then quake
                    Rough night

She laughed. "Yeah, he's what you might call 'intense.' Does that mean you've met him?"

At least he didn't mention her hooking up with Rhys, although she had a sneaking suspicion that might just be good manners on his part. She doubted much went on in this town without Note Man knowing.

> Everyone here
> knows E.P.

A thought struck.

"Hey, wait. How did you know I was up at the Lodge?"

> I watch

Oh, yeah . . . he def knew about her and Rhys.

"Like I told you before, that's creepy."

> I know
>
> But have nothing else

She went from feeling creeped out to feeling sorry for him. Like before, his loneliness and isolation seeped through the door.

"Too bad. We were just going to watch a movie."

> We?

("You slipped!")

*I know!*

"I meant *I* was just going to watch a movie."

> You're not alone?

"I'm never alone. I'm always with myself. You know: me, myself, and I?"

("Careful there.")

"If you want you can come in and join me."

("Are you *crazy*?")

*I need to throw him off. He'll think I'm just being friendly.*

("You?")

*Ha. Ha. And deflecting. Don't worry. He won't accept.*

> That won't
> Work for me

*Told ya!*

"I promise I won't look."

She waited for his response. And waited.

"You still there?"

Thinking

("That means he's considering it!")

Daley was thinking that wasn't necessarily bad, but it could be. Finally a note slipped through.

You need to

See a film

"Well, that's been the plan for tonight."

Specific film

Okay. What's the title?"

Private film

("Uh-oh.")

*Yeah.*

"We're not talking a porno, are we?"

Ha! No.

Home movie

"Whose home?"

The clan

"Are you in the clan?"

Regrettably yes

("This could be interesting.")

"All right. I'm game. When?"

Tonight?

"Are you telling me you have it with you?"

Must see it at Lodge

Only plays on player there

"You must be a Pendry if you're inviting me up to the Lodge."

Sneak in

("Oh, I don't like this, Daley. Don't like it at all.")

*I'm with you there.*

"I don't think that's such a good idea."

Will change your life

"I'll ask Rhys about it next time I see him."

No!

Must not tell

You know!

("That's odd.")

*No kidding.*

"Don't tell him I know about the film? Why not?"

Hasn't seen it

"You're telling me the son of the head of the clan hasn't seen a family film?"

Only 1st half

Too young. Must wait.

"Till when?"

Age 30

"But you've seen it all?"

I sneak & hide

*He's offering to let me see a family film Rhys hasn't seen? How weird is that?*

("Too dangerous, Daley. You could get caught.")

*What are they going to do? Shoot me?*

("Call the cops.")

*Remember what Sam Alvarez said: I've got a friend. Aren't you the least bit curious?*

("I'm damn near dying of curiosity.")

*Then let's do it.*

("No!")

*Fraidy-cat.*

"Okay," she said, "how do we work this?"

("No-no-no!")

At 2am go to lodge

Same door as yesterday

"Two in the morning? Seriously?"

("Much too late, Daley. Your beauty sleep!")

I will be near.

If you don't show, OK

"I'll be there."

("You'll be so ugly tomorrow.")

C.U. then.

Notes please

She bundled them up but had so many this time she had to split the pile to fit them back under the door.

("I wish to formally register my absolute total disapproval of this idiot, harebrained scheme.")

*Noted.*

("Now what?")

*I'm going to take a nap. Beauty sleep, you know . . .*

# 1

Daley did manage to catch a few hours' sleep. Her phone alarm woke her at one thirty and she was out the door fifteen minutes later wearing her baseball cap to hide the white patch. She didn't think driving would allow a stealthy approach so she walked. The starlight and rising moon proved sufficient to light her way along the deserted street and up the hillside road.

("Since it's obvious I can't dissuade you, I'm simply going to go along with this risky business.")

*Well, thank God! Does this mean the harassment will stop?*

("I was not harassing you. Merely attempting to persuade.")

*Yammer-yammer-yammer. Take a breath, will you?*

("I don't breathe—I don't need air to speak. But I'm stopping now. I'm simply going to shut up and pay attention.")

*Hallelujah!*

She found her way to the parking area and from there to the side door where she'd entered with Rhys. An overhang shielded it from the sky, casting it into deep shadow. She checked her phone and found she was right on time.

(What now?")

*We wait, I guess.*

("How long?")

*How should I know? Don't start, okay? I—*

"Ungh."

She jumped at the sound. Someone was in the deep shadow with her. A gloved hand thrust a typed sheet of paper at her. Another gloved hand held a penlight and trained it on the paper.

*Note Man.*

("I guess you're supposed to read.")

*Somewhere around 1990, Dylan Pendry, father to Elis and grandfather to Rhys, commissioned the making of a short educational film—not at all difficult to arrange in Southern California. It was originally on one reel and shown only to the Elders. A few years after his father died in 2001, Elis had the film digitized and divided into two parts which he then transferred to two specially coded DVDs that could be played only on the player in the Lodge. He then destroyed the film. Everyone in the clan has seen disk one. Only the Elders have seen disk two. I'm going to show you both tonight. I will mute the sound but the film has subtitles.*

*Turn your phone off—that's all the way OFF—then follow me and don't make a sound.*

"Got it," she said.

A soft "shhh" came out of the darkness.

A hand took the sheet from her. A dark figure in a hoodie waited until she'd turned off her phone, then the door swung open and he led the way in. No lights were on inside so he kept flashing the penlight behind him to show her the way. Just like last time, she went up a three-step flight to the lower floor and then around a corner and down a vaguely familiar hallway, except this time all was cloaked in darkness.

The farther into the Lodge she moved, the less she wanted to be here.

Instead of continuing straight ahead as she and Rhys had done before to arrive at the glassed-in room overlooking the town and the Imperial Valley, they turned right.

*Maybe this was a mistake.*

("What did I tell you?")

*I don't need to hear "I told you so" right now.*

("Well, nothing's keeping us from turning around.")

But now they'd arrived at a small, windowless, equally dark

room. A flash of the penlight revealed a half dozen chairs all faced toward a monitor on the far wall.

Note Man tapped on one of the chairs and, guessing that meant *sit*, Daley hesitated, then sat. The door clicked shut behind her.

("We're staying?")

*Well, we're here. It looks like it might be an AV room. We've come this far. Might as well see it through.*

And so she sat and waited.

# 2

Elis Pendry awoke with Hefina snoring softly beside him and the odd feeling that something was wrong in the Lodge. He couldn't put his finger on it but something somewhere in the building felt definitely *off.*

The display on the digital clock read *2:13.* He knew Cadoc wandered in and out of the building nightly at all hours and was used to that. No, this was something different.

He slipped out from under the sheet and padded to the closet where he kept the pistol—a small .32 semiautomatic. He'd never had to point it at a human being and didn't want tonight to change that. But he believed in being prepared for the worst.

Closing the door behind him, he flicked on the hall light and padded toward Rhys's room. A quick peek through the crack he opened revealed his younger son sound asleep. Farther on and across the hall he found Cadoc's room empty. No surprise there. Cad had been a nocturnal creature most of his adult life.

He made quick work of the rest of the second floor and found it deserted—as it should be.

Yet still the feeling persisted.

Leaving all the lights on, he headed down to the first floor which appeared completely dark, a good sign that Cadoc had left the Lodge and was wandering around outside. Where he went and what he did remained a mystery to Elis. Oh, he'd asked many

times, but never got a straight answer. *Out & about . . . Here &
there . . .* were about as specific as the notes ever got. Cadoc's in-
ability to communicate except through scribbling made a fluid
conversation impossible, and he quickly tired of writing them.

But Elis couldn't hold it against him—couldn't hold anything
against Cadoc. His skin was a horrible accident, something that
had never happened before and he prayed would never happen
again to any child of the clan. Elis couldn't help feeling responsible, though. His affliction had warped Cadoc into a compulsive
recluse, obsessed with keeping anyone from seeing his skin. Elis,
in a very real sense, had brought that on.

He lit up the central hall and trotted down the short flight to
the side entrance, the one everybody used. As expected, the Lodge
alarm was unarmed—Cadoc's doing. He habitually disarmed it
when he went out and left it off till his return. He'd permanently
disabled the CCTV camera over the door—his fear of being
photographed. Elis had had it replaced twice but Cadoc had
sabotaged it each time. He'd considered replacing it yet again but
why bother? He'd only disable it.

He reset the alarm. When Cadoc returned, it would beep to
let him know it was armed; he had the code to turn it off. But
resetting it now meant no one without the code could enter or exit
without setting off a howler.

Elis returned to the business floor and checked all the individual offices. Nothing wrong there. He headed toward his own
office but remembered the AV room off to the right. He frowned
as he approached the door. They usually left it open because it was
such an airless little space, but no one had made it a rule. He'd give
it a look before heading for his own office.

## 3

Daley heard a few metallic clicks behind her and then the screen lit
with an illuminated square that faded into a map of Southern California. Subtitles started crawling along the bottom of the screen.

WELCOME TO THE SALTON TROUGH WHICH INCLUDES
THE COACHELLA AND IMPERIAL VALLEYS OF SOUTHERN
CALIFORNIA, PLUS THE WESTERN HALF OF THE MEXICALI
VALLEY AND THE COLORADO RIVER DELTA IN MEXICO.

The map changed, still Southern California but not the Southern California she knew. Baja looked much, much longer. Or did the Gulf of California reach farther north?

BUT MILLIONS OF YEARS AGO IT WAS ALL UNDERWATER, AN
INLAND SEA THAT CONNECTED TO THE PACIFIC OCEAN. WHAT
WE NOW CALL THE GULF OF CALIFORNIA BETWEEN BAJA AND
MEXICO REACHED ALL THE WAY UP TO THE SAN GORGONIO
PASS.

The view descended toward the inland sea. As it neared the surface Daley noticed large creatures floating on the water and gliding beneath. Dinosaurs? Possibly, but their images were blurred.

THE VISITORS LIKED THE SEA AND SPENT MILLIONS OF YEARS
THERE.

Visitors?
*Pard, do you have any idea what they're talking about?*
("Not a clue.")
She looked around. *I should ask—*
("Maintain silence—*please!*")
*Okay, okay.*
And now some sort of hole in space had opened over the water and the blurry forms began to flow through.

BUT THE VISITORS WERE CALLED AWAY.

*Is this crazy or what? I thought those were dinosaurs but instead they're . . .*

("Aliens from . . . what? Another star? Another dimension?")

*I didn't know we'd be watching a sci-fi film.*

("I think it's the clan's religion, Daley. Remember how Doc Llewelyn told you yesterday afternoon that 'the clan has its own unique religion.'")

*And this is it? They believe in visitors from another dimension? I think somebody's been watching* Ancient Astronauts *too much.*

("It's hardly unprecedented. The core beliefs of Scientology and Dormentalism are basically space opera.")

She couldn't believe Rhys bought into this.

The screen changed again to show a river running from the east and emptying into the water.

AFTER THE VISITORS' DEPARTURE, THE SEA CHANGED. THE
COLORADO RIVER WAS LARGER THEN AND EMPTIED INTO
THE INLAND SEA.

An animation now showed silt being deposited in the sea, building up, gradually narrowing the gap until the northern half was divided from the Gulf of California.

EVENTUALLY SILT FROM THE COLORADO RIVER DELTA
COLLECTED TO FORM A NATURAL DIKE AT WHAT IS NOW THE
MEXICALI AREA BETWEEN THE WATERS OF THE GULF OF
CALIFORNIA AND WHAT WE CALL THE SALTON TROUGH.

More animation showed the landlocked body of water shrinking to the size of the current Salton Sea.

MILLIONS OF YEARS PASS DURING WHICH THE WATER IN
THE TROUGH DRIES UP, THEN GOES THROUGH CYCLES OF
FLOODING AND DRYING UNTIL IT SETTLES INTO ITS CURRENT
CONFIGURATION WITH THE SALTON SEA AS THE ONLY BODY
OF WATER.

And now a live aerial shot of the Imperial Valley with its green checkerboard of farmland.

THOUSANDS UPON THOUSANDS OF PEOPLE LIVE IN THE TROUGH. THE VISITORS ARE FORGOTTEN BY ALL BUT A FAITHFUL FEW. BUT THE VISITORS CAN RETURN WHEN CONDITIONS ARE RIGHT . . . WHEN CELESTIAL BODIES ALIGN AND—

The screen abruptly went dark along with the room and she felt a hand franticly tapping her shoulder, its urgency unmistakable. She started to ask what was wrong but a gloved finger pressed against her lips. Note Man pulled her to her feet and guided her to a corner on the same wall as the door.

That was when she noticed light along the door's edges. Someone was out there and they'd turned on the lights. Most likely that was what had alerted him.

Again the finger pressed against her lips and she nodded to signal she'd got the message: *Keep quiet.*

("Something's gone wrong.")

*Ya think?*

A hand pressed down against the top of her head and she figured that meant to drop into a crouch, so she did. Note Man lifted a chair and set it in front of her, then disappeared into shadows on the far side of the room.

("We're staying here then?")

*Do you see another choice? We can't run, so we hide.*

The door clicked then and Daley froze and held her breath. Light from the hall poured into the room as the door swung inward.

*If he turns on the light . . .*

She couldn't see the intruder, but whoever it was didn't enter the room—just took a quick look, then retreated. But left the door open and the hall light on.

("Looks like we're going to be stuck here awhile.")

*At least we're still undercover, as it were.*

("I'm glad you don't wear perfume.")

*Why not?*

("Well, while he was hovering at the door—we'll assume it was the head of the household, Elis Pendry—it occurred to me that in this small room, any hint of perfume would be instantly noticeable.")

*That's why I don't wear it.*

("Please, Daley, think who you're talking to?")

*What?*

("I know you almost as well as you know yourself—maybe better. You don't wear perfume because it never occurs to you.")

*Yeah, well, that too.*

Still in a crouch, they waited . . . and waited.

After what seemed like a very long time . . .

*Damn! It's been—what—half an hour now?*

("Exactly nine minutes.")

*No way.*

("I can use your internal rhythms as a clock.")

*This is getting to me. If I don't get out of here soon—*

The hall light went out.

("Won't be long now.")

More waiting, and then Daley jumped as a hand touched her arm and tugged her upward. As she rose, Note Man wrapped gloved fingers around her wrist and led her out into the hallway. He left her standing alone while he entered Elis Pendry's office. Starlight and moonlight filtered through the big windows, silhouetting his hoodied figure as he hurried about inside.

("Does he seem agitated to you?")

*Well, yeah, and why not? We almost got caught. Probably be worse for him than us.*

("You seem to think you have a 'Get Out of Jail Free' card from Deputy Alvarez. I wouldn't count too heavily on that.")

*Can't hurt.*

Note Man returned within a minute and ushered her back the way they had come. They paused at the door while he disarmed an alarm, and seconds later they stepped out into the night. They paused briefly in the shadowed doorway where she took a deep, grateful breath of fresh air.

The finger pressed against her lips once more then gently steered her out into the starlight.

*I'm guessing this means "Go home."*

("So it would appear.")

So she hurried down the hill.

("Who is Note Man, do you think?") Pard said.

*No idea, but he sure knows his way around that Lodge.*

("Well, he did say he belongs to the clan, so maybe that explains it.")

*You think clan members are given the Lodge's security code?*

("Maybe. Or maybe for a guy who spends his nights 'watching' and 'listening,' maybe he's found them out.")

*Whatever. He knows the code. But what I want to know is what's on disk two.*

("So do I. But let's face it: Can it be any more bizarre than disk one? Visitors from Out There treating Earth like a vacation resort and crawling in and out cosmic wormholes to get here?")

*I don't see how, but according to Note Man, one is the disk they let everybody see. What's on two that they're hiding from everyone but the Elders—even Rhys?*

("At least until he's thirty.")

*Yeah, what's up with that? He's a grown man. What can possibly be on disk two?*

("You have to wait till Note Man shows up and ask him—*if* he shows up again.")

*He damn well better. This is making me wish right now I hadn't seen disk one, because I can't stop thinking about what's on two. Should never have gone up there. And don't say it.*

("Told you.")

# 4

Elis felt logy the next morning, mainly because he hadn't slept right. After satisfying himself that all was well in the Lodge, he'd returned to bed. But even though the feeling that something was amiss faded away, he couldn't find restful sleep. He remembered hearing Cadoc come in around three—usually he never heard him—and after that he alternated between fitful slumber and wide awake.

Rhys looked perfectly chipper at breakfast. Why not? He'd been sleeping like the proverbial baby when Elis had looked in on him.

Saturday was Maria's day off, so breakfast was do-it-yourself this morning. She'd left some sweet rolls that required only a quick trip through the microwave to make them as good as fresh.

"You're up early for a Saturday," Elis said, tearing one of the steaming rolls apart.

Usually Rhys slept in on weekends. Hefina slept late every morning, and Cadoc never ate with the family. So usually Elis had the breakfast table to himself on Saturdays and Sundays. Nice to have company for a change.

Rhys shrugged. "I was awake, so why not?"

As they ate in silence, Elis still mulled over what had happened last night. The uneasiness had faded and never returned, but he couldn't escape the feeling that he had missed something.

"So," he said, "you actually have some extra time this morning?"

Rhys eyed him over his coffee cup, his expression wary. "Am I going to regret saying yes?"

"A favor, if you will: Run the configurations for me."

His eyebrows rose. "Now? On a Saturday?"

"Finish your breakfast, of course. But before you involve yourself in whatever you're going to get involved in today, run the star configurations for me."

"Any reason I can know about?"

"I'm not sure I even know it myself. Last night I felt some something . . . for want of a better word, I sensed something *off* in the Lodge. I have no idea what it was, or even *if* it was. But I just want to see if something's changed in the heavens."

"Um . . . sure. I'll get right on it."

Rhys's eyes didn't literally roll, but Elis sensed the virtual roll. He'd learn the truth soon enough, learn that his father wasn't crazy, and that the Visitors were real. Not long now . . . If everything Elis was working so hard to arrange came together as planned, come the equinox the whole world would know about the Visitors.

When Rhys headed downstairs, taking coffee and a couple of rolls with him, Elis stayed behind. He didn't want to hover over him, so he waited at the breakfast table until . . .

His phone vibrated: Rhys.

*"Dad, maybe you better come down here."*

Okay, he's found something. And it sounds like something he doesn't like.

With a mixture of dread and anticipation, Elis headed down to the first floor. He found Rhys at his workstation, staring at the screen. And there, centered on the display . . .

### THE DUAD MUST CEASE

Rhys didn't look up as he spoke. "All last week it said 'must go'—every freaking day. Now it says 'must cease.' What does that even mean? And what happened to make it change?" Now he looked up, his expression stricken. "Did you know about this?"

"I had no idea."

"Yet you wanted me to analyze the configurations on a Saturday. You have to know something."

"I wish I did. I told you about that odd feeling I had during the night, that something was wrong. By this morning I began to have my doubts as to whether or not it was real, so I wanted to see if anything was reflected in the analysis. It appears it *was* real."

Rhys tapped the screen. "I don't like this 'must cease' bit. It sounds, well, sinister, a sense of finality to it. I don't want anything to happen to Daley, Dad."

"Nothing's going to happen to anyone."

"Oh, really? A few days ago you saw 'must go' on the screen and sicced the porthors on her."

"Not on her—her *store*. There's a big difference. The last thing I want is to see someone hurt. That's not what the Pendrys are about, and you know it."

The screen went dark as Rhys powered down his workstation.

As he rose, he said, "That's what I've always thought, and I'm trusting you'll stick to that."

"I think I'm insulted that you feel you need to say that."

He watched Rhys leave, then turned back to the dark monitor where he still saw *THE DUAD MUST CEASE* on its screen.

Elis had known since the instant he saw the girl's hair that she was the Duad and had to be eliminated. Now the stars were confirming that. No surprise. But what about last night? Something happened here, something he wasn't supposed to know about. But what? Had there been a trespasser?

If only Cadoc hadn't disabled the CCTV camera, Elis might have a clue about—

Wait . . .

Elis wanted to kick himself. A year and a half ago he'd attached a motion-triggered, wireless Minicam, little bigger than a button, with a fish-eye lens, to the base of the dead CCTV camera. It recorded all the comings and goings from the Lodge and none of the dead space between. For a while he'd monitored it from the app on his iPhone, but had soon wearied of checking it. When he upgraded the phone, he never bothered replacing the app, and essentially forgot about the camera.

Until now.

He'd left his phone upstairs on the breakfast table. He hurried to retrieve it.

# 5

Daley almost overslept the shop's opening time. That damn film had kept replaying in her head all night. But she managed to grab a quick shower, run across the street for a coffee, and reach the front door in time to unlock it at exactly 10:00 A.M.

("I don't know why you were in such a hurry,") Pard said. ("Not as if we've got a crowd of people lined up waiting to get in.")

*A matter of principle. The sign I put out front says "Open at 10 A.M.," so that means I open at ten A.M.*

("I'm proud of you.")

*Really? Why?*

("Well, you usually take a rather laissez-faire attitude toward schedules.")

*Only between games when my time is my own. I feel, I don't know, responsible for this place. And if I don't do it, it won't get done.*

The glazier hadn't been by yet, probably because the entire Imperial Valley was a mess of broken glass, and so the blue tarp still stood in for the front window. Since Daley couldn't watch the street through the glass, she opened the front door and leaned in the doorway.

*I hope nobody gets the wrong idea.*

("Like what?")

*I'm thinking I look like an Amsterdam hooker.*

("What do you know of Amsterdam hookers?")

*I've seen pictures.*

Daley watched the street. Pretty good foot traffic out there. She imagined with the coming of spring that more tourists would be making their way south to soak in one of the various springs at this end of the desert: Borrego, Jacumba, and of course Nespodee.

A fair number of locals were trailing in and out of the food market, along with members of the various families of the Pendry Clan. Everybody had to eat, and it didn't look like the Pendrys had any dietary restrictions. At least she'd seen no evidence of any in the way Rhys had scarfed down pretty much everything in sight at dinner the other night.

Off and on, when she wasn't thinking about that film and what might be on disk two, she thought about Rhys, wondering what he was up to. She had no doubt she'd see him again. But after last night's text about their relationship becoming an item, they needed to be discreet.

A few tourists wandered in and out of Healerina without buying anything. Around midday two native women pulled up in a pickup and brought in a number of dream catchers. Pard moved off to his spot where the window used to be.

"Juana sent us," the older of the pair said.

"Where's Juana?"

"She couldn't make it today," said the younger. "But she wanted us to check to see if you needed to restock any dream catchers."

Daley gestured to where they were arrayed on the wall. "Not now. Business has been slow. Is Juana okay?"

The younger said, "She has duties at the reservation this morning."

"Oh, good. I thought her mother might have taken a turn for the worse."

They both stared at her with puzzled expressions.

"Mother?" said the older.

"Yeah. The one in the hospital with the horrors."

Now they looked at each other.

The older said, "We're Juana's sisters. Our mother died years ago."

"No, wait. She told me—"

Both were shaking their heads.

"Our mother is long gone."

("Well, now, isn't that interesting,") Pard said.

*Isn't it, though?*

After they'd driven off, she resumed her spot at the shop door. Pard moved up beside her.

("So . . . all those times you ran into her in the hospital, she wasn't there for her mother, she was there for you.")

*Sure seems that way. But why?*

("Her duty to 'help and guide you,' I assume.")

*She didn't have to lie.*

("I'm sure she didn't want you to think she was stalking you.")

*When all the time she was doing just that.*

("I'm wondering . . . the 'guide you' part . . . didn't she encourage you to leave LA?")

*Yeah. That night she dropped me at Gram's place.*

("Right. Get out of LA, away from the 'loudmouth crazies' . . . find an out-of-the-way small town where you can work discreetly.")

*She made a good case for getting some experience under my belt before a small audience.*

("But it's not like she gave you a list of possible venues. She brought you straight here.")

*But you're the one who fell in love with the place.*

("Guilty as charged. I felt an immediate homey vibe.")

*Got to admit it's been growing on me.*

("Only the Pendrys have been less than welcoming.")

*An interesting way to say "hostile."*

("But not all of them, need I remind you?")

She smiled. *No need.*

("Everyone else in town has been very open, and it's been a good place for us. We've had two definite cures and possibly saved that girl Wynny's life. And yet . . .")

*And yet what?*

("And yet I still can't escape the feeling that Juana steered us here for reasons that go beyond 'help and guide,' that she wants us here for a very specific reason.")

*What possible . . . Oh, you don't mean that film, do you?*

("I don't know how she could know about the Pendry film, but then, I get the feeling Juana knows an awful lot of things she doesn't share.")

*Amen.*

Daley didn't like the idea of being part of anyone's agenda, even less so when she had no clue as to what that agenda might be.

She jumped at the sound of a hoarse, terrified scream. One of the tourists, a middle-aged man, was staggering across the street, arms waving wildly before him like a blind man. He dropped to his knees and screamed again. His scream was joined by a high-pitched cry as a woman—his wife?—ran to him.

Pard said, ("Let's go see,") but Daley was already moving.

She reached him right after his wife, who was screaming, "Timothy! Oh, God, Timothy, what's wrong?"

He screamed again and fell over onto his side. As he began to curl into a ball, Daley grabbed his hand.

*Can you check him out?*

("We've never witnessed a case but it looks like the horrors. I'll take a peek. Keep a grip on him.")

"Does he have any medical conditions?" Daley asked the wife, more to distract her and give Pard time to break through than to learn anything useful.

The woman shook her head, panic in her eyes. "No. Healthy as can be! Is this—oh, God, don't tell me this is the horrors!"

Other people were gathering around as Timothy curled into a progressively tighter and tighter ball.

Pard said . . . ("Contact! Taking a look.") . . . and disappeared.

A big, hyper-muscled, buzz-cut guy pushed through the onlookers, growling, "Back off, people! Give him air!" He dropped to one knee by Timothy's head and pointed to the wife. "Who're you?"

"I'm his wife."

Then to Daley, "And you with the weird hair?"

Daley bit back a *Fuck you!* and said, "Just trying to help."

"You got medical training?"

"No, I just—"

"Okay, then, back off. I'm taking charge here."

Daley didn't want to release Timothy's hand until Pard had had enough time.

"Who the hell are you?"

"Certified EMT, and I got this." He jabbed his index finger at her nose. "Now back off."

Daley backed off and had to break her grip.

"What's his name?" the guy said to the wife.

"Timothy—Timothy Blaine."

As the EMT started shouting Timothy's name, Pard re-appeared.

("Damn, I needed more time. Just a wee bit full of himself, isn't he.")

*Just a bit. What'd you find?*

("This fellow's mind is filled—as in *crammed*—with the most horrific images. But to him they're not images, they're real. He feels as if he's just been swallowed into a pit of hell and can't see any way out.")

*The horrors.*

("Right, the horrors. It's finally reached Nespodee Springs.")

She shivered. *It seems so random.*

("It does. But not to worry. I'm pretty sure I can shield you from it should it strike.")

*Good to know. But can you do anything for Timothy?*

("I didn't have time to find out, but I may not be able to help.")

*Why not?*

("Those images . . . they're not from him. He's not generating them. They're coming from outside.")

*Outside? What's that mean?*

("Either he's tapped into something horrible, or something horrible has tapped into him.")

## 6

It took Elis half the morning to access the Minicam. He'd hardwired it to the CCTV power supply upon installation, so he was sure it was still operating. But the camera app hadn't transferred to his new phone, so he'd had to hunt it down online and install it anew. Then he had to find the right access code. Smartphones and apps were not his forte, but he finally managed to access the video memory.

So now he sat in his upstairs study and explored that memory.

The Minicam's SD card could store an hour's worth of video, then it began overwriting. But since it recorded only when triggered by motion, it stored only a snippet at a time. He had to scroll through all the snippets to find whatever it recorded early this morning. If nothing else, it would have caught Cadoc's comings and goings. Fortunately they were all date-and time-stamped, and he quickly zeroed in on the most recent, slowing as he approached March 6.

All right, here was last night, the night vision clearly showed Cadoc leaving at 10:02 and returning at 11:37.

Odd . . . he hadn't been around when Elis had wandered the house after two A.M.

The date shifted to Saturday, March 7, and showed Cadoc leaving again at 1:31 A.M. this morning.

Okay, that explained his absence.

He returned less than twenty minutes later and backed into the shadows of the doorway alcove, but the infrared showed him quite clearly. He didn't enter, simply stood there. Why?

At exactly two A.M. a young woman appeared. Elis's gut coiled as he recognized her: the Duad, the Pairing, the interloper who called herself "Daley."

What was she . . . ?

Cadoc handed her a sheet of paper and held a light for her. Elis wished he could magnify the image to reveal what was written, but that lay well beyond the app's abilities. After she'd read it, he took it back and led her inside.

Cadoc . . . what . . . why? What possible reason could he have for giving her entry to the clan sanctum? Had she somehow seduced him like she was seducing his brother? What sort of siren was she? What did she want here?

It struck him then that the two of them had been in the Lodge when Elis made his search. Where had they been hiding? He'd searched everywhere.

The AV room . . . he remembered the door had been closed. But he'd looked in and . . .

No, he'd just glanced in. He'd had such low expectations of finding anything he'd trusted the light from the hall instead of turning on the room lights. They could have been in there, but why? Were they having a movie night? Or—

He jolted upright in the chair.

Oh, no! Oh-no-no-no-no-no!

He dashed downstairs to his office and flew to the safe. He punched in the combination and yanked open the door. Relief flooded him upon seeing the disks where he'd left them, then drained away when he realized they weren't *how* he'd left them.

He always left disk one on the right—he was right-handed and since disk one was used far more frequently than two, he always shoved it back on the right. But it sat on the left now.

And on the floor before the safe . . . familiar gray flakes.

Elis felt sick. His own son . . . Cadoc had betrayed him . . . betrayed not just his father, but the entire clan.

How had this happened? Like everyone else in the clan, Cadoc had seen the first half of the film, but never the second. That was shown only to Elders or to firstborns who'd reached thirty and were in line to be elevated to Elder status. Due to his compulsive reclusiveness, Cadoc had recused himself from consideration as an Elder, so that had put Rhys on track.

So how had Cadoc even known about the second half? Its existence had always been kept a secret; otherwise all the families would be clamoring to see it. And that would never do. The hoi polloi of the clan had to be protected from its contents.

Because they would not be able to keep their mouths shut. Some might even consider it their duty to expose the plan. And that would tear it. A leak would prove catastrophic. Worse, it would bring the population of the entire Imperial Valley storming through Nespodee Springs and into the hills to drag all the Pend-rys from their homes and rip them to pieces.

But Cadoc . . . somehow Cadoc had learned of the second half. More than *learned* of it, he had *seen* it.

What other explanation could there be? Cadoc was a phantom, a wraith, a spirit in the night, wandering the darkened halls at all hours. His nightly rambles had undoubtedly revealed a way to eavesdrop on the Elder gatherings, to peep on the AV room during the regular viewings of the second disk. Undoubtedly he'd found a way to spy on his father's office and memorize the sequence of combination buttons that opened the safe.

All bad enough, but all forgivable.

This, however . . .

What could possibly have possessed him to align himself with the Duad against his own clan?

And the worst part, Elis thought, is that I've been warned time and time again over the past few weeks, but was too lackadaisical to act. I let Rhys's protestations that the Healerina woman was not the Duad persuade me and put me off, turn me hesitant. The warnings in the configuration analyses kept growing progressively stronger and yet still I dithered.

And then this morning: *The Duad must cease.*

That had come after the Duad's invasion. The analysis had issued a virtual gut punch: *Do something decisive or forever suffer the consequences.*

The Duad had seen the entire film. She knew the plan. No question about what had to happen. But first Elis had to lay the groundwork, set the stage.

And then she must . . . *cease.*

# 7

Elis knocked on Cadoc's door and then entered his quarters with-out waiting for a response. He found his son, a shadow within the shadows, seated at a table in the center of the room. As usual, the room-darkener shades were pulled. The daylight seeping around them provided the only illumination.

"Ungh?"

"You betrayed me, Cadoc. Not just me, your entire clan—your *blood*, Cadoc."

"Ungh?"

"Let's not play games, son." He held up his phone. "You were recorded early this morning letting that woman, that charlatan, that threat to everything we believe and hold dear, into the base of our operations."

"Ungh-ungh!"

"Don't deny it! I don't know what hold she has on you or what spell she cast over you, but it's not bad enough that you allowed her in our sanctum, *you showed her the film*!"

"Ungh-ungh!"

Elis stepped forward, jabbing a finger at the silhouette of Cadoc's head, where his face should be. "*You* haven't earned the right to see the second half, and yet you show it to an outsider?"

"Ungh-ungh!"

Elis felt on the verge of tears but forced them back.

"I'm so disappointed in you, so disgusted with you, so *ashamed* of you, I-I-I'm almost at a loss for words. This is the worst sort of betrayal. If I didn't have a meeting in San Diego on a matter crucial to the future of the clan that demands immediate attention, I would gather the Elders and bring you before them tonight. As it is, I am forbidding you from further contact with that woman. You are confined to your quarters until I return tomorrow."

With that he stepped back into the hallway and slammed the door.

Both levels of the Lodge had been modernized and updated when they had to rebuild it in 1940, and it had undergone a number of renovations since then, but the locks on the doors had remained unchanged—the original lever tumbler locks from the old days. Elis had searched out the ornate original key to Cadoc's room, and used it now. He prayed the antique lock was still functional. He nodded with satisfaction as his turn of the key was rewarded by the sound of the bolt clanking into the strike plate.

Cadoc began pounding on the other side.

"I meant what I said, son. We'll deal with you when I get back."

Cadoc had an en suite bathroom. He usually stocked in fruit and snacks on Friday so he'd have something to eat until Maria returned on Sunday morning. And even if he didn't, he'd survive.

Now . . . to find Kendrick.

## 8

"Whatta y'want done, Mister Pendry?" Kendrick said as he slipped into the passenger seat of Elis's Land Rover.

Wishing to avoid all connection with Jeff "Karma" Kendrick beyond being his employer, Elis had driven into Brawley and bought a couple of prepaid phones. He'd called Kendrick on one of them and arranged to meet him out in the desert.

Normally he wouldn't trust a man like Kendrick, a sociopath if he'd ever met one. But he sensed a certain core of . . . what? Certainly not decency. Call it loyalty, for want of a better term. He'd been loyal to the Gargoyles—a ruthless enforcer, by all accounts—and would no doubt be with them still if the leadership hadn't been disbanded by arrests and lengthy jail terms. Kendrick had done a stretch himself, and avoidance of any and all gang-related activity had been a stipulation of his release. Otherwise, back inside.

Like a dog, he was loyal to the pack.

Ordinarily that wouldn't be enough to convince Elis that Kendrick was the man for this. The dead trespasser at the tower, however, changed everything. Had he really tripped and fallen to his death in the shaft? Elis doubted it. The barrier was high enough to make that unlikely. Much more likely the man had sneaked past Kendrick who decided to hide his dereliction. Only by chance had Elis caught him in flagrante delicto.

"What makes you think I want something done?"

Kendrick snorted a sharp laugh. "You don't call me up on a Saturday and ask to meet out in the middle of nowhere just to chitchat. You need something done and I'm the only one you know who can take care of it. And hey, I'm here to listen."

Elis would have preferred to hear him say, *Whatever you want, consider it done*, but Karma was too streetwise for that.

"I suppose you have a point. I'm satisfied with how you handled the trespasser. His current whereabouts remain a mystery."

Kendrick gave a sharp nod but said nothing. Casual. As if to say, *All in a day's work*.

"I'd like someone else's whereabouts to become a mystery, if you follow what I'm saying."

"I follow."

"Interested?"

"Depends on who."

"Are you familiar with the new shop owner in town—the woman who runs the place called 'Healerina'?"

A slow turn of his head. Yes, he was interested.

"I know her."

That might not be good.

"'Know' her?"

He scratched at his beard. "We talked a little once or twice. Seen her with your boy. What's your beef with her?"

"If there's a conflict here, we can end this right now, and this conversation never happened."

He stared through the windshield. "Whatta y'mean, 'conflict'?"

"I mean if she's a friend—"

He laughed. "Oh, she ain't no friend."

"So, you don't have feelings for her?"

"Yeah, I got feelings for her, but they ain't good feelings."

This was looking better and better.

"I'm glad to hear that. I would like her gone."

"'Gone' as in . . . ?"

"Gone as in I'd rather not see or hear from her ever again. I don't think I can make it much clearer than that."

A smile. "Yeah, that's pretty damn clear. And you want her gone as of when?"

"My son and I have to travel to San Diego tonight. We'll be back tomorrow. When we return, I would like her to be, shall we say, a memory and nothing more."

"Okay, tell me why I should do this?"

What was he saying? Oh, yes . . .

"For the money I'm offering you: ten thousand dollars, half up front, half when she's gone."

There. No dickering. A lordly sum. Known in business as a pre-emptive bid. And Elis could tell the number struck home because Kendrick let slip the slightest twitch when he heard it.

He sat silent a moment, then: "I might need a little help."

"You handled the trespasser without help."

"Yeah, but he fell and that was all she wrote. Just a matter of disposal after that. This gal won't go quiet. Might involve some getting rough."

Elis preferred not to know details. She'd be here when they left tonight, she'd be gone when they returned in the morning. No need to know what transpired during the interim.

"Before involving another, you might do well to consider an old saying: Two can keep a secret if one is dead."

He gave Elis a suspicious look. "I like that. But you'll be in on the secret."

Good point—and a little scary. Best to head this off at the pass.

"Not quite. I'll be on the other side of a mountain range in a San Diego hotel when she disappears, so my son and I will be above suspicion. I will have no idea what transpired back here in Nespodee Springs. Nor will I want to know."

"Your kid's sweet on her. That why you're doing this?"

"I always try to do what's best for my family." No lie there, ex-cept this time *family* meant the entire clan. "Do we have a deal?"

"Yeah, we have a deal."

He handed Kendrick the envelope he'd prepared.

"Here's the first half: fifty hundred-dollar bills."

Kendrick hefted it and lifted the flap to make a quick fan through the bills. Elis handed him the other prepaid phone.

Kendrick grinned. "A burner?"

Was that what they called them?

"I wrote down the number of mine. Call me when you've settled the matter."

Kendrick tucked the envelope and phone inside his shirt, then opened the passenger door.

"I better get movin'. If I'm gonna get this done tonight, I gotta start makin' arrangements."

Wondering what sort of "arrangements" he needed to make, Elis watched him stroll back to his pickup and drive away with a cloud of dust in his wake. Then he closed his eyes and took a deep breath.

He'd done it . . . arranged the murder of another human being. Never in his darkest moments had he dreamed himself capable of such a thing. He tried to balm the guilt and, yes, a modicum of self-loathing, with the thought that she wasn't just another human being, she was something more or perhaps less. A *Duad*, the product of *Pairing*, an impediment to the return of the Visitors, and thus a threat to the entire clan.

As such, she had to . . . cease.

And as head of the clan Elders, it fell to him to make it so.

# 9

"San Diego?" Daley said. "I can think of worse places to spend a Saturday night."

Rhys's exasperation was almost comical. "With my *father*? Are you kidding?"

"Why not?" She fought a grin. "He looks like a fun guy."

"*Fun?*" That broke through his outrage and started him laughing. "Oh, you have no idea!"

He'd come by the shop and immediately started venting his frustration over his father's dragooning him into an overnight trip to San Diego that couldn't be put off.

"Just out of curiosity," she said, "what's so important in San Diego that can't wait? Or is it a family secret I'm not allowed to know?"

"It's a family secret you're not allowed to know but I'm gonna tell you anyway, because who are you going to tell? And I can't see how it would matter if you did."

"I could tell my two hundred thousand Instagram followers."

His eyes widened . . . "Two hun—!" . . . then narrowed . . . "Wait . . . I searched you out on Insta and you're not even listed."

"Oh, yeah. Forgot."

"I don't need you trying to make me crazy, Daley, because my father's doing just fine in that department. Okay, so here's the deal, and it's not really a family secret: Someone approached my father claiming to have a stash of Nikola Tesla's old papers that supposedly contain the key to the tower technology."

"The broadcast power thing?"

Daley's brain immediately red-lined into scam alert. *Why didn't I think of this?*

("Because you're reaching for higher rungs on a different ladder.")

*Yeah, but why didn't it even* occur *to me? When Rhys took me to that demo and nothing worked the way they'd hoped, the grifter part of my brain should have gone into high gear and started figuring angles I could use to separate the Pendrys from their money—even if I never acted on them.*

("I would think Elis Pendry is too smart.")

*But that's the secret: You get to smart people by telling them exactly what they want to hear, by affirming what they already believe. The Pendrys want to believe that the tower will broadcast electric energy. You tell them it absolutely will, but not without a missing secret component that Tesla kept hidden and you've only just now discovered.*

"Right," Rhys was saying. "The broadcast power thing. This fellow says he's got papers from Tesla's Colorado Springs place— that's where he had an experimental lab before he moved to Long

Island. These papers contain diagrams and technology he didn't have a chance to work into the Wardenclyffe tower before the money ran out. Supposedly this is the last piece that, once in place, will make everything work according to plan."

*What did I tell you?*

("You nailed it, I'm sorry to say.")

*Instead of riding a bike, I learned to swindle people. They're a lot alike in how once you learn, you never forget.*

She gave Rhys a level stare. "You realize, don't you, that he's being scammed."

He threw his hands in the air and walked in a circle. "Of course he is! I tried to talk him out of it but he's determined to go. And everything has to be on the down low because the energy companies are supposedly out to stop this guy by any means necessary."

*Another tried-and-true technique: We've got to keep this secret. Loose lips sink ships. If word gets out you'll queer the deal. And now he's added the ever-reliable "they." "They" want to stop him . . . His life is in danger if "they" find out.*

"Also, the guy says he'll be in San Diego tonight and tonight only. If we don't do the deal, then he's hopping a plane to Osaka to talk to a Japanese businessman who's very interested."

*Wow, this is touching all the bases. Set a deadline and start the clock ticking. Now or never, baby. You miss this window, it closes forever. He who hesitates is lost. You snooze, you lose, and so on. I'm impressed. This guy is a pro.*

Daley said, "So why does Pops want you along?"

"He *says* because I'll be joining the Elders one day and I should know how to deal with these things. But I think the real truth is he has his doubts about the guy and wants a little backup."

("I think he could take more imposing backup.")

*That makes two of us, but I'm not saying anything.*

"At least San Diego's got better restaurants than Nespodee Springs."

"I was hoping you and I would wind up in a nice restaurant tonight. And normally I'd have blown him off, but I think he needs a voice of reason and skepticism along."

"And that will be you?"

"That will be me." He stepped closer and lowered his voice. "I was really hoping to see you tonight."

As he started to reach for her she stepped back.

"No PDA, okay? We're under constant scrutiny, it seems."

He glanced around at the pair of browsers idling through the shop and sighed. "Yeah, you're right. How about tomorrow night? Dinner? I know a little Italian place in Brawley that serves Sunday gravy with spaghetti and meatballs."

Her mouth immediately started watering. "I love Italian food. You're on!"

He started for the door. "Call you to firm it up when I get back."

"Don't have too much fun without me."

He exited laughing.

*Well, looks like we've got another exciting Saturday night in Nespodee Springs ahead of us.*

("I don't mind. I've got a number of projects I'm working on. By the way, we need to turn the clocks ahead before bedtime because daylight savings time starts two A.M.)

Oh, right. Her phone and the cable box would reset themselves, but not her microwave.

*Got to remember to do that.*

("I'll remind you.")

*I have no doubt you will.*

("'Spring ahead—'")

*Yeah, yeah, I know.*

The tarp over the window space was giving her a closed-in feeling. She stepped into the doorway and checked out the street.

Quiet now. Earlier, the big excitement had been the ambulance that had raced in from the El Centro medical center and spirited the horrors victim away.

*I wonder how that guy's doing.*

("If he's like any other horrors victim, not well. Nobody seems to be able to get a handle on treating it.")

*And you say it's from "outside"? Outside what?*

("I'm not sure. The horrific visions afflicting them are not generated by a disturbed mind. They bear no connection to . . . how do I say this? . . . they're totally beyond human experience. That's why I said 'outside.' I'm afraid I can't be more specific than that.")

Daley would have pressed him further except she spotted Karma Kendrick standing across the street, staring her way.

*Oh, look. Mister Muscles is strutting his stuff.*

Before he walked on he flashed a grin that sent a chill straight to her marrow.

# 1

Awright. Time to take this uppity bitch down a few pegs. No, make that *all* her pegs.

Karma had stood out front of the Thirsty Cactus Saturday afternoon and watched Pendry and his kid drive out of town. The kid had been behind the wheel which put Pendry on the same side as Karma. They'd locked eyes as the car passed but they was both too savvy to nod or give any sort of sign that something was on between them.

With Pendry gone, the plan was on.

Pendry had said to do this solo, but Karma knew better. Yeah, Daley might be a lightweight but bitches like her could be slippery as eels, and some was a lot stronger than they looked. They say you don't bring a knife to a gunfight. But if you're smart, you don't bring a gun neither. You bring a fucking cannon.

That was why Karma had Benny Mendoza along. Benny was big and tough and mean as they come. Pendry had said two can keep a secret if one is dead, but two can also keep a secret if they're both equally guilty.

Karma hadn't completely leveled with Benny. Told him he'd been paid two Gs for the job and he was splitting even steven—*after* the job was done. A grand was a big payday for Benny, especially for something he'd probably do for free because the plan was to wrap up the bitch and take her out in the desert and have some fun with her before they finished her and put her in the ground. Karma was really looking forward to doing anything he wanted to that fine little body.

*I just don't think we're a good match . . .*

Those words had been locked in his head. He kept hearing her say that over and over. He knew what it meant: *You ain't good enough for me.*

You wanna match, slut? Well, guess what? We're gonna match up real fine, you and me. And then we're gonna see how you match up with Benny. We'll take our time with you. We got all night to get our jollies.

So midnight had come and gone a couple hours ago and here they was at her back door. Tonight's big, fucking, fat-assed moon was lighting up the sky. Luckily it hung more toward the front of the building so the back here was in shadow.

Karma's pickup sat straight below with their boots in the cab. They'd climbed up the steps with gloves on their hands and socks on their feet. T-shirts and work gloves made for a funny look, but Karma had insisted on gloves. A peek through the window by the door showed everything dark inside. So now Benny stood ready with the duct tape while Karma worked on the lock. He'd learned to pick in the Gargoyles. Kicking down a door would do in most cases, but sometimes you had to be sneaky. Like now.

The gloves slowed him down, but finally the last pin fell, the cylinder turned, and they stepped into a kitchen.

Karma took the duct tape and had a flashlight ready but left it off because now the moonlight was their friend, lighting up the front room through the big window there and letting them see where they was going. They padded into it and saw a dark doorway to their left. Karma led the way. As soon as Benny was in beside him, he lit the flashlight.

She woke with that deer in the headlights look. "Wha—?"

Benny didn't hesitate. He jumped on her and got her in a choke hold just as she started to scream. She kicked like a wildcat and Karma admired those long flying legs as she grabbed at Benny's arms, but no way she was gonna break that hold.

It looked like everything was under control and just a matter of a few more seconds before she started going limp. Karma was getting ready to start tearing off strips of tape when Benny suddenly let her go and fell off the bed. He hit the floor with a thud and didn't move. Karma gaped in shock.

"Benny—what the fuck?"

But still he didn't move, and the bitch was screaming now—not that anyone was around to hear her. She jumped off the bed and ducked by him. He made a grab for her but with the flashlight in one hand and the tape in the other, he couldn't get a grip. He raced after her, managed to grab a hunk of her hair and yank her back, but she turned and kneed him in the balls. He couldn't help it—he let her go. But at least he'd put himself between her and the door.

He heard a drawer open and utensils rattle. He couldn't see a fucking thing so he fumbled along the wall, found a switch, and hit it. An overhead light came on and showed her charging him with a big kitchen knife.

"You!" she screamed. "I should've known!"

Knife fight? His turf.

The way she held the blade said she had no idea what she was doing, so he couldn't help but smile as his reflexes took over. He dropped the tape and flashlight, blocked her wild, awkward slash, grabbed her wrist and spun, trapping her arm under his. In a heartbeat he twisted the blade from her fingers, spun back toward her, and drove it into her chest.

He watched in shock as she staggered back against the wall, her face white, her jaw slack. She looked down at the knife handle jutting from the left side of her chest, then back up at him, disbelief filling her eyes as she began a slow slide down the wall. She landed on her butt, then fell to the side. Her mouth worked a few times but no sound came out. And then she just lay there, her blue eyes wide and staring.

"Aw, shit!"

He hadn't meant for that to happen. His muscles had acted on their own. This hadn't been the plan at all. They were supposed to do her out in the desert, not here. All fucking Benny's fault.

With his balls still hurting, he limped back to the bedroom ready to kick the shit out of Benny who still lay on the floor.

"Benny!"

No answer.

He turned on the light and found Benny looking at the ceiling with the same forever stare as the bitch.

Dead! The two of them . . . both dead!

He knelt beside Benny and checked him over. Not a scratch on him. What—he die of a heart attack or something? At his age? Sure as shit looked like it. He couldn't fucking believe it. How could this happen?

How does this shit always happen to me?

Okay, keep cool. Don't lose it. He and Benny was both wearing gloves, so nobody left any fingerprints. It wouldn't be easy, but he could lug Benny down to the truck and—

Wait-wait-wait. If he took Benny with him, the sheriff and the county cops and staties too, no doubt, would be looking for whoever killed the bitch. But if he left Benny here, they'd have their answer: Benny broke in, she fought back, he killed her, then had a heart attack or a stroke or whatever. Case closed.

Karma liked it. Neat. All wrapped up and tied with a bow. Pendry would like it too. If she just disappeared, there'd be search parties and people wondering for weeks and months if there'd been foul play or some such shit. But this way nobody had to wonder nothing: Yeah, there was foul play, all right, but everybody would know who'd committed the foul.

He turned out the bedroom light and returned to the kitchen where he grabbed the tape and flashlight. He took another look at the bitch. Her legs was spread in a V and her T-shirt—now all red-soaked around the knife handle—had ridden up during her slide down the wall, showing her pink panties. Man, he'd been so looking forward to plowing into all that. Now she was just dead meat, growing cold.

He turned off the kitchen light and slipped out through the back door, leaving it unlocked behind him. When he hit his pickup, he set Benny's boots at the bottom of the stairs, then drove away as slow and quiet as he could.

Out on the road, he called Pendry on the burner.

When he picked up, Karma said, "It's done."

A pause, then a sigh, *"You're sure?"*

"Course I'm sure. She's on her kitchen floor with a knife in her heart, put there by the dead guy in her bedroom."

*"What? This was not—"*

"This is better. Worked out perfect. We got a fall guy. It's all taken care of. All questions answered."

Another pause. *"They damn well better be. Lose that phone."*

"Yeah." Like he needed to be told. "See ya around." He cut the call.

What a fucking night.

He needed a drink something fierce. The Cactus was closed by now, but he had a six of Lone Star in his fridge and he heard it calling his name.

# 2

Though the voice was inside her head, it seemed to be coming from far away.

("Daley . . . Daley, can you hear me? Come back to me, Daley.")

Daley blinked in the darkness and vaguely made out Pard kneeling beside her.

"Pard?" Her voice sounded like a frog croak. "Oh, I'm so glad you woke me. I had the worst nightmare ever . . ."

Daley realized then she was on the floor. She put out her hand— why did it weigh a ton?—and felt . . . linoleum? How'd she get to the kitchen?

("Daley, don't waste your strength on speech. And I want you to move as little as possible. That wasn't a nightmare.")

*Not a—?*

("Listen to me: You're on the kitchen floor, but you're not flat. I need you to get flat . . . flat on your back. Just scooch your buttocks a little and let your upper body slide the rest of the way down.")

She did the best she could and soon she lay flat. Why did she feel so *weak?*

("There. That's it. Good.")

*My nightmare . . .*

("As I said, not a nightmare. Karma Kendrick really was here with a friend and they attacked you and Karma stabbed you in the heart with a knife.")

What? Pard had to be kidding.

*In my heart? No . . . I'd be dead.*

("You should be, and you would be if I hadn't decided awhile back that your anatomy needed certain modifications.")

*What sort of—?*

("I'll explain everything later.")

*Why didn't I bleed to death?*

("Because I wouldn't allow it. Now we'll go over everything after—")

*No! Now, Pard.* Now! *What happened to me?*

("Very well. I suppose it won't hurt for you to lie flat awhile longer. What do you remember?")

She tried to organize her thoughts. Everything was a jumble.

*I remember waking up with a light in my eyes, and then someone choking me. I remember you telling me to squeeze his arm, and then he let me go and I ran in here. Last I remember I was on my feet in the kitchen.*

("Karma Kendrick and a friend named Benny—")

*How do you know his name?*

("I heard Karma call him that after you went down. They sneaked in, Karma held the light while Benny put a choke hold on you. While you were holding his arm, I went inside him and caused a fatal heart arrhythmia.")

*Fatal? You killed him?*

("It's what you do to someone who's trying to kill *you.* That was why he stopped choking you: He died. You ran but Karma blocked your escape. You pulled a knife out of a drawer but he took it away and used it on you. Then he took off.")

She lifted her head just enough to look down at her body. Enough moonlight filtered from the front room to outline the handle of the knife jutting from her chest.

"Oh, God!" she croaked as her head dropped back.

("I've got everything pretty much under control.")

*"Pretty much"? What about this Benny guy?*

("I'm assuming he's still on the floor of your bedroom. I know Karma left without him.")

An awful thought: *Is he coming back?*

("I think he left Benny behind so he'd catch the blame for your murder.")

*I've got a dead body in my bedroom?* She was wondering how she'd explain all this when she realized: *I suppose it could be worse. I mean, that could be my body in there now. But why on earth did he want to kill me? Just because I wouldn't go out with him?*

("They brought along a roll of duct tape, Daley. I don't think they had killing in mind. Or at least not right away.")

As that sank in, Daley's queasiness graduated to nausea.

*I think I'm going to be sick.*

("Please don't do that. You could disturb the knife.")

Daley swallowed back her rising gorge, and after a moment the nausea subsided.

*I need to know right now, Pard: Why am I still alive?*

("Since joining you I've been concerned how, despite many paired organs, the human body has only one heart—a single pump. If something catastrophic befalls the pump—oh, let's just pick something at random, say, a four-inch knife blade puncturing its left ventricle—you have no way to provide oxygen to your cells and they quickly die.")

*You're going to tell me you grew me a second heart?*

("No-no. That would be beyond even my prodigious abilities. But I should mention that multiple hearts are not unknown in nature: the giant squid has three. Anyway, I did install a backup system by gradually building up layers of skeletal muscle around your superior and inferior vena cava and your ascending aorta.")

*Meaning?*

("Should your heart stop—which it did—I can still pump blood through your lungs and out into the system. It's nowhere near as efficient or as powerful as the heart itself, which is why I have you lying flat.")

*What's that got to do with it?*

("When you're flat, my stopgap measures don't have to work against gravity to maintain sufficient blood flow to your brain. I can keep you alive while I repair the damage to the real pump and get it back online.")

*And to think I used to criticize you for being anal.*

("Apology accepted.")

*But once you've fixed me up, what do we do?*

("What do you mean?")

*Well, I won't very well be able to accuse Karma of murdering me. And we've got a dead body in my bedroom.*

("You can say Benny attacked you and suddenly dropped dead.")

*That's the kind of news that makes national headlines. I don't want Healerina to have those kinds of headlines.*

("It's the kind of news that will stop Karma from coming back some other time and finishing the job once he learns you're not dead. You're a witness against him, after all.")

*There's got to be another way.*

("Maybe there is, but right now I'm primarily concerned with the damage in here. Why don't you put that devious mind of yours to work while I make repairs?")

*I'm on it.*

Pard faded away.

## 3

("Okay, we're ready,") Pard said as he materialized, once again kneeling beside her. ("Here's how we're going to work it: Before I restart your heart, you're going to remove the knife to allow me to form a good clot under low-pressure conditions from the auxiliary pump.")

*Auxiliary pump . . . what am I, the* Titanic?

("Well, you did almost sink. Now—")

*I'm not ready to remove the blade.*

("It won't hurt. I'll do a nerve block to—")

*I want to leave it in and go see Karma.*

("Why on earth would you do that? What can you hope to accomplish?")

*I think I can scare the shit out of him.*

("Well, maybe you can and maybe you can't, but it's a moot point since there's no way for you to get there.")

*I'll drive.*

("You can't get to your car, Daley. The auxiliary pump can't maintain enough blood pressure for you to stand, let alone walk down those steps.")

*So you say. I am* pissed, *Pard. That son of a bitch* murdered *me, and if he thinks he's just going to go on with his life as if nothing happened, he's so very wrong. He murdered the wrong gal.*

("I feel your anger, Daley—literally and figuratively—but facts are facts. You can't—")

*I'm going to sit up now, Pard, and you're going to work your ass off pumping enough blood through my system to make this work. Got it?*

("Is there no way to dissuade you?")

*Absolutely none.*

("All right, then, cap'n. Damn the torpedoes and full speed ahead.")

*That's the spirit.*

("But I feel I must-must-must warn you that if you fall and land on the knife handle, the blade could rip your heart in two, and then even I can't save you.")

*Thanks for the warning.*

("Well, it's not as if I have no stake in this. Just don't say I didn't warn you.")

Daley rolled onto her side, then pushed herself to a sitting position and leaned back against the wall.

The room spun, faded out, then came back into focus. When

she felt half stable, she reached for the kitchen chair that stood within reach, and pulled it over. Slowly, carefully, she used it as support to get to her knees, wait some more, then onto the seat where she could lean gasping against the kitchen table and wait for the world to right itself.

("You're sure you want to go through with this?")

*Absolutely.*

("You are one determined young lady.")

*A word I heard a lot growing up was "stubborn."*

("Yes, well, that too.")

Struggling, she pushed herself slowly to her feet and stood leaning on the table while black blotches nearly blotted out what little of the darkened kitchen she could see. After a few deep breaths she staggered toward the door with Pard walking beside her. When she reached it she slumped against the jamb.

*I feel like I'm a hundred years old.*

("I wish I could help you, but . . .") He waved a hand and it passed right through her.

*I can do it.*

She pulled the door open and lurched out onto the landing.

("Please reconsider, Daley. If you fall here, it's all over.")

He had a point.

She lowered herself until she was seated on the top step, then descended one tread at a time on her almost-bare butt.

*I go from feeling ancient to going down the stairs like a toddler.*

("But at least you won't fall.")

When her bare feet hit the ground, she hauled herself upright and staggered to her Subaru. She never locked it here in Nespodee Springs, and left the keys under the front seat, something she'd never dream of risking in North Hollywood.

After struggling into the driver's seat, she closed her eyes and leaned back, gathering her strength.

*How are you doing with the auxiliary pumps?*

("Barely keeping up. I don't know how you're doing this.")

*I need to do this.*

She started the car and then drove out of town to the trailer park. From her unsteady, wavering course, anyone watching would think she was drunk. Karma had bragged about his double-wide next to the big dish, so she had no trouble finding it. She pulled to a stop just past it and swung her feet out onto the ground. Was it her imagination, or had standing become just a little bit easier?

*I seem to be getting stronger.*

("No, your blood vessels are adjusting to the low pressure, but they can do only so much. I'm worried about your brain. If it doesn't get sufficient flow, you'll pass out.")

*Can't let that happen.*

("Don't I know.")

She shuffled to Karma's door, and stopped.

*How do I look?*

("I can only see what you see, remember?")

*Okay, how do you* think *I look?*

("You're just inside the moonshadow. If you take a step back, you should be illuminated by very pale light.")

Good. She wanted to be sure Karma could see the knife handle.

*Got it.*

She tapped on the door—she wished she had the strength to pound on it, but it simply wasn't there—and stepped back.

Heavy footsteps sounded inside and the door swung open to reveal Karma Kendrick holding a can of beer.

"Who the fuck—?"

He stared, then dropped both his jaw and the beer as he screamed and fell back. He landed on his butt and kicked-scrambled back until he slammed against the opposite wall.

"You scream like a girl," Daley said.

As if to reinforce her, he pointed to her chest and screamed again.

"Why did you kill me?"

He whimpered and kicked his feet as if trying to push through the wall.

"I can't stay dead, Karma. With all the healing crystals in my shop working for me, I can't die—or at least not for long. I'll always come back. And now I'm back for you."

More whimpering as a dark stain spread across the crotch of his jeans

"I'm not in the business of hurting people, but I made an exception for your friend, Benny."

"Y-y-you know his name?" he said, high-pitched and barely a whisper.

"I know everything, Karma. I stopped his heart because he was trying to kill me. But he only *tried*. You . . . you succeeded."

Daley paused, unsure where to go from here. In her anger she hadn't thought this all the way through.

But apparently Pard had. ("I have an idea. Get me some skin contact.")

*What are you—?*

("Trust me. I'll explain later.")

How to do this . . . ?

Daley reached out to him. "Give me your hand."

A whine. "No!"

"I will let you live if you give me your hand now, Karma. *Now!*"

His hand shook like he was having a seizure as he crawled her way and stretched it toward her. Daley grabbed it and squeezed.

("Now hang on as long as you can and tell him this is what awaits him.")

*What—?*

("Here I go.")

Karma's expression flashed from one of puzzlement to abject horror as his eyes flew wide and he began to scream and thrash. In her weakened state Daley could not hold on for long and he quickly broke free and slammed back against the wall of his trailer.

*What did you do?*

("Gave him a short dose of the horrors—re-created from memory. I leave the rest to you.")

*Got it.*

"You've just seen your future, Karma," she said when his screams subsided. "Your *eternal* future."

He moaned. A pitiful sound.

"Unless . . ."

He quieted and listened.

"Unless you take Benny's body and yourself away—far away. I don't care where you go but I never want to see you again. If I do, I will stop your heart dead as I did Benny's and send you to the hell I just showed you. Understand?"

He nodded spasmodically.

"You will be gone before sunup." She started to turn away, then turned back. "Did somebody put you up to this?"

He shook his head.

"All your idea?"

Vigorous nodding.

("Do you believe him?")

*Not sure.*

("I detected an instant of hesitation before he shook his head.")

*I have to sit before I pass out.*

Trying for as normal a gait as possible, she walked to her idling car and collapsed behind the steering wheel.

Pard appeared in the passenger seat.

("I'm very impressed. I don't know if you managed to 'scare the shit out of him,' but you most definitely scared the piss out of him.")

*I need to lie down.*

("Well, your bedroom is occupied by a corpse at the moment. And I'd like to remove that four-inch knife blade from your heart as soon as possible.")

*Where do we do that?*

("Get back on the road, then pull off into the desert. After you lie back, we'll get it done.")

*In the car?*

("We don't need an operating room.")

Daley got her car rolling, then pulled off the road and took it very slowly into the desert. She did *not* want to bounce. When her headlights picked out a flat spot a few hundred feet in, she stopped the car and sat, shaking. She lowered the windows.

*I need air.*

("I understand.")

*You want me to lie flat?*

("As flat as possible. That way I can lower your blood pressure before you pull out the blade.")

She began lowering the seat back. As it reached max recline, she said, "I'm scared."

("Not to worry. I've got it all under control.")

"Famous last words. Right up there with, 'Hold my beer and watch this.'"

Pard leaned over her. ("Hey, whatever happens to you happens to me as well.")

"Remember that."

("Okay, quiet now and just follow my instructions. I want you to grasp the handle with your left hand but don't do anything else until I'm ready.")

He disappeared.

("Okay. I want you to pull it out slowly, and pull it straight up toward the ceiling.")

"Ohhhhhh, I don't know . . ."

("Do it. I'll make sure you don't feel a thing.")

Clenching her teeth, Daley did as instructed, slowly pulling straight up. Pard had been right about not feeling anything.

("That's it. Keep pulling. The point is free of the myocardium and I'm starting to clot the wound.")

Daley kept pulling and soon enough the point came free of her chest. She tossed it through the open window and into the desert.

*Good riddance.*

*Can you start my heart now?*

("Almost ready. I can seal the myocardium with minimal loss of blood now because the heart wall isn't moving.")

Daley touched the slit in her chest and jumped a little because her hands were so cold. The cut pierced straight through the upper part of her left breast. Her finger came away bloody.

*My boob is bleeding.*

("I'll stop that as soon as I finish here.")

*I'm scarred for life. My beauty is ruined. There goes my nude modeling career.*

("Yes. But at least you'll be able to talk about the time you were stabbed to death.")

*Can't wait.*

She lay still and trembled. Finally . . .

("Okay, I'm ready to restart your heart.")

*Stop talking and do it.*

And just then she felt a thump in her chest like something inside had kicked her, and slowly she became suffused with warmth, her fingers tingling with renewed circulation. She gave it a few seconds, then sat up with no dizziness.

And suddenly, without warning, she began to cry, huge wracking sobs quaked through her.

And just as suddenly, Pard was beside her with his arm around her.

("I was wondering when it would hit you. Cry it out.")

She shook her head, not knowing why, simply an automatic response. He put his other arm around her and hugged her tight.

("No shame. You've just gone through a terrible ordeal, one you shouldn't have survived. Your home was invaded, your body violated, and all for no reason beyond you being you. Let it out.")

And she did let it out. Not only fear and hurt, but helpless rage as well. She'd been *murdered*. And if not for Pard eliminating Benny, she would have been raped and *then* murdered.

Finally the sobs abated. As she got control again, she realized something . . .

"Hey, I can feel your arms."

("Well, it just feels like you feel them. I'm fooling certain of your nerve endings into thinking they have pressure against them.")

"Okay, you can let go now." The sensation eased. "But . . . thanks."

("What's good for you is good for me, so you know I'm always here for you.")

"What do we do now?"

("Drive a little deeper into the desert and find a spot to watch a spectacular sunrise, then go home.")

"Good plan."

She drove but it didn't take long for exhaustion to land on her like a falling safe. So she stopped, leaned back, and closed her eyes.

"Wake me when the show starts."

# 4

The moon had set and the sun was rising as Karma stood over Benny's open grave. He'd dug down in the same spot he'd used before and laid him on top of the *Light* reporter. He wasn't taking no chances of another dead one coming for him. He hadn't killed Benny, so he wasn't worried about him. But the reporter . . . who knew?

He stood there, vibrating. Man, he'd never been so scared in his entire life as when he opened his door and saw the dead bitch standing there in the moonlight with her eyes all sunk in and the fucking knife sticking out of her bloody chest.

If she'd just been standing there, no knife, he coulda told himself he'd been wrong and only thought he'd left her dead back in the apartment. After all, he hadn't checked her for a pulse or nothing 'cause, like, what the fuck he know about taking a pulse?

But the knife, man, the *knife*! She had the same fucking knife he'd used on her still buried up to the handle in her heart. And then she'd shown him hell . . . horrors beyond anything he'd ever imagined. He thought for sure she was going to drag him kicking and screaming into the down-below to keep those horrors company for all eternity.

But no, she'd let him go . . . gave him a second chance.

Well, he wasn't gonna fuck this up. He had Pendry's five grand, which he deserved to keep for not ratting him out—he'd never ratted on anyone and wasn't gonna start now. He had nowhere to go, so he guessed that after he filled up this hole he'd just get in his truck and start driving, and keep on driving till he was as far from here as he could get.

He pulled the chip out of Benny's phone, pocketed it, and tossed the phone into the grave. Did the same with his burner phone. Later on he'd hold the chips over a flame and melt them a little, like he'd already done with that reporter's phone.

He pulled the knife from his back pocket and held it up in the dawn light and watched it shake in his hand. He'd been heading to her place to get Benny like she'd told him to when he'd spotted her car stopped off in the desert. He'd pulled over, killed his lights and engine, and watched from a distance—a safe distance.

Nothing happened, except he thought he saw something catch the moonlight as it flew out the driver's window. After a while she drove away. When she was gone he checked out the area and found the knife on the sand, still sticky with her blood.

The knife he'd killed her with. She must have known he was watching. She meant for him to have it. Why? He had a feeling he'd find out.

He couldn't get it out of his head that she was some sort of goddess. He didn't know her goddess name but had no doubt she'd risen from some sort of hell and he'd gone and pissed her off. Maybe the fact he was still alive and walking this earth was a sign. He'd always believed in signs. He was forty-six years old next month and hadn't done nothing with his life. Well, nothing good, anyways. Maybe this goddess or whatever she was was telling him to finally get his shit together.

# 5

Daley stepped inside her back door and stared at the spot on the kitchen floor where she'd died.

Okay, not officially dead. Pard had told her she hadn't truly died, he'd only made her look dead to fool Karma. Yes, her heart had stopped but he'd maintained enough blood circulating to keep her brain alive.

Pard appeared beside her.

She said, "I wish I could send you into the bedroom to see if Karma did as he was told."

("I'd love to do that for you, but unfortunately—")

"—you can only see what I see. Right. Okay, let's go."

Taking a deep breath, she marched around the corner, through the front room, and into the bedroom and . . . no body.

"Well," she said, "if he did that, he probably did the disappearing act too."

("He looked scared enough to do anything you told him.")

She stared at the bed. The predawn nap in the car hadn't been restorative. Emotional and physical exhaustion still weighed on her, but somehow, getting back into the bed where someone had choked her . . .

("If it will help, I'll lie down with you.")

"I thought you couldn't read my thoughts."

("I can't except when you think at me. But I can sense your feelings and—")

"Okay, okay. Lay with me."

("I can't lay with you but can lie with you.")

Normally his grammar fixation torqued her, but right now, as far as she was concerned, he could be as anal as he needed.

She flopped onto her back and stared at the ceiling. Pard lay down beside her. Not so bad here with company. She'd get over this.

"Tell me, Pard: Is there any injury to me you couldn't fix?"

("I can think of zillions. Can't do much about catastrophic injuries, I'm afraid. A hollow-point slug through your heart would cause hemorrhaging from multiple tears I couldn't stop. Same with a torn aorta. Or a serious brain stem injury. I could go on . . .")

"That's plenty, thank you. You're saying I can take a lot of punishment but I'm not invincible. So, if I'm reasonably careful, I can expect a long life?"

("A very long life. In fact I don't see any reason for you to die at all. Or even get old, for that matter.")

She bolted upright. "Whoa-whoa-whoa! What? You're saying I'm immortal?"

("I'd prefer a different pronoun: *We* are immortal—as immortal as we want to be.")

"I don't believe it."

("What you believe is irrelevant. I'm going to keep you alive for a long, long time, Daley.")

"But how?"

("Maintenance—constant maintenance. Remember: I'm conscious down to the subcellular level. I keep an eye on things. I keep your arteries clean, maintain the organs and tissues, replace damaged or dying cells. I'm in the process of lengthening all your telomeres to keep your cells from aging.")

Daley was still having trouble buying into this.

"Where's the catch?

("No catch. While you live, I live, and I've grown rather fond of living.")

"Still . . ."

("Juana told you the old Cahuilla saying about alarets' victims: 'Of a thousand struck down, nine hundred and ninety-nine will die.' You might take that to mean that one *won't* die. Ever. You're that one.")

Daley flopped back to stare at the ceiling again. Her life seemed to be coming apart at the seams. Everything had seemed so much simpler when she'd gone to bed last night. Now . . .

"This is going to take some getting used to."

("Take your time. You have plenty of it.")

"Ha. Ha. But if you're right, I guess there's no hurry to do anything. Except maybe find out if someone sent Karma after me."

("I don't see any love lost between you and Elis Pendry.")

"Well, yeah, he's not a warm cuddly type, but what motive could he have?"

("His son has a crush on you.")

"You think he kills every non-clan woman Rhys takes a shine to?"

("Well, no. But if someone was indeed behind the attack, we have to stay on alert. Or . . .")

"Or what?"

("Get outa Dodge, as they say.")

That didn't sit right with Daley. She was getting to like Nespodee Springs.

"That might be good advice if I'd been working a game here, but I've been a straight arrow. Not ready to turn tail and run."

("Good for you.")

"And don't you get the feeling that something's going on in this town, something bubbling under the surface? Maybe it's got something to do with that Pendry film. I want to see the rest of it. I mean, what's on the second disk that needs to be kept secret?"

("And I'd like to get another look inside a horrors patient. Something going on there too.")

"Good. We have an agenda." She closed her eyes. "Now let's get some sleep. Looks like we've got a big week ahead of us."

# THE SECRET HISTORY OF THE WORLD

The preponderance of my work deals with a history of the world that remains undiscovered, unexplored, and unknown to most of humanity. Some of this secret history has been revealed in the Adversary Cycle, some in the Repairman Jack novels, and bits and pieces in other, seemingly unconnected works. Taken together, even these millions of words barely scratch the surface of what has been going on behind the scenes, hidden from the workaday world. I've listed them below in chronological order. (NB: "Year Zero" is the end of civilization as we know it; "Year Zero Minus One" is the year preceding it, etc.)

*Scenes from the Secret History* is FREE on Smashwords.

## The Past

"Demonsong" (prehistory)*
"The Compendium of Srem" (1498)
"Wardenclyffe" (1903–1906)
"Aryans and Absinthe"* (1923–1924)
*Black Wind* (1926–1945)
*The Keep* (1941)
*Reborn* (February–March 1968)
"Dat Tay Vao"* (March 1968)
*Jack: Secret Histories* (1983)
*Jack: Secret Circles* (1983)
*Jack: Secret Vengeance* (1983)
"Faces"* (1988)
*Cold City* (1990)
*Dark City* (1991)

*Fear City* (1993)

"Fix"** (2004) with Joe Konrath and Ann Voss Peterson

## Year Zero Minus Three

*Sibs* (February)

*The Tomb* (summer)

"The Barrens"* (ends in September)

"A Day in the Life"+ (October)

"The Long Way Home"+

*Legacies* (December)

## Year Zero Minus Two

"Interlude at Duane's"+ (April)

*Conspiracies* (April) (includes "Home Repairs"+)

*All the Rage* (May) (includes "The Last Rakosh"+)

*Hosts* (June)

*The Haunted Air* (August)

*Scar-Lip Redux* (August)

*Gateways* (September)

*Crisscross* (November)

*Infernal* (December)

## Year Zero Minus One

*Harbingers* (January)

"Infernal Night"** (with Heather Graham)

*Bloodline* (April)

*The Fifth Harmonic* (April)

*Panacea* (April)

*The God Gene* (May)

*By the Sword* (May)

*Ground Zero* (July)

*The Touch* (ends in August)

*The Void Protocol* (September)
*The Peabody-Ozymandias Traveling Circus & Oddity Emporium*
(ends in September)
"Tenants"*
*The Last Christmas* (December)

## Year Zero

"Pelts"**
*Reprisal* (ends in February)
*Fatal Error* (February) (includes "The Wringer"+)
*Double Threat* (February–March)
*The Dark at the End* (March)
*Signalz* (May)
*Nightworld* (May)

* available in *Secret Stories*
** available in *Other Sandboxes*
+ available in *Quick Fixes—Tales of Repairman Jack*